# A Yuletide Kiss

A
Yuletide
Kiss

SABRINA JEFFRIES
MADELINE HUNTER
MARY JO PUTNEY

KENSINGTON
PUBLISHING CORP.

www.kensingtonbooks.com

KENSINGTON BOOKS are published by

Kensington Publishing Corp.
119 West 40th Street
New York, NY 10018

ISBN-13: 978-1-4967-3130-2 (ebook)

ISBN-13: 978-1-4967-3129-6

First Kensington Trade Paperback Printing: October 2021

10 9 8 7 6 5 4 3 2

Printed in the United States of America

# Contents

# When We Finally Kiss Good Night

## SABRINA JEFFRIES

*To my husband, Rene, who's always been my rock,
even when times are hard.
I love you forever!*

# Chapter 1

Konrad Juncker prodded the exhausted post-horse pulling his rented gig down a snowy lane. Normally, he'd reach Sanforth before nightfall easily, but not now that it was sleeting. The sign with a white rose at the turn from the main road could only mark the site of the exclusive inn he sought, which his friend Thorn, the Duke of Thornstock, had once described to him.

"Just a bit more, and you can rest," Konrad muttered to the horse.

He hoped he was right. His stomach grumbled, his eyebrows were crusted with ice, and even his greatcoat failed to keep him warm. The horse struggled a few hundred yards more and suddenly the lane widened to reveal a circular drive with an impressive building nestled in the evergreens. There was an entrance arch and a sign with the words THE WHITE ROSE. This had to be the place.

Still, it didn't look like a fully functioning inn. It seemed deserted, with no ostler bustling to attend to his horse, no noise from within to indicate people eating or drinking. But why should that be? The storm had come up suddenly—no one would have had time to gather their mounts and head off. They would have been stuck here . . . as he clearly was.

He'd been told it had a sizeable stable. That had to be through the other archway he could see. Even the horse pricked up its ears as if it knew this was to be its home until the storm abated and the roads cleared.

Konrad climbed down, tied the horse to a post, and entered the stables. There wasn't a single groom about, although there were a couple of nags in the stalls. While that was a good sign, it didn't explain the lack of people.

So he trudged back out and through the snow to the front of the inn. Hearing what sounded like voices coming from the other end of the archway—finally—he headed that way.

He shivered as he walked along the passageway, beyond which sleet fell steadily. As he came out into what proved to be an alley behind the inn, he spied two young women and a man of about sixty laboring to drag a rather stalwart fellow . . . somewhere.

"Good God," Konrad couldn't help saying as he strode toward them. "Is he drunk? Dead?" Or worse yet, murdered. It would be just Konrad's luck to have stumbled across a criminal act in progress.

He'd expected the man to answer, but it was the older of the two women who blinked over at him while snow continued dusting her heavy wrap and blond hair. "Neither, I hope. We found him outside in this state. He seems quite ill."

Konrad approached her and the brown-haired girl who was probably a maidservant, judging by her youth and her apron. Each was tugging on one of the prone fellow's arms while the old gentleman attempted to lift the man's legs.

Now that Konrad was closer, he could hear the ill chap mumbling and see his flushed face. "Where are you taking him?" Konrad asked.

"To a room, of course. Although how we'll get him onto the bed, I don't know."

"Let me deal with dragging him." Moving between the two women, Konrad hoisted the stranger up. As the women let go, he locked his hands around the fellow's chest, enabling the older gentleman to finally lift the chap's legs off the ground. "Tell me where you want him."

Once again, it was the blond woman who answered. "Go straight back to the end of the alley. I'll take care of the door." He heard the creak of snow and ice being shoved aside by the door opening. As he and the other fellow half lifted, half dragged their burden along the alley, the woman said to the girl, "Alice, go light a fire on the hearth to dispel the cold and damp."

"Yes, Mrs. Waverly," Alice said.

Ah. So the outspoken woman was the owner of this place. Thorn had told him of her.

As Konrad and the old gentleman maneuvered the fellow into the bedchamber, Konrad grumbled, "This chap must weigh thirteen stone."

"At the very least," Mrs. Waverly said as she drew back the covers.

Still, they finally got him on the bed and rolled him to his back.

"Help me get his coats off, Peter," Mrs. Waverly told the old gentleman as she unbuttoned the feverish man's greatcoat.

"I'll do it," Konrad said and brushed her aside. Peter lifted their patient's shoulders so that Konrad could pull the coat off his arms. Then they dragged the sodden, heavy wool out from under him. More buttons and pulling, and the frock coat and waistcoat followed. The woman threw a blanket over the man, then hung the coats on pegs.

She turned to Konrad. "Thank you for your help, Mister . . ."

"Juncker. Konrad Juncker. I assume you are the keeper of this fine inn, Mrs. Waverly." He figured a compliment couldn't hurt.

Apparently, Mrs. Waverly didn't share his belief. "Yes, I own this place. But at present it is closed for the holidays."

Not ready to give up, Konrad kept a smile on his face. "I'll accept any shelter you have. Perhaps there is an extra place with the grooms? I'm happy to pay your price."

"That's not the issue. We're not only closed, but we lack provisions for guests at present. Nor are there any other servants here beside Peter and his granddaughter, Alice."

"I am sorry to intrude on what you probably thought would be a quiet few days, but I can't go back or forward. The road has become impassable. There is ice to the west, and it is beginning to fall here. You can hear it, even if you didn't see it while you were out in the cold."

The woman looked torn.

"I can do for myself," Konrad added. "I won't need servants."

She sighed. "Of course you can stay until the road improves. There are plenty of chambers above, off the gallery over the courtyard. Alice will show you to Room Four if you will fetch your own bag. Peter can see to your horses and equipage. You are welcome to dine with us, simple as our fare will be."

"Thank you."

With a nod to Mrs. Waverly, Konrad followed Alice and Peter to the front of the inn to get his valise. Then, as Peter headed for the stables with the horse and gig, Konrad climbed the stairs behind Alice. Even there he noticed touches that showed this inn catered to the wealthy—gilded sconces, beeswax tapers, wide stairsteps—things he'd never experienced in his days touring with the theatrical troupe.

"How did you hear of our 'fine inn'?" Alice asked, a bit tartly.

"My friend, the Duke of Thornstock, praised the White Rose once, which brought it to my mind when I was struggling on the road."

She relaxed a bit. "I know of His Grace. Sometimes he stops here on his way to Armitage Hall. He even has a pint while he waits for his horses to be changed." She looked back briefly as she climbed. "Mrs. Waverly is a good woman, you know. She was just hoping for some time away from the bustle. Generally, we're full up most of the year."

"Trust me, this wasn't where I wanted to be, either." He caught himself. "I'm grateful for the shelter, but I was headed for a comfortable country house in Sanforth owned by my friends."

"Sanforth, is it? We know people there. But no one in a country house." Her mouth dropped open. "Are you visiting the Duke of Armitage? Oh, that's right, the Duke of Thornstock is your friend, too. Now there's a family—three dukes as half brothers! Are they as wild as they sound? You must know them fairly well if you were invited to—"

"Ah, look, Room Number Four." He halted, not wanting to engage in this discussion. He knew firsthand how gossipy village folk could be, and he didn't want to betray any secrets he shouldn't. "I take it this is mine?"

"Oh, yes." She blushed furiously. "And me going on and on so I nearly passed it by." She unlocked the door. "There's a bed-chamber and separate sitting room. They've been closed up these past two days, so they may need airing. I'll get the fire going, make up the bed, and fetch you fresh water for washing up. That's about all I can manage before dinner."

"I can build a fire and fetch my own water if you tell me where the well is."

She looked taken aback. "That would be a help, thank you."

As he doffed his damp greatcoat and hung it on a hook, she took clean linens from a chest underneath the bed. The hearth was in the sitting room, so he went in and grabbed the tinderbox, then set about building the fire. Once the logs were stacked with the kindling, he struck flint to steel until a spark caught on the charcloth. A minute later, he had a nice fire going.

He caught Alice watching him through the connecting doorway.

"For a gentleman, you're very good at that," she said.

He returned to the bedroom. "That's because I'm not a gentleman." When she looked perplexed, he said, "I work for a living."

She eyed him skeptically as she fluffed the pillows. "Making fires?"

He laughed. "No. Writing plays." Or rather, pretending to write the popular plays his best friend, Thorn, actually wrote.

"Like ones in a theater?"

"Exactly like those."

But Konrad wouldn't be "writing" them much longer. Thorn planned to pen new plays under his own name, so he no longer needed to pay Konrad to stand in for him. Even though Konrad had put aside a great deal of the money he'd earned, what would he do when it ran out? He must have a plan for his future.

He could fall back on acting, but he'd had his fill of traveling the country, and competition among actors was fierce in London, the only place where acting paid a living wage. Besides, he didn't know how long his credit in the theater community would last once Thorn revealed that *he'd* written the Felix plays and not Konrad. That was also why Konrad might have no luck selling his own plays. Even if he thought he could write them, the theater community might not agree.

His poetry, which was where his heart was, would never make enough to support him unless he found a wealthy patron, and he didn't like the idea of going hat in hand to his rich friends. His novel was only half finished. The words for it didn't come as easily as they did for his poetry.

"So, these plays you write," she said, beating at the feather mattress to fluff it up, too. "Are they for theaters in London?"

"Yes. You could go see them if you ever travel there."

She eyed him askance. "London might as well be in China for all the good it does me."

Damn. He was thinking like a gentleman, worrying about what work to do so he could remain in London while this poor girl had never even been there. Servants generally only traveled with their masters or mistresses, and even then only a few did, although paid companions like Flora might be taken along.

Flora? What had him thinking of *her*?

Well, he *had* seen her in London last month, looking as lovely eight years later as she had at nineteen. Just the sight of her had brought it all flooding back: dances and long talks and furtive touches during their month of half flirtation, half courtship. It had made him want to start up with her again, even though little had changed in his life, and her life had only changed for the worse.

He'd squandered his one chance at making amends. He'd had so many questions and hadn't asked a single one. Nor was he likely to see her again.

God, he had to stop thinking of her. He stepped forward as Alice finished with the sheets. "Let me help you put the pillowcases on."

"How kind of you, sir," she said and circled around to the other side.

Then something seemed to catch her eye outside the window. "There's an equipage coming up the drive, I think."

He joined her there. "It looks like a carriage. A rather large one."

Alice began clucking her tongue. "Oh, I'd best go tell the mistress, but she ain't going to be happy about it." She hurried for the door. "That's the last thing we need right now."

All he could do was agree.

# Chapter 2

Miss Flora Younger cleared a spot on the carriage window with her gloved hand and tried to make out what lay at the other end of the drive. "I fear the White Rose Inn is abandoned."

"Poppycock!" Lady Hortensia Whitmarsh, Flora's employer, peered out of her own window. "No one abandons an inn. It would be terribly rude to travelers."

"I doubt that was the intention," Flora said dryly. "And I can't see anyone around. Not that beggars can be choosers at the moment. Shelter is shelter."

"We are not beggars. And we can choose to go wherever we jolly well please. I shall simply tell Braxton to drive on until we find a more felicitous abode." The viscountess knocked on the ceiling. "Braxton! Braxton, my good man!" When no answer came, she muttered, "Damned fellow is pretending not to hear me again."

Flora stifled a laugh. "He's nearly deaf."

"Only when he chooses," Lady Whitmarsh grumbled.

"Yet you keep him on."

"Of course. He's the best coachman I've ever had."

"Exactly." Flora had long ago given up on following the winding roads of Lady Whitmarsh's mind. "Braxton would only come this way because it's our last chance at shelter."

"Perhaps," Lady Whitmarsh said, though she began to retie her boots. The poor woman's feet had a tendency to ache in cold weather, so she often undid her half boots when the two ladies were traveling. Apparently that helped.

Flora buttoned up her cloak of forest-green velvet, a castoff of her ladyship's, and pulled the hood over her head in anticipation of having to disembark. "Now I wish I'd worn my other gown when we set out from last night's lodgings."

"Pish, you wanted to make a good impression on the guests at the house party. Nothing wrong with that. And this gown is such a pretty thing, with the flourishes and furbelows you embroidered on it. It's nice for the season, too, with all the ivy and holly leaves."

"Yes, but it's too thin for this weather. I should have worn my heaviest gown, no matter how outdated—or unseasonable—its design."

"If we're forced to stay here tonight, you should get the footmen to take your trunk off the top of the servants' coach." Lady Whitmarsh paused. "Although you're probably better off with the bag you packed for use at inns. We'll rise early tomorrow to go on to Armitage Hall."

"I fear we won't be going anywhere soon," Flora said. "It will take time for the ice and snow to melt."

"Very well. We'll delay our departure until tomorrow afternoon. But we shall leave in time to arrive at the duke's."

"I still say—"

The carriage shuddered to a halt, and the door opened so Braxton could thrust his head inside. "We're here, m'lady."

"Didn't you hear me knocking for you, Braxton?"

Used to Lady Whitmarsh's grousing, Braxton didn't so much

as frown. "Not with that icy wind rushing past my ears. It's damned near a gale out here. Got the carriage as close to the building as I could manage."

"That was very good of you, Braxton," Flora said.

"Thank you, miss, but you both should still watch yourselves. There's a slippery bit right by the entrance."

Lady Whitmarsh frowned. "What we should do is wait for the footmen to help us past the 'slippery bit.' They must be behind us somewhere."

"Sorry, m'lady, but they stayed at the last inn where we changed horses," Braxton put in. "James don't drive well in bad weather, so I told him not to press on."

Lady Whitmarsh blinked. "Without consulting me?"

"Aye," Braxton said unrepentantly. "I wanted us to go as far as we could before the road got impassable, and forgive me, but there was no time to waste arguing with your ladyship."

"I see." She drew in a steadying breath. "Well then, I suppose we'd better hope someone is here to help us."

The viscountess and her coachman had been together so long that they fairly ignored each other's complaints. Most of the time Flora found their grousing vastly amusing. But right now, she was in no mood for anything but a hot cup of chocolate and a rest by a warm hearth.

After they disembarked, Braxton did his best to shield them from the wind with his outstretched arms while they slipped past him into the covered passageway. She heard voices coming from the other end.

Excellent. So the inn *wasn't* abandoned. Flora might get that warm hearth after all.

Within moments, a pretty woman hurried toward them from the far end of the passageway. "I'm Jenna Waverly, owner of this inn. I suppose you're looking for shelter." She sounded—and looked—bone-weary.

Before Lady Whitmarsh could get them ejected with one of

her typically tart remarks, Flora said, "We are, as a matter of fact. We'd be most grateful, for I don't think our coachman is willing to go any farther on the roads as they are."

"I can give you tea and a bit of respite and food for the night, but that's all I can manage. I generally keep the inn closed during the holiday to allow my servants a chance to be with their families."

"What a droll idea," Lady Whitmarsh said. When Flora scowled at her, she added, "We're happy to pay. And how refreshing to find a female innkeeper. There ought to be more of you." Relief stole over Flora at the viscountess's ingratiating tone, until Lady Whitmarsh added, "I would even make your inn a regular stop on my travels if I came often to this godforsaken part of England. Fortunately, I do not."

"What her ladyship is trying to say—" Flora began.

"Why not let her ladyship speak for herself?" said a familiar voice. "She seems to be doing an excellent job of it already."

When the gaze of the man approaching met Flora's, her insides knotted up. Only one man had eyes as dark a blue as a starlit night. It was Konrad Juncker in all his larger-than-life, sinfully handsome, untrustworthy glory.

Her heart sank. How could that be? Could he be following them? Perhaps he'd learned the truth about "A Discerning Lady," who often criticized his plays for *The London Society Times*. Unless . . .

She narrowed her gaze on Lady Whitmarsh. Flora wouldn't put it past the woman to be playing matchmaker. Still, the viscountess hadn't approved of Juncker or his plays even *before* she'd met him, and it would have taken a masterful schemer indeed to have arranged this. Even Lady Whitmarsh couldn't control the weather.

The innkeeper glanced from Flora to Konrad. "Do you know each other?"

"You could say that." His eyes locked with hers. "We met

years ago, but only recently became reacquainted in London. Mrs. Waverly, may I introduce Lady Hortensia Whitmarsh and her companion, Miss Flora Younger?"

The viscountess nodded at Mrs. Waverly. "If you're allowing *him* to stay, then you should certainly allow us to do so."

Mrs. Waverly raised an eyebrow. "I'm allowing him because he promised to take care of his own needs. I also close the inn at this time of year to give myself a respite from running the place. Only a couple of servants and I are here to wait on you, and we are already running low on provisions. So if you stay, you will be expected to help cook meals and such."

"I have servants of my own in—" Lady Whitmarsh began before Flora nudged her. The viscountess shot her a questioning glance, then slumped as she apparently remembered. "It's only Miss Younger and I."

"And her ladyship's coachman," Flora put in, fighting to ignore Konrad. "I'm sure Mr. Braxton will be happy to give aid in the stable and anywhere else you need assistance. I can take care of Lady Whitmarsh's other needs. We'll manage, Mrs. Waverly."

"Very well. I'd have Alice show you to your rooms, but she's looking after another guest."

"Tell me which rooms you wish to assign to Lady Whitmarsh and Miss Younger," Konrad said, "and I can take them up. Oh, and if you can explain where the well is, I'll fetch water for their rooms when I'm fetching it for myself."

"Why, thank you, Mr. Juncker. How kind of you." After Mrs. Waverly pointed behind her and described how to reach the well, she added, "The ladies will be upstairs on the same side of the inn as you, in a suite marked Two. That will make it easier for Alice to tend to all of you. Now, if you will excuse me, I must return to my patient."

Patient? Flora watched the innkeeper go, questions swirling through her head. How many people had asked for shelter here, anyway?

She hoped there were enough to keep her from stumbling over Konrad everywhere she stepped. Judging from the sudden gleam in his eye, he seemed to have a good rapport with Mrs. Waverly already.

An unwanted jealousy stabbed her. Of course he did. He regularly enticed women of all ages with that crooked smile of his.

"Shall we, ladies?" He swept his hand to indicate a closed door behind him.

"Flora, why don't you go on with Mr. Juncker and see whether our accommodations will suit," Lady Whitmarsh said. "I have to . . . er . . . make sure Braxton is aware of our decision to stay and get him to carry up our luggage."

Flora tried to read Lady Whitmarsh's expression. Never before had her employer gone out of her way to inform Braxton of anything. Or, for that matter, had Flora examine their "accommodations." It only reinforced Flora's suspicion that Lady Whitmarsh was up to something.

Konrad watched the woman leave, then moved to open the door, waiting for her to go through before he gestured to the stairs. "Why do you let her treat you like a servant?"

"I *am* a servant, for all intents and purposes," Flora shot back as she climbed the stairs ahead of him. "Anytime you do something for someone because you're paid and not out of the goodness of your heart, you're a servant. Besides, it's better than being treated like a post-horse, to be used for a stretch and then abandoned."

When Konrad swore under his breath, she took less pleasure in his reaction than she'd expected. But at least she'd made it clear where they stood now, instead of simply lapsing into one-word answers as she had when briefly encountering him a month ago.

"In Bath," he said, "I was constrained . . . I could not . . ." He muttered something she couldn't make out. "Never mind. It hardly matters now."

It mattered to her, but she wasn't about to ask him to elaborate. He would give her some excuse, and she would want to believe him. In the end, it would simply lead to more unhappiness for her.

"What are you doing here, anyway?" she asked.

"The same thing you are, most likely. Hiding from the weather."

"Hiding is certainly in your character," Flora mumbled as they reached the top. It was warmer up here, so she pushed her hood off her head.

Then she wished she hadn't when he moved to stand in front of her, his icy look chilling her again. "What did you say?"

"Never mind. It hardly matters now," she said, echoing his earlier words.

A muscle flexed in his jaw. "If you must know, I'm on my way to the house party at Armitage Hall."

"The Duke of Armitage invited you, too?" Dread settled in her chest. After being trapped here with Konrad, she'd be trapped there as well.

"I do happen to be his half brother's closest friend, despite my lowly station."

The sarcasm in his words stung a little. "Yes, so lowly that all of London knows your name. False modesty does not become you, sir."

"Trust me, my modesty is more genuine than you know."

"If you say so." She started walking along the gallery, hardly noticing where she went. "But I wasn't trying to insult you. After all, Thornstock doesn't live at Armitage Hall. I assumed Lady Whitmarsh and I were invited because of my friendship with Armitage's new wife, Vanessa. I didn't realize Thornstock or the rest of the family might be there, too. That's all I was remarking on."

Belatedly, it occurred to her that Lady Whitmarsh most certainly could have engineered both invitations—one for Flora and one for Konrad. But why would the woman wish to match her with Konrad? Lady Whitmarsh didn't even like him.

It made no sense. Perhaps Flora was reading too much into her employer's behavior.

Konrad came up beside her, and her foolish heart started thumping. Why must he still do this to her? It had made sense for her to react like a schoolgirl at nineteen, but she was a woman of the world now, the companion to a viscountess. He shouldn't affect her like this anymore.

He dropped his voice to a murmur that hummed along her skin. "Perhaps we should call a truce."

"I didn't know we were at war."

"The ice in your eyes whenever you look my way seems to imply otherwise."

"What were you expecting—warmth? You disappeared from my life without a word to go become a famous playwright. You led me to believe—" She shook her head. "I am not discussing this with you. I have to ready her ladyship's room . . . and mine."

"I'll help you."

"I don't need your help."

"Do you even know how to start a fire?"

Of course not. And he was obviously aware of that, judging from his smug look. Oh, how she hated it. "Do *you*?" she shot back.

"I do. And what I meant by 'truce' was we should put our past grievances aside for the sake of getting through these next few days in an understaffed inn."

"Next few days!" Her stomach knotted up. "Do you think we'll be forced to spend Christmas here?"

"Possibly. Why? The good part about being stuck so close to Sanforth is that the guests at the house party will also be unable to leave. So our plans to enjoy the season with our friends are merely postponed."

"I hope you're right. Vanessa told me the family puts up something called a Christmas tree for their festivities. She hasn't seen it, though, so she couldn't describe it for me, and I was so looking forward to seeing it."

"If it's anything like the one my parents used to put up every year, it's beautiful." When she eyed him askance, he added, "Christmas trees are a German custom. My father was German, and all of Armitage's siblings were raised in Germany. But every tree is different, so I can't describe it in detail either."

"Now you're making me even more upset that I might miss it."

Then it hit her that he'd mentioned his parents. She'd known nothing of them. She was about to ask some probing questions when he said, "Anyway, back to our truce... Will you agree to one?"

She looked him over, noting his bright blond hair, fashionable in its disarray, and his finely tailored clothes, from his tailcoat of dark blue superfine wool to his chocolate-colored top boots. No one could deny he was attractive, but that appearance now came with a full measure of rakish charm.

He was no longer the man she'd thought he was, if he ever had been. He was famous now, and so posed no danger to her. She wasn't about to take up with a man who had so many admirers that she'd have to fight them off, even if his speaking glances *did* hint at the secret embraces he might give her if they were alone.

A pity they could never be alone, no matter how much she was tempted.

Oh, dear, what a foolish thought. "Fine," she said. "I suppose a truce sounds... wise."

Very wise, as long as she could reconcile herself to the man he was now, and finally set about forgetting the man she'd once known.

He released a heavy breath. "In keeping with that, I—"

"Oh, there you are, Mr. Juncker," a girlish voice said from behind them.

Frustrated by the interruption, Flora turned to find a buxom maid staring at Mr. Juncker with adoring eyes. Drat it, he had already entranced another female.

Flora swallowed her ire and pasted a smile to her lips. "You must be Alice. I'm afraid my employer and I will be staying here until the bad weather lets up and the roads are clear enough for travel. We're to be in Room Two, I believe. Isn't that right, Mr. Juncker?"

Konrad had a gleam in his eyes, the same one he'd had downstairs when Mrs. Waverly had assigned the suite to her and Lady Whitmarsh. A suite on the same side of the inn as his room.

Oh no. "What is *your* room number, Mr. Juncker?"

"Four." He flashed her a decidedly mischievous smile.

"You're nearly right next to each other," Alice said and pointed across the open space to the other gallery. "See?"

Flora stifled a groan. Only one door separated Room Two from Room Four. Good Lord.

He bent his head to whisper, "It's a good thing we called a truce."

Or the worst thing. She had a feeling she would regret that agreement before the day was over.

# Chapter 3

Konrad had known he was in trouble the second he'd heard Flora's melodious voice downstairs. It affected him the same way it had when they'd first met in Bath. Or even the more recent time he'd seen her at the theater, when the sound of her laugh had drawn him unwittingly to the Whitmarsh box.

In any pitch, her voice sang to him like the poetry he poured onto paper. He could listen to it all day.

He caught Alice staring at them. "Miss Younger and I . . . um . . . know each other. We met years ago, so we're old friends."

"Speak for yourself," Flora said. "I am not in the least old."

With a chuckle, he gave her his most courtly bow. "I am duly chastened. I never meant to imply that you are." He deliberately let his gaze play over her high brow, her impish nose, and the best part, her Cupid's-bow lips, which he wanted to kiss. "Not a wrinkle in sight. So I'd be daft to think it."

Alice snorted. "You'll need to watch this one," she told Flora. "He's got a silver tongue."

"And is bold as brass," Flora said, though she wore a wisp of a smile.

"Don't you worry about your door being so close to his," Alice went on. "The suite has two entrances. So you could always use the one down at the end."

"You don't have to look so relieved, Miss Younger," Konrad said, gaining a laugh from both women.

"Here," Alice said, "I'll show you where it is." She started to circle the gallery with Flora in tow. She didn't get far.

"Alice!" shouted the innkeeper from downstairs. "Come down here! We've got more arriving."

"Oh, Lord," Alice muttered. "Here's your keys, miss, but the rooms are unlocked on account of no one being here." Pressing two keys into Flora's hand, Alice retraced her steps to the stairs. "Coming, mistress!"

Konrad offered Flora his arm. "We'll find the other entrance together. I can build a fire while you make up the beds." He eyed her closely. "You *do* know how to make up beds, don't you?"

"Of course," she said and reluctantly took his arm.

She smelled of orange flowers, and her dark blond hair, now that she'd pushed off the hood of her cloak, was a feathery haze about her head, threatening to escape her hairpins entirely at any moment.

He wouldn't mind helping it escape. He had never seen her hair down, and he badly wanted to. It would surely be glorious.

*Stop it, man! You went down this road once and it didn't end well.*

Still, fate had given him another chance to make amends, and this time he wouldn't squander it. He owed her an explanation at the very least, but only that, nothing more. Or he'd find himself in an endless circle of making amends, then mucking it up by courting her when he had naught to offer. She deserved better.

Once they passed his door and hers, they spotted a door at the far end, also marked Two.

When they entered, leaving the door open for propriety's sake, he let out a whistle. "You have quite the suite here. Lady Whitmarsh will be pleased."

"Only if it's ready for habitation by the time she gets up here," Flora said and looked around. "Where are the sheets?"

"Under the bed." He turned his attention to the fire.

She knelt to pull a chest out. "How did you know?"

"I got here first, remember? My room is already done." He began to stack up logs and kindling in the fireplace.

But instead of starting on the bed-making, Flora wandered the room, apparently checking to see what amenities it held. "Oh! There's even a closet." She opened a door, then gasped. "It's not a closet. It's a whole other room."

"That's usually what is meant by a suite," he quipped.

Flora disappeared for a few moments. When he heard her come back, he discovered she'd removed her cloak to reveal a gown of scarlet taffeta with pretty green leaves embroidered all over it. Yet none of it was as beautiful as the smile lighting her face. One glance at that smile, and he was slain.

Damnation.

"There's a sitting room adjoining this," she said cheerily. "And another bedroom for me. It's small but quite lovely. Oh, and now I know why there are two doors labeled with the same room number. The other is for *my* bedchamber."

"Excellent." It meant they might be bumping into each other often.

God help him, he was hopeless. He must not dwell on that. Instead he concentrated on starting the fire.

Flora sat on the edge of the bed. "Where on earth did you learn to do that?"

"A fairy taught me," he joked.

"That sounds like something you'd say. Even after all the time we spent together in Bath, I could never make out who you really were. Nobody could. You were always so cagey with everyone, deflecting questions with jests."

When he didn't answer, she shook her head. "You did it just to intrigue us, didn't you? It worked on us young ladies—we thought it delightful. But the matrons thought it quite mysterious, and that was not a good thing in their eyes."

He rose and dusted off his hands. "No doubt."

"Speculations ranged from your being an American—which could explain your German name yet lack of a German accent—to your being a rich count or some such who met Thornstock abroad."

The flash of mischief in her eyes stirred old feelings in him he desperately wished were dead. Then a curtain came down over her features, and he was locked out once more. He understood. This time he meant to tread more carefully himself. He could make amends without promising anything.

He could, damn it.

She went on. "That made sense to us. The duke did grow up in Prussia. But Thornstock was as cagey about the truth as you were. He told us almost nothing. To be honest, your mention of your German father a few minutes ago was the first I'd heard of him."

He kicked himself for even mentioning his family. Nor was he about to tell her of them now, though she seemed to be waiting for him to do so. Instead, he revealed something less painful. "The truth is, I met Thorn in a provincial theater in Bristol."

Given how she leaned toward him, that did *not* put her off. "Were you both attending a play? Or had you already started productions of the Felix plays?"

He hesitated. He was tired of lying for Thorn but couldn't stop until he knew whether Thorn also meant to claim those plays for himself. Still, Konrad could reveal enough of the truth to keep him from temptation. Once she realized how far below her rank he was, she would let him be. Her parents might be destitute—the only reason that explained her working as a companion—but they were still gentry, and he definitely was not.

"Actually," he said, "I was in Bristol with my theater troupe, performing the part of Benedict in *Much Ado About Nothing*. I learned to build fires by spending summer nights outdoors while traveling with the troupe. We generally cooked over an open flame, so someone had to build a fire. Most of the time, it was me."

Her mouth dropped open. Clearly, she'd expected any explanation but that.

He turned away to avoid seeing her regard for him, such as it was, plummet. "That is why, as I told you earlier, my modesty isn't false. I come from humble beginnings. I would probably still be traveling with the theater company if Thorn hadn't met me."

"But . . . but when *we* met, your manners were polished. You fit in."

"Good actors generally do." He shrugged. "I'd been playing the part of gentlemen on the stage for five years at least. More, if you include my roles when I was a youth. There are still gaps in my knowledge about etiquette and manners, although I can usually cover those up by watching someone else."

"So what were you doing in Bath?" she asked.

Was she asking out of genuine interest or out of anger that he had pulled the wool over her eyes years ago? "Thorn had . . . er . . . read my unfinished play and thought it showed promise. He fancied himself a patron of the arts, so he wanted to bring me into London society as a playwright rather than an actor. He hoped the social whirl might inspire me to finish my play. Our trip to Bath was to make sure I could blend in. A writer has to, you know. He must be a part of the world without drawing too much attention to himself."

Ah, he spun such a nonsensical web. His and Thorn's trip to Bath had really been a test to see if Konrad could convincingly play the part of a playwright in society. It wouldn't have helped Thorn if Konrad had behaved more like a provincial actor of no consequence than a wit Thorn had "discovered" in Bath.

"So I was just practice for you?" she whispered behind him. "Our flirtations were merely you seeing if you could fit in with London nobility?"

Hearing the catch in her throat, he rounded on her. "No,

damn it." She wore a look of betrayal. God, he'd never wanted her to feel that. "You were definitely not 'practice.' If I were to call you anything, you were my respite. I could be myself around you, because you never looked down on me. Do you know how freeing that is?"

"I have some idea." Before he could probe that statement, she approached the bed and grabbed a sheet. "I suppose I should start this if Lady Whitmarsh is to have any sleep tonight."

That sparked his temper. She wouldn't talk to him as freely as he talked to her. It was maddening. "Why do you let the viscountess bully you?"

"Bully me?" She faced him with an unreadable expression. "She's not nearly the harridan you seem to think. She merely turns cranky when her plans are upset—like when an ice-and-snow storm keep her from her destination."

"Ah," he said, although he wasn't convinced.

"She and I understand each other." Flora looked away. "She has never once tried to put me in my place, something any other employer would have done. *She's* the one I can be myself around without fear of punishment."

If Flora had been setting out to wound him, she'd certainly succeeded. He had once wanted to play that role for her. He stepped as close as he dared. "Did you ever feel comfortable enough to be yourself around *me*?"

Her eyes shone amber in the firelight. "Of course." She caught herself and returned to making the bed. "Or as much as any woman can be when she thinks she's being courted and fears she'll make a bad impression."

"You mean," he said bitterly, "when first we met, you were behaving exactly like every other woman hunting a husband. You said what you thought I wanted to hear."

Her lovely face clouded over. "Not entirely. But I was young and more circumspect then. I was in Bath to find someone to marry, pure and simple. Or at least, that was my parents' hope for me. It was the reason they agreed to let my great-aunt take me under her wing and champion me in Bath society, where I might have a chance of making a decent match."

That caught him off guard. "Lady Hyde was your great-aunt? You never said what her connection to your family was."

Flora finished making the bed. "She was my mother's aunt. Mother wasn't heir to her fortune, of course, because my great-aunt already had sons. So helping me find a good husband was something Great-Aunt Hyde could do to aid my family. She offered to give me a substantial dowry, as long as I . . . I attracted a suitable fellow. Since my parents and I were the quintessential poor relations, it was very generous of her."

His head reeled. He'd thought that Flora shared her chaperone's high station, which had made Flora far above *his* station. That was why he'd been careful not to make any promises or compromise her. He hadn't been looking for a wife then. He'd barely been able to take care of himself, much less a family.

He still wasn't, not entirely.

Suddenly it hit him exactly how much her words revealed. "So when I, a very unsuitable fellow, toyed with your affections, I upset the apple cart. Is that why you're a paid companion now instead of some man's bride?"

Her cheeks flamed. "It was a long time ago."

"That's not an answer," he said.

Taking up the other set of sheets, she walked through the next room and into her bedroom. Though he knew it unwise, he followed her. He had to discover how much he'd wronged her by going about with her in public and then leaving without offering marriage.

Back then, he hadn't really known the significance of such things. Cut off from his adopted theater family, he had been lonely, and she had seemed to like his company as much as he liked hers. Now, however, after years in high society, he understood that when it came to young ladies, his every action had consequences.

Like being here in her bedchamber, alone, with the door to the passageway closed. He should leave.

He couldn't. He had to know everything she was concealing.

When she shivered, he glanced around. Unlike the other two rooms in the suite, this had no fireplace, and her bed was small. A lump stuck in his throat. This was what he'd unwittingly brought her to. "If you're chilled, you might wish to don your cloak again."

"It gets in the way. I'm fine."

The hell she was. "All this time," he murmured, "I assumed I merely hurt your feelings by leaving without so much as a fare-thee-well. But it was worse than that, wasn't it?"

She snapped the sheet over the bed. "It doesn't matter."

"It matters to me." He moved to stand between her and the bed. "You should have been married by now, with three or four fat, happy children in your nursery. When I saw you last month, I couldn't believe you weren't. I'd assumed—"

"*Assumed?*" Her eyes flashed at him. "Why do men *assume* so very much about women? My only hope of marrying well was my great-aunt's offer of a dowry. She'd already made it quite clear she wouldn't give it to me unless I chose a worthy husband and not some fortune hunter. She certainly wasn't going to waste it on . . . on a man of dubious background, even if you *had* offered marriage. And had stayed around."

"But once I was gone, why wouldn't she . . . why wouldn't *you* just—"

"Find another man? It wasn't that easy. In her eyes, in everyone's eyes, I had proven myself unworthy of her money by choosing to give my affections too easily and quickly to a man . . . unworthy of me."

Great God. "Did you agree I was unworthy?"

"Not at the time, no." She skirted him and went to the other side of the bed to continue making it. "I was fond of you. I enjoyed our time together. And you were the good friend of a wealthy duke. How could you not be . . . worthy?"

"Forgive me, Flora, I had no idea that you were pinning your hopes—"

"On you?" she clipped out. "Of course you didn't. You were long gone, off to London to find fortune and fame. Without, as you said, 'so much as a fare-thee-well.'"

"The lack of a farewell wasn't my fault," he protested. "Thorn, like your great-aunt, got worried when he saw that you and I were drawing attention. He'd just gone through his own sticky situation with a young lady, and he didn't want something similar to happen to me. He knew I had no money, that his . . . *my* play might never be finished, and even if it was, might not succeed in the London theaters. So after a couple of weeks in Bath, he had our bags packed and put into the carriage without my knowledge, then told me we were leaving."

She nodded. "It was probably just as well. If you had stayed, I might have . . . we might have—" She shrugged. "It doesn't matter. After you left, rumors circulated that you were a fortune hunter. I didn't believe them. We'd had such a . . . a strong connection. You wrote heavenly poetry. To me, you seemed more like a prince than a pauper."

She'd found his poetry "heavenly"? He shouldn't be so pleased, but he was. His poetry meant far more to him than his pretend plays, since it came straight from his soul.

With stiff movements, she tucked the sheet under the mattress. "I made matters worse by defending you. I was sure that any day you would come waltzing into the Pump Room and put the gossips in their place."

"I did go back to find you," he put in. "After the production of my fourth play, I returned to Bath for a week to discover discreetly where you'd gone. But nobody knew. I had let too much time pass, and people had forgotten." So he'd frozen his heart in an ice house, determined not to let anyone else in.

"Of course they'd forgotten." She snorted. "Wasn't your fourth play *The Wild Adventures of a Foreign Gentleman Loose in*

*London*? That originally came out in March of 1806 or thereabouts, long after my great-aunt and I left Bath. It was the one..." She trailed off as she apparently realized how hard he was staring at her. "What?"

"You've read the Felix plays?"

A strange alarm crossed her face before she masked it. "Some of them. I could hardly avoid it. They were published from here to beyond."

She'd read his—*Thorn's*—plays. He had to know why. "Did you ever see them on the stage?"

Her cheeks flamed as scarlet as her gown. "Only that last one, the charity performance of *The Wild Adventures, etc.,* where you and I encountered each other. Lady Whitmarsh isn't fond of travel these days. And even when we go to town, it's not during the season. She doesn't like how crowded the city gets."

"So I've heard," he said dryly.

"From whom?"

"Vanessa. We are grand friends, you know."

"She's happily married now," she warned, "so—"

"*Friends*, sweetheart." When the misspoken endearment seemed to lighten her mood, he went on hastily. "Nothing more, even if she was interested, which she is not. Besides, I am equally friendly with her husband." Now, anyway. He stared Flora down. "Does it bother you that the duchess is my sometime confidante?" He hoped it did, though he hated himself for it.

"Certainly not," she said. "Why should it?"

Why should it, indeed? Still, she'd read what she thought were *his* plays, and more than one, too. That had to mean something.

He wanted to ask what she thought of them, but whatever she said would have more to do with Thorn's writing than his. So he didn't.

Instead, he asked, "How much longer after I left Bath did you and your great-aunt stay?"

She picked up a pillow and stuffed it into a pillowcase. "A

week or so. Great-Aunt Hyde was so angry over my 'foolish behavior' that she told me I was needed at home, and we left. That
was the sad end to my life in high society."

After tossing the pillow to the headboard, she unfolded a coverlet and arranged it neatly on the narrow bed. "Once I got home,
I couldn't bear more than a week of listening to my parents rail at
me over how I'd lost my plum chance. I answered an advertise-
ment, and Lady Whitmarsh hired me, thank heaven."

"Hard to believe that our small flirtation caused all of that."
He had more to answer for than he'd realized. "I will never understand high society. You and I didn't even have a proper kiss,
for God's sake."

She gaped at him. "Yes, we did." She looked wounded. "Have
you forgotten the night we stood on the balcony and watched the
moon come up?"

He advanced on her. "A *proper* kiss. That was a simple peck on
the lips."

"Which is precisely what a 'proper' kiss is," she said archly.
"Anything more would be decidedly *im*proper."

"You have a point." He came up to cup her cheek, exulting
when he let him caress her buttery-soft skin. He wanted more,
*needed* more. "Do you even know what an improper kiss is?"

"I can . . . well imagine." Her breathing grew labored, and she
wouldn't look at him.

He tipped up her chin, and her beautiful eyes met his at last,
widening as he bent closer. "No need to imagine—I'll show you."
Then he bent and pressed his mouth to hers.

At first he contented himself with exploring her lips, gauging
their suppleness, letting himself sink into them. Before he knew
it, he was sinking his tongue between them and relishing how she
angled her head up to receive his forays into her mouth.

God, she tasted of Christmas, of cinnamon and cloves, mulled
wine and plum pudding. He caught her head in his hands to kiss
her more in earnest, drinking up her every sweet moan, letting

himself enjoy them because he feared he might only get this one chance.

So no matter how unwise it was and how unlikely this kiss could come to anything, he meant to make good use of these stolen moments with her. Before she found out how low a fellow he truly was.

# Chapter 4

Flora covered his hands with hers, meaning to pull them away. Instead, she just left hers there, like a half-meant caress. The trouble was she wanted to fully explore his *improper* kiss. She'd never had one, and it thrilled her with every bold thrust of his tongue.

Her mind shouted, *Danger, danger, imminent danger!* But she didn't care. For once in her life, danger appealed, especially when it took the form of his masculine hands cradling her head, his masculine scent of woodsmoke and leather engulfing her senses . . . his masculine kiss searing her and tempting her and . . .

Oh, how wicked it was! She loved it. No one had ever dared to kiss her in this cheeky fashion. Her head spun and her pulse thundered in her ears until she thought she might faint.

As if he feared the same thing, he slipped one hand from beneath hers to slide it about her waist and hold her flush against him.

He drew back long enough to murmur, "*That*, sweetheart, is an improper kiss."

She barely got out the words, "Most improper," before he was kissing her again with long, slow thrusts of his tongue. Flora nearly swooned, like a tipsy maiden at her debut, but she caught him about the neck to steady herself. Of course, that led to her sliding her hand through his thick, silky hair, which led to *his* kissing a path down her cheek to her ear, where he playfully seized the lobe in his teeth.

Trying and failing to catch her breath, she had just smoothed her hand down his surprisingly muscular neck when she heard a sound in the sitting room.

"What do you think *you're* doing, you little rascal?" said the unmistakable voice of Lady Whitmarsh.

In a panic at the thought that they'd been caught in a compromising position, she turned toward the door, but Konrad snagged her hand just as she registered that no one was there. Besides, the viscountess would never call Konrad a rascal. If she caught them kissing in her bedchamber, she'd call him something far harsher. Blackguard. Scoundrel.

Heavenly Seducer.

Flora frowned. That was her own term for him, especially after that amazing kiss. Then she heard a faint meow, and relief flooded her.

But not for long. The meow grew more pronounced. The cat was walking their way, devil take it! And Lady Whitmarsh was soon to follow.

She pulled her hand from Konrad's and tipped her head toward the door leading out to the passageway. His nod showed he understood. But before he left, he bent to whisper in her ear, "Until later."

Then he was gone, thank heaven. He'd even managed not to make much sound as he opened and shut the door. Meanwhile, with one whisper he'd left her in a heightened state of awareness, craving more of him.

How did he do it? *Why* would he do it? Just because she was handy? Or because he'd missed her for all these years?

A mew alerted her to the entrance of the cat, a small tabby with gray stripes and quizzical eyes. Flora, who'd always liked cats, said, "Well, aren't you a little slyboots?"

As if in answer, the cat jumped up on the bed.

"He is, isn't he?" Lady Whitmarsh came in, clearly not suspecting anything, if Flora were to judge from her broad smile. "Mrs. Waverly said his name is Ivan. Followed me right up the stairs and into my room. Did you see we have a sitting room that could also serve as a dining room? This inn is quite lovely. I'm not sure about the lack of staff, but I suppose we can endure it for one night."

"I fear it may be more."

"Nonsense," the viscountess said with a wave of her hand. "I spoke with Braxton, and he assured me that if it were at all possible for us to leave tomorrow, he would take us."

Flora picked up the kitty, which, to her surprise, allowed it. As Flora stroked him, he began to purr. "You are clearly a lady's cat, Mr. Ivan. You like to flirt." Just like someone else she knew.

*Until later*, Konrad had said. The very promise of it made her shiver deliciously.

"So, what did Mr. Juncker have to say?" Lady Whitmarsh asked.

Flora started. Was the viscountess reading her mind now? That would be alarming. "What do you mean?"

"He accompanied you up the stairs, didn't he? I'm sure you had a conversation of some kind."

A relieved breath escaped her. Oh yes, and what a conversation it had been, too. She still couldn't believe he'd once been part of a theatrical troupe. He'd acted ashamed to admit it, but she thought it fascinating. A man as talented as he, snatched from a troupe to remake himself as a playwright. Astonishing!

She was still dying to know *why* he'd been in the troupe and where his parents were. Had they been actors, too?

When Flora said nothing, Lady Whitmarsh stepped close to brush Flora's sleeve with her hand. "You're getting cat hair on your gown."

Flora sighed. "What does it matter? No one but the guests here will even see my gown."

"And Mr. Juncker. Surely he's the only one who matters."

"I'm not certain he even noticed," she said dully.

"I knew it!" the viscountess cried. "He was in here with you when I came up."

Flora blinked. "What? No! Why would you think that?"

Obviously noting her agitation, Ivan jumped out of her arms, and Lady Whitmarsh narrowed her gaze on Flora. "Because I assume you only took off your cloak once you were in the room. That means he couldn't yet have seen your gown. But you said he didn't even seem to notice it, which implies he did see it."

She scrambled for a believable answer. "Well, I . . . um . . . I took my cloak off while he was building your fire, and we had a few moments of conversation. That is all."

"Is it? Hmm." With interest lighting her face, the viscountess sat down on the bed. "Tell me everything. Spare no detail."

Flora lifted an eyebrow. "I thought you hated him."

"I did, but only because he broke your heart years ago in Bath." She sniffed. "Not that you deigned to tell me the whole tale even after I finally got us tickets to one of his plays, but it was enough. Then I asked around about him . . . and learned things that changed my perspective."

"You certainly kept your own counsel about it," Flora grumbled.

"I always do, until I'm sure which way the wind blows. If you still hated him, I didn't want to interfere." She laughed. "But any gentleman who offers to bring pails of water up two narrow flights of stairs for a woman is worth his weight in gold."

"I'm not sure he *is* a gentleman," Flora said. "And he hasn't brought the pails up yet, either."

"If he doesn't, I shall consider striking him from my list."

"What list?"

"Of all the men worthy enough to marry you, of course."

Oh, Lord. Flora dropped onto the bed next to Lady Whitmarsh. "Why are older women always trying to find a man worthy of me? What do I have that makes *me* such a catch?"

"A big heart, my dear. A trusting soul, and a practical mind. All of those are more important to a successful marriage than fame or fortune. Or even beauty, which you have in abundance."

Flora eyed her suspiciously. "Are you trying to marry me off?"

"Of course. A woman as fine as you deserves a fine man. And those plays probably made him rich."

Her stomach began to churn. "Please tell me this isn't your way of gently dismissing me from your employ."

"Don't be absurd." Lady Whitmarsh patted Flora's knee. "As far as I'm concerned, you can serve as my companion until we both wither on the vine. But I'm not so oblivious as to assume that caring for a woman of advanced age is your life's ambition."

"I beg your pardon," Flora said stoutly. "I am perfectly content in my post." She *was*. She really was. Most of the time, anyway.

"There's more to life than taking the safe path to avoid being hurt."

"That's not what I meant," Flora said, although it partly was. "I make my own money, and I answer to no one but you, who, by the way, are exceedingly entertaining to work for."

Lady Whitmarsh considered that. "Most women of my consequence would find that description appalling." She broke into a smile. "But I like it. I like to entertain where I can. You and I share a similar sense of humor, after all."

Then the viscountess sobered. "Unfortunately, since I am a good thirty years your senior, you will almost certainly outlive me. Trust me, you do not want to be alone at my age. *I* don't want to be alone at my age, which is why I hired you. And will probably hire someone after you marry, too. I may even allow you to pick your own successor."

"*If* I marry, you mean."

"Not a bit. I saw how Mr. Juncker stared at you during that party at Thornstock's last month. It was clear he hadn't forgotten you any more than you had forgotten him. I suspect he cares for you more than he lets on." Lady Whitmarsh seized her hand. "So, what did he say during your few moments of conversation?"

Flora narrowed her gaze. "I suppose you'll plague me about it until I tell you everything." Well, except for how alarmingly much she'd enjoyed his kiss. "But I will do so only if *you* tell *me* what you learned about him in town that convinced you to like him." She lifted an eyebrow. "I doubt you approve of his reputation for debauchery."

"So you know about that," the viscountess said cautiously.

Flora jumped to her feet. "Of course I know about that. Everyone in London knows about that. The whole blasted world probably knows about that. He isn't exactly what one would call 'discreet.' "

"Yet you like him."

"I like the Konrad Juncker I met in Bath." Flora drew in a heavy breath. "He was not a rakehell then."

"Are you sure he is one now?" The viscountess leaned closer. "Because my staff questioned the servants at the Albany, where he lives, and they said that when Thornstock wasn't in town, he stayed in his rooms. Even when he didn't, he most often attended theater performances, apparently looking for ways to improve the productions of his plays. He must have succeeded. They're very popular."

"They are, even if I don't like them that much."

"I prefer his poetry."

"So do I. But I daresay poetry doesn't pay as well as playwriting." Honestly, she didn't know for certain. She'd written nothing but prose. And songs, but she could only write the melodies. She took the lyrics from poems. She did enjoy *reading* poetry, especially his, but she would never tell *him* that, since his head was no doubt swelled already. "Not that I have anything to say about what he writes."

A knock sounded on her door.

Lady Whitmarsh smirked at her. "It appears I won't have to take Mr. Juncker off my list of eligible gentlemen after all."

Flora hurried to open the door, praying he wouldn't give them away by word or deed. Konrad was standing there with two large pails of water. Good heavens. What a strong fellow he must be!

"You see, Lady Whitmarsh?" she called back to her employer. "I told you he would be here with those pails." She stepped to the side so he could enter. "Mr. Juncker is quite the gentleman."

He leveled a mischievous gaze on her. "And I always keep my promises."

She knew only too well he wasn't talking about the water, either. *Until later.* Oh, dear, she really needed to put *that* hint of a promise out of her mind.

He brought the water over to a washstand in the corner. He even filled her pitcher. Ignoring Lady Whitmarsh, he said to Flora, "This should last you the night, Miss Younger."

After tucking the pail out of the way, he finally faced the viscountess. "I can fill your pitcher, too, Lady Whitmarsh, if you wish."

"I-I'll fill hers from the rest of the water in my pail," Flora said, praying that she wasn't blushing enough for him—or her employer—to see. "You should keep a pail for yourself."

"I'll get mine. Eventually." He stared so intently at her that his words implied another meaning. Good heavens. That roused her blood as surely as if he'd run his finger down her throat. And then lower.

"Besides," he went on, "I'm sure our new arrivals will need water, and I enjoy keeping busy."

"Very well," Flora said. "Then thank you."

"Yes," the viscountess added. "Thank you, indeed. And what's this about new arrivals? How many? Who are they?"

"There's a gentleman named Faringdon, another named Matthews, and a lady by the name of Miss Macleod. Along with a few servants. That's all I know."

Lady Whitmarsh looked full to bursting from the effort of holding back her opinions about his limited information, but she merely walked to the door that led to their sitting room. "Then I'll show you where the washstand is in my room."

"I hope to see you at dinner, Miss Younger," Konrad said with a wink.

"We can hardly avoid that," Flora said, "unless twenty more people descend on the inn seeking shelter."

"The roads are too bad for that now," he said. "No one is out and about with the ice everywhere."

Lady Whitmarsh sighed. "But it will be gone tomorrow, don't you think?"

"I doubt it." Konrad picked up the pail. "We may end up spending Christmas here."

Another knock sounded. Wondering who it might be, Flora opened the door. It was Braxton, huffing and puffing.

"I brought your bags up, miss." Braxton put them on her bed before she could help him, although it was clearly a struggle for him.

"Oh, thank you, Braxton," Flora said. He looked awfully red in the face. The footmen usually managed the baggage.

"I'll get her ladyship's after I sit a spell," Braxton said.

"Give me a moment," Konrad said, "and I'll bring up her ladyship's bags for you. You just have to show me which ones are hers."

The viscountess arched an eyebrow at Flora as if to say, *You see?*

Braxton said, "Oh, no, sir. I wouldn't ask that of a gentleman."

"Clearly he's *not* a gentleman, thank God," Lady Whitmarsh said. "No gentleman would readily offer to do such work, so you might as well take advantage of it."

"Lady Whitmarsh!" Flora said.

"Her ladyship is right." Konrad chuckled. "And truly, Braxton, I don't mind. Especially since I believe the actual gentlemen who've arrived are being expected to do their part as well."

Konrad carried the pail into the other room and returned a few moments later. "Come on, Braxton." They left.

As Lady Whitmarsh went to freshen up, Flora began to unpack. Her room had a decent-sized armoire for clothes. A pity she couldn't stuff Konrad in it and forget about him entirely. But she would probably end up taking him out just so he could kiss her again.

Good heavens, what a thought. She was no silly girl giggling over the officers in the village square. She was a grown woman, and he was markedly flirting with her, the same as he'd done in Bath. But if he didn't mean any of it, she mustn't encourage him.

Why was he behaving this way with her? She would have to be bold and make him tell her. Otherwise, the events of Bath would play out just as they had before, and this time she feared she wouldn't get over the heartbreak.

# Chapter 5

For the next hour, Konrad hauled water pails and made sure his post-horse and Lady Whitmarsh's horses were comfortable. It wasn't as if the ladies could do anything about that. Although Peter was in charge of the stables, he had to be feeling overwhelmed by now, and helping out there was the least Konrad could do under the circumstances.

But the whole time he was busy, he could only think of Flora. How lush her body had been under his hands. How tender her lips. How badly he'd wanted to lay her down on a bed—any bed—and show her how much he desired her.

He ought to know better. His prospects hadn't changed. He could only offer her a tumultuous future with a former actor and sometime poet.

Worse yet, any day now Thorn might unveil the subterfuge Konrad had been part of, leaving him with only his savings and a bad reputation for misleading theater management. People wouldn't blame Thorn. They would blame *him*, since he'd done all the lying, something he'd never been comfortable doing.

He hated not being able to tell Flora the truth about the plays.

He had no right to kiss her, touch her, if he couldn't be honest with her. How could she trust him to take care of her when her assumptions about his future were rooted in a lie?

Someone caught him on the gallery to tell him dinner would be served at five p.m., so he headed for his room to dress. He paused outside Flora's door and actually considered entering and kissing her senseless again. All the chaos in his world settled into place when he held her.

Then he heard someone coming up the stairs and continued on to his room. He must gain control over his desires. He wasn't a green youth anymore, for God's sake.

When he went down to dinner, he found all the guests in a large public room off the passageway where travelers generally dined, apparently. As he approached the table, he got a better look at their new fellow guests: a gentleman named Faringdon, whom he'd met earlier in the stables, and Miss Macleod, sitting beside him. They seemed to know each other, but he couldn't be certain.

He took a seat to the left of Flora. Lady Whitmarsh was on Flora's right. She nodded regally to him, though Flora stared straight ahead. Actually, she was staring at Faringdon, quite a good-looking fellow, curse him.

Their hostess was nowhere to be seen, probably still dealing with the unexpected patient who'd landed in her lap. Alice was there, looking very matter-of-fact as she served up what appeared to be chicken soup. He liked chicken soup. They could serve it every day he was here, and he'd be content.

Loaves of bread had been sliced and set at intervals down the table, along with little pots of butter. Since the other two fellows had already taken some slices, he did the same. He knew it would be poor manners to dip the bread in the soup, but he was sorely tempted. Still, the crusty bread had a smooth flavor and the butter was delicious, so he was satisfied.

Honestly, he would be satisfied with sawdust bread as long as Flora sat next to him, her scent of cinnamon and oranges lightly flavoring the air. He only wished she weren't ignoring him, pretending to be very engrossed in the meal.

He noticed she dipped the side of her spoon into the soup, probably something they taught gently bred young ladies to do. Seeing her follow proper etiquette despite the informal circumstances put a dent in his pleasure. Thorn had taught him as much as possible about the finer points of deportment, but there was always more to learn.

What had he been thinking? Even if he could manage the many other difficulties of his future, she would never countenance marriage to a man like him. He might not be a green youth anymore, but she was no schoolgirl, either. She dealt in practicalities now, as should he. And he didn't want to end up being a source of embarrassment to his wife.

"Mr. Juncker," Lady Whitmarsh said as she leaned forward to look past Flora. "Do you intend to continue writing the Felix plays? They seem quite successful."

That began a bit of discussion about what everyone did for a living, thank God. The last thing he wanted to talk about was his unsettled plans for the future.

Flora remained silent. She might have read all the plays, but that didn't mean she'd approved of them. Not that he cared. He'd only written a few lines here and there, at most a scene or two in each.

"So?" Lady Whitmarsh prodded. "Have you started writing the next one?"

"No. And I never will," he bit out.

Flora looked at him, her eyes wide. "Never?"

Was that disappointment he saw on her face? Hard to tell. "The seventh, which will open next April, was the last I wrote. I am done with Felix." In more ways than one.

"Then what will you write next?" Flora asked. "I'm sure your many admirers would be delighted by anything you offered."

Did he imagine it, or did he detect a bit of an edge in her remark about his "many admirers"? "Perhaps. Fortunately, I have

the final say, which is that I intend to stop writing for the theater."
Damn, now she and Lady Whitmarsh would want to know why.

To his surprise, rather than asking that, Lady Whitmarsh said,
"I am glad to hear it. Your poetry outshines your other writing by
far. You write *good* poetry, well-respected among other poets, and
not that drivel written by Henry James Pye." She shook her head.
"I don't know why you would even waste your time writing plays
when you could be England's next poet laureate."

That was a surprising remark, coming from Lady Whitmarsh.

"Henry James Pye was made poet laureate in exchange for
doing political favors," Flora said as she buttered her bread. "You
can hardly expect him to write good poetry, too, no matter how
*he* fancies his abilities." When Konrad's gaze shot to her, she
blushed. "I read it somewhere."

"*The London Society Times,* perhaps?" he asked.

This time her gaze shot to *him*. "Why . . . er . . . would you ask
that?"

"Because that gossip rag hates everyone, especially me, although it did speak the truth about Pye."

Before Flora could respond, Lady Whitmarsh asked, "Do you
deem it a 'gossip rag' because women write some of the pieces?
Or because the writers are simply not fond of your plays?"

"Not 'writers.' Only one writer." He stared hard at the viscountess. "I'm sure you have read A Discerning Lady's reviews."
And since Lady Whitmarsh disliked him in general, she might
very well *be* "A Discerning Lady," taking her disapproval of him
out on the plays she thought he'd written.

Then again, if she had a bad opinion of him as a person, why
not write bad reviews of his poetry, too? Why say she admired it?

"Should I assume you haven't seen the plays performed?" he
asked the viscountess. "Other than at that charity performance, I
mean."

"You shouldn't assume anything." Lady Whitmarsh finished
off her wine. "Assumptions are always unwise."

Konrad poured her another from one of the bottles on the table. Perhaps it would encourage her to say more so he could figure out whether she'd written those reviews. The damned things drove Thorn mad. "I asked because I noticed that the 'Discerning Lady' seems to have only read the plays, rather than seen them performed. I thought perhaps you had done so as well."

"How could you possibly tell that this reviewer only *read* the plays?" Flora asked, with a barely detectible glance at Lady Whitmarsh.

Aha. He might be able to get the truth out of Flora later. "The script of a play isn't the play itself. A play is designed to be performed. That means the director and stage manager have some influence on how it succeeds as a performance. If someone reviews a play and makes no mention of how certain scenes were staged or actors handled their lines, that person is reviewing the script and not a play."

Flora's eyes widened. "Oh, yes! Now I understand what you mean. That charity performance differed markedly from how I pictured things when I read the play. I mean, the script. On the stage, Felix was always moving furniture or yawning or nudging someone. That wasn't in the script—or not all of it, anyway."

Their discussion was cut off by the entrance of Mrs. Waverly and Alice, who was lugging a large kettle of stew. Within moments she had it dished into serving bowls, which were set on the table along with serving spoons.

"Apparently, we are expected to serve ourselves," Lady Whitmarsh murmured.

"We're lucky to have lodgings at all," Flora whispered. "We can hardly complain."

He chuckled. Flora was right, but he suspected Lady Whitmarsh wasn't used to keeping her comments to herself, no matter what the circumstances.

After they'd dined on what was surprisingly good mutton stew, Mrs. Waverly gave a long speech about how everyone would have to pitch in with chores. He readily suggested he could haul pails up and down the stairs from the well as he'd been doing. The other gentlemen offered to do so as well.

But her next request was a bit harder to swallow. Apparently, they'd eaten the last of the meat, so she suggested that the men might wish to hunt.

He stifled a groan. It was one thing to haul pails and build fires. It was quite another to go looking for small creatures to murder. He had nothing against eating them once they were killed. But he had hunted so rarely, he wasn't sure how to do it effectively. Especially since he wasn't particularly handy with a gun.

The few times he'd hunted with Thorn and other gentlemen, he'd spent his time joking and drinking to cover up his basic discomfort with the process. Gentlemen learned to shoot from an early age. Men like him did not. Surely that stalwart fellow across from him, along with Peter, was more than capable of bringing in enough game for everyone. But under the circumstances he felt honor bound to volunteer.

Then Miss Macleod offered to hunt as well, and he was glad that he had. Besides, if he couldn't adapt to this situation, he could hardly fault Lady Whitmarsh for her lack of ability to do so.

Apparently, however, the sick gentleman Konrad had dragged in would not be joining them, either for the hunting or for their meals. Mrs. Waverly was keeping him isolated as he was gravely ill.

So far, the women had been spared any duties. But that changed when Flora offered to help in the kitchen. It was decided that Flora would make pies under Alice's supervision, since the one thing the inn had plenty of was apples and a few other items, like cheese and butter.

Only with an effort did he contain his amusement when he saw the startled expression on Lady Whitmarsh's face. Still, to his surprise the viscountess agreed to make bread if someone would show her how.

Now *that,* he would have to see. He doubted Lady Whitmarsh had ever darkened the door of her own kitchen, much less made bread. He wasn't even sure he would want to eat any bread made by her.

But he would enjoy watching her try. For that matter, he would vastly enjoy watching *Flora* bake a pie. He liked pie, and he liked Flora. The combination was nigh on to irresistible. Too bad he had to go hunt first thing in the morning, while she was baking.

Flora rose to go speak to Alice, and as he watched her, Lady Whitmarsh slid over into Flora's seat. "Let her be," she murmured.

He scowled at her. "I beg your pardon?"

"I see the way you look at my companion. Let her be."

"Or what?"

"Or you will have me to reckon with."

He was on the verge of telling Lady Whitmarsh he could take on a presumptuous dowager any day of the week when Flora returned, eyeing them both with concern. And in that moment, he knew he could not let Flora be. Not until whatever lay between them was settled for good.

Flora barely managed to keep silent until she and Lady Whitmarsh left dinner. But once they were climbing the stairs, Flora, with a quick backward glance to make sure Konrad was nowhere about, asked her employer what he and she had been discussing.

Apparently her ladyship was more than eager to tell her. "I have ensured that your young man will pursue you, if that is what you wish of him."

"He's not *my* young man," Flora said mechanically. "And how could you possibly ensure such a thing?"

They came out onto the gallery, and Lady Whitmarsh leaned close. "By telling him to leave you alone, my dear. No man will stand for being thwarted by a busybody like me in his pursuit of the lady he desires. And Mr. Juncker most definitely desires you." When Flora colored, the viscountess winked. She actually winked, as if she thought this a vastly amusing game! "I mean that he desires you to be his *wife*, of course."

"I don't think that's what you meant at all," Flora said.

With a self-satisfied smile, Lady Whitmarsh marched toward her room.

Flora kept pace with her. "Because I'm not so sure he *does* desire me, at least not as his wife. He's had nearly a decade to offer for me if that was what he wanted." She didn't believe his excuse—that he'd returned to find her and hadn't been successful. He'd certainly waited long enough to look for her, after all.

Lady Whitmarsh halted to unlock her door, but before they could enter, Miss Macleod called out from behind them, "Miss Younger!"

Flora paused and waited for the woman. As Miss Macleod caught up to her, she said, "I hate to ask this, but I need help with . . . undressing."

"Oh, of course!" Flora said. "We're all in the same situation here, aren't we?" She turned to Lady Whitmarsh, but before she could even speak, the viscountess said, "Go on, then. It's fine. I can wait."

"It won't take long," Flora said, for she could see the exhaustion in her employer's eyes. For all her stalwart nature, Lady Whitmarsh could tire easily in winter.

Some time later, after helping Miss Macleod undress and then Lady Whitmarsh, Flora was able to get her own clothes off with the viscountess's help and settle in for the evening, comfortable in nightgown and stockings.

Thank goodness she'd had the forethought before dinner to put a few of the bricks provided by the inn into the fireplace for her and Lady Whitmarsh. Now Flora got cozy beneath the sumptuous covers in the warmth created by the heated brick at her feet. She opened *Don Sebastian; or, The House of Braganza, An Historical Romance* by Anna Maria Porter and forced herself to begin reading the first of the two volumes.

On any other night, she would have found the story engrossing, since it began with the death of one prince and the birth of another. But she was in no mood to read right now. She was still reeling from Lady Whitmarsh's remarks to her after dinner.

The viscountess *was* playing matchmaker, and Flora wasn't sure she liked it. Konrad had clearly charmed her employer somehow. But the man had certainly become a feckless fellow as his popularity had grown. How could he be determined not to write any more plays? Didn't he realize how fortunate he was to have any sort of profession at all in these hard times? What did he plan to do, return to acting?

Forcing herself to stop dwelling on the strange revelations he'd made at dinner, Flora returned to reading her new book, and managed to lose herself in it for nearly two chapters, when she was interrupted by a knock at the door to the passageway.

It must be Alice, coming to stoke up the fire and make sure she was warm for the night. She threw on her wrapper and opened the door.

But it was Konrad, still fully dressed. He even had his greatcoat on and had clearly been outside, for snow dusted his shoulders. And he was staring at her, or rather at the hair tumbled down over her shoulders.

*Until later,* he'd said. Apparently *later* had come.

Self-conscious, she brushed her hair back out of the way and pulled her wrapper more closely about her. "What do you want, Mr. Juncker?"

"There's no one out and about right now, sweetheart. You needn't stand on ceremony. Most everyone has gone to bed, exhausted after a day of harrowing travel."

Boldly, she met his searching gaze. "But not you."

He looked behind her at the lit candle beside her bed and the book next to it. "Nor you, apparently."

"I was reading."

"I can see that." His voice roughened. "And I was too restless to sleep. After years in the theater nursing my plays to fruition, I get that way sometimes."

"So you went outside in this awful weather?"

"I was hoping to find evidence of thawing. Sadly, I found none. I fear we'll be stuck here for tomorrow at the very least." He glanced over to the closed connecting door between her bedroom and Lady Whitmarsh's sitting room. "May I come in?"

"Are you mad?" she whispered. "If her ladyship were to get up and find us together with me dressed like this—"

"Then come to my rooms. I have an independent sitting room just like the one you and the viscountess share, only smaller, and I will be sure to close the door between it and my bedchamber. We can . . . talk."

Talk? She doubted that. Although the thought of being with him without talking was almost too much to resist. "About what?"

He turned sober very quickly. "I don't want to discuss it out here."

"Well, I don't want to risk being seen in my nightclothes going down to your rooms."

"You didn't used to be so cautious."

"And you didn't used to be so wild." Although she did enjoy that bit of reckless abandon in him, she wasn't about to admit it. It didn't bode well for his future. Or hers, if she took up with him again.

"Just put on your cloak," he said, clearly exasperated, "and no one will guess what you're wearing beneath. If anyone sees you in the passageway, you can tell them you went down to drink a glass of sherry. We fellows were certainly making short work of the inn's excellent port after dinner. According to Mrs. Waverly, despite the scarcity of food there's enough ale, wine, and spirits in this inn to keep us celebrating until Twelfth Night."

"Good heavens, I pray we are not here until then."

"So do I. But I must speak to you. It's important."

She eyed him skeptically. Yet he didn't so much as smirk at her. He was serious. And she had questions of her own she wanted answered. "Very well. But not for too long."

After donning her cloak, she let him guide her past Mr. Matthews's room and on to his own. To her vast relief, he'd been right about everyone being abed.

Nor had he lied about having a sitting room. As soon as they were inside it, he took off his greatcoat and hung it on a hook beside the small fireplace. Then he closed the door to his bedchamber.

"Feeling less worried now about being caught together?" he asked.

"Marginally so. But it's late, and we both must rise early, so you'd best say your piece."

"At least sit down. You look like a hare about to bolt."

She felt like a hare about to become a snack. Warily, she perched on the small settee, watching as he began to pace.

After the seconds stretched out into minutes, he halted in front of her. "I'll come right out with it. Do you happen to know who the 'Discerning Lady' from *The London Society Times* really is?"

She felt the blood drain from her face. Had he guessed? He must have guessed.

"Given your expression," he said, "I assume that the answer is yes."

"I can explain—" she began.

"No need. I can easily figure it out. I'm sure that harridan you work for saw it as her duty to plague me with bad reviews. She seems always at the ready to protect you, and no doubt that was her fiendish way of doing so."

"Wait, wait." She jumped to her feet, feeling all at sea. "You think *Lady Whitmarsh* writes them?"

It was his turn to look confused. "Doesn't she?"

When Flora turned away, her heart racing, she cursed herself for not simply agreeing with him. But she'd never been adept at lying, and she sure as the devil would never convince *him* if she tried. He'd always seen right through her.

As he was doing this very moment. "Are you saying that *you* write them?" He scrubbed his face with his hands. " 'A Discerning Lady' is *you*. I should have seen it before. I'm such a fool."

With her stomach in knots, she watched as Konrad walked over to the fireplace, then back so he could glare at her. "Of course it's you. You're the only person in the world who has reason to take revenge upon me, and this is a most fitting revenge." He bowed like an actor at the end of a play. "Bravo, Miss Younger. Bravo."

# Chapter 6

$K$onrad knew it was absurd of him to be angry—he hadn't written but a fraction of the plays. Yet the idea that she had been so furious at him she'd written bad reviews of the six Felix plays didn't sit right. It wasn't fair for her to take her ire out on a man's writing. For all she knew, her reviews had battered his confidence. Instead of merely fueling Thorn's bad temper.

Flora was gaping at him now. "Revenge! I didn't write the reviews for *that* reason. How can you think it?"

"For one, your reviews all disparage my plays."

"N-not entirely." She thrust up her chin. "I complimented them. A bit."

"A bit?" Thinking of Thorn's rage over her reviews, he scowled. "Not the parts I read."

"You didn't read the entirety of the reviews?"

Honestly, he'd read very little, just enough to see why they rubbed Thorn the wrong way. If he'd known *she* was the one writing them, he would have read every word. "Why would I want to bash my head repeatedly against a stone? The first hit was bad enough."

"I wasn't trying to . . . to *hit* you, for pity's sake. I was simply being truthful. You can't possibly fault me for that."

"Being truthful, right. It had nothing to do with wanting revenge on me for leaving Bath without offering marriage. Or without even saying good-bye."

She thrust out her chin. "No, it did not. I take great pride in writing unbiased reviews."

Now she was insulted, which wasn't what he'd meant to do. But seeing her in that nightgown and wrapper earlier, her hair pouring over her shoulders like dark honey, had made him want her all the more, even knowing he couldn't have her and couldn't even support her if he *could* have her. It had infuriated him.

Which wasn't her fault, of course. "Nonetheless," he said, fighting to soften his tone, "according to you, I'm the reason you lost any hope of gaining a respectable husband. No one would blame you for lashing out."

"What sort of person do you think I am? I was not 'lashing out.' I didn't wish revenge on you at all."

"Then why write the reviews?"

She crossed her arms over her chest. "First of all, *The London Society Times* paid me. You may have noticed yours aren't the only works I've reviewed."

"Actually, no, I didn't notice, because I had no idea you were the author. Indeed, I only knew about the reviews at all because—" *Thorn gave them to me.* No, that would rouse her suspicions. "Because a friend showed them to me. Not much of a friend, eh?"

Her eyes narrowed. "Now I wish I'd brought them with me, so I could show you the good parts."

Now he wished he'd read every one from beginning to end. "You said you wrote the reviews because the newspaper paid you. It can't have been much, though. Reviewers make a pittance."

She shrugged, as if to acknowledge the truth of that. "To be honest, I read the first play out of curiosity. Your poetry had so . . . enthralled me in Bath that I couldn't wait to read your play."

Ducking her head, she fiddled with the tie of her cloak. "Forgive me for saying so, but I agree with Lady Whitmarsh in believing your poetry to be better."

He was so intent on watching her fingers and praying that her cloak would magically fall off that it took him a moment to realize what she was saying.

His gaze shot to her. "I . . . er . . . don't know how to answer that. Thank you? How dare you? It's a conundrum, I confess."

A ghost of a smile hovered over her lips. "I mean, your plays do have scenes of sheer beauty, when your characters are almost Shakespearian in their descriptions of what's around them. Those are the parts I like best."

How could he fault her critique? He'd written those parts. "So it's the comic scenes you dislike," he said, suppressing a grin.

"Not entirely. There *was* a scene in which Felix stole fireworks on Guy Fawkes Day—"

"Yes, and someone threw a smoldering rushlight into them and caused an explosion. I wrote that!"

She looked at him oddly. "I *know*. I read it."

He caught himself. If he wasn't careful, he would blather everything, and he'd promised Thorn he would keep their secret. After all the money Thorn had paid him, it was only fair. "It's just that Thorn's wife doesn't like that scene." God, he sounded like a fool. "She says the chemistry is wrong."

"Well, Olivia would notice that, wouldn't she? She's a chemist. But nobody would know except another chemist, so it hardly matters to the average reader. Or playgoer." She regarded him with a soft, almost tender, gaze. "Or me."

"Then you have excellent taste in poetry, bad taste in dramatic literature, and a deplorable knowledge of chemistry."

That got a chuckle out of her. "I confess the last is true. As for the rest, I'm sorry I didn't . . . like your plays all that much."

"Wait, did you say you didn't like my plays all that much? Forgive me, I'm still stuck on the part where you said my poetry enthralled you in Bath." And now he *really* wished he had those reviews in front of him, if only to see whether she'd enjoyed just the parts *he'd* written.

"Very amusing, sir." She nodded toward the door. "I-I should probably go."

"Of course." He paused. "But before you do, there's one more thing. I brought something back for you from my walk."

Striding to his greatcoat, he dug pieces of greenery out of his deep pockets. When he returned she was looking at the small branches with raised eyebrows.

"There's plenty more of the holly behind the inn," he said. "Having seen it embroidered on your gown today, I thought you might like some for your room. It's fairly clear we won't be leaving tomorrow. The ice and snow haven't melted one whit. So I picked some in case we're trapped here through Christmas."

"Thank you," she said, her genuine smile warming the frost around his heart. "Although you do know it's considered bad luck to hang greenery anywhere inside before Christmas Eve, don't you?"

"Are you superstitious?"

"No. But given the bad luck that has stranded us here in the first place, it's probably unwise to tempt fate."

"I don't see it as bad luck," he said, reaching up to tuck a long lock of her hair behind her ear. When she met his gaze with a slumberous one that fired his senses, he added in a low voice, "I rather enjoy the company."

"If we aren't able to leave here before Christmas," she said, even as her breath quickened, "people will blame *you* and your early greenery hanging for it."

"Then keep it to yourself until Christmas Eve. And this, too." He held out a sprig of mistletoe. "Now that I know where it's growing, I'll get more when we're hunting tomorrow. I'll put it in the stables, and you and the other ladies can make decorations early Christmas Eve."

"Decorations? You mean, like kissing boughs?"

"Yes," he murmured. "Like kissing boughs. Or, if you prefer, you can just hang the mistletoe. Like this."

And holding the mistletoe over her head, he bent to kiss her. Good God, she had such a sweet mouth. He pressed the mistletoe into her hand, so he could hold her close, the way he'd been itching to do ever since this afternoon.

Fortunately, she made no sign she wished him to stop. On the contrary, she looped her arms about his neck and stretched up so he could kiss her more boldly, more thoroughly.

Then he realized her cloak was open to reveal her wrapper and nightdress. Hungry for more intimate caresses, he slid his hands inside and burrowed them past her barely closed wrapper to her thinly covered breasts.

She drew back, but didn't pull away entirely or even drop her arms from about his neck. "Are you . . . quite sure you should be doing that?" she whispered.

But her eyes shone in the firelight, and a powerful thrill shot through him to be touching her so carnally. "I'm not sure of anything," he said as he cupped her pert breasts, which were just the size to fill a man's greedy hands. "Do you want me to stop?"

"I don't know."

"Close your eyes." When she did so, he thumbed her nipples erect, even as his flesh grew erect, too. "*Now* do you know?"

"Ohh . . . that's . . . lovely." Her eyes shot open. "I can't believe I said that!"

"I can. I always knew you would be sensual—with me, at least." He bent to nuzzle her ear, then her neck, all the while teasing her breasts with his hands. "It's in every subtle move of your hands, in the way you purse your lips when you're thinking. I never forgot the last time we danced at Bath. Your sweet smiles, your bright eyes, your body moving in perfect harmony with mine . . ."

He drew back to shift one hand to her cascading locks, so he could stroke the magnificent mass. "I have waited for *years* to see your hair tumbled down to your hips. It's so soft, sweetheart, just the way I thought it would be."

She thrust out her lower lip. "It won't curl. And curls are the fashion."

"I don't care about fashion." He drew up a hank of her hair so he could kiss it. "I only care about you."

The minute he saw her pale, he knew it was the wrong thing to say. She pushed away from him. "Like you cared about me in Bath? Wait, is this . . . your revenge on *me* for those reviews?"

"No! How could you think it?"

He reached for her, but she stepped back, wrapping her cursed cloak about her. "How could I not, when you were accusing me of wanting revenge only moments ago?"

"Sweetheart—"

"Don't call me sweetheart when you don't mean it."

"I do mean it," he said hoarsely.

She stared him down. "Are you courting me? Is that what you're doing?"

"I . . . It's not that simple."

Her expression of pain and resignation cut him right through. "It never is." She shook her head at him. "I've heard stories of the women you flirt with, the women who worship you." She reached for the door handle. "I'm not going through this again."

"Here, at least keep these." He bent down to pick up the holly and mistletoe she'd dropped and offered them to her. "I'll get more for you and the others tomorrow."

She nodded, but at least she took them. Then she was out the door, hurrying down the passageway in her forest-green cloak. Only after he was certain she'd arrived safely in her room did he close his own door.

Well, he'd certainly made a hash of that. But she'd looked so damned beautiful in her nightdress and wrapper that he'd been unable to resist taking a few liberties, certainly more than he'd ever taken in Bath.

He had no right, given his situation. If he thought he could trust her to keep Thorn's secret, he would tell her the truth in a heartbeat, but she'd been keeping secrets of her own, and who was to say she wouldn't expose him and Thorn as payment for what they'd done to her in Bath? She was a clever woman, perfectly capable of engineering a complicated scheme of revenge.

But if he didn't tell her, he would lose her for certain . . . if only because she didn't want to suffer that pain again. This was the classic "damned if you do, damned if you don't" situation. He'd always thought that such a dilemma was ridiculous—surely one could always settle somewhere in the middle.

Except that in this case, one couldn't. There was no middle when it came to trust. He either trusted her with everything or trusted her with nothing. Because these half measures would be the ruin of him.

# Chapter 7

Flora's hands ached from peeling, coring, and now slicing apples. How many apples did it take to make a pie, for pity's sake? She had a newfound appreciation for Lady Whitmarsh's cook.

Did Konrad have a cook? Or a valet? Or even a footboy? Was he in debt to half of London or had he invested in the three percents? She had no idea. That was the trouble with Konrad—he asked all the questions and gave very few answers.

Well, that wasn't entirely true. He'd told her he'd spent time in a theatrical troupe, which was more than she'd known before. But last night he hadn't admitted to wanting her for anything beyond bed-warming, and that should give her pause.

Alice came up beside her. "Excellent, miss, you've got them all done. We should have enough pie to go around tonight."

Flora would have thought the apples she'd peeled would provide enough pie to "go around" ten times over, but she wasn't about to question the logic of a young woman wielding a mallet. "What's that thing in your hand for?"

"The pestle? You'll be using it to break down that sugar cone there. We'll need a bit for the bread and the rest for the pies."

"I can do that," Flora said gamely. After last night's frustrating discussion—and other things—with Konrad, she was more than ready to thrash something.

"Let me show you how." Alice hit the sugar cone with the mallet in such a way that a portion came off, which she then pounded to a powder. "I'll take a little for the dough Lady Whitmarsh is working with Mrs. Waverly," she said as she scooped it into a bowl. "You can do the rest of the cone. I'll come back later to show you how to make the crust."

Flora nodded and began pounding. To her surprise, though it was hard work, it soothed her. By the time she was done, she felt more like herself again. She could ignore Konrad. Surely she could manage *that* at least.

Alice came back to show her how to make pie crust by cutting flour and butter together, then adding a bit of ice water. "Whatever you do," Alice said as she rolled out the crust, "once you've put the water in, don't work it much. Do most of your working while it's just the flour and butter. That's the secret."

*The secret to what?* Flora wanted to ask, but also didn't want to appear as stupid as she felt. She'd never dreamed that cooking was this complicated. At least now she knew what *not* to become if something ever happened to Lady Whitmarsh.

After Alice placed one crust in a pie pan, she layered the apples with the sugar and spices inside the crust without using a measure of any kind, and though Flora tried to make note of the amounts, she feared she would forget. Especially since Alice had a unique system. It was "you pile the apples up this high," "add a good handful of sugar," "with just a pinch of cinnamon and a touch of nutmeg," and "a squeeze of lemon."

When Flora ventured to ask how much a "squeeze of lemon" was, Alice said, "a *hard* squeeze." As if that solved everything. Then Alice placed the second crust atop the fruit, sugar, and spice mix, trimmed the edges, and pricked holes in the crust to "vent."

"Done!" Alice dusted off her hands. "Now, miss, do you think you can do what I did?"

"I hope so," Flora said, though all of it had been shown her so quickly, she wasn't sure she'd memorized the instructions.

"Good. I must start preparing the breakfast for the gentlemen so it'll be ready as soon as they finish their hunt."

And off Alice went. That girl would make a soldier on the march blush with shame, she was that energetic.

Flora did what she could. She was careful with the crust. When it didn't hold together as it should, she added a bit more water, and then a bit more again. By the time she was done, it seemed a bit . . . wet? In the end, she hoped the cooking would dry it out. But her pie did end up looking far different from Alice's. More lumpy on the top.

So for the next one, she tried to work the butter and flour more, having remembered what Alice had said about turning it into tiny bits.

Lady Whitmarsh came up to watch.

Flora glanced at her. "Aren't you supposed to be making the bread?"

"It's rising," she said, "whatever that means. Apparently, it takes a while. So I thought I'd come help you."

Flora lifted an eyebrow at her. Lady Whitmarsh gave a rueful laugh, then whispered, "I have no idea if I'm doing any of this correctly, do you?"

"Not really. But when we arrive home, I believe you should double Cook's pay. And perhaps that of the kitchen staff as well."

"You may be right," the viscountess said. "What are you doing now?"

Flora had already kneaded the flour and butter enough, so she was adding the water in carefully. "I'm mixing this. What does it look like?"

"Like you're doing it wrong. I had to be more vigorous with the bread. Mrs. Waverly herself said that, and I should think she'd know more than a kitchen maid."

"I'm not so sure. Alice insisted that I shouldn't work the crust too much."

"Well, that doesn't even make sense, does it?" Lady Whitmarsh said with a wave of her hand. "Bread and pie both have crusts and both use flour and water. So I don't see why you can't treat them the same."

"Lady Whitmarsh?" Mrs. Waverly called out.

"Forgive me," her ladyship said, "I must tend to my duties." Then with a peal of laughter, she hurried back to Mrs. Waverly. She wasn't taking this seriously, and who could blame her? The weather had turned everything upside down.

But Flora wasn't at all certain she agreed with the viscountess regarding bread and pies. Both might have crusts, but once cooked, they didn't taste at all alike.

So she rolled out the pie crust. She thought it had turned out rather well this time. Or at least it looked more like Alice's. As she worked, she found herself humming a melody she'd been trying out in her head lately, a spirited tune that made her smile. It was certainly appropriate for the season, though she hadn't come up with any words for it.

"What are you humming?" asked a deep male voice, making her jump.

She scowled at Konrad. "Stop that! You gave me quite a fright!"

"Sorry," he said, without appearing the least bit repentant. "So?"

"What?" she asked.

"The tune you were humming. I've never heard it before."

"That's because I invented it." Having him next to her made her nervous. He looked rumpled and red-cheeked from being outdoors and far too attractive for his own good.

She squeezed the lemon juice in—fairly hard—and sprinkled some cinnamon, too. Wait, had she already put lemon juice and cinnamon in the pie? She'd put in the apples and sugar for certain.

"Do you do that often?" he asked. "Invent music, I mean."

"Often enough. I work the melodies out in my head, and then I write them down. The hard part is coming up with words. My tunes are songs, not symphonies, so I need words."

"Perhaps I could help. I write poems, you know."

She eyed him askance. "I do. You're hardly modest about it."

"Should I be?" He grinned. "I've been told by a very reliable source that my poems are 'heavenly.' Some have even gone so far as to say my poetry 'enthralled' them."

"Whoever told you that has terrible taste," she teased. Oh, why was it so easy to joke with him, even after he'd made her angry?

"Superior taste, in my opinion." He gazed down at the pie. "That looks good. I think. I've never seen a pie before it was cooked." He dusted off her shoulders. "I believe you've got more flour on you than in the pies."

"It's not flour," she said matter-of-factly. "It's sugar." Pounding a sugar cone was hard to do without getting some of it on oneself.

He tasted his fingertip. "Good God, so it is." He bent close to whisper. "If you need someone to get it all off you, I'm happy to oblige later. I like sweets."

Oh, he was so wicked, immediately provoking her to imagine him licking her. Everywhere. The very idea intoxicated her. And that annoyed her. She leaned up to whisper, "Fortunately, a gentleman filled my pitcher with water yesterday. So I have no need of you for that."

"No good deed goes unpunished, as they say. Though I'm glad to hear you call me a gentleman." He reached up to tuck a wayward lock of hair beneath her cap, and her blood heated, just from that gesture.

"I exaggerated," she quipped.

He laughed. "At least it's warm in here with the ovens going. There's an icy wind blowing around the inn. And still no sign of thawing."

She shook her head. "I'm not going to get to see that Christmas tree, am I?"

"The roads might clear tomorrow. You never know."

"Always the optimist."

"*You* used to be an optimist."

That was before he'd broken her heart. "I like to think I'm pragmatic now."

"Then perhaps we should give you something to be optimistic about. I think your 'song' sounds perfect for a Christmas carol. It might raise people's spirits if you could sing it for them."

"Me? Here?"

"Why not?" He bent to whisper in her ear. "As I recall, you have a lovely voice. I remember your displaying your talent a number of times in Bath."

Her breath faltered. Oh, Lord help her. The man was a walking seducer. One whisper and her very bones were in a puddle.

"Does Lady Whitmarsh ever allow you to 'exhibit'?" he asked. "You know, at social occasions."

Deliberately, she started work on another pie. "Sometimes, if I wish. I still play the pianoforte."

"They have a pianoforte in the room where we dined last night. All that's left is for us to turn your melody into a Christmas song. You can play and sing, and I will sing, too, just not as well as you."

She narrowed her gaze on him. "You sing?"

"Of course. No respectable former actor could do otherwise."

"Is that what you plan to do instead of writing another play? Acting?"

Her question seemed to sweep his good mood away. "Perhaps. But probably not."

"Will you write something else, then?"

"I haven't thought that far ahead. Right now, I merely want to enjoy Christmastide, if I can." He turned away. "And eat some of that amazing breakfast being put on the table. Do you want any?"

"I have two more pies to make. The servants will get some, too, you know."

"As well they should. And I'm looking forward to eating at least half of one tonight."

"You might want to rethink that idea," she said in an undertone. "I have it on good authority that they may not be at all edible."

"I'm sure they'll be fine once they're baked." He glanced across the room, then added, "They have to be better than Lady Whitmarsh's bread."

"Well, at least with pies, they're not necessary to the meal. Bread is."

"True."

"Now go on," she said, giving him a little shove with her floured hand. "You'd best eat that breakfast before it gets cold."

"Fine," he said. "But only if you agree to meet me later so we can work up our Christmas carol."

"Meet you where?" Drat it, she should have said no.

"In that room where we dined last night. Where the piano-forte is. You can play your melody, and I will put the words to it."

"Very well. Let me finish my pies and give them to Alice to bake—since I doubt they want any of us near an oven. Then I will join you. *If* Lady Whitmarsh doesn't need anything."

"Excellent. I will await your arrival, madam, with bated breath." He strolled over to the table that held the breakfast for the hunts-men and cried, "This will do for now, but where, I ask you, is the figgy pudding, ladies? We brought you back a brace of rabbits for tonight's repast, so we expect figgy pudding!"

Flora couldn't prevent the smile stealing over her lips. He was such an odd duck. That was what had drawn her to him in the first place. He was nothing like the gentlemen in her provincial town up north. He was a showman at heart. And that only made her like him more.

"What's figgy pudding?" Alice asked as she walked up.

"I haven't a clue," Flora said. "You'll have to ask *him*."

He looked over at her and winked, and she shook her head. What was she to do about him? It was clear to see he liked her, and yes, desired her. It was equally clear he wasn't bent on mar-riage.

Although at the moment, did she care? She wasn't likely to receive any offers in her present situation, and she wasn't getting any younger. Perhaps she *should* have an affaire de coeur. It was risky, to be sure, but he was the only man who'd ever tempted her, the only man who made her laugh and sigh. And sometimes cry.

Should she take up with him again? Or should she hold him at bay and keep her heart safe? As he'd said last night, "It's a conundrum."

And one she still hadn't figured out how to solve.

As Konrad waited for Flora in the public room, he jotted down some possible lines for their carol. While he'd been touring theaters, he'd heard various versions of one particular carol sung in the West Country. He could use that as a starting point, and throw in a few other bits—and take *out* the part about wishing someone barrels of beer.

After he'd moved words around and added things, his mind started wandering to Flora. How could it not? She was even more delightful as a mature woman than as a fine lady fresh out of the schoolroom.

He knew he was toying with her affections, and she deserved better. But if he told her the truth—that he didn't know if he could support her, that his whole life had been a lie, that he had no future—he feared it would be the end to any relationship between them. He couldn't bear that.

Why couldn't they just enjoy this time with each other while it lasted?

Because that would never be enough for her. Hell, he wasn't even sure it would be enough for *him*. He might have changed in recent years, but he hadn't changed enough to doubt his interest in her. It had endured all this time. He didn't think it would suddenly wane now.

"You look pensive," Flora said lightly as she came into the room. "It's uncharacteristic of you. And a bit worrisome."

"Very funny." He rose to feast his eyes on her, a vision of loveliness in her simple sky-blue gown. She had worn more practical attire this morning, of wool or fustian or some such. "You look much less . . . like a cook."

He must have conveyed how desperately he wanted to ravish her, for her cheeks pinkened. "I should hope so." She walked over to the pianoforte. "I didn't know how long we would be doing this, so I changed into what I mean to wear at dinner. No point in being rushed."

"Or spending the rest of the day covered in flour and sugar."

She chuckled. "That, too. Besides, Lady Whitmarsh said she would change for dinner, too, to make it easier for me." Her face shone in the winter light seeping in through the two windows. "I think she knew I was meeting you."

"And she didn't disapprove?" Konrad asked.

"No." She cocked her head. "I do believe you've won her over, just by being your usual charming self."

"Ah," he said.

He wanted to walk up and kiss her, but that would not do. This part of the room was too public for that. Anyone on the gallery that jutted out above could look right down into the dining area where the pianoforte was. He could pull her underneath the gallery, but then he risked one of the guests or servants entering and seeing them together.

Best to just keep this friendly and not . . . intimate. "I've been considering lines for our song. But I need you to hum your tune again."

She smiled. "Wouldn't it be easier if I just play it?"

"I bow to your superior intellect, madam," he said, then grinned at her.

Her knowing glance only tempted him more. This was killing him, being so close but not able to kiss her, touch her, show her exactly what she did to him.

He mentally pinched himself. *Mustn't lust after the lady, sir. You still have nothing to offer her. And it's ungentlemanly.*

Then again, he wasn't exactly a gentleman.

She glided over to the pianoforte, the very picture of elegance,

and sat down on the bench there. It took her a moment to get situated, during which he considered a number of things.

Taking down her fashionable chignon. Or, failing that, coming
up behind her to kiss the bit of back and neck showing between
her coiffure and her gown. Or, the thing he wanted most, reaching around her and under her arms to fondle her sweet breasts
until she sighed and gave herself to him body and soul.

Bloody hell. He had to stop this.

She started playing her tune, which provided him with enough
of a distraction to shift his thoughts elsewhere. Barely.

He began singing, "I wish you a happy Christmas / La la la la
la la la la / Fa la la la la la la la / And a bountiful New Year."

"No, no," she said. "It should be '*We* wish' because it's a song
for more than one person to sing. Ideally, you and I both will be
doing it."

"Right. And in case you couldn't figure it out on your own, I
don't have any words for the second and third line. But two lines
seem short for the chorus."

"Hmm," she said. "For now, why don't you just repeat that
first one? It would fit."

"Good idea. At least until we come up with other lines." He
made some notations on his paper. "Another thing. I don't like
'bountiful New Year.' But if I use the typical greeting of 'a happy
New Year,' then I'd have to take out the 'happy' in the first line. I
don't know what to put in its place."

She frowned. " 'Pretty'? 'Cheerful'? 'Enjoyable' won't scan, I suppose."

"No, but 'joyful' would. 'We wish you a joyful Christmas.' "

They looked at each other, and both shook their heads no. "I
don't know why, but I don't like that," she said.

"The same for me. It's the '-ful' part of the word. It's why I don't
like 'cheerful' as a choice, either. It doesn't trip off the tongue. But
'cheery' might work."

"What about 'merry'? I could swear I've heard that before."

"Oh, of course, 'merry.' I tend to forget that greeting, because no one in London uses it." He made a notation. "I'm imagining the singers as those boys who go around caroling and begging for treats during the season. So, 'Now bring us the . . .' What do they usually ask for?"

"Figgy pudding?" she said and laughed. "What *is* figgy pudding, anyway?"

"It's hard to explain, if you haven't eaten it. It's like plum pudding—"

"But with figs?" Her face lit up.

"Actually, no. Good guess, though." He sat down beside her on the pianoforte bench. "It has honey and nuts and fruit. I suppose sometimes it must have figs. I remember hearing people in the West Country talk about it, but I only tasted it once, while we were touring. It was delicious." He added in a whisper, "Not quite as delicious as your lips, though."

He'd been hoping for another blush, but instead got an arch look. "I suppose you use that one on all your women."

"All *my* women? I don't have any women."

"That's not what the gossips say."

"To hell with the gossips. Given how they treated you after I left Bath, how could you give them any credence?"

She blinked. "So you're saying it's not true."

"I'm saying there's a vast difference between flirting and actually doing the deed," he said irritably. "Yes, I've kissed a great many women, but I rarely went beyond that. I had a vested interest in making my reputation sound salacious. Salacious writers get noticed in the press. Boring ones do not." And Thorn had definitely been paying him to get noticed in the press.

She still looked skeptical, but he was done defending his actions. He'd behaved as he had for many reasons, and they had all landed him here. He regretted some and knew others had been necessary. He refused to apologize for the latter.

So he changed the subject. "Do you ever write or visit your parents?"

She started. "Why do you ask?"

"You said they were angry about your losing your 'plum chance.' Did they have someone in mind for you in Bath? Or were they just talking in general about a future man you might capture with your great-aunt's promise of a dowry?"

She shook her head. "You make me sound like a lady of the evening."

"Sorry, I didn't mean to. But the way you described the inter- action made it seem as if—"

"They wanted me to marry my rich second cousin, all right?" she snapped. "I refused. That's all."

"Judging from your reaction to my question, that's not all."

She sighed. "My refusal of my cousin was why my parents let my great-aunt take me to Bath—so I could appreciate what a 'catch' he was." Her tone turned bitter. "They thought to make me see firsthand how difficult it would be for me to find a reliable husband of any worth."

Damn. "And I gave you a good view of that, didn't I?"

"I suppose. Although out of all the men I danced or conversed with, *you* were the most interesting."

When she nudged his foot with hers, he felt it clear to his bones. "Just not 'worthy.'"

"Not to *them,* anyway. If I wasn't going to marry my cousin, then Thornstock was the sort they were angling for."

He ached to stroke her leg, pressed right up against his on the bench with only a few layers of fabric between them. But not here. "You never answered my question. Do you still write to your parents or visit them?"

She shrugged. "Once or twice a year. I write to my sisters more frequently. Including the one who *did* end up marrying my cousin."

He laughed, and so did she. It was the sort of helpless laugh someone gave when they saw no way out of their predicament.

"Now you know about *my* family," she said. "I want to know about yours."

He stiffened. "We should finish the song. We're well on our way."

"Coward."

Hell, yes. A complete coward when it came to showing her that she'd been right to have considered him a scapegrace and a scoundrel.

For the next two hours, they tried his various lyrics, some of which he knew from the West Country versions, but most of which he had come up with on his own. The lines he thought would be the chorus ended up as the verses.

"We still need words for the middle two lines of the verses," he pointed out.

"I disagree. The repetitious lines in each verse make it more of a chant."

"Do we *want* more of a chant?"

She nodded. "Chants are common at Christmas in church. Besides which, the song is supposed to be sung by boys demanding treats. The repetition emphasizes the demand aspect."

"You're right. I hadn't thought of that."

"Well, you've been writing plays and poetry. I write songs, although, to be fair, I don't generally do the words." She shot him a shy look that resonated throughout his randy body. "That's your area."

"I don't know about that. You write reviews very feelingly."

"Yes, but they don't rhyme, do they? I'm hopeless when it comes to rhymes. Or poetic language in general. You're much better at it." She returned her gaze to their scribbled notes. "In fact, that's one thing I'm curious about. Given your upbringing, I can't figure out how you are so good at using poetic language."

"What do you mean?" he asked, though he feared he knew precisely what she meant.

"I'm only saying you couldn't have had much of an education

growing up, if you were traveling from place to place all the time. So how did your language become so polished, and your knowledge of literature so wide ranging?"

"My parents taught me."

"Yes, but being in the theater doesn't automatically—"

"I don't mean my adoptive parents in the troupe. I mean, my actual parents." When confusion clouded her eyes, he added, "The couple in London who gave me my name. Those parents."

# Chapter 8

Flora could only stare at him. "What...what do you mean? What happened to them?" She held her breath. Would he tell her? Every time she'd asked about his family before, he'd changed the subject.

He left the piano bench and began to roam, as if staying still might bring the past back too clearly. "I should start at the beginning. My father emigrated from Germany to escape his—quite frankly—awful family. Despite being a Latin professor and well-read in a variety of languages, he had difficulty speaking English. Speaking it is different from reading it, you know."

"So I've gathered," Flora said.

"When he first came to London, my mother, who lived next door with her own mother, helped him with his English. She was a Sunday school teacher and took in pupils on the other days. Both were well-educated and read a great deal."

"They sound perfect for each other."

"They were. They fell in love and got married." A wistful expression crossed his face. "I heard the romantic story from Mother so many times, I could recite it in my sleep." He stared down at her with a faint smile. "When I was born, they started me reading early. They were happy. *We* were happy."

His voice hardened. "But since my father was rather opinionated and believed he knew best, he refused to be inoculated against smallpox. My mother refused as well, because he'd done so. But she did take me secretly to have the variolation procedure performed. I had a mild case. I don't think my father ever knew it was the procedure that caused it—he assumed I caught smallpox from someone at Mother's school, which I attended."

After pausing as if to regain his composure, he went on. "A couple of years later, when I was nine, smallpox swept through our part of the city, and they both died, along with my grandmother next door."

The shock of the statement brought tears to her eyes. "Oh, Konrad, I'm so sorry! That sounds awful. And utterly unfair." She wished she could give him more comfort, but what could she do to soothe the pain of his losing both parents as a child? "So that is how you ended up in the theatrical troupe?"

"Not quite. Since my parents were still fairly young, they had made no will, not that it would have mattered, since they had no money. They didn't even own the small house we lived in, which had been rented to them. And that's why I was sent to the workhouse."

A chill ran down her spine. Everyone in England knew how bad London's workhouses were. "Had you no family or friends who could take you in?"

"Mother had no family other than my grandmother, and since Father had been estranged from his family in Germany and no one knew how to reach them, they were not a choice. My father was wary of strangers, so we hadn't formed strong ties to anyone in the community. The ones who did know us were in the same predicament—ravaged by smallpox. Plenty of them died. And the orphanages were full. The workhouse was where one sent orphans in that case."

She caught his hand as he turned to walk away. "How long were you in the workhouse?"

He shrugged, though his fingers gripped her hand as if belying his nonchalant response. "Two years, one month, three days. I counted every one. After a while, the work is so tedious you have to do *something* to keep your sanity. I entertained my fellow orphans by reciting funny bits from Shakespeare—Father had been keen on memorization, and I was keen on the Bard."

"Isn't everyone?" she said lightly, though her heart was breaking for him. At eleven, she was still being coddled by her governess and taken for long walks in the village by her mother.

He sat down on the bench next to her. "Anyway, one of our 'taskmasters,' as we dubbed them, heard me reciting from *Much Ado About Nothing* and told a friend of his who had a traveling theatrical troupe. The Bakers—the couple I now think of as my second parents—came to the workhouse and asked me if I thought I would enjoy treading the boards and traveling. When I said yes, they took me away with them. And that, sweetheart, is how I ended up in a traveling troupe."

"Well!" she exclaimed. "That is quite a story. Add to it the story of Thorn's discovering your talent, and it would make a fine novel."

"Or a play, even," he said lightly.

"Did you enjoy traveling with the troupe?"

"Every minute of it. I could do accents of all kinds, and I could speak well enough to pass for nobility, so I got most of the 'young lord' roles. Since I was tall for my age, I played Romeo several times."

She chuckled. "Of course you did. No wonder you're such an accomplished flirt."

"Am I accomplished? You seemed to disapprove of my flirting earlier."

She stared at the keyboard. "Only because you use it indiscriminately."

"Perhaps so." He took her hand in his. "But you're the only

person I've told about how my parents died, about how I landed in the workhouse. Not even Thorn knows."

She gazed up at him, wanting to believe him as he went on. "You're the only woman I've ever courted seriously, and the only woman whose words can destroy me . . . or inspire me. I have no right to say such things to you, given my present circumstances, but I need to say them so you'll understand why I seem mercurial."

"What do you mean, 'given my present circumstances'? What are your circumstances? Do you mean the fact that you don't wish to write the Felix plays anymore?"

He released her hand to stand again, this time with his back to her. "The fact that I *can't* write the Felix plays anymore," he said in a resigned voice. "They've run their course. No one wants another, trust me."

"That's not true!" She rose, too. "Don't let *my* opinions of them sway you. Many Londoners enjoy them. Vanessa thinks they're brilliant."

"I'm sure she does. She . . . has an affinity for such dramas. But other people grow weary of seeing them performed." He faced her, his jaw stiffening. "*I* grow weary of writing them. Unfortunately, I can think of no other plays to write. I have a half-finished novel I can't seem to complete. And poetry will not support me, much less a wife."

She caught her breath. He was warning her off, telling her they couldn't be together because of . . . of money. A lack of money. "Is that a proposal of marriage?" she asked. "Because if it is, it's the worst I've ever heard."

"Flora—"

Someone cleared their throat. She and Konrad turned to see Alice standing in the doorway with a tray of funny-looking loaves of bread.

"It's nearly dinnertime." Alice glanced at her and then Konrad and gave a small smile. "I thought I'd put these out first, then set the table."

"Oh, we're done now," Flora said, without meeting his gaze. "Let me help you with that. And I can set a table as well as anybody."

Alice just nodded toward the bar that took up one part of the room. "Behind the bar are the plates, cutlery, and glasses. If you can take care of those, I'll go fetch the rest of the food. Mr. Juncker, if you would summon the guests, I would be most appreciative."

With a nod, Konrad headed out of the room with Alice. Thank heaven. Flora couldn't think with him around. He made her . . . excited and giddy and nervous all at once.

As she set the table, she considered what he had told her. Was he merely grasping at a convenient way to dampen her hopes . . . or did he really want to marry her but felt hampered by his uncertain future? Why bring it up, otherwise?

The other guests trickled in, with the exception of Mrs. Waverly and her patient, Lucas Avonwood, who finally had a name but was still recovering. So they passed quickly through and into another room to keep the others from being exposed to whatever he'd caught.

Flora's heart beat faster when Konrad brought up the rear. Their eyes met, and he gave her a look of such yearning that she wished she could bolt across the room and offer him whatever he wished.

Of course she couldn't. Not until she knew more of what he'd meant by his words.

He waited to seat himself until she'd sat down, and in a show of his own feelings, he sat beside *her*. Then he reached under the table to grab her hand and squeeze. She managed a polite smile for Miss Macleod when the woman sat down across from her, but the rest of her focus went to his hand in hers.

How thrilling to touch clandestinely under the table! They wouldn't be able to do it during the whole meal—they had to eat, after all, or someone would notice—but for these first few moments, it was a heady indulgence.

One that didn't last long, unfortunately. Someone started the bread going around, and then they had to part hands. It was almost necessary to do so, since the loaves were misshapen, which made them a bit unwieldy. Konrad finally took it upon himself to slice them.

Some were huge and doughy in the middle, with the edges much browner. Others seemed not to have risen at all. Those were hard enough to break the dishes. Alice had possessed the forethought to bring a large carving knife for slicing, which made it easier for Konrad, but when Flora took a slice, it was only to make her employer feel better.

To her credit, Lady Whitmarsh didn't blame anyone by word or deed for the sad outcome of her short career as a baker, although she spent the meal somewhat more quietly than usual. Meanwhile, Flora spent it dreading the arrival of dessert. She should have waylaid Alice to determine how the pies had turned out.

The meal commenced with little fanfare, but plenty of discussion about what to do for Christmas Eve tomorrow—it looked as if they'd be spending it in the inn. The men said they'd fetch boughs of greenery when they went hunting again the next day.

Konrad leaned over to whisper, "Shall I tell them I've already brought greenery in?"

"Don't you dare," Flora whispered back, frowning at him for good measure.

The rascal just laughed.

To cover for his nonsense, Flora told the others she'd be willing to make kissing boughs from the greenery, if anyone had enough ribbons. She could contribute a few herself.

Having overheard the group discussing the next day's festivities, Alice cleared her throat. "The mistress has a ham she's been saving for just such an occasion. We'll prepare that, for certain."

"My horrible bread would make good bread pudding if anyone is of a mind to make it," Lady Whitmarsh surprised Flora by saying. "I have no idea how myself, but I'm sure one of the more talented ladies here could do so."

"We'll see," Alice said. "I have a recipe for one. Been meaning to try it."

Alice set the pies on the bar, and Flora sprang up to go see how they'd turned out. Alice's looked delicious, of course. But the ones Flora had done were . . . strange. Only one pie looked at all as Alice's did.

The first appeared suspiciously lumpy, but otherwise edible. The second smelled lemony for some reason. She'd forgotten to prick holes in the top crust of the third, and it looked as if it had exploded. There was a big gash down the middle, with the insides oozing out a bit, although otherwise it seemed fine.

The last was perfect, thank heaven. Or at least it looked that way.

"Well?" Konrad called out. "May we have pie or not?"

Alice picked up the worst looking and murmured, "I'll bring this to the servants."

"You will not," Flora said. "They've had to put up with a great deal of inconvenience, so you should bring them *your* pie. That one, at least, will be edible."

"All right, then." Alice smiled. "It's good of you to do it, miss. They will surely appreciate it. And the other pies probably taste fine. They just look . . . different."

Different was certainly a kind word for awful. "We'll see," Flora said. "Can you slice a little sliver of each for me, so I can determine how they taste? I don't wish to poison anyone during my first attempt at cooking."

Alice laughed. "Of course, miss."

After doing that, Alice sliced and served up the rest. Flora noticed as she took her seat that no one had tasted theirs. Instead, they were all watching to see her own reaction to her assortment of slivers.

She ate a bite of the first. "Hmm. I don't think pie crust is meant to be as stiff as a playing card."

"The middle looks quite good, though." Miss Macleod took a bite of hers. "It's delicious."

The lemony smelling one was not only too tart to bear, but it had more cinnamon than she'd ever tasted in her life. Alice had given Konrad a slice of that, probably hoping that since it looked good, it might taste good. To Flora's shock, he was happily consuming it.

When he caught her staring at him, he said, "What? It's lemon pie. I like lemon pie."

"It's supposed to be apple."

He shrugged. "Lemon. Apple. It's still pie."

At that, everyone laughed and began sampling the pies. The general consensus was that overall, they weren't bad. Oddly enough, everyone liked the exploded one the best.

"It has character," Lady Whitmarsh said, as if that explained anything.

One thing was for certain. If cooking were part of being Konrad's wife—assuming he did indeed mean to offer for her—she'd be a failure before she started.

Even as she thought it, he got up to serve himself more of the lemon pie.

Flora shook her head. Perhaps her cooking skills wouldn't be a problem after all. She could only hope.

And try again. Why not? Surely the inn's larder had mince on hand for pies. Many cooks put it together in jars on Stir-Up Sunday—the Sunday before Advent, when the plum pudding was also put together—using brandy to preserve the fruit, suet, and nut mixture. She should ask Alice.

If they had mince on hand, Flora would like to try putting together a couple of mince pies for Christmas Eve or Christmas Day. And if she could, she'd ask Alice to help her get the pie crust perfect.

Right now she needed something—anything—to remind her of Christmas in the midst of this dreary weather. She suspected she wasn't the only one.

\* \* \*

When Flora rose, Konrad did as well, determined to find a way to finish their conversation in private. But Lady Whitmarsh immediately stood and told Flora she needed her help with something. Short of warning the viscountess to keep her nose out of it, which might lose Flora her post, Konrad could only watch as the woman he'd always wanted walked off with the woman who had the right to monopolize her time.

The others were still at the table, and since he couldn't talk to Flora anyway, he decided to reveal what he'd been thinking about doing for Christmas Eve. After he explained what Christmas trees were, the other guests were enthusiastic about his idea of putting one up secretly for Flora. Her disappointment at not being able to see the tree at Armitage Hall had spurred his imagination.

Apparently, it had spurred theirs as well, for they had a number of ideas about how to decorate the tree. As they were discussing it, Alice walked into the room to clear away the remaining dinner dishes.

"Alice!" he called out to her. "Can you spare a bucket? And does the inn happen to have any Argand lamps?"

"Why?" she asked suspiciously.

Briefly, he explained the idea of a Christmas tree. Had no one in England read the story in the papers years ago about Queen Charlotte's tree?

"Sounds dangerous," she said. "Putting lamps near a tree."

"Usually people use little candles," he said, "but I wasn't sure if you'd have many of those. Don't worry—the lamps won't set the tree on fire. I'm quite used to dealing with lighting on a stage." Especially after years in the troupe and then roaming London's theaters. "It's a favorite pursuit of mine."

Sometimes he had no choice. Theater managers always came to him when a scene was difficult to stage, and Konrad either had to guess what change Thorn would tolerate or figure out on his own how to get whatever effect was needed. Konrad enjoyed the challenge.

"Besides," he added, "the tree will stay green for several days, certainly too green to catch fire."

"If you say so," she said, obviously still skeptical. "We do have a bucket you can use. I don't know what an Argand lamp is, but I'll ask the mistress if we have any. We do have ordinary lamps if they will suffice."

"They will. They don't give off as bright a light, but I'll take whatever you have."

With a nod, she went out.

The conversation turned to other decorations—kissing boughs and greenery to hang. They discussed hauling in a yule log, but that was determined to be a bit too cumbersome. Besides, neither he nor Faringdon was enthusiastic about hunting both game in the morning and masses of trees, logs, and branches. So they kept the plans somewhat simple.

Konrad left then, hoping to catch Flora alone upstairs. After making sure everyone else was either downstairs or in their own rooms, he tapped lightly on Flora's door. When there was no answer, he tried opening the door, which proved to be unlocked, only to find Flora asleep on her bed, fully clothed.

Damn. She must have been very tired after all the baking and the music practice. Or perhaps the trip's trials yesterday had simply caught up with her. Either way, he was loath to wake her.

He did wish he could just stand here staring at her asleep on her side. She had the look of an angel, with her bronze-hued locks spread out on the pillow like a halo adorning her head. Her hands were even pressed together as if in prayer.

But prayer wasn't uppermost in his mind. He was more focused on his fantasy of stripping off her very fetching gown. As he unbuttoned and unsnapped and untied, he would kiss every inch of her flesh he revealed along the way. He knew she'd have the most luscious—

Voices sounded from beneath the gallery, warning him that people were heading for the stairs and would soon catch him eyeing the sleeping Flora like some wicked Peeping Tom.

He silently closed her door and hurried to his own bedchamber. Only after he was inside did he relax, secure that he'd escaped being caught gawking at her.

Now if only he could figure out what to do about her. Perhaps it was time he told her the truth about his connection to Thorn. If she understood why he couldn't yet support her or their children, she might be willing to wait until he could.

That is, if she wasn't too angry at him for not being the playwright she'd thought he was. At least he'd know once and for all whether she wanted marriage to him. He was tired of trying to convince himself *he* didn't want that, didn't want *her*. He wanted all of it—the home with a wife and children of his own.

He just didn't know how to go about getting it.

# Chapter 9

Late the next morning, Christmas Eve, Flora hummed the new carol she and Konrad had written as she finished cutting little crust stars for her mince pies. This time she'd had Alice coach her through the first one, to make sure she did it right.

Miss Macleod had been in the kitchen making tea cakes, too, with Mr. Faringdon's assistance, and Mrs. Waverly had popped in and out, checking on the ham that was boiling, so they'd had quite a pleasant time. Even Lady Whitmarsh had appeared earlier, offering to help with the kneading of the bread.

Konrad showed up once, but only to aid Mr. Avonwood in lifting the ham into the roasting pan. Apparently Mr. Avonwood now felt well enough to join the festivities.

Then with a wink at Flora, Konrad disappeared again.

Now all the women seemed to have disappeared, too. All that remained were the other men who'd gone hunting, who were eating a late breakfast and discussing guns, a boring topic if she ever heard one. Meanwhile, she kept hearing laughter and light steps going upstairs and down. What the devil was happening in the hall?

And why hadn't Konrad stayed to flirt with her? Dare she ask? Probably not. He might be avoiding her, and if that were the case, she'd rather not know. Still, a thread of disappointment ran through her. She'd expected him to attempt to kiss her yesterday, but he hadn't. What did that mean? And why must the scoundrel leave her with so many questions unanswered? Again?

No, everything was different this time from the way it had been in Bath. *She* was different, more in command of her feelings. Or at least she hoped she was. She could survive losing him this time. She *could*. Even if they had a quick affaire de coeur.

She scowled. She mustn't think that way. It was unladylike. And wicked, besides.

Lady Whitmarsh came over to watch as Flora finished what she was doing. "Those are so pretty. Did you cut them yourself?"

"I did. I'm rather pleased with how they turned out."

"As well you should be." Lady Whitmarsh waited until Flora handed off the pies to Alice for baking, then took her by the arm. "We should go upstairs and start working on those kissing boughs, or no one will have time to make use of them."

"I agree entirely." Though it was odd how her ladyship was walking arm in arm with her. The viscountess had never done so before. "You seem chipper."

"I'm merely looking forward to making the kissing boughs."

"Me, too." Especially if it meant she'd get a kiss or two from Konrad. Even a chaste kiss was better than none. Oh, she was becoming so shameless.

"You'll be proud of me," Lady Whitmarsh said. "I gathered up all the materials we'll need and spread them out on our sitting room table. But we only have enough mistletoe and ivy for three boughs. That should be enough, don't you think?"

"Honestly, we don't have time to make more, anyway."

"Where shall we hang them?"

That discussion continued as they headed for their suite.

It took nearly two hours to put together three beautiful kissing boughs by forming balls from limber young tree branches, then weaving the ivy and mistletoe through. Topped off with pretty red bows, they ended up looking quite pleasing.

Flora stood. "I'll fetch someone to hang them for us." Ignoring Lady Whitmarsh's protests that she needed Flora's help dressing—nearly three hours before dinner—Flora hurried down the stairs and headed for the public room, where she hoped to find the men putting up greenery. But before she could reach the door, Konrad came out.

"Good afternoon," he said, looking surprised and pleased to see her. "Where are you off to?"

"I need someone to put up our kissing boughs. I thought surely there would be men in the public room who could help me."

"I'll find someone for you," he said firmly. "But first, I want to show you something."

He opened the door for her, but when she entered, she saw nothing out of the ordinary, just the same room they'd been using for meals. Then he walked behind her, and she turned to catch sight of Miss Macleod tying sprigs of holly and berries onto a tree, of all things. The spruce was stuck in a bucket full of what looked like split logs standing on end to keep it upright.

Miss Macleod smiled and murmured something about checking on her cat—Flora didn't even know she *had* a cat—then fled through the door.

Meanwhile, Konrad had ducked behind the tree, turning up what looked like several low-lit lamps hanging from hooks on the wall at different heights. She watched in awe as the fires grew brighter, together shining a magical light through all the branches. As she neared the tree, she could see that the shimmer on the branches came from multiple pieces of jewelry and shiny ribbons, not to mention shiny holly, all of which reflected the steady lamplight. There were even silver spoons twisting on strings, thus adding to the glittering beauty.

Oh. Good. Heavens. She gazed at him as he came to her side. "This . . . is a Christmas tree?"

"That's exactly what it is."

"You did this? For *me*?"

"Yes." His eyes shone almost as brilliantly as the lamps. "To be fair, I didn't do all of it. The other ladies found items to decorate it with. There may even be more to come. So while I did indeed begin the project for you, in the end we will all gain joy from it. I hope." He smiled. "I'm still working on one of the effects."

"But it was your idea," she said. "You decided to do it."

"I didn't want you to miss seeing a Christmas tree," he said with a shrug. "I daresay the Armitage one will probably be grander, with little candles and presents and the like, but this is the best we could do on such short notice. And the spruce had to fit under the balcony, so we could hide it from you."

Tears filled her eyes. "It's amazing!" He offered her his hand-kerchief, and she blotted her eyes with it. "No one has ever done anything so lovely for me, not even Lady Whitmarsh."

"I should hope I'd do better than the viscountess," he said with a grin. "Although she did promise me she could keep you away until it was done, and she came very close to honoring her promise."

She wasn't about to argue that point with him. Not now, not after this. "I daresay I have some things I could put on it myself. I keep a sewing box on hand in case something should happen to Lady Whitmarsh's lady's maid. There are buttons in it and pins I can use to fix them on the branches and perhaps even—"

"So you like it," he interrupted in a husky voice.

"I love it!" She faced him. "Truly, Konrad, I do. It's pretty and elegant and magical. What more could I ask of a Christmas tree?"

She stretched up to kiss his cheek, and he caught her head in his hands. "I think it deserves a proper thank-you kiss, don't you?" he rasped.

She glanced around to make sure no one else was in the room. "Or even an improper one."

That was all it took to have him hauling her into his arms and kissing her for all he was worth. The room spun and her heart hammered as he once again showed her the meaning of pleasure.

Voices sounded overhead, and though she knew no one could see them underneath the balcony, she pulled away. "I suppose this isn't private enough for even a proper kiss."

"No," he said tersely. "Promise me you'll come to my sitting room tonight, after everyone retires. I need to talk to you, and this isn't the time *or* the place for that. Besides, I still have to complete my other effects."

"And I still have to find someone to hang the kissing boughs. It shouldn't take long."

"*I'd* hang them for you if I didn't have to finish up the tree—I want it to make a grand entrance tonight."

She laughed. "If that tree is so magical that it comes marching in here, I swear I will *eat* a kissing bough."

"Don't say that. Mistletoe berries are poisonous, and I'm also employing an angelic organ for the tree's entrance."

"Now you're just teasing me," she said airily. "And on that note, I believe I shall make my grand exit."

He caught her hand before she could leave. "Tonight then?" he prodded her in a low voice. "Once everyone has retired?"

She nodded. It was a mistake to agree, but she wanted to know what was so important. She also wanted to have his hands on her again. Good Lord, her cheeks were heating at just the thought of it.

And she didn't dare consider what he might wish to talk to her about. Because if it wasn't a proposal of marriage, she wasn't sure she wanted to hear it.

She'd rather follow Lady Whitmarsh's generally sage advice: *It's best not to leave former loves dangling in the past. Either pick them up and start again, or cut them off.* She would cut him off if she had to. But she'd already spent years in his thrall, so before she did any cutting, she wanted to do some seducing.

At least that way she wouldn't be spending the *next* eight years wondering what it would have been like to share his bed.

\* \* \*

Late in the afternoon, Konrad stood nervously awaiting everyone's entry into the public room. He'd hung a sheet up to cover the tree so that Lady Whitmarsh and Flora could unveil his creation once everyone had come in. In front of him was a hastily created glass harp, sometimes called an angelic organ, made of wineglasses filled with different levels of water. He'd seen it used at a theater once and had been determined to employ it himself in staging.

Alice had made him swear he wouldn't break any of the wineglasses as he tapped them with his sticks—it was the only way her mistress would agree to the scheme. He didn't know how to play a tune—he just wanted an airy, lighthearted tinkling to go along with the twinkling lights.

It seemed to take forever for everyone to enter and gaze about them at the other decorations—the greenery hung everywhere, the kissing bough, and the lovely centerpiece Alice had hastily thrown together for the table.

Once they had, he began his speech. "When I was a lad, on Christmas Eve my German father insisted upon our having a Christmas tree, which remained up until Twelfth Night. Yesterday, Miss Younger expressed disappointment that she would miss seeing the one she knew to be planned at her destination."

His eyes sought her out. "So I created one in her honor. But in the process, it became something more, a project we all took part in, which showed our determination to celebrate the season in our own ways. And we have Mrs. Waverly to thank for making it possible by giving us shelter when we needed it." He picked up one of the wineglasses, which actually held wine. "So here's to Mrs. Waverly for her kindness in taking us in."

Everyone echoed his toast.

Then he lifted his glass again. "And here's to us, for creating a Christmas celebration where there was none."

When they all had toasted to that as well, he said, "Now, without further ado . . ." He began tapping the wineglasses so they tinkled nicely. "Here's to the Christmas tree!"

On that cue, Flora and Lady Whitmarsh dropped the sheet.

To his alarm, the room fell utterly silent. Then he saw that they were staring at the tree transfixed. He "played" the angelic organ more enthusiastically, and his audience burst into applause.

Flora made her way toward him, beaming at him. "They love it," she whispered. "And your angelic organ makes a heavenly sound indeed. But tell me—can it be played like an actual musical instrument, with notes and such?"

"It can."

"Then I will definitely have to learn how to play it. Later you must explain to me how it works."

She reached for a glass, and he said in an undertone, "That holds only water, sweetheart. But you can have some of *my* wine."

"I am perfectly capable of fetching my own glass of wine, Mr. Juncker," she said in a teasing tone. "Besides, I believe Mr. Avonwood made negus."

Konrad stared after her as she darted away. Why the hell would Avonwood make *negus* of all things? That was not a man's drink at all. Too watered-down and sweet. But the ladies would like it, and that was essential for a party of this sort.

Konrad quit tapping the angelic organ and headed into the crowd, which included guests and servants alike. He was stopped by this one and that one, asking how he made the lamps work so well or why he'd used spoons on the tree or what the instrument with the glasses was called. He lost sight of Flora until they were beckoned to sit at the table, and she ended up across from him.

The meal was a feast: bread that appeared much improved from last night's meal, baked ham and root vegetables, roasted ducks with bread stuffing, and boiled potatoes with butter and cream. For dessert, they had pie again—mince this time—and something Miss Macleod called tea cakes. When he complimented her on them, she pointed out that Flora had made the mince pie he'd eaten a large slice of.

He looked at Flora in surprise, and she said, "Apparently I can make something other than 'lemon pie.' Although, to be fair, I did use a jar of mince made up by the inn's cook ahead of time."

"I'm sure you could have made the mince yourself, if necessary," he said.

One of the gentlemen laughed. "Very wise compliment, sir!"

"Now, it's time for our celebration entertainment," Mrs. Waverly said. "If everyone hasn't dined *too* well to sing." Amid a chorus of protests, she added, "Alice will be fetching the others to join in as well. We'll start with Lady Whitmarsh's reading of the Christmas story. Then Mr. Juncker and Miss Younger will begin the singing with a song they wrote themselves."

As soon as Lady Whitmarsh had finished reading, Konrad rounded the table to give Flora his arm so they could take the stage, as it were. Flora sat at the piano as he introduced their song.

"We didn't entirely write this one," he explained. "When I traveled in the West Country, I used to hear various versions of it with widely differing lyrics and music. But Miss Younger and I wrote additional verses, and Miss Younger wrote the tune all on her own."

The servants wandered in, taking seats wherever they could find any.

"You'll pick it up as it goes along," he added, "but the first line of each verse is repeated twice more, and the chorus is the same every time."

He walked around to stand behind Flora, where he noticed that from this angle, he could see quite a bit of her décolletage. Damn. He'd better keep his eyes on the audience or this song would end in scandal.

They began singing, "We wish you a merry Christmas," and it didn't take long for the others to catch on. The fact that the song ran to eight verses didn't seem to bother anyone.

After that, the gentlemen began "Adeste Fideles" at Mrs. Waverly's bidding while Flora continued to play. For the next couple of hours, there was singing, playing—not just by Flora and not just the piano—and plenty of drinking, although definitely not by Konrad. He knew only too well that he intended to have a serious conversation with Flora later that night, and he wanted to be able to make sense when he did so.

The celebration was in full swing—with even some dancing going on—when Braxton came in to announce that the weather had grown markedly warmer, and water was dripping off the icicles on the eaves. He felt fairly certain that they'd be able to leave in the morning.

That put an end to their party. Everyone wanted to pack their bags—in case Braxton was right—and leave as early as possible. Flora left the room with Lady Whitmarsh, shooting Konrad a backward glance as if to say that she still expected to see him later.

He certainly hoped so. And he hoped as well that Flora would change into something more sedate. Because there was no way on God's green earth he'd be able to concentrate if he could see her breasts so nicely served up.

# Chapter 10

Once all was quiet, and the viscountess had gone to bed, Flora slipped out of her bedchamber, dressed rather scantily. The only thing under her cloak was her nightdress, stockings, and slippers.

When he let her in, his sober expression showed he dreaded this conversation, which boded ill for the outcome. Perhaps she should just proceed with her plan. She'd already dressed for seduction, after all.

"We should have this discussion in the adjoining room," she said. "This one shares a wall with Mr. Matthews, and we don't want him to overhear us."

He eyed her closely. "You want to talk in my bedchamber."

"I hadn't thought of it that way," she lied smoothly, "but yes."

"It's cold in there. There's no fireplace."

"You'll keep me warm somehow, won't you?" Without waiting for an answer, she breezed past him, through the doorway, and into the inner sanctum.

Clearly, it was a man's room, untidy and littered with braces, breeches, and boots he'd discarded while changing. With a mumbled curse, he followed her in and began picking up clothing, which wasn't what she wanted.

"You needn't tidy up for me," she said. "I know Alice hasn't been able to clean the rooms. Besides..." She waited until he looked at her, then untied her cloak and let it slip to the ground to reveal her nightdress.

His jaw dropped. Literally. Then his eyes raked every inch of her, from her slippered feet to her knowing smile. She could almost swear he growled low in his throat, like some savage animal scenting a snack. "What are you up to, sweetheart?"

"Giving you your Christmas present. And hoping you'll give me the same one."

He didn't bother to ask what she meant. "Why would I do that?" he asked, though he approached her with deliberate steps.

"Because it's what we both want."

She swallowed hard as he reached over to tug on her loosely gathered chignon, bringing it tumbling down. His gaze centered on a tendril that had caught on her barely covered breast. "I'm not sure you *know* what you want."

After pushing his coat off his shoulders, she unbuttoned and removed his waistcoat with trembling fingers. "Oh, I know. I want you to seduce me. I may not be aware of exactly how that works, but I know I want it to happen."

He set his lips in a line. "God, woman, you will put me in my grave," he rasped, still seeming to hesitate.

"If I do, will you promise to haunt me?"

A muscle twitched in his jaw. "Every damned day of your life."

Then he was kissing her, his hands unbuttoning the placket of her nightdress, so he could shove the garment off her shoulders and then down. It caught halfway down her upper arms, leaving her trapped, with her breasts exposed. He drew back to stare at them while he swiftly removed all his clothes except his stockings and his breeches, which were bulging for some reason.

She started to pull her nightdress back up so she could get it off over her head, but before she could, he brushed her hands away and bent to suck one breast while he fondled the other.

"This is what you get for being a tease," he growled against her breast before turning to suck the other. "How did you know I can't resist you? Never could."

"I didn't know," she said, his words thrilling her. "But I did hope."

He took care of the nightdress problem by whisking it off over her head, leaving her naked but for her stockings. "God, Flora . . ." he choked out. He ran his hands lightly over her body, as if trying to choose which part to fondle first. "We were supposed to talk."

"We will. Later." Then she ran her hands over *his* flesh. Oh, goodness, he had such a chest. She'd never seen a naked male chest in real life, and certainly not one as well-crafted as those on statues.

And his arms! My my. There was a reason he could haul all those buckets up and down stairs with ease. His arms were thickly woven with muscle, like ropes on a ship, for pity's sake.

Then he showed her exactly *how* strong they were when he lifted her and tossed her back on the feather mattress as if she were no more than a handkerchief. Her breath quickened, especially after he tore off his breeches and drawers. But she only got the merest glimpse of what lay beneath before he joined her on the bed, half covering her with his body, their naked limbs entwined.

Wait, why did he have something protruding from between his legs? "What is this?" she asked as she laid her hand on it.

He groaned. "You really don't know how a seduction works, do you?"

"To be honest, no. But you can teach me, can't you?"

"It would be my greatest pleasure, Miss Younger," he said as he covered one breast with his hand, teasing it deliciously.

"So will you tell me what this is, then?" She stroked along the length of his flesh.

"Only if you stop doing that before I go out of my mind."

She didn't stop. "I rather like the idea of driving you out of your mind."

"Of course you do." He moaned. "You're a . . . Delilah in the making, handling my prick . . . I mean, my . . . er . . . member so deftly."

"Then I'm doing this right? I'm touching your member correctly?"

"If you did it . . . any more correctly, I'd . . . go up in smoke." He slid his hand down between her legs. "But two can play that game."

He slid his finger along the place she sometimes touched furtively in the night. She didn't know whether to be outraged by the intimacy of his doing it . . . or to be craving a great deal more.

"Am I doing this right?" he drawled, mocking her earlier question with his. "I'm touching you correctly?"

"Yes, oh, yes" was all she could eke out. She threw her head back and closed her eyes. He was . . . quite proficient at this.

Even as he sucked her breast and did wicked things to her privates, rubbing and fondling them, thumbing the tender spot at the top, he was also slipping his finger up inside her . . .

Her eyes shot open. "Are you sure you should do that?"

"Absolutely certain." He bent close to whisper, "In a moment, I'll be placing my 'member' in there instead."

"Really?" she said, rather shocked. "Is that how it's supposed to be done?"

He chuckled. "That's how. Trust me."

She did. At least about this, she did. It was good he'd taken over the seduction. Because she obviously knew nothing about how to manage it.

After that, there were no words. He played her below, as if she were a violin and he the bow. All the while, he sucked her breasts so exquisitely she wanted to break into song.

She threaded her fingers through his hair, his gorgeous bright locks, and pressed up against his hand down below. It felt awfully good when she did.

Next thing she knew, he was kneeling between her legs. "Are you sure you want this?" he asked, his gaze burning into hers. "Because we can stop right now."

"No. I mean, yes, I want this and no, don't stop." She squirmed beneath his caresses, seeking more of the pleasure. "*Please* don't stop."

"Whatever my lady wishes," he said, a bit smugly.

Then he slowly pushed himself inside her. It seemed like an awfully tight fit, but that didn't bother him in the least. If anything, he looked beatific.

Once he had himself inside her, he reached down to thumb her sensitive spot, and *she* felt beatific.

"Flora . . ." he rasped. "You have no idea . . . how often I've imagined . . . doing this with you."

She arched up against him below, reveling in how it felt to have his flesh slip further in. "I dreamed . . . of you at night."

"I missed you."

"Me, too."

When he started moving inside her, she gasped. It was different than she'd expected. *Better* than she'd expected. She gripped his arms and gave herself up to the rush of sensations . . . the thrill of the unknown . . . the excitement building in her body until it reached a high note, then cascaded over her, like the music of his angelic organ.

And as it did, he thrust one more time into her, then threw his head back and apparently reached his own high note before collapsing atop her. For a moment, they both just lay there replete, still joined below in a way she would never forget.

Then he kissed her cheek and murmured, "Merry Christmas, sweetheart."

It was a merry Christmas indeed.

Konrad lay on his back beside Flora, his senses still in full riot at the pleasures they'd shared. He looked to where she lay sleepily snuggled up against him, her hair a glorious tangle, her body every bit as long-limbed, elegant, and beautiful as he'd always expected.

The stirring in his prick made him groan. God, he wanted her again. And again and again, for the rest of their lives. How was he to part from her? No one else would ever make him feel this joy. He was quite sure of that.

"Are you all right?" she whispered.

"More than all right." It was true . . . for the moment. He could hardly tell her he didn't know whether to exult that she was his or sink into despair that he might not be able to keep her. He should have insisted that they discuss their future first. "What about you? How do you feel?"

"Wonderful." She beamed up at him. "Simply wonderful."

"It . . . didn't hurt?" He knew she'd been an innocent from how tight she was. But he didn't care—he'd take her any way he could get her. He just wasn't sure she felt the same.

"Not so much hurt as . . . well . . . It was a bit uncomfortable at first. But you made sure that went away." She ran her fingers over his chest.

He choked back a laugh. "You might want to stop doing that, or we'll be having our second round of gift-giving, so to speak."

"I wouldn't mind." She rolled over. "But we still need to have that talk you promised, and I gather it's not something you can discuss when her ladyship is around."

"No." Lady Whitmarsh had surprised him by offering to take him to Armitage Hall in her carriage. He'd accepted, even knowing he might have to change his mind after tonight.

He watched Flora as she left the bed and felt a palpable loss when she slid into her nightdress and slippers, then pulled on her cloak, explaining she was cold. He wanted more time alone with her, as much as he could have without ruining her reputation.

Climbing out of bed himself, he put on his drawers and shirt. "You're probably too tired for this discussion tonight, but—"

"I'm certainly not too tired, and if we don't have it now, I'll go mad wondering what you want to say." She wouldn't look at him as she twisted her cloak ties into a bow. "Although I can guess. And I want you to know it won't change a thing if you decide not to marry me." She met his gaze. "I will never regret tonight. I wanted a night with you, even if it was only one."

"Good God, is that what you thought I was going to tell you? That I wouldn't marry you? What sort of scoundrel do you think I am?" He strode up to catch her by the shoulders. "I want nothing more than to marry you. But you may not want to marry *me* when you hear that . . ." He paused, trying to remember how he'd rehearsed this speech.

"That what?"

"That I've been lying to you for years. That everything you know about me is false. By telling you the truth, I'm breaking a solemn promise to a friend, one I have kept ever since you and I first met."

She lifted an eyebrow. "You mean, you aren't really Konrad Juncker but instead are a secret spy for the crown? Ooh, perhaps you're secretly a prince from Russia!" Her eyes twinkled at him. "That would be worthy of your plays."

"Not *my* plays. None of them are my plays." When he saw her shocked expression, he forced himself to go on. "I've never written a full play in my life. Thorn wrote all of them, almost entirely."

Her mouth fell open. "Thorn? The Duke of Thornstock—*that* Thorn?"

"Yes."

Looking overwhelmed, she turned to walk into the other room.

He followed her, determined to say it all. "What I told you two days ago—how Thorn brought me to Bath to see how well I behaved in society—was only partly true. He hired me for the role of author of his plays, to keep his family—and his stepfather, an ambassador at the time—from being embroiled in scandal. Dukes aren't supposed to write for money."

When she said nothing, he blathered on. "That's why we were

really in Bath. He wanted a month to coach me in acting the part."

"Of playwright," she said.

"Yes."

"And poet, too?" She faced him, her eyes the color of fire.

"No. The poetry is all my own. But while I did write a scene or two here and there in the plays, mostly they're his."

She let out a breath. "I see."

"Do you?" That's all she had to say about it? *I see?*

Thrusting her hands toward the fire, she said grimly, "You're not planning on writing any more plays because *he's* not going to write any more plays."

"Not any more Felix plays, no. But he wants to write new plays, and with his stepfather dead, he wants to put his own name on them."

She paled, as if realizing precisely what that meant. "Where does that leave you?"

He dragged in a heavy breath. "He hasn't been clear on that point. That's why I accepted Sheridan and Vanessa's invitation, so I could see Thorn to hash out what, if anything, he expects from me. It's been hard to get his attention since he married. But I suspect I have no gentlemanly choices for a profession. And that, my sweet Flora, is why you probably won't wish to marry *me.*"

# Chapter 11

That wounded Flora deeply. "Do you really believe me to be so small-minded? That I'll only care about you if you're a famous playwright?"

"No!" He thrust his fingers through his hair. "And definitely not after you and Lady Whitmarsh explained how little you like my—*Thorn's*—plays."

She started to apologize, then realized she had nothing to apologize for. "I'm sure you found that conversation amusing. I dreaded telling you about my reviews, and now I learn it wasn't even you who wrote the plays." She sniffed. "No wonder you didn't seem upset."

"You're angry at me," he said warily. "I don't blame you."

"I'm not angry." When he lifted an eyebrow, she realized that wasn't true. He'd lied to her ever since Bath, even while they'd spent time together in Bath. And here. Worse yet, he'd had this . . . this weight on his chest for the past few days and hadn't even let on. "All right, perhaps I *am* a little angry. But more because you kept the truth to yourself even after you realized Thornstock might cut you off."

"He's not cutting me off. He's . . ."

"Paying you *not* to write plays? I doubt he's doing that. Why did you feel you couldn't tell me?"

"Because I made a solemn promise to my friend. I already said that."

She smiled thinly. "How nice to know where I stand with you: right below the duke."

"But I've broken my promise to him by telling you, so clearly you stand first," he said irritably. "Besides, taking you into my confidence would have made no difference. It's not as if you can solve my problem. Once the last play is produced next year, Thorn won't have any use for me." He stepped closer. "Possibly before that, if he claims authorship of the plays. Either way, I'll soon have no more income. And no respectable profession with which to get any. After all, I can't apply for a post using imaginary credentials."

It was beginning to dawn on her what this conversation was about. "If Thornstock isn't writing any more Felix plays, you could ask him not to reveal he wrote them. Except for telling *me*, you kept his secret and you did what he paid you to do. Now it's his turn to keep up the fiction. He ought to let you keep those plays on your list of accomplishments."

"I won't ask that of the man who already gave me eight years of fame and funds," he said stiffly. "He deserves to finally have his work recognized."

"Then why not ask him to at least delay telling anyone of his authorship? I'm sure he would do so. He's your friend. That would give you a chance to get a post in the theater world and show them what you can do before everyone finds out the truth."

"The only post I could have in the theater now is as an actor, which pays abysmally."

"Even if you're good at it? Because you obviously are, given that you convinced all of London you'd written plays you had not," she said archly. "You were successful in the traveling troupe, weren't you? They don't let just anyone play Romeo."

"Traveling troupes pay even less than London theaters. Besides, that's no way to live for a family man with a wife and children."

"True." She was encouraged that he spoke of having a family as if it were a foregone conclusion. "Aren't there other posts in the theater?" She racked her brain to think what those might be. "Oh, I know. Why don't you do what you clearly do quite well—become a stage manager? I overheard several of the other guests say that very thing. You already have the connections. You could even still write poetry or finish your novel, if you wanted."

He enjoyed that kind of work, but that didn't matter. "Be honest, Flora. You would never like being the wife of an actor or even a stage manager. You'd have to give up all your friends, all of high society, for me."

"If you can do it, I certainly can."

A pitying expression crossed his face. "It's not the same, sweetheart. I always knew my time in society would end eventually. Why do you think I tried writing other things and saved as much of the money Thorn paid me as I could? I wasn't taking any chances, not after my parents left me penniless. Even so, that money will only go so far without a decent income."

He clasped both her hands. "It's enough funds for me alone—I could be an actor or a stage manager—but for you? I can't offer you the sort of life you deserve, the sort of life you've been living until now."

She tugged her hands free. "You have somehow gained the wrong image of what a paid companion does. Even as generous and prone to include me in everything as her ladyship is, my future is subject to hers." A sadness crept into her voice. "What if she dies suddenly? You'd marry me then? Even though I might be past the age of having children, even though you might have found someone else less haughty than you apparently think I am?"

His eyes looked haunted. "You don't understand."

"I understand you've convinced yourself that because of Thornstock's decision to claim authorship of his plays, you now can't have a wife, a profession, or a future. If that's true, it's not fair, and you know it." A thought occurred to her that stole her breath. "Unless you're just using the situation as an excuse not to marry me. Unless this is your way of casting me aside as you did before."

"Damn it, Flora, I do want to marry you, but I can't until I've found a way to make an income sufficient to support you in the manner to which you've become accustomed."

"In other words, you don't believe I really know what I want," she said wearily. "You think I'm lying when I say I'm perfectly content to marry a stage manager or a clerk or whatever you choose to be."

She reached out to clasp his arms. She wanted to shake him, hard. But the big lummox probably wouldn't even budge. "If I had wanted to marry a man of rank and fortune, I would have married my second cousin when my parents pushed him on me. I want to marry *you*, not the playwright you've pretended to be for so long. I want 'in sickness and in health, 'til death do us part,' not 'as long as you stay in high society.' What has high society ever done for me but give me misery? It's you I want. Nothing more."

For a moment, he seemed to relent. Then, although he didn't move an inch, he withdrew from her, as clearly as if he'd left the room. "You claim that now, but you've never lived in squalor, never been without money to buy essentials, never had to worry about your next meal. I have. And I refuse to do that to you."

Her heart plummeted. "Are you saying we can only marry when you reach some arbitrary rank or find a gentlemanly post?"

A muscle worked in his jaw. "I see no other choice."

She snorted. "I do. I love you, Konrad. I think I always have, foolish as that probably was." She released him. "But I waited eight years for you to want my love, to come looking for me. I'm not waiting for you to hurt me again." With that she headed toward the door.

Then she paused to look back at him, aching for the man she knew she would love all her life. "Just don't fool yourself that it's me you're worried about. It's you and your fear that you're unworthy of happiness or love, that the world is just waiting to take everything from you once more and leave you alone in your misery, an orphan boy in a workhouse who had a stroke of good fortune and now has none again."

She took a steadying breath. "But you're not unworthy. You're a good man—talented, amusing, and not remotely pretentious. That's what all those people saw in you, *liked* in you. Until you believe it, however, I'll never make you accept that *I* believe it."

Then she walked out. She did have *some* pride, after all.

She'd never completely relinquished hope they could be together some day. But hope was a fragile thing, and hers had been battered beyond endurance. It was time to find a way to enjoy the remainder of her life without him.

If she could.

Konrad watched her leave. He didn't stop her, didn't call her back. Nor did he care he was half naked, and the fire was about to go out. What she'd said rang in his ears, tilting him off-balance.

What if she was telling the truth? What if she did actually love him, the way his parents had loved each other? What if she really didn't care about his income or status?

If that were true, then he'd thrown away—again—the only person who'd ever suited him, the only one he'd ever wanted to marry. Somehow he knew that this time she wouldn't return.

*I waited eight years for you to want my love, to come looking for me. I'm not waiting for you to hurt me again.*

When he'd left Bath years ago, he hadn't realized how badly he'd wounded her. Even then he should have ignored Thorn, should have listened to his own instincts. Thorn had been cynical about women at the time, but would he really have dismissed Konrad from the unorthodox post of pretend playwright if Konrad had insisted on marrying Flora?

He'd never know. Now here he was, letting Thorn dictate his life and future again. Konrad released a curse. Why the hell *was* he doing that? Flora was right—he *was* putting Thorn above her, even knowing that Thorn meant to end their arrangement.

*I love you, Konrad. I think I always have.*

Konrad rubbed his stubbled chin. He didn't think he had always loved her. He *knew*. The same way he knew he had no right to ask her to wait for him. It wasn't fair to her or to him.

So, no more of that. She believed in him. If she could do that after all these years of being ignored, then he could damn well believe in her and her love for him.

Since he'd already proved his worth to her, it was time he proved his worth to Thorn, time he asked the duke to help him in his quest for a post, no matter how modest. Because if he continued to let fear govern his actions, he would never gain the woman he loved. And that was unacceptable.

# Chapter 12

After saying their farewells to everyone at the White Rose Inn—
and a special thank-you to Mrs. Waverly for taking them in—
Lady Whitmarsh settled their account, and she and Flora climbed
into the carriage. At once, the viscountess ordered Braxton to
drive on.

"Wait," Flora said, "I thought you invited Mr. Juncker to join
us." Indeed, she'd been both anticipating and dreading the long
drive with him.

"I did. But he decided to leave early this morning in his rented
gig. He told me that since he hadn't yet seen you, I was to tell you
he'd meet us at Armitage Hall."

The words made her despair. "He won't be there."

"Why not?"

She sighed. How much to reveal? "He and I quarreled last
night."

"Which partly explains why I had to awaken you this morning." Lady Whitmarsh's tone implied that she expected to be further enlightened on that score.

Flora ignored her. "That's why I suspect he is *not* going to show up at the house party."

"But he said he was. And I believe him—he seems to be a man of his word."

"Except when it comes to me," Flora said. "The last time he promised to meet me somewhere, he didn't show up, remember? In Bath? When he left my life for *years*?"

"Ah, but you were both young. Young people often act rashly. He doesn't seem the sort to be reckless anymore."

True. If anything he was overly cautious, even more so than she. *Except in his bedchamber. There was little caution there.* Just remembering it made her pulse rise, curse him. She could only pray she wasn't giving any outward sign of her new status as a fallen woman.

"I gather that my words didn't exactly set your mind at ease," Lady Whitmarsh said. "Since we have a couple of hours before we arrive and can learn which way he went, why don't you tell me what you quarreled about?"

Flora hesitated. "I don't know. It involves secrets of a friend of Mr. Juncker's that he shouldn't even have revealed to *me*."

"Yet he did."

"Not at first. And only because it was of great importance to . . . well, whether we married or not."

"Now you simply *have* to tell me," the viscountess said. "Marriage is involved? I cannot advise you if you can't explain."

Flora debated the issue in her head. But Lady Whitmarsh had always been a vault when it came to secrets. She'd kept Flora's for years. And Flora could desperately use some womanly advice.

"Fine," she said. "But you cannot reveal any of this to *anyone*. I mean it."

"Of course! You know I am always discreet."

That was actually true.

It took Flora most of the journey to reveal the situation to Lady Whitmarsh. She left out the part about making love—that would not go over well with the viscountess, who would never believe that Flora had done the seducing.

But Flora revealed everything else, even to the extent of telling Lady Whitmarsh how Konrad had ended up in a theatrical troupe and why. She felt fairly certain that her ladyship wouldn't look down on Konrad because of his humble origins. The woman was rather open-minded that way. She always judged people by their character.

At least Flora *thought* she did. Lady Whitmarsh had a habit of being unpredictable. And her long silence right now was alarming.

"That, my dear, is a tale worthy of a play on its own. Are you sure he didn't just make up the whole thing about his playwriting?"

"I don't believe he did. It explains so much. How he knows about stage lighting, why he's so well-read, why Thornstock was championing him. Haven't you wondered how he got to be such good friends with the duke in the first place?"

Her ladyship snorted. "I just assumed Thornstock enjoyed mixing with the artistic sort. It's not unusual, you know. I myself was infatuated with my harp instructor before my debut. Until Papa found out and sent the fellow packing."

Flora tried imagining the viscountess infatuated. She couldn't. "Unfortunately, what I feel for Mr. Juncker is more than an infatuation."

"I gathered that," Lady Whitmarsh said. "But you did ask a bit much of him. You asked him to trust you, but you weren't willing to trust him. He and the duke have worked together for years— he must be the one to decide how that situation should be handled."

"So I should wait until he arranges every part of his life the way he thinks it must be?"

"No, of course not. You could be dead by then. But you have no part in the situation between him and Thorn—only the situation between him and you. Entirely different."

Flora relaxed. "Thank goodness you agree with *that* at least."

"I agree with everything you said, except the part about telling him he should make demands of his friend of many years. You wouldn't like it if he tried to tell you how to behave with me, would you?"

She caught her breath. "He did try, actually. And I set him straight."

"As well you should. I'm not saying you're wrong in what you told him last night, mind you. I'm merely prescribing caution. What if he thinks the only way to have you is to burn his bridges with the duke? Burning bridges is never good, my dear. People need their friends."

They did. That was true. And as they neared Armitage Hall, she began to worry. What if he *had* taken her words too much to heart and demanded too much of Thornstock? She trusted Konrad, but not the duke, no matter what Lady Whitmarsh might say.

The carriage reached the entrance to an impressive Jacobean manor house, and servants came running out to see to the horses, the carriage, the viscountess, and Flora.

She could scarcely contain her awe as a footman helped her down. She'd known that Vanessa's husband was witty and courtly, two characteristics she admired. She'd had no idea he was also possessed of such a property. They could probably fit a huge Christmas tree inside their house.

Vanessa was waiting to greet her, all smiles, and Flora approached her pretty friend with a smile of her own. They hugged—it had been a month since they'd last met, after all.

"I'm so glad to see you." Vanessa's blue eyes shone with the truth of her words, and her black curls looked quite bouncy. "I worried you'd had trouble on the roads. Mr. Juncker said they were rather messy."

Flora caught her breath. "So he *is* here."

"I told you," Lady Whitmarsh said with a superior air.

Vanessa glanced between them, clearly aware something was going on. "Yes, he's here. While he waited for Thorn to rise, he told us all about being stranded at an inn with you and some others."

"Is he inside, then?" Flora asked, relief flooding her.

114 • *Sabrina Jeffries*

Vanessa nodded. "He and Thorn are closeted in Sheridan's study. They said they have business to discuss."

"Good Lord," Flora muttered. "How long ago did they start talking?"

"I'm not sure. It's been a while, though."

Oh, no. That did *not* sound good. "Can you take me to him? It's important."

"Very well."

When Flora looked back at her ladyship, the woman said, "Go on with you. Don't worry about me. I am dying to see this creation, the Christmas tree, when it is properly done."

Fortunately, at that moment Sheridan's mother came out to greet the guests, and Flora was able to leave the viscountess in good hands.

"Is something wrong?" Vanessa asked, trying to keep up as Flora hurried inside.

"No. But I urgently need to speak to Konrad...I mean, Mr. Juncker."

"Ah. So it's 'Konrad' now, is it?" Grinning, Vanessa took the lead and marched down a hall ahead of her. "I did hope, but I wasn't sure you would be amenable."

"I am, trust me. I'm not as sure about him."

Vanessa chuckled. "I think you'll find he shares your feelings. His face lit up whenever he mentioned you."

"Oh, no." *Please don't have done something rash, my love.*

Looking a bit bewildered, Vanessa halted outside a door and knocked. When no one answered, she opened the door. Flora saw Konrad and Thornstock, lounging in two comfortable chairs, drinking cups of what smelled like chocolate. They didn't look at odds.

Yet. Not that she'd be able to tell from Thornstock's demeanor. She'd met him a few times in Bath when he was young, and then recently at a party at his house. He'd been markedly different on that occasion. As a young man, he'd been a handsome, dark-haired rakehell who'd seemed a bit arrogant. As a married man, he'd still had all those qualities. But they'd been muted, and what shone through now was a willingness to be kind.

At least she *hoped* that was what she'd sensed.

Both men jumped to their feet when they spotted her.

"Why don't you go in," Vanessa murmured, "and I'll make sure the others of your party get settled?"

"Thank you." Flora walked inside, her stomach aflutter. "Your Grace, please don't listen to a word Mr. Juncker says. He is . . . laboring under a misapprehension."

Thornstock stared at her. "I hope not. He was just saying he wants to marry you. That you are quite a woman, and that he is in love with you."

"He is?" she whispered, her gaze meeting Konrad's.

"He is," Konrad answered, with a softness in his eyes that thrilled her. Then he smirked, the rascal. "But do go on, please. I'm curious to know what misapprehension I'm laboring under."

Her gaze narrowed on him. "The idea that I won't marry you unless you accost His Grace and demand that he give you your due."

Both men laughed.

"I see what you mean, Juncker," Thornstock said. "She is every bit as fierce as my wife."

"Sometimes." Konrad smiled at her. "In certain situations."

"I know better than to ask what those are," Thornstock said. "But let me put your mind at ease, Miss Younger. Your fiancé said his piece, and I agreed with him. Besides, I knew this discussion was long overdue, so I'd already been thinking about ways we could continue our . . . unusual partnership."

"It turns out I *was* laboring under a misapprehension, just not the one you thought," Konrad said. "Thorn doesn't want to lay claim to the Felix plays at all. It has something to do with his wife and the character of Lady Slyboots—"

"That's neither here nor there," Thornstock said hastily. "Juncker has agreed to continue on as the author of those plays, whenever and wherever they are performed. And I will continue to pay him for that service."

"In the meantime," Konrad said, "over the next few months, I will profess loudly that I am tired of writing plays. Thorn has already begun his new and original play, wholly unrelated to Felix, and he means to talk to Vickerman at the Parthenon and ask that I be stage manager for it. Vickerman will of course agree since Thorn is a duke. But I suspect that will only be the one time. If I do badly—"

"That won't happen. You're an excellent stage manager." Thornstock looked at her. "Truly, he'd be doing them a favor. Vickerman has complained about his own stage manager to Juncker countless times. If Juncker can show his expertise in that area, he could probably just move smoothly into that post at the theater."

Konrad came to her side. "Thorn's new play has a number of extravagant scenes that Vickerman will probably not know how to stage, but I will be able to make them feasible."

Thornstock smiled at her. "More importantly, we intend to work together for a very long time. Who knows? One day Juncker may decide to write a play after all. He's the creative sort. It's not beyond the realm of possibility."

"It certainly isn't," she said, her heart swelling within her chest. "He's very talented. We wrote a Christmas song together, you know. Konrad . . . I mean, Mr. Juncker wrote the lyrics."

Thornstock clapped Konrad on the back. "You should perform it for us at dinner! It's Christmas, old chap. The perfect time for it."

Konrad lifted an eyebrow at Thornstock, and the duke shook his head. "I can tell when I've overstayed my welcome." Thornstock bowed to Flora. "Miss Younger, I shall see you later, of course. Be sure to bend this fellow to your will. Otherwise, he will run amok, and my sister-in-law won't approve."

Flora smiled. "Knowing Vanessa, she would° probably run amok with him."

"True," the duke said. "She certainly leads my half brother a merry dance." He nodded to Konrad, then was out the door.

Konrad wasted no time in pulling her into his arms and kissing her as if they stood beneath a mistletoe bower. After several moments passed and they both became rather overheated, she drew back. "We probably should save this for . . . well . . ."

"When we marry?" he murmured. "Not a chance."

"I was going to say, for when we can have some privacy."

He chuckled. "Now *that* I can agree with. Although Thorn did offer to use his influence to gain us a special license, if you want. We can be married by the end of the week."

"Oh yes!" Then a sigh escaped her. "Lady Whitmarsh would probably be very hurt if I didn't let her help with a wedding."

"Probably. And Vanessa must be there. And Thorn. Not to mention Olivia, since she loves the plays so well."

"But we're getting ahead of ourselves," she said softly. "Do you really love me?"

A smile as broad as the sea crossed his face. "How could I not? Where would I find a woman so well suited to me? Who has sworn—and I believe her—that she cares naught for anything but me? You, my love, are my Argand lamp, shining through trees, in the night, in my dreams. You are all the ornaments on my Christmas tree. I love you until time stands still to honor our love."

His words warmed her soul. "I can see there's something to be said for loving a poet. I am not a poet, so I will merely say, I love you for all my life."

"That sounds poetic to me."

Then he kissed her again to emphasize it.

At last the ghosts of their shared pasts were banished. They could finally start anew.

# The Unexpected Gift

## MADELINE HUNTER

*This novella is dedicated to the medical professionals who have worked tirelessly during the last year to help others in their communities*

# Chapter 1

Deep snow defeated Jenna Waverly's best efforts to remain dry. It snuck in the tops of her boots while she trudged across the courtyard toward the stables. Icy cold tickled her legs. Ahead she could see the carriage house's roof through a haze of white, and beyond the fence the long field that today dissolved into obscurity.

Just as well that she had sent the servants home early this year. She had not stocked enough provisions to feed them all through Christmas if they had been caught here by the weather.

Steam from the little pail she carried provided welcome warmth to her left hand. The other hand carried a sack of bread and the last of the week's ham. That hand already felt numb even though she was wearing her warmest gloves.

She entered the closest stable and called for Peter. When he didn't answer, she set down the food on a barrel, then walked across the courtyard to the carriage house. Since the inn had closed to guests yesterday, there was no reason for Peter to be about, but she called for him anyway. No answer.

She checked the stable stalls and saw that one of the inn's

horses was gone, too. It would be like Peter to decide to hunt when he saw the snow. He liked to be more than prepared, and at his age had seen a few bad storms over the years.

Back outside she stopped and looked past the fence into that white blur. She shouldn't worry about him, but she did anyway. The same years that gave him experience with storms made him less strong to withstand them. She laughed at herself. She could picture his gray eyes gleaming with mockery if she scolded. "You call this a bad storm?" he'd say. "I've been in storms where you couldn't see a foot in front of you."

She was about to move on when something shifted in the haze past the fence. She squinted. Perhaps Peter was returning.

She opened the back gate and waited, snow quickly covering her cape and melting in her boots. The movement grew more visible and became a large, shapeless dark shadow in the heavy snowfall. Then the shadow took form and Peter emerged, walking in front of the horse.

He raised an arm to hail her.

"Did you get anything?" she called.

"More than I expected," he called back.

"You stayed on my property, I hope."

Peter wasn't particular about land boundaries when he hunted. She'd received a pointed letter about that from the steward of Mr. Beloit, whose vast lands bordered her own to the east.

Peter drew closer through the drifting snow. She squinted to see what he had bagged, but no hares or fowl dangled from his saddle. Instead a much larger form hung over it.

"Hard to see what is what in a snowfall like this," Peter drawled. His voice sounded loud in the silence the snow created. "His honorship should not miss a few rabbits anyway."

"I don't see any rabbits."

"I was distracted." He dropped the horse's reins and kept coming toward her. "Just as well I trespassed a few yards if I did. Come see why."

He helped her to trudge the twenty feet to his horse. The animal whinnied and shook its head and another snowfall joined the one coming from the skies. She angled around the horse, expecting to see a deer. Only deer were not black and didn't have human hair. An unconscious man hung across the saddle.

She brushed snow away to get a better look. Peter joined her and lifted the man's head. She faced a drawn visage that appeared both too slack and too pink. It was probably a handsome face on a normal day. She felt his cheek and found it oddly warm and dry.

"He was lying in the snow. I've no idea where his horse is. Could have been nearby but I couldn't see much in all of this. Weren't easy getting him up here, but there was no leaving him."

"I wonder who he is," she said.

"Some damned fool who tried to beat the storm by riding cross-country is my guess."

"Was he thrown?"

"More like he just fell, the way his body was. He looks sick to me and maybe he was overcome by fever."

"His greatcoat appears very fine." Other observations also told her this was a gentleman. His dark hair had been fashionably cut and dressed and the edges of the collar that she could see appeared to be the best linen.

"His boots are better than good, too," Peter said. "You want me to bring him into the barn? There's no knowing what he has if he's sick. Some hay will make sure he doesn't freeze to death at least."

"That will never do. He should be near a fire for warmth. Bring him to the inn. I will see to him."

She led the way back to the inn. Like Peter and the horse, the building's cross timbers first looked like dull shadows, then stronger ones, than clear lines on the white-washed walls. The inn appeared impressive from this side, and even better from the front, what with the way it rambled on either end and displayed good-size windows on its two levels. She felt a lot of pride in this establishment that she had bought with her small inheritance. Better an inn than opening a girls' school or living off the puny income from investing in the funds.

She was glad this man had not perished from the elements. It was only right to help him. Still, she knew this unexpected guest would intrude on her own plans.

She closed the inn for five days every Christmas specifically so she would not have any lodgers. This was her time for calm and repose, for peace and quiet. No patrons, no servants, no bustling about making strangers happy and no smiling in the face of complaints and demands. She looked forward to these days all year.

She relished this rare time for herself. And maybe, just maybe, Selwyn would visit this year. His recent letters implied he might. Of course, he wrote that every year, and he rarely came. She did not allow her anticipation to grow on his account anymore, but she still hoped.

She glanced over her shoulder at the long dark form hanging across the saddle. Her annual respite had just been ruined. If this man was seriously ill, she'd be lucky to get rid of him by the New Year.

They entered the alley behind the inn. When they reached the back portal, Peter stepped away and eyed the body. "I guess I could drag him. No way I can carry a dead weight this size."

Jenna lifted the stranger's head. She gave his cheek a little tap. To her surprise his eyelids rose. Vacant blue eyes gazed out. "He is conscious. Maybe he can walk with our help. Get him down."

Mumbling something, Peter grabbed at the coat and slid the body off the horse. "Stand up, now!" he yelled while the horse moved toward Jenna to avoid the weight leaning against its side.

"We will never get him up the stairs. We will put him in Mr. Chauly's chamber in the brewhouse," she said. It was also the closest chamber with a bed and a fireplace.

She hurried around the animal and took one of the man's arms. He spoke softly. Incoherently. He accepted enough of his own weight that she and Peter could walk him like a drunk toward the door. Suddenly one of his boots dragged, then the other, and he sank to the frozen ground.

Jenna crouched down beside him. "Can you get up if we help you?"

No answer. Sighing, she grabbed one of his arms. "We will have to drag him out of the cold. Take the other arm."

Peter did so and they heaved against the weight of the man. Inch by inch they slid him toward the brewhouse door. Normally Mr. Chauly, the brewmaster, lived there, but like most of the servants, he had returned to his family for several days.

It was a clumsy, slow business. Peter's granddaughter, Alice, arrived, but even with three they barely moved him. In mere moments the snow had salted the dark hair that showed under Alice's cap.

"Good God. Is he drunk? Dead?"

Jenna turned at the voice. A young man strode toward them through the inn, his coat covered in snow. He had very blue eyes and disheveled blond hair.

"Neither, I hope," she said. "We found him outside in this state. He seems quite ill."

The young man approached her. "Where are you taking him?"

"To a room, of course. Although how we'll get him onto the bed, I don't know."

"Let me deal with dragging him." Moving between her and Alice, the man grabbed the stranger under the man's arms, then slid his own around the chap's chest. He hauled the man up and locked his hands around the fellow's torso, which enabled Peter to finally lift the legs off the ground.

"Tell me where you want him."

"Go straight back to the end of the alley. I'll take care of the door." She strode there herself and opened the door to the brewhouse chamber. Peter and the new arrival clumsily carried the stranger in her direction. "Alice, go light a fire on the hearth to dispel the cold and damp."

"Yes, Mrs. Waverly," Alice said.

They finally got him onto the bed and rolled him onto his back.

"Help me get his coats off, Peter," Jenna said as she unbuttoned the feverish man's greatcoat.

"I'll do it," the other man said and brushed her aside. Peter lifted the sick man's shoulders so they could pull the coat off his arms. Then they dragged the sodden, heavy wool out from under him. More buttons and pulling and the frock coat and waistcoat followed. Jenna threw a blanket over the man, then hung the coats on pegs.

Jenna turned to their helper. "You have been a great help, Mister . . ."

"Juncker. Konrad Juncker. I assume you are the keeper of this fine inn, Mrs. Waverly."

"Yes, I own this place. But at present it is closed for the holidays."

"I'll accept any shelter you have. Perhaps there is an extra place with the grooms? I'm happy to pay your price."

"We're not only closed, but we lack provisions for guests at present. Nor are there any servants here beside Peter and his granddaughter, Alice."

"I am sorry to intrude on what you probably thought would be a quiet few days, but I can't go back or forward. The road has become impassable. There is ice to the west, and it is beginning to fall here. You can hear it already, even if you didn't see it while you were out in the cold."

Indeed she could. A light, rapid staccato sounded on the window. A horse might be able to make its way through snow, but if ice coated the road, it would be dangerous to both man and beast.

"I can do for myself," he said. "I won't need servants."

There was nothing else for it. "Of course, you can stay until the road improves. There are plenty of chambers above, off the gallery above the courtyard. Alice will show you to Room Four if you will fetch your own bag. Peter can see to your horses and equipage. You are welcome to dine with us, simple as our fare will be."

"Thank you." Mr. Juncker followed Alice out.

"I can do the rest," Jenna said to Peter. "Tell Alice to help the gentleman, then to come back to me. I'll need her help."

Peter hesitated. "Not proper. You and Alice and him. Not like he's family, and I'm not sure even then it would be proper."

"Are *you* going to care for him? Get him dry and warm? Cool his brow and feed him soup all night?"

Peter shifted and made a face. "I'll get Alice, but she's not old like you so—"

"*Old* like me?"

His face flushed. "You know what I mean."

Indeed, she did. Alice at nineteen was still a "girl" while Jenna had long ago ceased being one. "Before you tend to the horses, please bring me a nightshirt from my brother's trunk."

With Peter gone, Jenna set about pulling off the man's boots. " 'Old like you,' " she muttered to herself. "Six and twenty and I have one foot in the grave, I guess. That puts me well past girlish delicacies at least."

Only she wasn't past them entirely. So she unbuttoned the trousers with great care and covered the man's body while she slid the garment down. Her hand skimmed against his legs even so, and she noted a ragged scar on the left thigh, right above his knee. It made her pause a moment.

"I'm far too tired, you little minx."

The words were slurred. Jenna looked up to see blue eyes watching her from beneath heavy eyelids.

"You are very ill," she said firmly while she pulled the trousers to his ankles. "You are soaked to the skin. We need to remove the wet garments. Can you undress yourself?"

"Undress?" A crooked smile formed. "Well, m'dear, if you insist."

Suddenly he sat up and, after two fruitless grabs, dragged his shirt over his head. He tossed it aside, and, his chest naked, smiled at her for an instant before all awareness drained from his expression. He fell back with a groan.

"Goodness." Alice entered the chamber, wide-eyed. She peered at their visitor, her gaze lingering on his naked chest. "Quite impressive."

Jenna pretended she had not noticed, but of course she had. Alice might only be nineteen, but she possessed a country worldliness that appreciated a fine male form. What woman wouldn't? The lean strength of that honed torso made it hard to look away.

"He'd be handsome too if he didn't look ready to shoot the cat," Alice said. "Is he drunk?"

Jenna felt his forehead. "He has a fever, that is certain. Who knows what else. It might be best if you not come in here much. Bring me a pail from the kitchen, in case he does get sick, and another coverlet, and a basin of water with some cloths."

"I'll bring some soup, too."

Alice hurried away. When Peter arrived with the nightshirt he helped her get it on, then moved the man's legs onto the bed and dragged the bedclothes down from beneath his weight.

"There's some blood on the pillow." He bent and peered. "Head wound. He must have hit his head when he fell off the saddle. Probably explains why he was just lying there."

"I wonder if that horse is nearby. It would have his baggage."

"The horse has probably found some shelter by now." He shuffled to the door. "I need to take care of ours now, and that new fellow's. You send Alice if you need me."

Jenna tucked the bedclothes high around the stranger's neck, then turned to build up the fire in the fireplace. With any luck, after a rest this man would feel better and not need further attention. Not that he could leave now that the roads had turned bad.

Alice returned with the pail and water. "There's something you need to see, out in the courtyard."

"What now?" Jenna threw down the cloths and strode from

the chamber with Jenna by her side. Jenna brought her to the front portal and pointed through the window. A carriage approached, slowly making its way up the lane.

"More desperate travelers, it appears."

Jenna pasted on a smile and opened the front portal so she could greet the newest arrivals. This was not going to be the Christmas she had planned. Far from it.

# Chapter 2

They kept coming. The carriage carried the Lady Whitmarsh and Miss Younger, her companion. Lady Whitmarsh struck Jenna as a woman secure in her privileges as a widowed viscountess. Miss Younger, with her dark blond hair and brown eyes, appeared both quiet and sweet, but hardly a toady. Jenna suspected the two of them rubbed well together.

Then at dusk another carriage made it up the lane, its horses barely avoiding slips that would break their legs. That one delivered vivacious, red-haired Miss Macleod along with her coachman, Howell, and her servant, Craig. As best Jenna could ascertain, Miss Macleod's maid had remained in London with an illness so Howell and Craig served as her guards.

Just a few minutes after Miss Macleod had been sent to her chamber, a Mr. Faringdon rode up to the door with his manservant, Rob Matthews. There existed an easy manner between them that spoke of more than master-to-servant familiarity. Mr. Faringdon possessed a reserve that Jenna knew well, but Mr. Matthews seemed to draw him out.

Finally, nightfall halted the arrival of stranded travelers at the door.

One by one Jenna sent her guests above to settle themselves, and the servants to the quarters above the stables. All the while she calculated how she would manage this invasion. Not only would she not have an empty inn for Christmas, she would have a practically full one.

Between arrivals she dodged into the brewhouse chamber to check on her invalid. He appeared to be sleeping, but not calmly. He looked very sick, and uncomfortable. After one of those visits, she hurried down to the cellar to take stock of what food she had on hand. If the weather turned for the better tonight so that the guests could leave in the next day or two, she might just barely make do. If it didn't, these guests would eat her out of everything, and she would not have enough for the first day she reopened.

She explained her situation to each guest, but she wondered if they fully comprehended the problem. She could give them shelter, but not much else. If the weather did not break, they would find themselves eating little more than bread.

After the inn fell quiet and the guests settled in their chambers, Jenna brought Alice to the kitchen. "There is a bit of mutton left in the cellar's meat locker. We will make a stew to stretch it, and along with the soup, that will have to do."

"The stew will be very thin. I can put out some cheese, too."

Jenna pictured what was left of the cheese wheel. "We can spare some, but not too much. It may be needed tomorrow." Or even the day after. That would be a fine Christmas Eve meal—cheese, bread, and butter!

Together she and Alice got the stew cooking. Then Jenna removed her apron. "When you check the fires, inform our guests that a meal will be served two hours hence. Sit them in the large public room at the big table and start when they have assembled. I'll join them later. Now, I must see to our invalid."

She bundled back into her cape and strode to the back portal of the inner courtyard. From there she inched forward on what was now thick ice, sticking to the narrow space under the brew-house eaves. Once she opened the door, her heart sank.

Her patient showed no improvement. If anything, he appeared to be getting worse.

Beer.

He couldn't get the smell of it out of his nose. It permeated the air and leaked into his fitful dreams.

He emerged from one of them like a man thrashing against a drowning wave. As he did Marianne's face floated up in front of him, her expression sullen and afraid. *He will kill me, I think.*

*He won't. He is not that kind of man.*

*He will guess it all, though. He will know and never forgive me.*

Suddenly his eyes opened. Awareness slammed into him, bringing aches from his head to his feet. He was on a bed in a rustic chamber. A fire blazed, but it brought no warmth.

He shivered and pulled the bedclothes higher. It did no good. He turned on his side to curl up, and a pain pierced his head. He vaguely knew that he wasn't nearly cold enough to shake like this. The chill was inside him, not in this room.

He could see the chamber better now, and that fire. A woman bent there, feeding in fuel. All he could see was her rump. A nice one, from this view at least. The soft blue wool of her dress draped it closely, and her pose made her hips flare out from her waist. The moment of distraction that derriere afforded gave him heart for an instant. He wasn't dead yet, it seemed.

The woman straightened and cast aside her wrap. Too hot for her in here, but not for him. He still shivered. The way his body betrayed him was humiliating with this woman present.

She had blond hair, was of middling height, and her arms showed snowy skin that might be her finest feature. He kept examining her, because it seemed to help the chills a little.

As if she sensed his attention, she turned and looked right into his eyes. Her skin was not her best feature, he decided. Her eyes were. Dark, intelligent, and reflecting spirit and confidence, those green eyes assessed him while he shivered like a fool. He wasn't sure he had ever seen truly green eyes before. Normally they had a bit of brown in them, and the green appeared faded. Not hers.

She walked over and reached for something. Another blanket billowed out and down. It helped. A little.

"You are very ill," she said in a quiet, calm tone. Not a girl's voice. She was perhaps in her middle twenties. "You have a fever. It is getting worse. That is why you are shaking. Once it crests that should stop."

"Where am I?" He wasn't sure all of his words emerged through his chattering teeth. Damnation, he hated being helpless like this.

"The White Rose Inn. You were found on the ground, barely conscious, in the snow. There is no telling how long you were there." She reached down and felt his brow. A small frown flexed her expression for an instant. He found that brief caress comforting.

White Rose Inn. His mind was mostly fog, but he knew that was important. He was too tired to care why.

"I smell beer."

"This chamber is next to the inn's brewhouse." She pointed to the far wall. "It is right through that door." She lifted a cup and sat beside his shoulder, so close that his face almost touched her thigh. "I also have some here. You need to drink. Come. I'll help you to sit."

Her arm slid beneath his shoulders. The warmth of that limb against his body almost made him groan with relief. He only tried to sit because it meant her embracing arm would remain, bringing some heat. He instinctively nestled into her body with his head on her shoulder.

"That's good. A bit more."

He obediently drank what she offered, but his shaking meant a lot dribbled out of his mouth. She left her arm supporting him while she set the cup aside and wiped his chin. "You may have been delirious earlier. I don't know if you were sleeping or not.

You kept mumbling and moving about. I did not understand anything you said, but you were very agitated."

He shook his head. "Dreams."

"Ah. Well, that explains it. Now, you must rest." She removed her arm, to his regret, and stood. She lifted her wrap. "I will be back very soon. Would you tell me your name?"

His name? "Avonwood. Lucas Avonwood." He managed a steady voice. "And yours?"

"Jenna Waverly. Try to sleep, Mr. Avonwood."

# Chapter 3

Upon leaving the sickroom, Jenna saw Alice coming from the kitchen with the cauldron of stew. She fell into step.

"A shame you have to spend all that time with the sick man," Alice said. "You are missing all the fun. Our guests are a lively group."

"They are not complaining, I hope."

"They are all such fine types that no one is complaining yet," Alice said. "My guess is they will save that for your ears alone."

"Not after I address them, I trust."

She accompanied Alice to the dinner and took a place at the long table. Alice set out two large bowls of stew and everyone helped themselves.

Genteel conversation erupted now and again, but mostly her guests satisfied their hunger. At least she had wine, ale, and spirits in sufficient quantities. As for the food, it had been all she and Alice could do to muster a meal for these patrons, as well as the servants who were now eating in the kitchen.

Jenna ate sparingly, then called for attention. The conversations dribbled away.

"I am relieved that all of you are safe and warm, and hope that you have found the accommodations acceptable. I can promise you that we have enough fuel and the basics such as flour, milk, and butter. However, as you have been told already, because the inn was closed, there are not the provisions needed to feed everyone the way many of you may expect. This meal showed that."

"I think I speak for all of us in expressing gratitude that we have a roof over our heads and a warm fire in the hearth," Mr. Faringdon said.

"The problem is not only with food, unfortunately. I do not have servants in residence to attend to your needs. I regret this. The White Rose is known for the highest level of hospitality, but this is an extraordinary situation."

"You've that girl who brought in the stew," the viscountess said.

"I will be directing her in the kitchen, and she will build the fires and take care of necessities, but you should not expect her to come at your call. I'm sorry, but you will all have to do for yourselves, for the most part." She paused. "We are fortunate that our well is in our cellar, so no one will be forced into the frigid garden at least."

She watched the ladies' expressions reflect a new awareness of just what doing for themselves would entail.

Mr. Juncker noticed, too. "I'll carry water up for the ladies. I can tote two pails as well as one."

"We will both carry two," Mr. Faringdon said.

"You are so kind," Miss Younger said.

"If I may impose on the gentlemen one more way," Jenna said. "If you desire anything other than the barest of boards, you may want to hunt once the worst of the storm is over. It would be helpful."

"Of course."

"You have met Peter, who is in charge of the stables. He has firearms, and also wraps and warm garments. With the ice on the ground, it will have to be on foot. I will leave it to you to arrange how you will do this."

"Two together seems wise to me."

"We will set out in the morning."

To everyone's surprise, Miss Macleod announced that she would hunt, too. The gentlemen took that in stride, but Lady Whitmarsh's nose twitched.

"I also need to inform all of you that there is one more guest here, whom you have yet to meet. He suffered a mishap and was found lying in the snow this afternoon. He is in a separate chamber, away from the rest of you for now. He will stay there until I am convinced he is healthy enough for company."

"You mean he is sick, not that he had a mishap," Lady Whitmarsh said.

"He had a mishap and is also sick. I don't know which came first."

"It could be contagious."

"Hence his isolation. This guest will require my attention, which only makes the need for all of you to help yourselves more necessary."

"Perhaps I could also help with the cooking," Miss Macleod suggested. "I'm no expert, but I can chop vegetables and follow directions, and perhaps do a bit of baking."

"I'll help also," Miss Younger volunteered.

"You don't know how to cook," Lady Whitmarsh said.

"I can follow instructions. I can chop onions and such. It can't be hard. Or bake bread or pies. I should like to try a pie very much, in fact."

"I think bread is more necessary," Lady Whitmarsh said. "I will try my hand at that. It can't be too difficult."

"Have you done it before?" Jenna asked.

"No, but . . ."

Jenna trusted her guests would be kind when they sampled the results of the ladies' initial efforts. "I will show you in the morning, and I welcome your help. We will need several loaves for each meal."

"How many is several? Three?"

"It depends on whether there is any meat, doesn't it?" Jenna rose and draped her shawl around her shoulders. "I hope the hunters have good luck in the morning or we may be reduced to bread, soup, and cheese. Now I must see to my duties. Luckily there are ample supplies of wine, ale, and spirits, including port if any of you gentlemen are so inclined."

"Be careful on the ice." Alice offered the unnecessary admonishment at the portal to the back alley, while she handed over a pail of soup. "Here's a spoon and a shallow bowl, and some bread." She slid the handles of a cloth sack over Jenna's arm.

Jenna toed at the ground in front of her. Snow was falling again, but a slick covering of ice lurked beneath it. She wished she had put a simple roof over this far end of the alley, but Mr. Chauly, the brewmaster, said he preferred letting the light into his chamber.

"See if you can aid the ladies if they require it and show that nice Mr. Juncker where the well is." She took a deep breath and a short step at the same time. Her half boot slid a bit, but she didn't fall.

"He's already found it. He brought up water earlier for Miss Younger and Lady Whitmarsh," Alice said. "When will you be back?"

"It depends on how ill the gentleman is. When I left him he was having bad chills. That means a fever is spiking."

"I got that way once when I was young. Nothing would keep me warm. My mum got into bed with me and held me and that helped some. Odd that a fever would make you cold."

"It is the way sometimes." She took another step. "If anyone asks for me, tell them I am not available."

Snow dusted her cape now. A tree beyond the back fence twinkled, its bare branches covered in crystalline robes. Ice storms created great beauty along with great danger.

She noticed Alice had not left her spot. "Go in now. I don't want you getting ill, too."

"I'm waiting until you reach that door in case you need some-one to pick you up."

Jenna inched along, setting her feet down flat, holding onto the wall of the brewhouse. Finally she reached the door. Alice re-treated into the covered part of the courtyard, beneath the cham-bers.

She had hoped Mr. Avonwood would have improved, but that was not what she found. He still shivered under a mound of bed-clothes, huddled as near the fire as he could get. She set down the pail and sack and went over to add fuel. Then she examined him.

His lids half rose and his jaw tightened. She could tell that he tried to control the shaking. She found his coloring worrisome. His face was deeply flushed now. She touched his brow and found it dangerously hot.

She shed her cape onto the one chair, then pulled the bowl out of the sack and ladled some soup into it.

"I brought some hot soup and bread. You should try to eat something." She forced a brightness into her tone, one that hid her misgivings. She suspected that tonight this fever would reach a crisis. Then this man would either live or die, and nothing she did would matter.

He thought she was Marianne at first. He'd been dreaming about her during one of the fitful sleeps that would descend when the chills exhausted him. Then they would wake him again and the dreams continued in his head and sometimes in the chamber itself. Only when she spoke did he become lucid enough to re-member her as the woman who had tended him before.

He forced himself to remain awake. She helped him sit and propped some pillows behind him. Remaining upright sucked the strength out of him. She tucked the bedclothes high around his neck. Then she sat beside his hip and fed him the soup. Despite the weariness that soaked him to his core, he sipped at the spoon and allowed her to treat him like a child.

Her proximity formed an invisible blanket of sorts. He could smell the scent of her soap and other things. Foods, like this soup and the richer aromas of stew and bread. With each spoonful she leaned in, bringing her face close to his, so close that except in the presence of lovers he had never experienced such intimacy.

"You are too sick for this malady to be the result of your time in the snow," she said. "How long have you been ill?"

Hell if he knew. And yet . . . "I was out of sorts in the morning, but not ill as such." Mostly he had found the world out of sorts, not himself. It was as if he moved through spaces distorted and distant, experienced through an invisible veil.

She smiled. Her lips bowed when she did that.

He stared at the upturned ends, thinking them very charming. "You've a very pretty mouth."

"It is good to hear complete sentences," she said. "As well as false flattery. Hopefully that means you are getting better."

"It doesn't feel that way." He sipped more, only this time it dribbled down his chin. She wiped away the drops with a cloth.

The gesture arrested his attention. A wave of embarrassment fell before his fascination with her hand. A lovely hand, but he could see a roughness to its skin. On impulse he circled her wrist with his hand and examined her palm. She allowed it, although she flushed.

He looked around the chamber. "Is this part of the inn?"

"It is the brewmaster's chamber. With the only bed on the ground level. When you are better, you can recover further in a better one."

"Is the inn yours?"

She fed him more soup. Enough that he wondered if she would answer. The heat of the soup felt good going down. Warming. She offered some bread but he had no stomach for it.

Then she sat back, away from him. "It is mine. I inherited some money. Enough to live the kind of pecunious existence that

008000test

2

is just barely respectable. I chose instead to purchase this inn. I have made it a very good one. When you are better, you will see what I mean."

He nodded, but barely heard it all. Exhaustion was beginning to lower his alertness. "I am having waking dreams. Or not. Not clear. I see things in this chamber, but maybe I am dreaming even if I feel awake."

She fussed with the bedclothes again. "That is the fever, I think. It is—it is very high, and the chills say it will get higher. It may seem odd since you experience such cold, but I am going to use cool compresses on your brow, in the hopes of keeping the fever down." She looked at the bedclothes swaddling him. "It would be best if you are not so bundled up, but I know the notion of giving up those coverlets is horrifying."

"Would it help?"

"I don't know. I only think that if you are feverish, it can't be good to make you warmer."

He grabbed the top coverlet and flung it aside. "Then I will endure the shivers and take my chances." He began casting off the next one, but her hand stopped him. Her touch was cool. Refreshing. He turned his hand to capture that coolness. Again he felt the faint roughness, but the back of her hand was deliciously soft.

"Do not remove all of them. You should keep a normal amount. I will build up the fire more, so the chamber is comfortable for me and we will hope you do not suffer too much."

He got his arms under what warmth remained. She rose, walked away, then came back with a wet rag. She placed it on his brow. Through his wavering consciousness he saw her frown again. She noticed him watching and returned a smile.

He knew then that she thought he might die of this malady. He certainly felt as if he would. At the moment he didn't much care.

"My apologies. For this, Mrs. Waverly."

"None are required. Now, you must sleep. I will be here with you. You will not be alone."

"Won't your husband mind?"

"I am no longer married."

A widow, then. Probably the war.

He began to descend into dreams again. His last lucid thought was gratitude that this woman was willing to conduct a death watch for a stranger.

She doubted the wet compresses helped much. He just shook and shook and got hotter and hotter. She searched her memory for every illness she had ever experienced or witnessed. How does one cool a person who is shivering from cold, but burning up from fever?

She prayed that it all stopped before it damaged his brain. She had never seen that happen, but people spoke of it. Hopefully those were old tales without basis.

He had been ill this morning, that was clear. The way he spoke of his perceptions, he must already have had some fever. Yet he had ridden off, and cross-country at that. She pictured the moment when he'd stopped on the road coming from the east and considered the time to be saved if he followed the dry streambed diagonally to the road north. He had probably become sicker as he rode, his fever stoked by the cold wind and snow.

She did not think he'd fallen from his horse in a normal way. More likely he'd become so sick he slid out of the saddle and hit his head. He was fortunate Peter had found him.

The idea that her efforts might be futile saddened her. She did not know this man, and yet a sickroom created an unusual bond. One far deeper than that created by conversations in drawing rooms. Wordless. Elemental. She supposed matters of life and death did that.

She debated adding the extra coverlet again, but the unnatural dryness of his skin stayed her hand. She tucked the blanket along the side of the bed that abutted a wall, to stop any drafts.

He began talking. Mumbling. Whatever he dreamed caused

him agitation. His legs thrashed and his teeth gritted. He began fighting the bedclothes.

"No. You mustn't." She settled them atop him again. "Calm yourself."

As if he heard her, he stopped. She took the compress and dipped it in the cold water again and laid it on his forehead, then wiped it over his face.

She felt helpless. Worthless, and worried beyond all reason. He began thrashing again. She laid her hands on his chest and told him to stop. That seemed to help. Then to her surprise he thrust out his arm and grasped her hand against his chest. "Better," he murmured. "Warm."

It seemed to her that maybe, just maybe, he shivered less. She remembered what Alice had said about her mother. It couldn't hurt to try. It wasn't as if anyone would ever know.

She lowered the coverlet so only a sheet and nightshirt covered his chest. Then she leaned forward and placed her head and her body and her hands against him. His heartbeat entered her head and blood while she offered her own physical warmth to absorb his inner cold.

# Chapter 4

He was drowning. Then suddenly he was examining a rustic chamber through barely opened eyes. The vague scent of beer righted his mind and he remembered where he was.

No more chills. Rather the opposite. He felt so warm the notion of rolling in the snow took hold. Not a bad warmth, though. Too much, but not unpleasant.

The flames in the fireplace appeared to dance to a tune. They looked far away. The whole chamber did, as if he viewed it from outside a window. His head hurt now, and deep body aches made him uncomfortable. And the weight of the bedclothes—he reached to cast them aside, only to realize it was not a coverlet on his chest, but a body.

He looked down on a blond crown. Woman's hair. He sensed the swells of her body pressed against his own. She didn't move. Perhaps she was asleep.

His mind began spinning again. The woman was all that kept him from descending into delirium. He noticed her palms against his chest and felt her breath on him. Their shared warmth carried an intimacy that he recognized.

Suddenly he saw Marianne standing in front of the fire. He winced. Regret poured through him. He had failed her. Impatience crowded him, and the sure knowledge that he was supposed to be doing something to make amends. What? His mind groped through dreamlike wakening and the aches, trying to reach the duty now lost in fog.

*I was a fool. I know that, Lucas. Only now the broach is gone and when he finds out, how do I explain?*

*You don't. We make sure he never finds out.*

The broach. Yes, that was what he should be doing. Finding the damned broach. The Home Office officials thought he was visiting his family for the holiday, but instead he was using the skills learned in their service to track that broach.

Somehow the woman lying on him became Marianne. He laid his hands on her back in an embrace, to reassure her. To wake her and make another promise. She stirred in response, her body moving subtly against his. He hoped she did not wake now. Holding her like this was pleasant, and her human warmth did not suffocate the way sheets and quilts might.

Suddenly she started. For a moment she just lay there; then she turned her head. Green eyes looked up into his.

Not Marianne. Of course not. He'd left her in Wiltshire.

For a moment he and Mrs. Waverly remained immobile, looking at each other, not speaking of the intimacy born on this bed without their intention. An acknowledgment of it passed silently between them, though.

She sat up. She reached down and felt his brow, then his chin. "The chills have passed, but you are very hot now. Hopefully this is as bad as the fever will get." She lifted the coverlet and covered his chest. "If you are too warm you can remove it, but this chamber is drafty and it would be best if you didn't. I'll build up the fire more, so I can try to cool you down with compresses."

She spoke rapidly, efficiently, as if embarrassed.

"I thought you were someone else," he said, closing his eyes.

"Your wife?"

"Not married."

"Ah."

Her tone made his mind snap alert so the chamber became quite normal for a while. "That, ah, sounded like a scold."

"I am not a child, and I own an inn. There is little I have not seen, and I am well aware that unmarried men embrace women on beds quite frequently."

"They come here to do that, do they?"

"Sometimes. Most exercised great discretion. A few did not." She got up and brought over a pail of water. She set it down and bent to soak the rags. "I'm glad the chills are over. We need to try and cool you down, but while you suffered them you would have never tolerated the cool water."

She laid a compress on his forehead. It felt good. She twisted excess water out of another rag, then sat there with it in her hand, frowning slightly. "Can you do this yourself?" she asked, holding out the rag.

"Do what?"

"Smooth this over your body so it cools you."

He took the rag and pushed aside the coverlet and sheet. He dabbed at his chest where the nightshirt gaped. After a minute the notion of continuing exhausted him. He handed the rag back and closed his eyes. "Later."

"Later will not do. I will do it if you promise not to embrace me again."

Embrace her? Oh, yes. That. "No need to be indignant. I didn't get into bed with you, after all. You got into bed with me."

No response to that. No rag on his body, either. He slipped away, back into the dream that had not retreated entirely during this brief wakening. He was in the water again. The ocean. Only he wasn't drowning. He was swimming. The water felt very good. Cool. It smoothed over his body like an erotic caress.

\* \* \*

Jenna waited until Mr. Avonwood fell asleep, then set about wiping him down with water. She kept a keen eye out in case the chills started again, but blessedly they didn't.

His skin felt parched. Dry and hot. Not a drop of sweat showed on his face, or even on his legs when she folded back the heavy bedclothes. She would have to wake him when she was done and force him to drink.

When she had woken to find his arms around her, she had been surprised. Then stunned. Then embarrassed. When he came to his senses more, she would explain why she had lain beside him if he remembered it. Hopefully he wouldn't.

That human touch had been delicious, though. So delicious that she did not break away too quickly, but instead for a long moment savored the peace it brought. She felt her face flushing as she acknowledged that. How very sad to rely on a stranger for such closeness, and a sick, half-delirious stranger at that.

She peeled back the coverlet, then made use of the wet rag beneath the sheet, on his lower legs. Near his left knee her fingertips again skimmed a ridge of roughness. Curious, she lifted the sheet to see a long scar, ragged and red. Other than that he had nice legs. Admiration entered her mind before she could stop it. She felt her face flush again. Then she laughed at herself and replaced the sheet.

He appeared comfortable at least. Not thrashing about. The bath should have helped. His breathing seemed labored, though, and what she had done to cool him would not last long. She probably should do it again in an hour or so.

She slipped out of the chamber with her pail and knocked snow into it from the window ledge and eaves to spare herself a trip down to the well.

Then she placed the pail near the fire so the snow would melt and settled herself into the chair beside the bed to continue her vigil.

\* \* \*

"This is how you form a loaf," Jenna said. "Watch me." She took her wad of dough, flattened it, then turned in the sides. Lady Whitmarsh tried to imitate the movement, but ended up with a more clumsy, lumpish mound.

"It doesn't look like yours." She began to flatten it again. "At least Flora has done a fine job with the apple pie Alice helped her make. It is most elegant."

"It hardly is," Miss Younger said. "The crust kept breaking so it is all made up of pieces. Alice's is so much nicer."

Jenna grabbed Lady Whitmarsh's loaf before it could be smashed again. "Both bread and pie are fine. Once it is eaten no one will care about its appearance." She set three loaves on a board and moved them to the oven, then slid them inside, along with the pies. "Alice, keep an eye on these."

It had been a long night followed by a busy morning. That Lady Whitmarsh and Miss Younger had risen at dawn and, good to their word, come down to the kitchen to help surprised her. Even more surprising was that Mr. Juncker had stopped in the kitchen to chat briefly. Now flour covered the two ladies from head to toe; the aprons Alice had loaned them had not helped much. Miss Younger looked down and noticed.

"Just shake and brush it out the window," Alice said. "I'll do it for you if you want."

"I think I can shake it myself, but I should go up and find something cleaner now."

"I appreciate your efforts to help," Jenna said.

"Perhaps before we leave we will both know enough to feed ourselves," Lady Whitmarsh said with a little laugh that implied the notion struck her as most droll.

The two of them disappeared out the door.

"Seems to me they were more trouble than help," Alice said while she tried to collect the flour coating the table.

"They meant well and it was a good first effort. This afternoon you will be glad to have them when we prepare the dinner."

"If the gentlemen don't come back with some fowl or hares, it

will be a sad meal of nothing but those pies and lumpish bread."
Alice jabbed her thumb toward the oven.

Jenna bent over the open hearth to stir some porridge that
awaited the breakfasts of her guests and their servants. "Are you
sure your grandfather went with them? I don't want anyone getting turned around out there. One sick guest is enough."

"He led the way, all bundled up. One wonders how long the
other two will last, let alone Miss Macleod. Those fancy boots
aren't much good on ice."

Jenna poured herself some coffee and sat. A few minutes'
respite was in order. She also needed to remove herself from that
chamber for a while longer. A night of caring for Mr. Avonwood,
of forcing drink on him, of sitting and watching, and dozing off
only to start awake when he moved, had only deepened the emotions she had experienced when they'd mistakenly embraced each
other. As for bathing his body—she no longer flushed at the
memory of it. She probably knew his physical self better than she
knew her own by now.

"Alice, please put what is left of that soup in a clean pail so I
can bring it to Mr. Avonwood. I doubt he has much appetite, but
he must eat something."

Alice set about ladling the last of the soup into a pail. "How
is he?"

"Alive."

"Did you think he might not be?"

"His breathing turned bad. Rasping. I thought perhaps . . . but
near dawn it got better, so perhaps all will be well." She did not
describe how worried she had been, nor the hurried attempts on
her part to cool him again, to the point of removing the flannel
nightshirt from his arms. She reminded herself to go to the storeroom and retrieve fresh bedclothes. Her efforts had soaked the
ones on the bed now.

Alice set the pail on the table. "I don't suppose I'll be going to
Mr. Beloit's house on Christmas Day now, what with the weather
and all these guests."

Alice had been invited to spend the holiday with the servants at the manor house across the fields. Jenna took her hand and squeezed it. "If your young man can come for you, he will, and you will dance the day away in the servants' hall with him and eat the kinds of delicious food that we never have here. As for these guests, I am hoping the weather warms enough to allow them to move on."

"And if it doesn't?"

"Then we will all spend the feast day with strangers, I suppose."

"We should plan for that, so it isn't too sad."

"That is a splendid idea."

"Of course, I'm not sure they are all strangers to each other, even if they are to us."

"What do you mean?"

Alice shrugged. "I'm thinking the young ladies have met the gentlemen before, that's all. Don't frown like that. I'm sure there was no planning to it. More a coincidence. Nor do I think it was a happy one in all cases."

Jenna trusted the viscountess would keep an eye on things. Their hostess certainly couldn't. She forced herself to stand. "I will go see how my patient is faring now." She flung her cape on again, then took the pail, and another one with well water. She stopped by the storeroom for some bedclothes that she tucked under one arm, then made her way back to the brewer's chamber, inching along the wall.

She entered quietly and set the soup on the hearthstone. She set down the bedclothes on a tiny table.

"I seem to be naked."

The voice startled her. She turned to see Mr. Avonwood sitting up in his bed. Mostly naked indeed. His torso rose above the sheet bunched at his waist. Her gaze lingered a moment on the lean, muscular arms and chest that she had recently caressed with damp cloths. Then she looked in his eyes. Wide open now. So very blue. He was a very handsome man when he wasn't almost dead.

She strode over and placed her palm against his brow. "You are still too hot, but not like last night." She ran her fingertips down to his jaw and felt light moisture. A triumphant delight broke in her. "I don't think you are going to die on me after all."

"That is good to know." He kicked beneath the sheet. "You must have used a lot of water. This bed is very damp."

"I think some of that is from you, with the fever breaking. Are you cold now?"

He shook his head. "This is very pleasant."

"It shouldn't be. I will change the bedclothes, but you need to take care still." She pointed to the chair. "Can you get yourself over here, so I can fix the bed?"

"Not decently." He smiled slowly. A nice smile.

"Of course." She grabbed the clean coverlet. "Perhaps you can wrap yourself in this."

He took the coverlet and unfolded it. "I may need help." Another smile.

"Now I think you are being naughty."

"I'm too sick for that."

"Are you? It is a good sign, though. Far better than being half mad." She turned. "All you have to do is slide off the bed and onto the chair, then drape that around yourself."

Scuffling sounds came to her, along with the creak of the bed's ropes.

"I'm done."

She turned carefully. She really knew nothing about this man. He could be the sort to be *very* naughty, if not worse.

He sat on the chair, suitably covered. "It is very warm here by the fire."

"I'll be quick with the bed." She handed him the bowl and ladled the soup into it. "Eat this while I am busy."

Changing the bedclothes took some doing. It was a small

chamber and Mr. Avonwood was in the way. She had to keep moving around him and the chair to get the sheets tucked in and the pillows covered. While she worked at the head of the bed she grew uncomfortably aware that her posterior was all but in his face.

"Finished," she said a little breathlessly. "If you get under the sheet, I'll fix that coverlet. And bring you a clean nightshirt."

He just looked at her. She realized why and turned away.

"Done."

She turned to find the nightshirt on the floor, and Mr. Avonwood back as he had been, sitting up under the sheet. Only now he truly was naked. She blocked that image from her imagination. His eyes were closed, as if this activity had taken what strength he had mustered.

"Are you sleeping?" she asked very quietly, so as not to waken him.

"No. My head hurts. It helps if I close my eyes."

It relieved her that he continued to sound almost normal. "You appear to have finished the soup. Do you want something else to eat? We don't have much, but I could find something that is more substantial. Porridge, perhaps."

He shook his head. "Later, maybe." His lids rose briefly. "Why don't you have much? It is an inn."

She explained that she had closed the inn. "Only the weather brought others besides you, and now I am practically full but ill prepared. We are all making do as best we can."

"That was kind of you, to take them all in. To take *us* all in."

"I could hardly turn them away. There is at least a quarter inch of ice on everything. You can see some on the window if you turn your head. None of them would have made it much farther on the road, let alone to the next coaching inn."

"Nor found beds there if they had, most likely."

"Is that where you were going? To the next inn up the road, or to Leicester itself?"

He did not reply. She wondered if drowsiness had claimed him again. Then he frowned deeply. His lids rose and he looked at her with curiosity. "You told me your name, I think. I don't remember it. That is rude, but—"

"You were so ill it is a wonder you even remember we spoke. My name is Jenna Waverly, and this is the White Rose Inn."

His expression slackened. Softened. His lids dropped. He slid down on the bed so his head rested on the pillows again. "Thank you, Jenna Waverly, for your kindness."

He was alone when he woke again. He could not tell the time of day from the light coming in the small window. No sun, from the looks of it, so it could be anytime really, even dusk. Ice covered the lower half of the glass like an extra pane.

His head felt better. Not as sore, nor as foggy. He stayed lying down for a while, taking in the small chamber's details, most of which he had not noticed before. The fireplace held court on a stone wall, and he guessed that wall held another hearth on its other side. The brewhouse, she had said, was over there. He still smelled beer, but not as strongly as before.

While he examined the chamber, a small weight landed on the foot of the bed. A round face with round eyes peered at him. Then a tabby cat paced forward, right up his body, until the cat's face almost touched his.

He gave the cat's ears a scratch and it turned and angled to give him better purchase. Then, perhaps thinking they had made friends, the cat retraced its steps and curled into a circle at the bottom of the bed.

Other than the bed, the chamber only had one chair, a small table, and a large trunk. Personal items lined three shelves on the wall: a polished metal plate, several crockery tumblers, and what looked like a tea box. This brewmaster did not live in luxury, but this was a handsome space despite its small size. Since it was also private, the brewmaster enjoyed better lodgings than most servants did.

He wondered when Mrs. Waverly would return. Jenna. He

had a lot of questions for her. It would be rude to ask all of them right away. It would be awkward to pose some of them, ever, especially to someone who had nursed him while he walked along the abyss.

He considered getting out of the bed. The confinement made him restless, but his body rebelled at the idea of activity. His spirit won out, and he sat and turned, then cast off the bedclothes. He stood, naked, and the cool air washed over him.

It felt good. Refreshing. No chills. Mrs. Waverly's warning echoed in his head. He dragged the coverlet up and pulled it around like a cape, dislodging the cat. Then he tried his legs. Since they held him he walked the few paces to where his garments hung off pegs on the wall near the door.

He fished into his waistcoat pocket and found his watch. Eleven o'clock. He set the watch on the table so he would have use of it.

Noise came through one wall of the chamber. It sounded like horses and voices. The sounds moved away, as if someone had passed alongside the building. Perhaps some other guests had gone out, despite the ice. He wondered how many of them there were. Mostly he wondered if Steven Wickersham was among them.

His jaw tightened while he pictured the blond, blue-eyed scoundrel. The man was bad business. Anyone could see it. Well, any *man* could. The ladies, however . . .

His cousin Marianne would be blamed if that affair became known. That was how it always went, even if a lying thief had seduced a vulnerable woman. Society always blamed the woman. Marianne's husband definitely would. Lucas had not been able to spare Marianne marriage to such a humorless man, but he would save her from the man's anger if he could. She was like a sister to him and he owed her that much at least.

Suddenly aware that his illness had interfered with his mission, he forced himself to walk more, around the small chamber, back and forth. His legs felt sluggish at first, but their strength gradually returned. He was in front of the fire again when the door opened and cold swept in. He turned to see an old man with gray hair step inside.

"Well, now, she said you were getting better. You looked at death's door yesterday."

Lucas vaguely remembered this man. "Did you find me?"

"I did at that. Fool notion to ride cross-country in weather like this."

"It wasn't so bad when I started."

"Anyone could see those low, dark clouds to the west. You thought to outride them is my guess. You won't be doing that again, I'd warrant."

He would have succeeded, if each mile had not made his body weaker and his mind foggier.

"Thank you for your help, Mister . . ."

The man waved the gratitude away. "Everyone here just calls me Peter. I came to tell you your horse has been found. It sought shelter in a copse of trees that we came upon while hunting. None the worse for it. Animals know how to survive such as this. I'll brush him down good and make sure he is fed and warmed up. I'll bring your bags to you soon."

It would be good to have the bags. He could hardly live in borrowed nightshirts.

The cold blasted again, and one of those nightshirts arrived on Mrs. Waverly's arm.

"I was telling him we brought back his horse and baggage," Peter said.

"I'm more impressed by the four hares you left in the kitchen," Mrs. Waverly said. "The chicken bones in the soup cauldron have given up all that they can." She set the nightshirt down on the bed. "If you rose from this bed, that is a wonderful sign, Mr. Avonwood. Once you are thoroughly impatient with being an invalid, we can declare you healed. Just don't do too much too soon."

As if she called forth the remnants of his malady, his strength began leaking away. A wave of light-headedness had him pressing his hand against the stone hearth wall for balance.

She gripped his upper arm. "Peter, help me get him back into bed."

"I'll do it. You leave, or at least turn away. He's got no clothes on under that coverlet."

Mrs. Waverly flushed and turned her back on them. Peter insisted on supporting him to the bed. He sat and dropped the coverlet. This time the cool air chilled more than refreshed. Then the nightshirt came over his head. Once decent, he lay down again and pulled the sheets over himself.

Low talk mumbled near the door. Then a soft palm pressed his brow. Sleep started to descend again, defeating the brief rally he had enjoyed.

"That fool cat has taken up residence," Peter said in the distance. "I'll get him out of here."

"Oh, Ivan," Mrs. Waverly said.

"He can stay," Lucas muttered. "I don't care."

No one moved the cat.

# Chapter 5

"You must eat now." Jenna issued the order upon visiting Mr. Avonwood in early afternoon. She found him sitting up in bed, reading a book. She glanced to where Peter had dropped the baggage. Mr. Avonwood must have seen his things upon wakening and risen to find something to do.

He set aside the book. "I will eat, if you promise to release me from gaol soon. I am much better now."

He certainly appeared so. His color looked normal and his blue eyes sparkled. Unless she was wrong, he had also found a brush in his baggage, so even his hair appeared better. Several days' growth of beard made him more roguish than unkempt.

She set down the bowl of porridge and opened the cloth with bread and cheese. "I'll decide later. I don't want to risk the other guests."

"You risked yourself."

"That was my choice. If I allow you to mingle among them, they will not have a similar one."

"You could have just left me here to fend for myself. No one would have blamed you."

"You were not capable of doing that."

"But now you may succumb, too. If I had known, and realized what was happening, I would not have allowed it."

Such a masculine thing to say. Quite firm, he was, too. She bit back a laugh. "Mr. Avonwood, I am beginning to think you are not mending after all. If you were, you would hear how foolish that sounds. If you had known and not allowed it, you would not have needed my care in the first place."

He pondered that, as if not wanting to admit his attempt at taking the matter in hand had failed.

"Now, will you sit at this table, or do you need to eat over there?"

"If I eat here, will I feed myself?"

"I think it is apparent you can now."

"Pity. I rather like being fussed over by pretty ladies."

He had shown some nice smiles before, but the one he now gave her dazzled with its charm. She tried to meet it with sternness, but inside her body her heart did a silly little flip.

"I think the table would be best," she said, stepping aside.

He turned on the bed and pulled the coverlet over himself again. Awkwardly bundled, he rose and stepped over to the table, sat down, and bit into a piece of the bread. It came from Lady Whitmarsh's loaf, and it took a bit of chewing. He said nothing but did not bite again.

Jenna sat at the foot of the bed, petting Ivan, taking the opportunity to examine Lucas Avonwood. For a man at death's door last night, he was recovering quickly. A strong constitution allowed for that, of course, as did some maladies that had short but severe lives. The fever had been breaking in the morning, and now she wondered if it had done so entirely.

She stood and reached over to lay her palm on his brow. She had done this so often in the last day that she did not think twice, or request permission. Only when her palm met his skin did she realize that much had changed.

For one thing, he felt cool, not overly warm. If any fever remained it was very small. For another thing, since he no longer hung in semidelirium, he also no longer accepted the unspoken pact that he would barely notice her touch. Notice he did, and what had been in the past a need for practical information became an unexpected intimacy.

He did not jerk his head away. He did not startle. He allowed it, and looked at her, his gaze acknowledging all of the touches and the difference of this one. Then, to her astonishment, he placed his own hand over hers, drew it down, and kissed her palm.

She didn't know what to do or say. She stared at him like a fool, thinking she should run out the door but not wanting to. Or she might employ her repertoire of arch, clever responses kept in reserve for male patrons of the inn who flirted too much. At the least she should pull her hand out of his.

He released her hand and set to his meal again.

"There was bacon at breakfast, too, but it was all eaten," she said, stupidly.

"I don't think I would have wanted it anyway," he said. "Who are your other guests?"

Since a bit of conversation would delay a walk in the cold, she told him about her refugees.

"Faringdon is here? I didn't realize he had returned to England."

"Do you know him?"

"We met once many years ago. He is heir to a barony. He is not the sort to inform you of that."

"A viscountess and now a future baron. I have a most distinguished group of unexpected guests."

He just smiled at that. She examined him closely. "Are you titled as well?"

"Me? No. Why would you ask?"

She shrugged. The question had jumped out. Now that he was more himself, that self appeared far more impressive than it had when he was sick. There was something about him that had provoked the question. The White Rose often hosted members of the aristocracy, so she had grown accustomed to sensing that rarified air when it entered her inn.

"And that is all of them?" he asked. "No others?"

"Fortunately not. I am almost out of chambers."

"Did you expect others? Visitors, perhaps, if not patrons of the inn?"

"Alice's young man was going to come and bring her and Peter to his master's house for the holiday. Other than that, there should be no visitors or callers. Even the wagons that come by from local farms to sell us provisions will not do so until after Boxing Day."

"It seems a very lonely way for you to spend Christmas. All alone."

Perhaps not all alone. Before this storm interfered, there had been the chance that Selwyn would come. Not a big chance, and she wasn't sure that having him here would have been joyous. She doubted she could see him without having a row.

She felt guilty thinking that. "Not lonely. Quiet. Silent. Blissfully so."

"Ah. So we all ruined it for you."

"Thoroughly. However, I am resigned." She stood and flung on her cape, then collected his bowl. "I will return in a few hours. You are not completely well yet and should rest."

As soon as Mrs. Waverly left, Lucas opened one of his valises. He removed the necessities for grooming, then set the pail of water among the embers in the fireplace. He took down the polished plate, gave it a few buffs with the sleeve of his nightshirt, then propped it next to the window for what light it would reflect.

A half hour later, shaved, washed, and dressed, he left the sickroom to go and explore the inn. The cold shocked him when he opened the door. The entry to this chamber was not protected, but shelter waited a few steps away. He only slid twice while navigating the path there.

A back portal let him into a covered yard of sorts. Buildings flanked it and a second-story gallery of rooms provided a partial ceiling. He paced forward to some pillars. They supported that upper level, but also permitted an opening to the courtyard, like an atrium. Ahead the covered passage led to another portal and the front drive. A little chamber stood right inside that gateway. Probably when the inn was in use a servant waited there, to welcome and direct patrons.

He stuck his head inside the large public room to the right, then a smaller dining room behind its massive fireplace. He then followed a passageway that broke off on his left. He heard Mrs. Waverly's voice coming through a doorway, accompanied by some metallic clanging. The kitchen, he assumed from the odors reaching his nose.

He spied a door on his left and was reaching for the latch when the kitchen door opened and an elderly woman emerged. She paused and gave him a long look, then walked off toward the breezeway. After learning that the latched door was locked, he followed the passageway along until he reached a door. Upon opening it he saw the stables and courtyard. Up some stairs a series of doors indicated that servant quarters probably rose above the stables.

Peter came down those stairs and noticed Lucas. He ambled over. "Are you worried about your horse? I have him in that enclosed stable over there. He's doing fine. Better than you were."

"I'm relieved to hear it. This is a handsome establishment."

Peter laughed. "Far better than the staging inn I worked at when I started. Rude sorts there, horses as well as people. Always crowded, and those coaches rushing in and out. No, Mrs. Waverly runs a respectable inn. It's more like being a guest at a private home. There's dukes and earls who will travel longer just to reach us. 'Provide good beds and good food and the world will find you.' That is what she said when she came here." He winked. "They'll also pay well for all that goodness."

"Did you come here when she did?"

"Nah. I had been here about five years by then. The man who worked the place passed away, and the landlord sold it to Mrs. Waverly and her brother, as I understand it."

"I didn't know she has a brother. I hope to meet him."

"You won't, I'm thinking. A gentleman, he is. Doesn't care for this place, or for the work it needs. Smells too much of trade. He stopped by early on, stayed a fortnight, then left. I've rarely seen him since. Leaves it all to her."

Lucas did not like this brother who was too good to help with the inn, but who thought it fine if his sister labored to earn a living out of it. If the brother was a gentleman, due to his own father's birth, then she was a gentleman's daughter.

"You best be going inside now. Won't do to catch your death twice in as many days," Peter said before he walked across the courtyard.

Lucas returned to the passageway and saw that the locked door now stood ajar. As he passed he looked in.

It was a storeroom. Sacks of kitchen supplies rested against one wall, and folded linens rose on shelves lining the one opposite. Mrs. Waverly reached high to lift off some clean bedclothes. The movement stretched her dress's fabric over her breasts. She must have heard his step because she paused and glanced over.

"You are supposed to be resting," she scolded.

"I was bored."

"You had a book to read."

"I was still bored." He slipped into the storeroom and reached up. "Is this the one you want?"

He grabbed the linen and brought it down for her. She added it to some others, then hugged the clumsy pile.

"You said you were not a title, but Lady Whitmarsh said you are."

So that was the old woman who came out of the kitchen. "She is wrong."

"She said she knows your family. She asked me what the son of Viscount Hargrave is doing here."

"That was indeed my father, but I am the second son. So, no title. I would not lie to you after all that you have done for me."

She glanced around, as if suddenly realizing that they stood close together in a very small, dark space. Her color rose. "You should return to—"

"Not yet. I'm sure I'll get tired soon enough, but for now it feels good to be out of there."

He looked around the storeroom's shadows. She kept it tidy. Some big baskets sat on the floor beneath the linen shelves. They contained wrapped packets of various shapes.

"What are those?"

"Items left by the transport companies who ply this road. The wagons give them to us, and our neighbors retrieve them here. It saves them from having to journey into town, or back to the last coaching inn."

"Do you accept the mail as well?"

"Only if someone sends a letter in my care. I am not an official postmistress."

He would have to examine the contents of those baskets more closely.

He realized that Mrs. Waverly was examining *him*, and quite critically. "I'm not convinced you are healthy enough to be wandering about my inn," she said. "Is your fever gone completely?"

"I don't feel feverish, but then stepping outside was more refreshing than frigid, so perhaps I am still somewhat warm." He caught her gaze with his own. "Why don't you check?"

She hesitated, then tucked all those bedclothes under one arm and reached up with the other. Her palm pressed his brow. Her skin felt neither warm nor cool. He enjoyed the connection, and the way her concern brought her leaning body very close to his.

His illness had breached formalities between them, and her expression turned very soft when she saw to his care like this. Soft and pretty. Not much light came through the cracked door, but what did made her eyes appear large and dark. Her touch had his body reacting in a way that said he definitely was on the mend.

She caught him gazing at her and snatched her hand away. She rearranged the bedclothes so the pile formed a soft shield in front of her. "You are still a little warm. I expect it will pass by tomorrow, but for now you should not join the other guests for meals. I will bring dinner to your chamber."

His spirit rebelled at the notion of spending hour upon hour alone in that sickroom. "I would prefer to move to a chamber here. I promise to make myself scarce at least until tomorrow."

"The remaining bedchambers are even smaller than where you currently reside."

"At least you don't have to slide over ice to get to them."

She appeared to debate for a moment, then shrugged. "I will show you what is available." She took one step, then halted. She raised her eyebrows. "You are in the way."

He reached for the pile of linens. "Allow me to carry those."

He stepped aside and she brushed past him, her arm and shoulder skimming against his chest. Together they walked up the nearby stairs across from the kitchen. Above, the passageway widened and formed a gallery that surrounded that atrium created by the pillars. He peered over the balustrade and looked down on the inner courtyard.

Mrs. Waverly took him to the end of the gallery, where it met a balcony that looked over the public room. "You can have this one," she said while she opened a door. "The bedchamber is unimpressive, but it does have a small dressing room so it is not as cramped as it first appears."

He paced inside, to the window that overlooked the back alley that his old chamber faced. From up here he could see beyond the enclosing fence, to fields and trees that stretched for miles. That was where he had been unhorsed, he assumed.

The chamber held a bed, table, and chair along with a small fireplace. An opening in the long wall gave way to the small dressing room.

"It will suit me fine. I will move my baggage."

"I will leave it to you." She led the way back to the gallery. "I will take those linens now."

"Show me where to put them and I'll spare you the burden a few more feet."

She hesitated, then paced along the balcony toward the front of the building. Right past the end of the balcony railing, she opened a door. "Just set them in there."

He stepped over the threshold into a spacious chamber with a large fireplace and a good-sized window. The shadows of the inn disappeared in here, even with the overcast day. A large bed stretched below the window, and two upholstered chairs flanked the fireplace.

More windows, on the side of the building, cast light over a desk covered in papers. Several chairs hugged a table set against the opposite wall. The colors and fabrics gave it a domestic, cozy air. A variety of small items and pictures said this was not a guest room. There was nothing anonymous about it.

"This is a very fine chamber. I would much prefer to stay here than in the other one you showed me."

"That is not possible. This is where I live."

He looked back at where she remained one step out of the room. "I know."

"As such it is not hired out to anyone. Not even duchesses."

It was not a duchess he imagined sharing this space with. From the way she regarded him, she knew that.

He set down the linens, then looked around her chamber again. She decided that perhaps his last few sentences had not been the overture they seemed to be. He did not appear flirtatious, although she had to admit he looked quite fine now that he had shaved and dressed.

Standing tall like this, well on his way to recovery, he appeared very different. Seeing him as his normal self had startled her, and altered what stood between them. He was no longer the helpless invalid, and she was no longer the person in charge of his infirmity. Instead he had become a handsome, vital man and she responded like the woman she was.

In part that was because the last day had not disappeared, either. It colored how they treated each other and affected the air between them. A bond forms in such a situation. Vulnerabilities are exposed that most women would never see, especially in a man like this.

"It is conveniently situated," he said. "I can picture you here, after a day of acting the hostess to paying guests. You must see this as a refuge."

She felt stupid holding a conversation from the doorway. She entered a few feet and tried to see her home the way he might. "Refuge is a good word." There were days, especially during seasons when people traveled a lot, when she entered this space, closed the door, and all but collapsed with relief.

She liked her inn. She was proud of it, and of how quickly it became known among the best society. She did not mind the work, either. She enjoyed the baking in particular and seeing to all the details that made the White Rose one of the best inns in the land.

Sometimes, however, the daily duties weighed on her spirit. Something would happen that reminded her of how different she had expected her life to be. A lady would go down to dinner in a fine new dress, and she would devour the luxurious trims and fabric with her eyes. Her own wardrobe was hardly poor—the inn's reputation required quality garments. But it had been years since she had indulged herself in anything other than respectable, plain, and practical dresses.

In this refuge, however, she could reclaim something of herself again. She would turn her back on the accounts on the desk and for a few hours do nothing at all practical. She would read by the fire, or just dream of the life she might have had.

Mr. Avonwood gazed out the window. "One can almost see the road."

She stepped up beside him and looked as well. "On a clear winter day you can." Right now the view was no more than a palette of whites and grays, and yet beautiful in its own way. "The trees appear magical with the ice coatings, but you can tell the lane remains treacherous. I doubt we will see improvement on that count by morning."

"Meaning you are stuck with all of us."

"I don't think any of you will be pleased with that. You all had somewhere else to go, and tomorrow is Christmas Eve. Being stranded here will not make for a merry holiday."

"I won't mind."

"I don't think I will, either."

Silence beside her had her looking over at him only to find him looking at her. His gaze captivated her. Her thoughts scattered and an internal thrumming hummed through her body. Memories came, of falling asleep while she warmed him and waking to find herself in his arms.

"Perhaps the others will agree with us, that it will be pleasant for everyone to remain here another day." He averted his gaze and walked to the door.

"Mr. Avonwood, if you promise to rest this afternoon, perhaps you will feel well enough to take your meal in the private dining room this evening," she said on impulse. "I intend to do so myself, and you can join me but remain apart from the others, lest some of them worry about your malady still being contagious."

"Don't you worry about that, too?"

"It is very late for that. Nor do I think you pose a danger to me now."

He reached for the latch. "I'm not sure that is true, Mrs. Waverly."

# Chapter 6

He retrieved his belongings and settled into the chamber at the corner of the gallery and balcony. As he closed his door he could not help but note that he was mere steps from Jenna's own chamber.

He threw himself on the bed. Not that rest came easily, even if his body told him it was needed. He would much prefer to follow her around, watching her while she performed her duties, admiring her pretty face and very competent management of this inn.

He wondered if he would find her so interesting if he had never been ill. That malady had stripped him of more than strength and health. The fever had robbed him of his armor and made him dependent on the kindness of someone he did not even know.

Only he did know her now. It was the kind of knowing that rarely forms, even after many years. The forced intimacy had drenched his spirit down to his soul.

It was odd to experience that connection with someone whose life and character he knew little about. Hell, she could be an ally of that scoundrel Steven Wickersham. If Wickersham had been coming here, and good evidence had said he was, it might well have been to see her. After all, the inn was not supposed to be open now. While Wickersham may not have known that, maybe he did. Perhaps it was not open so he could visit, and Mrs. Waverly could hand over the jewels he had sent her.

He didn't want to believe that, but it was very plausible. He would have to remember that if he ever found himself getting poetic again, while gazing into Jenna's deep green eyes.

Jenna added mustard to the sauce. The scent of the hares roasting on their spits permeated the kitchen. Some roots and apples braised in a pot to the side.

Alice opened the oven door and used the big paddle to bring out the bread. Lady Whitmarsh's did not look nearly as lumpish this time. She and Miss Younger had helped prepare the meal, but now had gone above to dress.

Alice set out the big bowls and platters. "I'll make up the guests' table now, then come back to deal with this one for the servants."

"I'll take my meal in the private dining room, along with Mr. Avonwood. If you could set for us as well, I'd appreciate it. I'll be at this hearth until mealtime."

"He is better, then?"

"Much better. Tomorrow he will mingle with the others if he wants. He still needs rest, but I don't think he is a danger to anyone now."

As she said it, she remembered their last words in her chamber, and his insinuation that he might be a danger to *her*. He had not meant due to his malady. Mr. Avonwood in his health was given to subtle flirting. He probably charmed women as a matter of course and had merely reverted to his normal ways now.

She wished she in turn could return to her own normal way of responding. One unwelcomed admirer had said that she could chill the blood with the look she gave after an advance had been made. There was no room for being ambiguous, however. Nothing but trouble, then. As the inn's owner, she could be vulnerable.

She had not chilled Mr. Avonwood's blood, however. Nor had he made her feel vulnerable, except in the most pleasant way. She had no reason to trust him, but she did not think he would abuse their . . . friendship. Not the right word, since they barely knew each other the way typical friends did. How odd to have this more soulful knowing of a person she had barely conversed with.

A low hiss had her looking at the sauce, and hurriedly giving it a good stir so the bottom wouldn't burn. A fine thing that would be, to daydream so much that she ruined dinner.

She stepped to the shelves and brought down a small platter, then set a large cutting board on the worktable. She lifted a big cleaver from the wall. When she turned back to the table, she realized she was not alone.

Mr. Avonwood lounged near the door, his shoulder holding up the wall, watching her. He had dressed for dinner. His clean cravat gleamed in the lamps' glow.

"Are you preparing for battle?" he asked.

"Only with these hares." She set down the cleaver and made a pad out of a thick cloth.

He was beside her at once. "I will do that. You might burn yourself." He took the cloth and used it to lift the spit off its wheel.

"Set it on this board."

Once he did, she pushed the hares off the spit's rods. Using the cleaver she chopped each one into portions. Some went into the bowl for the servants, and she laid a few pieces on the small platter. The rest she arranged on the large platter for her guests.

"They be gathering," Alice announced upon returning. Footsteps indicated the servants were arriving, too. "I'll bring up the bread and come back for the meat once you're done with it."

"What can I do to help?" Mr. Avonwood asked.

Had it been any other man, she would have suggested his best help would be making himself scarce. Instead she gestured to the large platter. "If you hold this near the fire for me . . ."

He did so and she spooned the roots and apples around the hare, then ladled sauce over it all. They had all the platters dealt with just as Alice returned to carry food into the public room.

The servants began filing in. Mr. Faringdon's manservant, Rob, found them all plates and cups. It appeared Alice had the servants doing for themselves, too.

Jenna lifted the small platter. Mr. Avonwood reached for it, but she held it away. "That will never do. Although, you could bring that small basket of bread with you."

Out the door they paraded. Across the chilly inner courtyard. Through the public room, where several interested pairs of eyes watched their progress. Through the door to the private dining room.

Alice had laid the table and set out a bottle of Portuguese red.

"Are you hungry?" Jenna asked while they took their chairs.

"Starving." He stretched over the table and inhaled deeply. "Especially now. It looks and smells delicious. I find it hard to believe that your cook does better."

His praise pleased her. "Far better. Delicacies beyond your imagination come out of that kitchen. You must visit when he is here, so you can see. He allows me to bake if I have the notion to do so, and if we are very busy he will accept my help preparing the less important parts of the meal. The significant dishes are all his, however. Which means that I have no idea if this sauce is going to enhance or ruin things this evening."

She served them from the platter while he opened the wine and poured. There wasn't much talk after that because Mr. Avonwood ate as if he indeed was starving.

Eventually he slowed down. "I think your sauce is excellent." He continued their conversation as if fifteen minutes of serious eating had not interfered. "I would think you would be far too busy to bake."

"I enjoy it. I do it for my pleasure, as a little holiday amidst my duties."

His gaze narrowed on her. "You are not a typical innkeeper."

"I suppose not. That is by design, however."

"Why did you choose to do this?"

She heard the unspoken question beneath the verbal one. *Why aren't you married and at home with your family instead?* Normally she would find that an intrusive, even impertinent curiosity, but she didn't now. He was a stranger but not a stranger, and she experienced the same curiosity about him.

"My father was a gentleman, but the sort who was careless with both his purse and his land. He was a good man who nonetheless had large debts when he passed."

"It is a common enough story."

"Offspring left all but destitute are common enough, too. However, some money had been left to me by an aunt. I took it and bought this inn. I knew it would be a step down, but I preferred making my own way to living off the small amount the inheritance would bring if invested in funds."

"You more than proved you had a good idea. This is a very fine establishment."

"I made a decision to create a superior inn, one that the best of society would find agreeable. My guests are just that: guests. I am their hostess. They might be visiting a lodge owned by one of their friends. All of this brings me far more income than a normal inn would provide. It also means this is a place that I am proud of."

He poured them more wine and settled back in his chair. His handsome hand fondled the glass he held. She tried not to stare at how sensual that looked. "Are you totally alone? No family at all?"

She hesitated and did not know why. Perhaps a small sharpening of his attention made her pause. Maybe the way his hand mesmerized her interfered.

"I have a brother. The inheritance was mine, but I bought this for both of us." A mistake, that. Perhaps the worst she had ever made. "He soon decided that it did not suit him to stay here. He prefers London, and the country homes of his friends."

"Is he making his own way, too, only on a different path?"

"I expect so. He visits on occasion, but not for long. He is the sort who would never admit to employment, so I don't ask." She stood, walked over to a side table, and returned with the plate waiting there. "There is a piece of pie left from last night, if you want it. Also some ginger cakes that I made this afternoon. I should warn you that one of the young ladies made the pie, and it was her first effort."

He politely complimented the pie but seemed more genuine after he ate a cake.

"So now you know everything about me," she said.

"I doubt that. We are more than what we do."

"Yet what we do helps make us who we are. What do you do, Mr. Avonwood? Attend balls and dinner parties? Sit in boxes at the theater?"

"That must seem a frivolous life to someone like you."

"Perhaps, but enviable, too."

"Is it a life you would like to have? You seem a person who needs more purpose than that."

Would she want it now? She had once. Memories came to her, of dances and assemblies and laughing with friends and being lighthearted. But she could not deny that his use of the word *frivolous* had sounded right to her.

"Do you prefer a purpose, too, Mr. Avonwood? Besides the pursuit of pleasure? Did some purpose bring you across those fields yesterday, or merely a Christmas house party in Leicester?"

He finished the cake before responding. He looked over with a charming smile. "Why do you ask?"

"Something compelled you to risk a cross-country ride in that weather. I do not think it was something . . . frivolous."

His smile turned self-deprecating. He laughed lightly and looked at her while he drank his wine. Then he leaned in toward her. "I will tell you even though it is a private matter. I am in pursuit of someone."

Disappointment squeezed her heart. Stupid, but there it was. His impatience to reach his destination had a very common purpose, but a most compelling one.

He was on his way to see a woman.

A shadow filmed her eyes when he said it. As if she knew all the rest, and that this inn had been his goal. That wasn't possible, and yet . . . "I am looking for a man. It is a family matter."

The spark returned with one blink. "I did not mean to pry."

"You have a right to be curious. I'd be dead if not for you."

"I doubt that."

Only she didn't. She knew her care might well have made the difference. "You could probably sell this place and go up to Town if you wanted," he said, to change the subject from his mission. "The reputation you have built for it will make it more valuable than when you took it on."

"I have thought about that."

"The scheme has no appeal?"

She looked away and licked her lips. He watched the tiny tip of her tongue sweep up. She returned her attention just as he averted his own from the eroticism of that nervous action. "If I tell you something, you must promise not to hold it against him. Not that you will meet him, but—"

"Who?"

"My brother."

"I promise."

"I learned two months ago that he mortgaged it. The inn. I had it in both our names, so he would have—so he would not be without any property. And he . . ." Vexation tightened her expression. She reached for her wine and drank a solid swallow. "So I can't sell it and go up to Town, even if I wanted to."

"He didn't tell you?"

"Goodness, no. Nor did he ask, which he should have. I daresay when next I see him I will be hard-pressed not to start a big row over it. I think it was very unfair, since the money had been mine."

"Most unfair. Does anyone know?"

She shook her head and drank more wine.

The scoundrel. He had decided that he really did own half of the property, and as a man had the right to do what he chose with the whole thing. Right now he was probably living a good life in London, enjoying the clubs and assemblies with the money he'd obtained with that mortgage.

Eventually it would come due. Someone would have to pay it back, or the inn would be forfeited. Lucas doubted Mrs. Waverly made enough profit to lay aside such an amount.

The cowardly rogue.

She appeared distraught and absorbed by thoughts that probably were similar to his own. She forced a little, sad smile. "I don't know why I told you. It is just . . ." She shrugged.

He pictured her learning about this betrayal, and having no one to confide in. How many nights had she paced that chamber above this dining room, fretting over the impossible situation her brother had created for her?

He reached across the table and took her hand in his. "You needed to tell someone, that is all. Do you know where he stays in town? Can you write to him?"

She shook her head. "He takes chambers when he is in London but vacates when he travels. Scotland for grouse season and such." She sighed. "Well, I'll just have to find a way to fix it. Eventually he will have to return here. Maybe he will come with enough money to pay the loan back."

She had not removed her hand, or even seemed to realize he held it. Then suddenly she was staring at it. She glanced up into his eyes, then looked down at their hands again.

"I think I told you because I have seen you at your worst and thought you would not judge me too harshly if you saw me the same way," she said.

"I would be an ungrateful lout if I judged you at all. I am glad you confided in me. We share a special sympathy, I think. One that even old friends might not understand."

"Yes." Her expression turned sweet and soft. So sweet that he succumbed to impulse. He leaned over the table, cradled her chin in his hand, and kissed her.

What a wonderful surprise that kiss was. Astonishing and moving and just what her spirit needed. Thinking about her brother and that mortgage had dragged her mood low, but now she soared on the wings of excitement.

The sounds from the public room had been clamoring in the background, but they retreated when his lips touched hers. He knew what he was about, so that kiss, while gentle, was not tentative. She vaguely thought that she should pull away, but the notion did not stay long. She was enjoying herself too much for propriety to make much impression.

He stopped just as her physical reactions became insistent, pressing on her consciousness and absorbing her attention. He simply sat back in his chair. She realized that he still held her hand.

"I have been wanting to do that for a long time," he said. "Even when I was sick." He did not apologize or make excuses. She rather liked that.

"It was a nice kiss," she said, then realized that whatever she was supposed to say, it wasn't that.

"I'm glad you think so. Perhaps we should . . ." He began to lean toward her again.

She veered back this time. "Probably not. The dinner taking place in the adjoining room is finished, from the sounds of things. Someone may venture over here."

The sounds of chairs scraping and a feminine voice saying good night penetrated her awareness. Then light footsteps advanced toward them. He released her hand.

The viscountess poked her head around the stone hearth wall, then entered. He stood and Jenna greeted her.

"I just wanted to say that the meal was quite good," Lady

Whitmarsh said. "Hardly the prisoner's fare you threatened."

"We can thank the gentlemen for that, but I am delighted that you are pleased."

"My coachman ventured out to the road before dark fell. He does not think we will be able to leave tomorrow, unless a serious thaw sets in overnight."

"That is unfortunate for you. However, we can have some festivities here if everyone is agreeable."

"The young ladies are of the same mind. I think they are plotting." She turned her attention fully on Mr. Avonwood. "You appear to be better. A little pale still, but your eyes are good."

"I am much improved, thank you."

She kept regarding him. "Your grandmother and I were friends. I was sorry to hear about your injury."

"The family made more of it than necessary. I fared better than most."

"Yes, of course. Well, we are nothing if not a stoic people." She smiled and began to turn. "These old bones think a warm bed is in order. I've sent Miss Younger up ahead with a warming pan. You must let me know if I can help you tomorrow, Mrs. Waverly. I find being occupied refreshing."

Jenna strained her ears to hear the viscountess's steps pace down the public room, then up the stairs to the balcony.

She stood. "I, too, should seek some rest. Tomorrow promises to be very busy for me."

He walked with her around the hearth to the door of the public room.

Mr. Faringdon and Miss Macleod still sat at the table, now head to head. Bootsteps overhead on the balcony said the others had retreated.

Lucas accompanied her to the stairs on the far end of the public room. By the time they reached the balcony no one was about upstairs.

"I think I will join the others when they hunt tomorrow," he said as they paced toward her chamber door.

"You mustn't. I forbid it."

"Forbid it, do you?"

She opened her door but paused. "You will risk a relapse if you go out in the cold for hours on end. Your restlessness today was a good sign, but you are not truly recovered yet."

He feigned chagrin and gave a dutiful nod. "Perhaps you are right. Even now, I feel less well than before."

"That is because you did not rest enough." She peered at his face in the dim light, checking to see if he had become drawn or whether the viscountess had been correct about his coloring.

"You are probably right."

His easy capitulation worried her. She instinctively placed her palm on his forehead, as she had so many times, then skimmed down to his jaw, to check for fever.

Suddenly his hand pressed hers against his face and his other arm encircled her waist. With one quick move he spun her into the chamber as if they danced, and kicked the door closed with his boot.

A different kiss this time. Less gentle and more demanding. His embrace brought her close and that unintended intimacy on his bed came again and again, in waves that alternated between contentment and yearning. She could feel the body she had bathed with water, now pressed against her own. The warmth of his arms created a nest in which she wanted to nestle forever.

His passion rose and hers joined it. She could tell he kept himself in check, but even so his kisses came harder as they wandered down to her neck and chest before claiming her mouth again. Wildness beckoned, and a savage pulse kept coursing through her, discouraging any concern with a reckoning.

A new kiss. Invasive. Consuming. His arms moved and his hand wandered. Caresses teased her toward recklessness.

One word, and he would stop. But the sensations he evoked enlivened her so much that she did not speak it. She did not want to.

A scratch on the door. The faintest knock. "Mrs. Waverly."
They both froze, forehead to forehead, catching their breath.
"Mrs. Waverly, are you awake?"
It was Miss Macleod.
He did not say a word but stepped briskly into her chamber and around the hearth wall.
Jenna felt her hair, and hoped its appearance was not too damning. She opened the door.
"My apologies," Miss Macleod said. "I didn't mean to intrude if you have retired."
"No need for apologies. I was going to read for a while. How can I help you?"
"Flora and I have been talking about tomorrow. We have some wonderful ideas for making the day festive, if you don't mind. Some of it involves the kitchen. We want to make shortbread, and Russian tea cakes, and a cake, and—"
Jenna laughed. "You had best go to sleep soon, if you want to do all of that. You must be up at dawn."
"Then you don't mind?"
"Not at all. I'll be in the kitchen very early and can help you."
"Oh, good. What fun this will be. The gentlemen are going to bring back evergreens when they go hunt, and we will have songs and games after dinner. We have it all planned."
"Thank you. I'm sure you will arrange a much better party than I would have done."
"I will say good night, then, so you can return to your book."
She wandered off. Jenna closed the door and leaned against it. She took several deep breaths, then ventured into her chamber.
He stood near the big window, beside her bed, looking out on the moonlight glistening off ice crystals hanging from the tree branches. He glanced over at her step, then opened his arms, inviting her back into his embrace.
She went, and he held her, embracing her from behind while they watched the beauty outside.

"Should I apologize?" he asked.

She shook her head. "I didn't mind nearly as much as I'm supposed to."

He angled his head and kissed her ear. "It seemed very right to me. Necessary."

She looked back at him and smiled. "I think you must still have a bit of fever if you think that."

"I do at that, but not the kind you mean."

She turned in his arms and savored the feel of their closeness. "Give me one more kiss, then take yourself off and get that rest you need."

His slow smile made her heart swell. "If I am there and you are here, who will take care of me?"

"You no longer need my care."

"I'm sure that I am not *that* well."

"You are being naughty again."

He gave her the kiss she had requested. "I think I made a mistake in leaving that sickroom. No one cared if you spent all night with me there."

Regretfully, she slid out of his embrace. "And yet it will be a scandal to be alone together now. So, you must go."

He made a big, comical sigh of resignation. "I suppose I must." He strode to the door but stopped and looked at her. "You spoke of your brother at dinner. What is his name?"

"Selwyn."

He cocked his head, smiled, and opened the door. He peered out, then slipped away.

Selwyn Waverly.

Steven Wickersham.

Hell.

He hoped he was wrong.

There was no way to know. He could hardly ask Jenna for a detailed description of her brother. Does he have blue eyes? Is his hair more ginger than straw? Would you say he stood as tall as me, or shorter? By the by, you wouldn't happen to know if he travels the realm seducing vulnerable women and stealing from them?

He stretched out on his bed and considered the evidence. This Selwyn had stolen from his own sister, from the sounds of it. That alone made him an excellent candidate for being Wickersham.

Wickersham had spoken of stopping at this inn when he left the last one. Jenna did not have much faith in her brother visiting, however. Also the inn was well known among the circles in which Wickersham had insinuated himself. The fact that this inn was his destination did not make Steven and Selwyn the same person.

He wanted to reject the idea. After all, Waverly was Jenna's married name, so her brother would not have it. There. It wasn't him. His mind tried to accept that, but he had to admit the rest lined up into a plausible theory.

Damnation. A fine thing that would be, to repay Jenna's kindness by accusing her brother of being a thief. And as for their friendship . . .

He shouldn't have kissed her. He should have seen this possibility sooner. He had been most negligent about his duty.

He never should have allowed that deeper connection with Jenna to form.

Only it had formed, through no intention of his. Or hers. It just happened. The result of his illness and her help. She could have left him in that chamber to fend for himself. It was common enough. She could have spared herself both the exhaustion of nursing him and the forced intimacy. She hadn't.

The result had been those kisses. So right. A fulfillment of something begun in his delirium. A new closeness, born of the bond formed during his helplessness but free to exist on its own now. If they wanted it to.

He stood and paced the small chamber. He saw no exit from his conundrum. Either he waited to see if this brother arrived and was the scoundrel known as Steven Wickersham. Or he rode away as soon as the weather allowed and broke his promise to Marianne.

A betrayal either way, of someone who mattered.

He pivoted, lifted the lamp, and abruptly left his chamber. He took the steps down. Maybe, just maybe, Wickersham was coming here for another reason and was not Jenna's brother, or even a possible guest at the inn.

He tested the door to the storeroom across from the kitchen. It had been left unlocked this time. When it opened, he slipped in and closed it behind him. He set down the lamp and crouched next to the baskets of packages. Jenna said these had been left by transport companies. Neighbors and travelers had their packages delivered here, using it as a mail drop for larger items.

He pawed through the packets and boxes, reading the directions. One clearly contained some books. Another felt so light as to perhaps have clothing inside. A few odd-shaped little bundles made no sense at all.

Then he found one that had come from Burrell. He had passed through that town while tracking Wickersham. The small packet had been directed to the care of the inn, but the name of its recipient was S. Williams.

Another S.W.

His consternation lifted. He saw the game clearly now. This man, whatever his name might really be, made sure the items he stole would not be found on his person. He sent them to an inn that he would pass on his way to his next seduction. They left his possession until he was well away and safe, when he would present himself at the inn and ask if something had been delivered for him.

He felt along the packet but could not determine what it held. Not heavy, though. Light enough that it might have been sent by penny post. Only it hadn't been.

He dug deeper, and found another package for S.W. Another basket produced a third. Perhaps there were others, in other chambers, or in the cellar. The ill-gotten proceeds of months might be waiting here.

If he was correct, this was no longer a personal matter, but a case for the courts.

Tempted though he was to open the packages, he stood and lifted his lamp. He opened the door and slipped out.

And almost walked right into Jenna.

His appearance startled her. He simply arrived like magic, backlit by that lamp. She steadied her tray while they faced each other across the passageway. Only when he moved toward her did she realize he must have emerged from the storeroom.

Why would he be in there?

"What do you have there?" he asked as if there was nothing odd in their meeting.

"Chamomile tea. It is for you. You should drink it before you retire."

"Were you bringing it to me?"

"That was my intention, but since you are here, you can carry it yourself." She offered him the tray.

He set his lamp on it and took it from her. She in turn removed her own light. Together they walked to the stairs.

"Were you in the storeroom?"

"I was. I was seeing if you had the spices for negus. I thought if we are planning festivities, it would be nice to make some. I prefer certain spices in mine. Cloves, for example."

It sounded plausible enough. And yet ... "The spices are in a small cabinet in the kitchen. I'm sure we have what you want."

"Then making negus will be my duty tomorrow, since you will not let me hunt."

His vague allusion to his illness almost had her reaching out to feel his face again. She caught herself in time, but his slow smile suggested he saw the impulse.

"You get a worried frown whenever you check me for fever," he said. "Were you going to again?"

"Not at all."

"You can if you want. I can hardly grab you since I'm carrying this tray."

"You might be the sort to risk my china, if inclined to grab."

He balanced the tray on one hand. "Or not."

They had reached the upper story and paced toward the balcony. A few sounds came to her, of movements and voices. Perhaps the young ladies were still planning the festivities in one of their chambers.

He stopped at his door. "I think you should have some tea, too. There are two cups. You need to watch your health, after the time we spent together."

She lifted the teapot and poured into one cup. "I will take mine in my own chamber." She lifted the cup.

"You are sure you don't want some conversation with that?" He opened his door as he asked the question.

She wasn't sure at all. The light from that lamp flattered him, and the emotions engendered by their earlier embraces made her wistful. No one was about. How easy to slip in and spend a few hours with him, learning the things that normally are learned first, before one's heart is touched.

She could not be that bold, however. That reckless. She rather wished she could be. It would be sad to have felt this connection only to watch him ride away with it unfulfilled.

"I must get my rest. Tomorrow I have much to do. You should rest, too."

And so they parted at his door. She walked away like the respectable woman she was. She felt his gaze on her back the entire path to her chamber, however. Only when she entered and closed the door did the yearning release her.

She sat in one of her chairs by her fire and drank her tea. She mentally listed tomorrow's duties and chores. That kept her from contemplating what she had just denied herself.

It also distracted her from the question simmering in her mind. No one keeps spices in a storeroom. So why had Lucas Avonwood been in there?

# Chapter 7

Noise woke Lucas. It came from outside. He left his bed and looked out the window. Down below the hunting party had returned. Faringdon carried a group of ducks, which he handed to Peter. Rob Matthews brought up the rear.

It looked like Juncker was dragging a tree.

Perhaps he intended to cut off part of the trunk for a yule log. Hopefully not. Freshly cut pine doesn't like being burned. It would smoke horribly.

He dressed roughly and grabbed the water pail, to go look for the well. But when he opened his door, water already waited right outside. Someone had taken pity on the invalid. He washed, shaved, and dressed, then went below.

Miss Macleod's guard walked past, clearly heading for the well in the cellar. Across the way noises came from the kitchen. He poked his head in.

The ladies were all cooking. Jenna poked at something in a large cauldron. Miss Younger was rolling pie crust while Miss Macleod sifted flour. Lady Whitmarsh held court at a second table, drinking tea at one end.

The viscountess noticed him. "Come in, Mr. Avonwood. My, you are looking well today. Doesn't he look well, Mrs. Waverly?"

Jenna turned from the hearth. "He does indeed. A miraculous recovery."

"No miracle, but a strict nurse." He ambled over to her and barely resisted the urge to embrace her from behind, as he'd done the night before. He peered into the cauldron. A large mass kept trying to float to the top of the simmering water, and she kept poking it down again.

"It is a ham," she said. "Another hour and out it comes."

"I saw ducks arrive back from the hunt, but no boar."

"I had this in reserve but decided I can replace it easily enough after the holiday. Duck sounds very good, too. Peter will dress them and bring them along soon." She angled her head toward the viscountess's table. "There is still some breakfast there. Help yourself if you want, or you can wait a half hour and eat with the gentlemen. I'll be making eggs for them."

He decided he couldn't wait. A day without much food had left a hole in him that needed filling, and even last night's dinner had not sufficed. He filled a plate with the fried potatoes, bread, and bacon on the table, and sat to eat.

Jenna brushed past him, heading for the door, a basket over her arm.

"Are you leaving that ham on its own?" he asked.

"I'm only going for the eggs and some other items in the cellar. I'll return soon."

He swallowed the last of his bread. "I'll help you."

He joined her, ignoring the way Lady Whitmarsh's eyebrow rose just enough to show curiosity.

"I don't really need help," Jenna said as they walked through the inner courtyard. "I don't want you catching cold."

"I won't. I am feeling quite myself today."

"Having a good lie-in can do that."

"Are you scolding me for not rising at dawn? If you had allowed me to hunt, I would have. Besides, those two servants were no better."

"The viscountess scolded them. Seems the male servants are having a very nice holiday, with few duties and much merriment. They have found their way into the brewhouse, too."

They nipped around to the cellar stairs and went down. Deep and underground, the air warmed with each step.

It was a good-size cellar, under the public room and private dining room. Some light filtered through two grates in the stone ceiling, and he judged the space extended under the back alley as well.

Jenna went to some straw and pushed it aside to reveal rows of eggs. She began lining her basket with them.

"Do you have chickens here? I haven't noticed any livestock."

"I buy these from a neighbor. Mr. Dormont comes by three times a week with as many as he can spare. When the inn is open we use a lot of them." She paused her movements. "I thought about having chickens, out in the south garden beyond the stables. It would be practical, and there is a pen there where we put the ones that I buy for meals." She shrugged. "I could also have a cow for milk to make cheese and butter, and not buy either from Mr. Lawrence. I decided all of that was too rustic for me. Becoming an innkeeper is one thing. Taking on husbandry is another."

"I'm sure your neighbors are pleased with your decision. Their commerce with the inn helps them."

"And they help me. It is a fair trade."

He left her to the eggs and strolled around the cellar. In one corner, he saw a meat safe, and beside it the tubs and racks for laundry. Shelves held crocks for cream at the opposite end. Bins with apples, carrots, onions, and other foods lined the walls of the cellar, which was cold enough to preserve, but not so cold as to freeze. The well stood in the middle, its top covered by a large, hinged wooden disk. A bucket hung from the armature positioned above it.

He peered into the shadows, looking for any more baskets with packages. He came upon a large wooden crate in a dark corner. Inside it held smaller crates. He slipped his hand in and placed his fingers under the corner of one. He lifted it slightly. Heavy. There appeared to be paper labels on them, but he could not make out whether they gave directions to leave these crates at this inn.

He would have to return to this cellar, alone and with a lamp.

Jenna realized she had far too many eggs in her basket. She began returning some to their resting places.

When Lucas had accompanied her down here, she'd thought it was so he could find the privacy to kiss her again. She had been waiting for him to do that for a long while now, slowing her movements to stretch out the time. Her whole body remained alert to the sounds or warmth that said he was behind her. She kept imagining him embracing her as he had in her chamber, holding her close, then turning her in his arms and kissing her soundly.

"Can you spare these?" His voice spoke next to her ear. His breath thrilled her. Only he did not embrace her. Instead he reached around and placed three oranges and two lemons in her basket. "Will they break the eggs? They are for the negus."

"I'll pad the eggs with the cloth."

A five count pulsed by, one heavy with their proximity and what might happen. Only no warmth came. Instead he walked away and continued to examine the cellar as if it held the secrets to a treasure.

"Have you never been in a cellar before?" In her vexation she cracked an egg that she handled too hard. She returned it to the basket, to be used first. "Other than having a well in it, this one is not remarkable."

"It is larger than most and allows you to manage this inn efficiently."

Yes, it did. Only she did not believe he was assessing how well the building enabled her business. She looked over her shoulder and saw him standing near what was left of the wine that Selwyn had sent last year. How excited she had been when that wagon came to the door with all those wooden crates. She had been even more delighted when she opened a bottle and learned it was excellent.

She had lost much of her enthusiasm, however, when she saw there were no duty stamps on the crates, and that the Portuguese labels appeared very clean.

Selwyn's explanation, when he visited last August, had allayed her suspicions. He had won the wine at cards, and had new crates made so the bottles would survive the journey north. A wine merchant's bad luck at the tables had saved her at least a hundred pounds. *Don't say I don't contribute*, he had said. *That will pay your servants for at least two years.*

Had Lucas been examining those crates, and wondering about them just as she had when they first came? Smuggling was common along the coasts, but less so up here. Still, some such goods must move inland. Kent and Cornwall couldn't use it all.

He paced away with some deliberation. She owed him no explanation, so she bit back the impulse to give him one.

He made his way over to her. "You appear mysterious here in these shadows. Mysterious and lovely. The faint light from those grates bathes you in silver."

"A fine thing if I have to go into a cellar to look my best."

He ran his fingertips along the hand that held the basket's handle. "You are always lovely, Jenna."

That touch sent little shivers through her. Surely he would kiss her now. Her pulse raced from the anticipation building in her.

He lifted the basket out of her hand. "I will carry it."

Together they mounted the stairs, up into the cold. It appeared Mr. Avonwood had recovered from his passing deliriums. Thoroughly.

\* \* \*

It had been all he could do not to set that basket down and pull her into his arms. Only a heroic effort at control had checked him. That and a need to sort out the ideas crowding into his head.

If he was even partly right, to kiss her again would be wrong, unkind, and dishonorable in the worst way.

They entered the kitchen and Jenna set to cooking the eggs. They had just finished when Faringdon and Juncker came in to partake. They ate heartily of eggs and bread and cheese. Juncker finished and strolled by the fire to sniff the big cauldron.

"Do you think you can lift that ham out of the water?" Jenna asked. She handed him a long-handled spoon and he poked at the ham.

"I suppose so, somehow. Where do you want it?"

"In the big pan over here." She handed him a long butcher knife. "This might help steady it."

Lucas strode over. "I'll help. It will be awkward for one person."

Jenna gave him a wad of rags. "It will be hot, but if you can grab it by the shank and use these to protect your hand, you should be able to manage."

"I'll prod it up so you can grab," Juncker said.

"Just don't burn yourselves. The water is very hot," Jenna warned.

Juncker took a few minutes to test how to move the meat in the cauldron. "I think I can get it now. Be ready." He pushed the ham up with the spoon then speared the joint and forced the shank above the water. Lucas grabbed it, lifted the meat out of the water, and swung it over onto the pan.

"And not even a drip on your fine coat," Juncker said with a grin. "I'm devising a surprise in the public room. You should come and see it."

"I'm going there now. I need port."

"It could be you can help me there, too, then, since you are so good at holding up things."

Intrigued, he followed Konrad to the public room and spent an hour helping him with his surprise.

When he returned to the kitchen with the port, the ham appeared very different. Jenna had trimmed off the skin and covered the huge joint in some basting liquid. "Just in time," she said. "It is too heavy for me and needs to go in that oven down there."

The fireplace held several ovens with heavy iron doors. The one she pointed to was low, and the largest. He slid the pan into the cavern and she shut the door. Then she pushed an errant strand of hair away and stretched, arching her back. "I believe I will rest for an hour, before dinner preparations must start."

"If you show me what to use, I'll mix and warm the punch."

She retrieved a heavy pot from the shelf, then set down a sugar cone. "This pot will warm it quickly if you set it on the hearthstone."

With that she walked away.

He poured the port into the pot, then scraped off some sugar. He cut the **oranges** and lemons and squeezed their juice into the port. Finally, he chose some spices from the small chest she'd indicated and tossed them in, too. He set the pot on the hearthstone.

While he waited for it to warm, he finally addressed the unwelcome ideas that had entered his mind while in the cellar. He suspected he already knew what he would find when he returned there. Wine, and a lot of it, none with customs stamps. The question was whether Jenna knew what was in those crates, and if she also knew it was smuggled.

It did not follow that she must. A wagon that brought packages could bring larger items, also to be left at the inn until the owner called for it. It would be a splendid way to move illegal goods. Jenna could have merely accepted the shipment and stored it until the owner came.

Or, she might have played a larger role. Who would suspect

her? A young woman running an inn for elevated society, treating her guests as just that, guests, instead of itinerant travelers hiring a bed? No one would guess she bought illegitimate goods. Even if that wine were found down there, he doubted the county magistrate would conclude she'd had a hand in its arrival in England.

He certainly didn't want to suspect her. And yet there it was, just as Steven Wickersham might be her brother Selwyn, she might be a partner in those thefts.

It was an ignoble thought. An ungrateful one. He was surprised how deeply disappointed it left him. Not in her, or in himself, but in the way it threatened to break that special bond he felt with her.

He tested the negus's warmth, then found a spoon and dipped it in and tasted. He threw in a bit more spice and added the lemon skins for good measure. This time when he tasted, he approved of the result.

He pictured Jenna above, having a respite from her generous efforts to make this day festive for her stranded guests. He found two cups on the shelf and filled them with the warm punch, put them on a small tray, carried them from the kitchen.

He could not ignore the evidence that said she might be involved in criminal activities, but that didn't mean he had to believe she was. He didn't, but admitted, as he mounted the stairs, that desire might be distorting his judgment.

"Here are some bits of ribbon," Jenna said while she dug around her sewing basket. "Will they do?"

"It doesn't have to be fancy. I'll make bows of these." Alice tucked the ribbons into an apron pocket. "I think Miss Younger will be amazed by what Mr. Juncker has done. We can all enjoy it, but I believe she was the reason he went to the trouble. I think he is sweet on her."

Jenna had to smile. How wonderful if two of her guests found romance in this unusual situation. That would be a very nice outcome for two very pleasant people. She hoped Alice was right.

"You said sparkly would be good." Jenna strode to her dressing table. "I have these ear bobs and broken necklace pieces. They are not expensive, but the paste jewels will catch the light."

"Those are perfect. Granddad is making little twine holders for apples that I'll put out, too. This is fun. Come out and see what else is going on." She beckoned Jenna to join her at the door.

Together they stepped out. The two coachmen knelt on the balcony, tying twine around posts in the balustrade.

"Lift on the left," a voice called.

The coachmen farthest from them sighed and pulled some evergreens through his twine.

"A bit more."

"Glad he's such an expert," one coachman grumbled. "Seems to me I was the one who had to show how to string it all together to make a long rope of boughs."

"He's a high opinion of himself, that one does," the other coachman said. "That's what comes of gentlemen favoring a servant too much. They forget their place, they do."

"Well, if he wants anything changed again, he can do it himself."

Jenna looked over to see it was Rob Matthews giving the orders. Swags of evergreens already decorated the windowsills and ran down the center of the large table.

With much creaking and groaning the men got to their feet and headed to the stairs. Alice followed, just as Lucas came up the other stairs down the gallery. He carried a tray.

"You are supposed to be resting," he said.

"As are you."

"Share some warm port with me and we can rest together."

An image came to her mind, of lying close to him on her bed, embracing for a few peaceful minutes. She flushed as if the negus had already been consumed. "Warm punch sounds perfect." She led him into her chamber.

He offered her a cup, then settled into one of the chairs near the fireplace with his own. "You appear happy, not exhausted."

196 • *Madeline Hunter*

"I am discovering that I am not sorry my inn became a refuge. I am enjoying the day and don't mind the work. It is different cooking for a holiday. A pleasure more than a chore." She strolled in front of the fire, sipping her punch. "I had forgotten about the joy of Christmas."

He leaned forward and took her hand. He guided her closer to his chair. He set down his cup, then removed hers from her hold and set it aside, too. "No one should forget that."

Yet she had. She could not pretend. It had been her own fault, too. "The holiday is about family and friends," she said.

Sympathy entered his eyes. He tugged at her hand just enough so he could turn and lower her onto his lap. "So you spent it alone. Always?"

"My brother came a time or so. He always writes that he will, but he rarely does. I'm sure he is enjoying grand festivities at the home of a friend. A quiet day with his sister can hardly compete. I'm not sure I would choose to visit a relative alone in an empty inn if I were given a choice."

"Perhaps you won't be alone. We may all still be here."

She shook her head, then rested it on his shoulder. "It is not thawing yet, but I could tell when I stepped outside that the weather is warming. I will be surprised if any of you remain tomorrow. So I will enjoy my Christmas tonight, and it will be a very fine one, too, the kind I knew as a girl, with songs and feasting and lots of that warm punch."

"Won't Alice and her grandfather at least be here?"

"I expect Alice's beau will find a way to come and get her and Peter. He is a very resourceful young man."

He held her in an embrace that warmed her physically and emotionally. Her heart glowed at this simple connection. For a few minutes they did share that rest that both of them were supposed to be taking now.

He gently kissed her brow. "I think that I will stay until your servants return."

Oh, how she wanted him to. She wished he would insist, and hold her like this, and kiss her and—

"You will miss whatever celebration you were planning to join."

"I will celebrate with you. I can't imagine better company. Also, I will be here in case you need help. It does not appear I gave you my malady, but we won't know for certain for a day or so. It is unwise for you to be alone."

She sat up so she could look at him. "That is kind, but you do not have to delay your plans because of me."

"I wish to. If you can tolerate me awhile longer, it would give me great joy to remain here."

His offer moved her. She laid her hand on his face, but not to check for fever. The idea of having him here for two more days brought new depth to her unexpected happiness. "I would very much like you to remain."

He returned the caress, his palm tracing down her cheek to her chin. Then his fingertips guided her head closer and his lips met hers.

She had been impatient for him to kiss her again and she did not pretend otherwise. How glorious that kiss made her feel. Alive and vital and so full of joy that she wanted to cry. Each press of his mouth on her lips, her neck, her pulse, lured her into sensations that left her aching with pleasure.

She knew what she was all but promising. Offering. After what they had just said, he would assume . . . She did not care. She wanted to lie in his embrace and experience the completion that his kisses promised. She could live forever on the memory of the next two days if she had to, she was sure.

He nuzzled her neck and kissed her ear. His caress smoothed up her hip and side until his hand rested on her breast. That felt so good, so right, that she lost her breath.

"Have you been alone since your husband passed?" The question came quietly, like a thought finding voice.

198 • *Madeline Hunter*

Her husband?

Oh.

Oh, dear.

She pretended she did not hear. She kissed him hard, so maybe he would forget he had asked. That seemed to distract him, because a new passion rose with her aggression. It occurred to her in the fevered kisses and groping caresses that followed that perhaps he thought she had answered him after all.

His fingers explored her breast, finding sensitivities she did not know existed. Her whole body reacted in scandalous ways. She pressed down on the thigh on which she balanced, seeking some relief for the insistent hollow pulsing there. His other hand began seeking the tapes of her dress.

"Ma'am?" Alice's voice penetrated the door.

In one quick movement he had her on her feet and pressed her cup into her shaking hands. He leaned forward and brushed her skirt into place.

"Come in, Alice."

The door opened very slowly, it seemed to Jenna. Alice peered around. Jenna glanced around, to see what Alice might be seeing. Mr. Avonwood sitting on a chair, his hands cradling his cup of negus. He appeared extremely calm. Almost bored. Jenna stood at least five feet away with her own cup.

No one would ever guess.

And yet, she couldn't help think that Alice in fact *did* guess.

"I wondered if you be wanting me to start the apples for the warm compote?"

"Yes, that would be good. I will come with you. I have much to do and should not shirk my duties any longer. Mr. Avonwood, thank you for bringing me some fortification. You make an excellent warm punch."

She strode to Alice and led her out of the chamber.

"Odd that he was sitting while you were not," Alice said as they walked to the stairs. "I thought gentlemen always stood if a lady did."

"I insisted he sit. He is still recovering from his illness and needs to rest."

"He appears well enough. I expect he is grateful to you."

"Grateful enough. Too much gratitude is a burden to receive."

"Well, I'm sure he will find ways to express it without being burdensome, being a gentleman and all. Like bringing you the negus, for example."

"Yes. That was thoughtful of him."

She glanced askance at Alice just in time to see Alice glancing askance at her in turn.

# Chapter 8

Lucas joined the others in the public room before dinner just in time to witness the revelation of Konrad's big surprise. Miss Younger and Lady Whitmarsh held the top corners of a large sheet in front of a glowing tree beneath the balcony. Konrad made a nice little speech, and the sheet dropped.

Konrad had outdone himself. The tree was alight from Argand lamps set near and behind it. A variety of decorations dangled from its branches, many of them subtly sparkling. The tree created a lovely focal point for the other holiday decorations in the large room. Boughs lined the windowsills, and a long rope of greenery hung in swags from the balcony. More lamps and candles and the high fire glowed, turning the cavernous space into an intimate and cozy environment.

He was more than a bit aglow himself, and it had nothing to do with lamps or imbibing negus. It was all he had been able to do this afternoon not to stride to the kitchen, grab Jenna, and drag her somewhere private so they could continue what had started in her chamber.

*Patience. Patience.* His mind chanted the word, but it didn't help much, even though he knew he would need that patience for longer than this meal. She had not answered his question about her experiences as a widow, but her kisses told him a lot, and he doubted she had been touched since her husband died.

He probably would have to wait until all these refugees departed before pursuing what he wanted to explore with her. He watched the party admire the tree while he battled a recurrent fantasy of being entwined with Jenna's softness.

"It is impressive," Faringdon said, sidling alongside him. The man spoke of the tree, but his gaze kept drifting to Miss Macleod.

"It appears Juncker has an eye for grand effects. His background in the theater, no doubt," Lucas said. "The lamps are a nice touch and affect the entire chamber."

Various sweets had already been placed on a sideboard. A cake and pies and a variety of little round sugar balls. Faringdon reached for one of the wine bottles set on a side table nearby. "Portuguese. From the Douro region, I expect."

Lucas eyed the bottle. It was not one of the ones from the crates in the basement. This one showed duty stamps. He really wished Faringdon had not drawn attention to the wine. It reminded him about those crates and his suspicions. Damnation.

Whatever arguments his mind might make for Jenna, his desire made even stronger ones. Of course she had nothing to do with smuggling. If she did, she would have left this place long ago. Why live in isolation at this inn if she had enriched herself illegally?

It was a completely rational analysis, but not the true reason he discarded her involvement. Mostly, he just believed in her. His heart did. The woman who had risked herself to care for a stranger was not the sort to engage in such trade. He knew the kind of people who did. He had met enough of them. Opportunists did that. People seeking easy money did. Men of weak character and greedy scoundrels did. Not women who cooked all day to feed stranded travelers and sat up all night with a sick man.

Konrad opened one of the wine bottles and poured. The party began.

Jenna walked over to him, lighting the chamber as surely as those lamps did. She looked beautiful. Her hair had been dressed with curls and knots and she had changed into a dinner dress of deepest crimson.

"The dinner will arrive soon. If you would all sit," she announced.

Lucas managed to sit beside her. Not that it was hard to do. Faringdon stayed close to Miss Macleod, and Konrad inserted himself neatly beside Miss Younger.

"You look ravishing," Lucas murmured to her while the conversation continued around them. She favored him with a dazzling smile.

The door opened and silence fell. Alice marched in, carrying a platter of ducks. Mr. Matthews followed with another mounded with ham. The coachmen came with two bowls each, and Craig brought up the rear with even more.

Jenna beamed at the appreciative reaction of her guests. She explained each dish and urged them to enjoy themselves. As bowls and platters moved around the table and guests tasted and commented, Lucas watched Jenna's expression. This was her Christmas, and her pleasure in sharing it with these strangers could be seen in her eyes and her smiles.

He helped himself to portions as the food passed him.

"It looks and smells delicious," he said to her.

"I expect you to devour every bit of it."

"I would rather devour you."

She giggled behind her hand and flushed. Across the table Lady Whitmarsh did not miss that melodic laugh, nor the sensual smile that Jenna gave him before using her fork on a bit of ham.

"You stay here, ma'am," Alice said as she lifted two empty bowls off the table. "I've the others to help with the scullery after the songs and such."

"What did you promise them this time?"

"A dram of that fine Scotch whiskey that you keep hidden in the storeroom."

"Alice!"

"It is going to a good cause. I don't want to spend 'til midnight scrubbing pots and I don't think you do, either."

No, she didn't. She wanted to thoroughly enjoy her unexpected Christmas and sing songs and flirt with Lucas. Or rather, enjoy how he flirted with her. It was a wonder everyone had not guessed what was going on, what with the way he looked at her. Each time he did it thrilled her down to her . . . well, it made for very lively responses.

"I think you are giving us away," she whispered to Lucas after biting into a Russian tea cake that he fed her.

"Do you think so? I have been the soul of discretion. I've all but ignored you since the meal ended. No one suspects a thing." He glanced around. "Except for Lady Whitmarsh. I fear she has drawn conclusions, and attributes bad behavior to me of which I only dream."

A delicious little spiral spun down her core at the thought of the naughtiness he wanted. "I expect she is shocked."

"I daresay she is more interested in her companion's virtue than in yours."

She twisted to get a better view of her guests. "You mean the special sympathy between Miss Younger and Mr. Juncker. Lady Whitmarsh doesn't seem to mind, and they are most obvious. What surprises me is the close attention Miss Macleod and Mr. Faringdon are giving each other. When I saw them the first evening, I would have sworn they did not like each other."

"I can claim no special knowledge, but I believe they had a history."

"What a fortuitous storm, then."

He leaned toward her. "I think so."

Very fortuitous. A gift, really. One that brought her this special friend, and refreshed emotions about love and joy and Christmas.

The meal clearly over, Jenna rose to her feet.

"Now, it's time for our celebration entertainment," she said. "If everyone hasn't dined *too* well to sing." Amid a chorus of protests, she added, "Alice will be fetching the others to join in as well. We'll start with Lady Witmarsh's reading of the Christmas story. Then Mr. Juncker and Miss Younger will begin the singing with a song they wrote themselves."

Once the story was read, the two young people rose and stood together. They sang a Christmas song that they had composed, based on some old traditions they knew.

The servants had arrived, and now clustered along the wall near the pianoforte. Mr. Matthews urged Faringdon to join them, and Konrad did as well. Miss Younger sat at the pianoforte, ready to play.

"Avonwood, come here. We need your baritone," Faringdon called.

They all began "Adeste Fideles," their voices rising to the high roof. With the second verse the ladies joined in. More songs followed, while guests moved and visited and enjoyed the evening.

After an hour, Mr. Braxton, the viscountess's coachman, went over to Mr. Howell. Together they and Craig disappeared, only to return shortly. Braxton called for attention. "There's warmer weather coming in. Craig here's shoulder says so, and so do the drips falling off the icicles hanging from the eaves. The road should be passable tomorrow."

"What wonderful news," Jenna said while her guests celebrated with another, final song. "They can all join the festivities at their intended destinations tomorrow."

"I don't think whatever they find tomorrow will surpass this."

"That is very nice of you to say." She gazed at the party dividing up and moving to the door, to retire and prepare for their morning journeys. "I am so happy they were here, even if they were inconvenienced. This was very special for me. The best Christmas in many years." She turned her gaze on him and looked deeply into his eyes. "You are special, too. I don't think I have ever enjoyed having a guest more."

"I am glad your guests made you happy, but I will not be sorry to see them leave."

Suddenly they were alone as the sounds retreated down the gallery and into chambers or into the kitchen. He leaned in and kissed her. As if she heard a question in that kiss, she laid her palm on his face and kissed him back. "Help me to snuff out the lamps and dampen the hearth fire."

He strode to the tree, took a lamp, and brought it to her. "Take this one and go above. I'll do the rest."

She grasped the lamp. She looked at it, then at him. A bit of fear entered her eyes, but determination took its place. "Will I get another kiss tonight?"

"If your door is unbarred you will."

She mounted the stairs to the balcony. He watched her crimson dress flow along the balustrade and disappear.

She couldn't sit still. Instead she paced, nervous and excited. To allow Lucas into this chamber tonight would be scandalous. If any of her guests discovered it . . . She paused near her desk and looked down at the account book. If she were discovered with a man in her chamber, she would be ruined. Her business would be, too. Only it probably was going to be ruined very soon anyway. She really didn't have much to lose.

That wasn't true, of course. She knew it, but she also didn't want to dwell on all those prohibitions against what she wanted now. Surely if a woman could know intimacy with a person she cared for, she would be a fool to refuse it. Life could become very dry and vacant if one only did proper things.

She pictured him below, dealing with all of those lights, extinguishing them one by one, ensuring the fire would burn down to embers quickly. It seemed to take forever even though she knew not much time had passed. She checked for the third time that she had not barred her door through habit, by mistake.

Should she undress? That would be too bold. Perhaps he did not intend to—She laughed at herself. Of course he intended to. She certainly did.

What should she say when he arrived? Something clever, she supposed. Only she didn't think she would be able to talk much at all, with her heart in her throat like this.

Suddenly her door opened and he was there, looking magnificent, so handsome and somewhat dangerous, with a very masculine tightness to his expression. His blue eyes found her at once.

She couldn't speak, as she'd feared. She couldn't even move. Desire pulled between them like a taut, tethering rope while they looked at each other. Then with four strides he was with her and she was in his embrace.

Such excitement. Unearthly pleasure. She experienced astonishment like a long series of discoveries.

Thrilling caresses and erotic touches. Even being undressed amazed her and sent her blood racing. Then embracing under the bedclothes, skin to skin, touch to touch—whenever she thought she had tasted heaven, he did something else that made her fly higher. He teased at her breasts until she grew frantic with need. He explored down below, robbing her of breath and thought. Sweet pleasure turned primitive. Desire grew desperate.

Then he was in her arms, above her, starting the completion she craved. Careful at first, but then a thrust. And a pause. Startled by the shock of it, she opened her eyes to see him looking at her. He said not a word and began moving.

The soreness did not matter. Even the sensations didn't all that much. All she cared about was holding him, feeling his skin beneath her fingers, and inhaling his breath as if it carried his life force. And, when it was over, she pressed her body against his so she could forever remember this extraordinary Christmas gift.

"How did you get this?" Jenna's fingers swept the scar while he held her close.

"The war."

"You were in the army?"

"Not exactly." He resettled her so he could speak more easily. "I was in Portugal before the Spanish invaded. I was among some government people there. We served as a rear guard to protect our citizens as they left. That was the result of a well-aimed saber."

"You are lucky to be alive."

"Luckier yet to have that leg. I was fortunate that a naval surgeon dealt with it. He knew more than most."

She nestled her head against his shoulder. "So that ended your government work, I assume."

Not exactly. "I still do some, for the Home Office. On the coast. Spies trying to come in, that sort of thing."

She didn't speak for a short spell. Then: "Smuggling, too?"

"Smuggling, too."

"It sounds dangerous."

"That is the problem with wars."

She kissed his cheek. "I will worry about you now."

"Do not. Smugglers are not very clever people. Greed will always be their undoing. It makes them careless. And I am very careful now about sabers."

She seemed to accept that. He had more to say, about other things, but decided now was not the time. The conversation awaiting would probably prove lengthy, and the day had already been long. Besides, right now he only wanted to lie here with her in perfect contentment and acknowledge with his hold on her how very precious he thought her to be.

# Chapter 9

The sounds of muffled voices and footsteps lifted her toward consciousness. Loud knocking on the door and a call brought her wide awake in a blink.

She bolted upright in bed. The bedclothes fell away, revealing her nakedness. Memories of last night jumped into her mind.

"Ma'am," Alice called. "I need to talk to you."

Her heart rose to her throat and her gaze darted to her left, then around the chamber. Lucas was gone, and with him all evidence of his being here. Even her own garments had been swept off the floor and laid on a chair. A dressing gown waited at the foot of the bed.

"I'm awake," Jenna called, grabbing the dressing gown and feverishly trying to jam her arms into the sleeves. She stood and hurried with the buttons. "Come in."

Alice entered, appearing very different from normal. No apron this morning, and no cap. Instead she wore one of her best dresses, and half boots that were never donned during the kind of weather that might ruin their leather. Mostly, however, she looked different because of the lovely flush on her cheeks and the bright excitement reflected in her dark eyes.

"Sean is here," she said as she strode forth. "He came in the sleigh, over the back fields. He wants to bring me and Grandpop to the Beloits, and he says that Mr. Beloit told him to bring you as well."

"That is generous of Mr. Beloit, but I couldn't possibly leave. My guests—"

"They are all almost ready to leave themselves."

"I would delay you far too long. I am not at all prepared. And I still have hopes that my brother will visit." She did not want to spend Christmas with Mr. Beloit, no matter what. Even if Lucas had not said he was staying, she would resist this invitation. She reached for her garments on the chair. "Help me to dress quickly. If our guests are leaving, I should see them away."

Alice set about helping her into her undergarments and her crimson dress. "I think you should join us. It is too sad for you to be here alone."

"I won't be sad, I promise you." *I'll be elated. Astonished. Delirious with happiness.* She walked to her desk with Alice following, working on the tapes of her dress. "I will write a quick note of thanks to Mr. Beloit for you to bring to him." She jotted a note while Alice caught her hair into a knot and thrust in a few pins.

"Do I look presentable enough?" Jenna asked.

"Enough for the five minutes we just spent dressing you. Everyone is so busy preparing to leave, I don't think anyone will notice our hastiness."

"You should go and finish packing for your time at the manor."

"I've had my valise ready for a week already. And ma'am, the money given to me is probably enough for Sean and me to get married. The guests were most generous. I expect you will find the same when you check their chambers for their appreciation."

Letter in hand, Alice turned on her heel and hurried out.

210 • *Madeline Hunter*

Jenna followed. She passed Mr. Juncker in the gallery, carrying his baggage down. Lady Whitmarsh could be heard giving instructions in her suite. Down below, the coachmen ate their quick breakfasts while they waited for their passengers.

Lucas strolled out of the public room and came to her. He glanced around before giving her a very warm, private smile. "I thought they might all leave before you woke if I left you sleeping."

"Alice needed me, or that plan might have worked." She strode toward the yard with him beside her. He appeared as neat and polished as he had last night at dinner, his collar and cravat blindingly white in their cleanliness. "I want to see Alice off, so she can enjoy as much of the day as possible."

"Is the sled for her?"

"It is and that is her intended at the reins." She grabbed her cloak off a peg by the door to the stable yard and swung it on. They stepped out to a yard lined with carriages and horses.

Alice came down the servant stairs, carrying two large valises. Peter followed halfheartedly. At the bottom of the stairs Alice dropped the baggage and turned, hands on hips, to glare at her grandfather. Sandy-haired Sean darted over and grabbed the bags.

Alice saw Jenna. "Tell him he must go, ma'am. He needs a day away, as much as I do."

Jenna stepped into the yard. "She is right, Peter. Go and enjoy some festive merrymaking."

"I needs be here for the horses."

"I'll feed the horses. We are only talking two mornings."

Peter chewed over that idea. "What if more unexpected guests arrive and you are all alone?"

"I will send them away. Now, off with you. I insist and won't hear any argument. It will spare me having to cook and give me a day or so of peace."

The whole time she spoke she felt Lucas behind her, standing aside like a curious observer. His presence affected her to the point that the words tumbled out and her breath came quickly.

She had enjoyed having these guests here the last few days, truly, but right now she did not want to be Mrs. Waverly. She wanted to go back to bed and be debauched all day.

Peter fortunately relented. He and Alice joined Sean and walked to the back of the yard, past the foundry. Outside the open back gate a fine sleigh waited, drawn by two horses. Alice climbed into the sleigh and Peter pulled the gate closed behind him.

"Now for the rest of them." Jenna turned on her heel and marched down the corridor.

Lucas went with her as far as the kitchen. "I think I'll pour myself some coffee," he said. "I have already taken my leave of them."

She heard confusion above, pouring out of Lady Whitmarsh's suite. She sidled closer to Lucas and stretched up to give him a quick kiss. "Wait for me in my chamber. I will join you as soon as I can."

Lucas watched the departures from a window overlooking the yard. Miss Macleod left first, with Faringdon at her side. She entered her carriage alone, while he and Matthews took to their horses. It did not appear that they all intended to travel together.

The viscountess and Miss Younger came next, with their coachman, Mr. Braxton, first ensuring the ladies were warm under blankets. Juncker, it seemed, had departed earlier that morning. Jenna waved them off with smiles and many last-minute words exchanged.

Once they left, Jenna stood in the center of a silent yard. The lady of the manor. The chatelaine now alone. The whole inn quaked with emptiness. She turned and strode back toward the building.

He returned to her chamber and watched the last carriage disappear down the lane from the window there. The sun was up now, but the west-facing windows kept the chamber shadowed. He loosened his cravat and unbuttoned his collar. He knelt to build up the fire.

When he stood Jenna was in the chamber, watching him. "Am I shameless if I think that getting undressed again is a very good idea?" she asked.

It definitely was not a good idea, but he was long past caring about that. He had made a decision about her well before he touched her last night. The only question was whether she would agree it was the right one.

He shed his coats and cast them aside. "Come here."

Such pleasure. Such bliss. He made it long and slow this time, a rising tide of sensation that eventually submerged her in unbearable pleasure. She inhaled his scent and tasted his skin and wrapped her legs around him while he moved in her, pressing her face against his chest and shoulder. Even the vague soreness seemed right and perfect. Later, their passion spent, they lay together under the sheets in the diffused morning light and she filled her mind with him and how he looked and memorized her emotions and reactions so she would never forget them.

He propped himself up on his arm and looked down at his hand as it moved slowly over her body. "You should have told me."

Her happiness dimmed a bit. "I thought when you said nothing last night, that you did not intend to speak of it at all."

"Last night I was secretly relieved you did not tell me. This morning..."

This morning he had had time to think about it.

"I could find no way to tell you that would not risk you..." She bit her lower lip.

"Stopping?"

She halted his hand so it rested on her breast. "I wanted this. Very much. It did not seem fair that I might not have it just because I was not really a widow. One might say I tricked you, I suppose."

He laughed quietly. "That is a turn in the usual story. Perhaps I should demand that you do the right thing by me."

The vague allusion caused her heart to flip, but the excitement died. He was making light of it for her sake, she knew. Because she *had* tricked him and led him into behavior that as a gentleman he would otherwise not have undertaken.

She didn't regret it. Not a bit. If she could keep him here a fortnight and never leave this bed she would and accept any scandal or scorn it brought her. Only she did not have even half that long, and she did not want to waste the time left with talk of her deception.

"Are you angry?" That was all that mattered. Did he mind so much that he turned from her? This morning had suggested not, but men could be inconstant in their reactions.

"Not at all. I would have been more careful had I known, but I don't think I would have been any less a scoundrel."

"You were not—"

"Shh." He silenced her protests with a kiss.

"I expect we should rise. The sun's movement says it is afternoon." As if summoned by his words, a bright beam suddenly pierced the windows and fell across the bed. "Also, I am hungry. Let us go and forage in the kitchen." He swung his legs and sat on the side of the bed. He reached for his clothes.

"If your stomach insists that we take leave of this bed, you will have to help me lace up."

"You need no more lacing today. We can run naked through the inn if we want. A dressing gown and shawl will do and be easier to get off you later."

He didn't dress much, either, skipping his waistcoat and cravat. In happy dishabille they descended to the kitchen. Jenna handed him a basket. "You will find pie, duck, ham and bread pudding in the large covered crate near the root bins. Bring some butter and eggs, too."

He went down into the cellar and filled the basket with her list. As he was leaving, those other crates drew his attention. He studied them for a moment while his Home Office agent mind intruded on his sated bliss. He turned away so his mind would close that door again.

When he reentered the kitchen, Jenna lifted the food out of the basket. "Should we eat in here, or go to the private dining room? It might be nice to sit by the fire there, with the boughs all around us."

"Since this is our Christmas dinner, boughs it will be."

"Open some wine while I make up a tray."

He chose a bottle from the assortment in the public room and carried it and two glasses to the smaller dining room on the other side of the fireplace. He had just opened the wine when Jenna arrived carrying a large tray. She set out the food and plates.

"This is delicious," he said after tucking into the cold meats.

"And not one minute of cooking on my part. I will be a little sad to give the kitchen back to the cook, but I think I will overcome my sorrow fast enough."

He eyed the half loaf of bread on the tray. "Is that yours, or Lady W's?"

"I am afraid to say it is hers. That is all we have left."

"That is because we all learned to identify yours and reached for it at once."

She picked up the loaf and broke off a piece. "She tried hard and improved quickly." She took a big bite and chewed. And chewed. "This isn't half bad." Dry crumbs decorated her lips when she spoke.

"Which means it is barely half good. I will fill myself with Alice's mincemeat pie." He reached for a slice.

"I believe that is Miss Younger's pie," Jenna said.

He bit in more gingerly than planned. "It isn't half bad," he admitted.

She giggled and took a slice for herself.

They enjoyed their makeshift meal while the sun burned through the windows. Outside, icicles fell off the eaves in noisy thuds, accompanied by the crystalline chimes of shattering ice. Jenna appeared bright with happiness, and lovely in her lacy undressing gown and long patterned shawl. The meal would be among his most memorable, he knew. Not because of the setting, but due to the company. The peaceful domesticity of this hour lured him into broaching the subject he wanted to discuss sooner than he might have.

"You outdid yourself dealing with the invasion," he said. "You promised little but gave much."

"I can thank Alice for that. Had she not been so clever in bribing the coachmen to help with scullery duties, I would be spending the day in bed."

"Um, you are anyway. At least that is my plan for the afternoon. I hope it is yours, too."

"*Sleeping.*"

"Oh. Thank heaven for Alice, then." He raised his glass.

"My refugees were appreciative of our efforts. Alice whispered her vails were inordinately high, as were the fees left in the chambers for the hospitality. I almost feel bad accepting payment, since I enjoyed myself so much."

"But you will accept, I trust."

"Of course."

"Do you always enjoy providing such hospitality? Are you glad you found this solution to your situation after your father's death?" *Would you miss it if you stopped?* That question would have to come soon if he continued down this path. Most women would not miss either the work or worries associated with this inn, but Jenna had built something here and that might be very hard to give up.

"It suited me. There are days when I don't like it much at all, however. Days when I think I would have been much wiser to just invest that inheritance in the three percents. I miss Town, for one thing. And although my guests are treated like houseguests, in truth I am their servant, am I not?"

"You are not bound here if you grow tired of it, are you? You could go elsewhere, couldn't you?"

"I have nowhere else to go. As long as this property is mine, this is my home." She peered unhappily into her glass, as if looking for images in the dark liquid. "Of course it might not be mine much longer. I wonder if Lady Whitmarsh will be needing a new companion soon."

"I don't think the two of you would suit each other." He reached over and took her hand in his. "A much better idea is that you come with me."

She looked at him, confused. Then her eyes widened in surprise.

"We would go to my family's home. You would be welcomed there, and you would have time to decide if I suit you for a permanent alliance."

She was rarely speechless, but she had trouble finding her voice. *A permanent alliance.* Perhaps she misunderstood. Maybe he only wanted—

"Are you proposing?"

"I am."

Goodness. She had not allowed herself to consider he might do this. Not even in their deepest intimacy last night would she permit that dream to emerge.

"Is this because of—"

"I was going to propose anyway. I am glad to be a gentleman about your surprise, but I am not doing this for that reason."

Her thoughts kept scrambling. She held his hand tightly because only that warmth kept her tethered to reality.

"Will you consider it?" he asked.

"Of course. I am considering it now, even if it looks as though I am shocked into idiocy. The very notion that you . . . that we . . ." Her eyes misted until she could not see. Through the film of tears she felt him guide her out of her chair and into his lap. He wiped her eyes with his handkerchief.

"Did you really think I could just ride away from you, Jenna? Kiss you good-bye and disappear? We are bound by more than fleeting pleasure, darling. I think you know that just as I do."

"I suppose that Peter and Alice could manage here once the other servants return."

"I think Alice can manage most anything and anyone."

"It wouldn't be the same, of course. Our patrons expect a lady in residence. One can't imagine one is at a house party if there is no hostess."

"If the beds are good and the food is fine, I think your patrons will still come up the lane."

In a matter of months that mortgage would come due, and she would lose this inn anyway. Could she just pack and leave it all in Alice's hands, and go with Lucas?

Her heart yearned to believe this was possible, but a sadness inside said it was too wonderful to be true. She should accept the gift of this love for what it could be, and not try to have it become something bigger.

"Promise to think about it," he said. "I'm not going anywhere soon."

"I promise, once I can think clearly at all."

"I confess I don't intend to help with that too much today." He eased her head toward his and kissed her.

Sweet kisses. Tender and loving ones, soft and searching. It was as if he tried to convince her of his sincerity with the way his mouth toyed with hers, and also claim her for his own when their passion began rising.

They grew absorbed in each other, as surely as if they were naked in bed. She sighed with contentment when his hands caressed her through the gown's folds and he held her face still for deeper kisses. They became lost in each other until the world disappeared. And so it was that she did not hear the steps in the public room until they were right outside the door.

She looked up in shock, to see who had intruded on her perfect day.

"Selwyn! You came after all."

# Chapter 10

Lucas froze at Jenna's cry of surprise. Then he turned his head carefully in order to see what she did.

A man stood at the door connecting the private dining room to the public one. Tall and blond, he stared in shock at Jenna. Then he turned a more dangerous glare on Lucas.

To say this was awkward put too fine a point on things. In his entire life he had never been found in such a compromising situation. Nor had he ever faced a man so ready to issue a challenge.

Jenna found enough sense to hop off his lap. She turned and fastened the two buttons he had undone in order to caress her. Then she took a deep breath and turned to face her brother with a bright smile.

"How wonderful that you were able to visit, Selwyn. I was looking forward to it, but with the bad weather had given up hope."

"It appears you found a means to console yourself."

Her smile wavered a bit, but she held her ground. "Yes, I did. A most unexpected means. This is Mr. Avonwood." She turned to

Lucas. "And this, as you may have surmised, is my brother, Selwyn Markham."

Lucas tried a smile. Selwyn glared all the more while he continued his conversation with his sister. "I had hoped to be here sooner but was stranded by the storm. I left early this morning to arrive before the day was done."

"The inn was full of people stranded just as you were. They only left a few hours ago. It was exciting in its own way, as we all took the role of refugees." She walked closer to him. "I expect you are hungry if you have been riding for hours. I will cook something—"

"No, you will not." Lucas's command stopped her before she took two steps toward the door. "I'm sure your brother would rather have your company than a hot meal." He lifted the basket. "I will go below and gather more food, while you two chat."

In order to leave, he had to wait for Selwyn to move. The man finally did, but the hot anger in his eyes did not bode well for the rest of the day.

Hell. Of all the years for her brother to actually show up on Christmas.

"Is he your lover?"

Selwyn's demanding tone irritated Jenna. Her initial embarrassment had passed, and she was not in the mood to be scolded by him or anyone. "Yes."

"Good God." He paced through the chamber, face red and eyes flaring. "To walk in and see you like that, with his hands on you . . . There is nothing else for it. I will have to call him out."

"I do not want you to do that. You must promise you will not."

"I hope you are not so foolish as to believe any lies he has told you. He found a woman of some means who had no protection and took advantage. I will not have you mourn him."

"It is not he whom I worry I might mourn, brother. I think he has had more experience with both pistols and swords than you will ever have. Put any notion of a challenge out of your head at once, for my sake and for yours. Here, sit down." She grabbed his arm and forced him into one of the upholstered chairs near the fire. "I will be right back."

She ran across to the storage room and moved some linens to reveal the Scotch whiskey. While she hurried back with the bottle she noticed it felt a good deal lighter than it had the last time she'd held it. Alice had given out more than a few drams.

"Here, warm yourself and drink this." She poured some whiskey and handed it to him.

Refusing to acknowledge her, he took the glass. She settled in the other chair. "I am so happy to see you. It has been too long."

He shrugged and drank more. "I have been busy."

"In London with your friends?"

"Not in Town much at all, actually. Not since the Season ended. North, to shoot grouse, then the Lake District for a spell, and the Midlands."

She pictured him laughing and having fun at the estates of the gentlemen he cultivated as friends. He could probably spend the entire year moving among them, visiting their fine homes and making free with their food and entertainment.

Of course, he would still need funds to do that. Those friends would not buy his shirts and coats. He would need to leave vails for the servants who helped him. If they all visited a tavern, he would feel obligated to pay for the drink.

She debated whether to raise the unpleasant matter of the mortgage with him. Perhaps she should wait until tomorrow. Why ruin Christmas Day with such things?

He finally turned his attention on her again. His blue eyes appeared less stormy, but his gaze raked her from head to toe. "Is it your intention to remain in dishabille all day?"

She rearranged the fullness of the dressing gown on her lap. "Actually, it is."

"When did you become shameless?"

She pretended to think that over. "I can't put an exact date to it. It crept up on me, perhaps a result of my increasing age."

"Where is Alice? Peter? You said they would be here with you."

"They have gone to Mr. Beloit's house for a couple of days."

He sneered and muttered a curse. "So you are here alone with him."

"Yes. Completely alone." Blissfully alone. "Except for you now, of course."

"I won't have it, damn it."

She said nothing to that. It would be nice if at least an hour could pass before they had a row.

"What did you say his name is? I'm so furious I didn't really hear."

"Avonwood. Lucas Avonwood. His brother is the Viscount Hargrave."

He heard this time. All the anger drained from his face. Shock replaced it.

Just then Lucas returned, carrying the big basket now full of food. Jenna jumped up to set out clean dishes on the table. Lucas lifted out bowls of ham, duck, and various side dishes and filled the tabletop with food.

"Oh, and I found this. I thought it would be a nice change." He produced a bottle of wine from the basket.

It was one of the bottles from the crates in the cellar. Lucas set it ceremoniously in the center of the table, then moved over a third chair. He bent to build up the fire while Selwyn didn't move a hair. With a big smile, Lucas then set out the food he had brought up.

"You must eat something. Come and sit. I'll open the wine."

Jenna took her own seat. She looked expectantly at her brother. Such a conundrum for him! Should he sit down to a meal with the man who'd seduced his sister, thus implying acceptance of the alliance, or walk away and lose the possibility of forming a connection with a viscount?

She was not at all surprised when Selwyn somewhat grudgingly pulled out the third chair.

"Jenna says you are Hargrave's brother," he said between bites of ham.

Lucas went to work on the wine's cork. "Yes. Do you know him?"

"I have been in his presence at parties hosted by mutual friends, but I have never been introduced."

The cork popped loudly. "We will have to rectify that."

Selwyn fed his stomach more before giving way to curiosity. "I'm surprised you are not spending the holiday with family."

"Normally I would, but duty called me away."

Selwyn's fork paused ever so momentarily before continuing its journey to his mouth. "Duty? Are you in the army?"

"No. However, I am sometimes given missions by the Home Office. My current one has been much delayed."

"Storms will do that."

"It was not only the storm," Jenna said. "He was very ill when he arrived here. At death's door. His recovery has been miraculous."

"Only because a saint did not leave me to my own devices," Lucas said, giving her a warm look.

Selwyn looked from one to the other, then back again. He flushed and dug into the duck.

When he had finished eating, he sat back and peered at them both with a frown. "I don't want to be rude but you have to admit, Avonwood, that this is most irregular. Arriving and finding the two of you like ... *this*." He waved in a broad gesture that encompassed their dishabille and insinuated much more.

"We were not expecting anyone to walk in the door," Jenna said.

"*Obviously.*"

"Yet we are both so glad that you did," Lucas said soothingly. "It permits me—here, let me pour you more wine. It is surpassingly good, don't you think? Surely the best Douro red I have ever had. It equals a fine Bordeaux. It permits me to become acquainted with you. I'm sure we have many mutual friends."

Selwyn blanched, but summoned another deep frown. "I'm not sure an acquaintance is appropriate. It would imply I approve of . . . whatever plans you have regarding my sister. In fact, I should be issuing challenges, not drinking wine with you."

"If you have not challenged me by now, you aren't going to. And you are so enjoying the wine. Why not wish your sister happiness in whatever plans I have?"

Her brother became the image of outraged shock. "I think not. She may be too naïve to recognize the blandishments of a man up to no good, but you and I both know that you are playing free with her reputation and livelihood. Such things always get out, and this inn will be deserted within a month when it does."

Lucas never dropped his vague smile, but his blue eyes turned to hard crystals. "Perhaps it is your livelihood that you fear for, more than hers."

"What do you mean by that?"

"The inn supports you both, does it not?"

"Now you insult me." Selwyn rose to his feet. "I must insist that you leave so I can speak frankly with my sister."

"Selwyn—"

"No, Jenna. He has no business in the conversation we must have."

Lucas stood. He poured himself another half glass of wine and set it on the large tray where Jenna had placed the dishes from their private repast. "I will take these to the kitchen." Arms loaded, he sidled over to Jenna and gave her a peck on the cheek. "Call if you need me, darling."

"What has he offered you?" Those were the first words out of Selwyn's mouth when the door closed behind Lucas. "I hope you had enough sense to demand property and an annual allowance."

Jenna glared at her brother. She had expected a scolding, not instructions on how to negotiate a mistress's due.

"He did make an offer, I hope?"

"Yes."

"Thank Zeus for that. I feared he intended to take his pleasure and ride off. I really would have had to challenge him, then."

"As I said, I don't think that would have been wise. I have no idea if he has ever dueled, but I suspect he would not lose."

Her brother paced around the chamber, then stopped at the windows and gazed out at the glaring white snow. "He must know you are not really a widow."

She was not going to explain any of that, least of all to him.

"I expect he will want to keep you in London."

"I don't know. Eventually, perhaps."

"What of the inn?"

"What of it?"

"Can you dismiss it so easily? I don't think you should sell. It does provide you an income and one never knows how long a man will remain fascinated."

She began to lose hold of her attempt to maintain some grace in a most uncomfortable situation. "It also provides you with income."

"Nonsense. I've rarely taken more than ten or twenty pounds."

"Selwyn, I received a letter from that bank in Leicester. I know what you have done."

He turned on her, surprised. Dismay etched his face for a moment. Anger replaced it quickly. "Damnation. I told them to communicate only with me."

"Perhaps they felt free to include me because my name is on the deed. Besides, where would they write to you? Your last chambers in London? A friend's estate? If I never know where you are, how would they? They needed to inform someone that the date is fast approaching when that loan has to be paid."

He didn't move. Nor did he look at her. Silence submerged them.

"Do you have the money?" She tried to control her voice, but anger strangled it. "Because I do not."

"I will. Soon."

"Soon enough?"

Nothing.

"Is any of it left, or have you spent it all?"

"Damnation, Jenna. I had expenses. A man can't be out in the world without some blunt in his purse. And I've made some . . . investments that will pay off soon. That should be enough to keep them at bay."

"No wonder you are so quick to grab hold of the notion that Lucas wants me for a mistress. It absolves you of losing this property that I bought with my own inheritance."

"That is a dastardly thing to say."

"It is the truth, brother. The sad truth." Her emotions had her on the edge of fury. If she lost hold of herself, it would not just be a row. It would be the kind of argument from which there is no turning back. Ugly, resentful thoughts already clamored for attention in her head. If she gave voice to them, the break with her brother would be total and complete.

She forced her legs to move. "I am going to my chamber to dress. You can take the suite if you want, although it is not prepared. Don't expect me to serve you. You know where the linens are as well as I do."

Lucas idled in the kitchen, waiting for the sounds of a huge row. When they never came, he ventured out to the private dining room. Both Jenna and her brother were gone.

He could hear footsteps above, in Jenna's chamber. He returned to the atrium just in time to see Selwyn carrying one of those big baskets up the stairs, with some linens atop the packages.

He took the balcony stairs and went up to Jenna's chamber. When he entered he saw her down on her hands and knees beside the bed.

"What are you doing?"

She thrust her arm under the bed. "Hiding my money box. I'd

never scolded him for helping himself when he visited, but he bluntly admitted it while we talked. Only ten or twenty pounds, he said. As if that doesn't matter." She climbed to her feet. "I was wrong to try to spare him our reduced circumstances. Wrong to add his name to the deed so he would not feel too diminished. He has used that money to play the grand gentleman without a care in the world for how very diminished I would be."

He went to her and took her in his arms. "It is understandable that you wanted him to have the life he expected. He is your brother."

She accepted his embrace but hardly turned pliable. He could feel the anger in her. "It is only that he is my brother that keeps me from telling him to leave."

He turned her face to give her a reassuring kiss and saw the sadness in her eyes. More had happened while he was gone than she had revealed. "What else did he say, besides admitting to have taken money?"

She lowered her gaze, embarrassed now. "He assumed—he thinks you made an offer to me, but not an honorable one. And he advised me to grab it." She pressed her hands against his chest. "Did I misunderstand? I could not bear it if that was what you meant and in my foolishness I expected more and you had no choice but to—"

"It was a proposal of marriage, Jenna. Nothing less. I love you and I want you beside me as a wife." He kissed her while inwardly cursing her brother.

She nestled against him. "I may never forgive him for ruining the best Christmas I have had in years. Such a gift you have been, one that has revived the best in me. My love might be fast and rash, but I can't imagine living without you."

"Then it is decided."

"There is still much to settle before I can leave."

"I'll take care of everything."

She stretched up to kiss him. "I suppose I should tell him the truth. I was too angry to do so before parting from him."

"I'll do it. I will enjoy breaking the news." He released her. "Do you need help lacing?"

She laughed lightly. "I will manage it."

"Then I will go find your brother."

After returning to the dining room to grab the bottle of wine and two glasses, he mounted the stairs again. The door to Lady Whitmarsh's suite stood open.

He poked his head in. Selwyn sat on the sofa in front of the fire, with the basket at his feet. Lucas collected himself, so he would not follow his inclinations and smash his fist into the scoundrel's face.

"Ah, there you are," he said, forcing a tone of *bonhomie*. He set the glasses on a table near a chair and poured. "It won't do to have this used for cooking. It is far too good."

Selwyn sneered with annoyance. "What in hell do you want?"

"I thought you and I should have a conversation about your sister."

Selwyn's expression relaxed. "Yes, we should. She is not very worldly, and I fear she does not know how to look after her own interests. Far better if we settle this between us."

"By all means." Lucas threw himself into the chair. While he sipped the wine, he absently toyed with a corner of the wine bottle's label.

"A house in London with servants, I think, with the property in her name," Selwyn said. "A carriage and pair. And two thousand a year allowance."

"I think I can manage that."

His easy acceptance emboldened Selwyn. Glints of avarice appeared in his eyes. "The house must be in Mayfair."

"No other address would do." He continued picking at the corner of the label. A fragment fell to the table, revealing another label underneath.

Selwyn noticed that bit of paper flutter down. It distracted him.

"Anything else?" Lucas asked. Another small piece of paper fell.

Selwyn's gaze kept returning to the table. "Well, since I am being so agreeable about the entire affair, I think a small settlement for me is in order, too. A few thousand at least."

Lucas picked up the wine bottle and examined the corner where he had exposed the underlying label. "I have a better idea. Since you are being so agreeable, I will not inform the Home Office that you purchased smuggled wine, affixed new labels to it, and brought it north." He set down the wine. "I spent close to a year in Portugal, and this is not Portuguese wine. It is, however, a very good claret from France."

Selwyn feigned shock. "I had no idea. I received it as payment for a gambling debt."

"Foolish of you not to make sure it was what the fellow claimed. Now you are the one in possession. The courts have a bad habit of seeing smuggling from France as treason. I'd say you will be lucky to be sent to the hulls."

"I was duped, I swear."

"You knew exactly what it was. Who wouldn't, with those pristine labels and lack of duty stamps? Even your sister guessed. That is why she does not serve it."

Selwyn toyed with his cravat nervously. He frowned deeply, as if to appear thoughtful, but fear showed in his eyes.

Lucas gestured to the basket. "Don't you want to open them? Some have been waiting a long while for you to come for them."

"They can wait."

"I insist."

Selwyn bent and fumbled through the packages, probably looking for the one least damning.

"How did you plan to explain to Jenna that you are the various men with the initials S.W. who sent all of that here?"

Selwyn shrugged. "I would have found a way." He continued to pick through the basket's contents.

Lucas leaned forward. "Why not start with the most recent one? The one that contains the broach you stole from Marianne two weeks ago."

Selwyn froze, his hand still thrust among the packages. "I stole nothing." His voice faltered. "It was a gift."

"No, it was not."

"It was. I wouldn't be so stupid as to steal from her. I knew she was related to Hargrave."

"She is our cousin. Now, find that broach and give it to me."

Selwyn lifted a long package and handed it over. Lucas opened it. The broach, all goldwork and jewels, fell onto his lap. He looked at the other parcels in the basket.

"I assume those are other objects that were stolen from women you seduced. It was clever, I will give you that. To accuse you would mean revealing their infidelities."

Face red, Selwyn said nothing.

"You have put me in a bad situation, Markham. I am duty bound to hand you over to the authorities. Only then you will probably hang. And you are Jenna's brother. Your death would be a very poor wedding gift."

"Wedding—"

"Yes, you ass. I didn't proposition her. I proposed. Are all of those packages the fruits of your thieving?"

"Um, not all." He reached down and lifted a large box. "This is perfume."

"That is just wonderful. The ones that aren't thefts are the result of more smuggling."

They sat in a tense silence. Selwyn stank of fear. Lucas barely kept his temper. If ever a man needed a good thrashing, this one did.

"I could return them." Selwyn offered the solution with a weak smile. "Just send them back, much as I sent them here. I could take them to Leicester and—"

"*We* could take them, you mean. You don't leave this inn on your own."

Selwyn swallowed hard. "We could bring them to Leicester and send them off. As for the perfume and wine—"

"You will give me the names of the men who sold them to you, and the bottles will be destroyed." A real shame, that. The claret was very good.

"I can't give you their names. They would probably kill me the next time I was near the coast."

"You won't be near the coast for years, so that doesn't signify."

"I won't?" He covered his face with his hands. "Oh, hell."

Lucas let him sweat a bit. More than a bit. The man was close to tears before he took some pity.

"Here is what you will do," Lucas said. "I will not brook any disagreement. If you object, or do not play your part with honesty and good character, I will indeed give you over to the Home Office, and to hell with you."

"What? What must I do?"

Lucas explained it to him.

# Chapter 11

She screamed into infinity while her entirety exploded with un-earthly pleasure. She heard Lucas's deep groan in harmony with her.

They stayed like that, joined still, wrapped in each other's spir-its. She savored each moment of profound intimacy while he held her against his body.

Slowly heaven gave way to the world. She snuggled closer, pressing her knees against his hips and her lips against his chest. One of his arms left her so that he could pull the bedclothes over her back.

"I guess that wasn't very discreet," she murmured.

"I'm sure he is asleep and heard nothing."

"If he doesn't like it, he can leave."

"I don't think he minds, and he will not leave. Learning about our pending marriage has him thinking anew about many things, including this inn."

She rested her chin on his chest and looked at his face. "What do you mean?"

"Well, since you will be coming with me, he has decided he should stay here."

She rose abruptly and sat back on his thighs. "Surely not. He never wanted anything to do with this inn."

"And yet he does now. I can't account for it, but he will brook no argument on the matter."

Jenna found it hard to believe what Lucas had just told her.

"It is to be a surprise, so don't let him know I told you first."

"I am astonished. It is the perfect solution to everything, however." She fell onto her back beside him while the pieces of the future fell into place.

"It does work out nicely, it seems to me."

"Perfectly. The servants return tomorrow, so I will be able to explain everything to them. Alice and Peter will manage the inn, and Selwyn will be the owner and host. Patrons of good breeding will still feel as if they are guests in the home of a gentleman, even if Alice is the cog that makes all the wheels turn." His arm came around her and she tucked herself against his side. "She can bring Sean here after they marry," she said. "It is what she wants. We will build them a cottage right outside the fence."

"That does sound perfect." His lips pressed her crown. "Do you think you can arrange it all tomorrow? I should like to leave the next day, or the one after at the latest. It would be nice to return to my family home for Twelfth Night."

Her mind raced with all that she needed to do. "I think so. I will need to have a right understanding with my brother, however. He can't be disappearing to visit some country house for a fortnight on impulse. If he is going to do this, he must be here."

"I am convinced that is his intention. In fact, I am convinced he will never leave this inn for more than two hours at a time."

That did not sound like Selwyn, but Lucas sounded very secure in his opinion. Still . . . "I don't suppose he has the funds to pay that mortgage. If he doesn't, this will be a very brief solution."

"He said something about selling his horse. It is new, and he paid handsomely for it."

"How handsomely?"

He told her.

"That will barely cover half of the loan."

"I will take care of the rest."

He continued to astonish her. She stretched up and kissed him. "You are too good."

"It is your character that is to be praised, Jenna. You gave aid to a stranger and offered care and warmth and eventually love. I've never seen the likes of it, let alone been the beneficiary of such goodness."

She held him tightly and felt her body begin the descent into sleep. "There is just one thing."

"What is that?"

"My brother never goes near the money."

"That goes without saying. Now, sleep my love. Soon this inn will be full of servants again, and you will have much to do before I take you away."

Take her away. To a new life with a new love. What a wonderful Christmas this had been.

# When Strangers Meet

## Mary Jo Putney

*This story is dedicated to Alicia Condon, Robin Rue, Beth Miller, and all the other great people at Kensington Books and Writers House who do the detail work that keeps my career afloat, leaving me free to pull my hair out while I do the actual writing! Thanks, guys!*

# Chapter 1

The carriage slid sideways in the soft snow, and Kate Macleod swore with a fluency that would have done her Scottish grandfather proud as she grabbed for a handhold. Her guard, Craig, always said that the musket ball in his arm that he'd acquired at the Battle of Salamanca made him a champion weather forecaster. He'd predicted that any snow they might encounter would be slight, but he'd missed the ice storm coming on the heels of the snow. The road was slippery and getting worse quickly.

The carriage lurched again. Outside, the swirling snowflakes made it difficult to see much of anything. A good thing her maid, Bridget, had stayed home with a streaming cold. She wasn't a good traveler at the best of times, and the lurching carriage would have had her pulling out her rosary and praying. Loudly.

They crested a hill, and a blast of wind shook the vehicle. At least if they went over, they'd land in soft fresh snow.

Kate knocked on the hatch in the roof, and a moment later, it slid open, showing Craig's worried face. "I think we must find an inn along this road, the sooner the better," she said.

"I asked at the last change of horses and there should be one soon, Miss Kate. The White Rose." He grimaced. "The snow is bad enough, but the ice is worse."

"Since you acquired that musket ball in Spain, it may not work in winter weather," she said. "Do your best to get us all there safely."

"Aye, that we will." The hatch slid closed.

The carriage lurched again as they headed down the other side of the hill. Kate grabbed the handhold again and hoped they would all reach the White Rose in one piece. Battered by the wind, the carriage lurched slowly onward. Until it crested another hill and a blast of wind shoved the vehicle and it began sliding out of control. Craig shouted, "Hang on, Miss Kate!"

Grimly, Kate obeyed and wished she'd stayed in London.

A blast of wind sent snow down Daniel Faringdon's neck despite the scarf wound around most of his face. He swore. "I'm rethinking my decision to ride rather than travel by coach."

"A carriage wouldn't be any better, just different," his companion, Robert Matthews, said dryly. "Look at that carriage on the hill ahead. The wind is pushing it all over the road. Passengers must be seasick by now."

Daniel squinted at the vehicle, which was barely visible through the blowing snow. "What we really should have done was stayed in London till spring arrived," he said morosely.

"You wanted to get this journey over," Rob pointed out. As Daniel's longtime friend, companion, valet, and whatever else needed doing, he also functioned as Daniel's conscience when required.

As usual, Rob was right. Daniel's unexpected inheritance of the Elland barony and property had come with a raft of unwanted responsibilities. The sooner he visited his family, the sooner he could stop worrying about how unwelcome he'd be.

Rob swore, and Daniel saw that the carriage ahead had swerved off the road, probably skidding on the ice. Now it seemed to be stuck.

"At least the carriage didn't smash, so with luck, no serious injuries," Daniel observed. "Maybe with our help they can get on the road again."

"And if we're really lucky, maybe they'll know where the nearest inn is," Rob said dourly.

"Agreed," Daniel said as he tightened his scarf around his face. "It will be getting dark soon so we need to find a place for the night."

By the time they reached the stranded coach, the driver and a guard were outside, trying to get the vehicle unstuck. Daniel waved as they approached. "Can we lend a hand?"

Both men turned and the smaller one said, "A hand would be welcome, or better yet your horses. If we can rig a harness, they might be able to pull the carriage free."

Daniel swung from his horse and Rob did the same. "We'll do what we can. Were any passengers injured?"

"No, the lady is fine." The man chuckled. "I had to restrain her from getting out to help." He offered his hand. "I'm Craig and this is Howell."

Daniel hesitated. Should he say Faringdon or Elland? He still wasn't used to being Lord Elland, so he'd stay with his real name. "I'm Faringdon and this is Matthews."

Howell nodded. "I carry ropes and other useful bits for this sort of emergency so we should be able to rig up a harness that will let your horses tow the carriage free."

Daniel saw movement behind the carriage window, but the glass was so iced up that the lady was no more than a pale oval face. She was probably praying that the carriage could be freed so she wouldn't have to walk to shelter.

Howell was experienced in rigging harness so it didn't take long to turn the riding horses into tow horses. A couple of good pulls and the carriage was back on the road. As Howell checked the condition of his team, Craig said, "Thank you kindly, sirs! If there's anything we can do for you?"

"Do you know if there's an inn nearby?" Daniel asked. "The nearer the better!"

242 • *Mary Jo Putney*

Howell spoke up. "Aye, the White Rose is less than half a mile from here. It's not a major coaching inn, caters mostly to private carriages. But it's a snug place to bed down for the night."

"As long as it's warm and there's food and drink!" Rob said fervently. "It's on this road?"

"It's on a lane off to the right. It would be easy to miss in this weather. Follow us and we'll lead the way."

"Thank you!" Daniel said.

The coach started off again, being driven with caution. Daniel and Rob followed. They would never have found the inn if not for their guides.

"Our good deed repaid," Daniel remarked as they trailed the carriage along the rutted lane. "We never would have found the inn in this snow."

The outlines of a wide, half-timbered building emerged from the blowing snow. The stables and carriage house were at the right end of the inn, and the wide doors were open. The carriage had been parked in the courtyard and was rapidly being covered with snow. Presumably the lady in the carriage had been ushered safely inside.

Daniel and Rob dismounted and led their mounts into the stable, where Craig and Howell were grooming and feeding the team that had pulled the carriage. It was a relief to be out of the wind, and the warmth and scent of the horses were welcoming.

The newcomers were approached by an old man with white hair and beard and an unlit clay pipe clenched in his teeth. "I'm Peter, the head ostler." He cackled. "The only one at present."

"I'd say good day, except that it's a miserable day out there," Daniel said. "Do you have room for two more guests?"

Peter pulled the pipe from his mouth. "The inn is officially closed for Christmas, but the mistress won't let anyone freeze to death in the cold. Not much food and the only servants are me and me granddaughter, so not much service, either." The ostler's eyes glinted. "If that don't suit, there's another inn ten miles or so north."

"The White Rose will suit us very well, Peter," Daniel said, having dealt with far worse accommodations in the past. "What stalls do you want us to use?"

"Down there, take your pick."

The stables were dim, but there was hay and bedding and everything else needed to make horses comfortable. It was a relief to be out of the bitter wind and biting chips of ice and snow. Daniel found it soothing to groom his mount, who'd certainly earned some pampering after his stalwart efforts on the day's journey.

Rob was equally busy with grooming and feeding. After they'd provided hay and water and horse blankets, Rob said, "Time to see just what they have in the way of food and drink."

"Anything warm will do, and I can heat it up myself if necessary," Daniel said. "I hope they haven't run out of provisions, because with this weather, we'll probably be here for at least another day."

"Bound to be better than camping out under a tree." Side by side, the men headed indoors.

Once they stepped inside, they took off coats, hats, and scarves, shaking off the snow before hanging their garments on pegs. "Time to find the mistress of the house." Daniel stepped into the narrow passage that ran the length of the building and was immediately drawn into the kitchen on the left. It was warm and well lit and there was a pleasant scent of soup in the air.

A petite, dark-haired young woman glanced up from the pot she was stirring. "I'm Alice, sir. Are you looking for lodging?"

"That we are. I'm Faringdon and this is Matthews. Do you have space for two more guests?"

"Aye, though we're close to full up. I have a good-size room with two beds available." Alice added a handful of dried herbs to the soup. "I'll take you to your rooms in a few minutes, when I've finished seasoning this soup. There's tea if you want it while you wait."

She nodded toward the table on her right. A large teapot was warmed by a knit blue cozy, and several mugs, sugar, and a cream pot sat beside it.

A young lady sat at the end of the table clasping a mug of tea in both hands for warmth. She was well dressed, if somewhat bedraggled, and Daniel guessed that she was the passenger from the carriage. She was a striking young woman. Somewhere in her early to mid-twenties, with rich auburn hair, and a face that was rather more than pretty.

She glanced up with a friendly smile, one refugee from the storm greeting two more. Then she stared at him, her face shocked.

After a long moment, she clattered her mug onto the table and leaped to her feet. "*YOUUU!*" she spat out, her hazel eyes golden with rage. "Daniel Faringdon, yes?"

He blinked, equally distracted by her rage and her very fine figure. "I am. Do I know you?"

If she'd been a cat, her tail would have been lashing. "Have you forgotten that you married me seven years ago in Bombay?"

# Chapter 2

Staring at the furious Kate Macleod, Daniel felt the blood drain from his face as splintered fragments of that chaotic night blazed to life in his mind. A slim young girl with red hair and an Indian shawl wrapped tightly around her, terrified and desperately trying not to show it. A passionate need on his part to save her from a horrible fate.

Now the past had come to stunning life. He drew a deep breath. "We need to talk. Alice, is there a place where the lady and I can confer in private?"

Eyes wide, the maid said, "The private parlor, sir. Go left down to the public room. The door to the private room is on the left."

He nodded thanks as Rob said, "Miss Alice, could you show me to the room Faringdon and I will be sharing? Since you've no help, I can carry up water and set the fire and such other tasks."

"That would be most welcome, sir." The maid wiped her hands on her apron. "If you'll come this way."

As the two left the kitchen, Daniel poured himself a mug of

the tea, not wanting to forego the warmth that he desperately needed. "Will you accompany me to the parlor, my lady?"

"You're right that we have much to discuss," she said grimly as she topped up her tea. She led the way out and along the corridor to the public room, where a long table had been set up. A couple of men were sitting by the fireplace, sharing a drink and conversation. Ignoring them, she opened the door into the private parlor.

The room was more elegantly furnished and was clearly used for a private dining and parlor. A fire was laid, so Daniel knelt and struck a light, nursing it into a proper blaze.

He rose and retrieved his mug of tea, then sat in one of the wing chairs by the fireplace. Kate had taken the other wing chair and was watching him with narrowed eyes.

She'd grown in stature and confidence, not to mention beauty, in the intervening years. And she also looked as if she wanted his guts for garters. This was going to be . . . interesting.

He swallowed half the tea in one long gulp. There was nothing like tea to strengthen a Briton's nerves. "Where shall we begin?"

Kate drew a deep breath as she collected herself. It was most unlike her to lose her control as she'd just done, but this situation was beyond shocking. She'd instantly recognized Daniel Faringdon because his face had haunted her for seven years. He was tall, dark haired, and handsome with a faint scar on his left cheekbone just to make his looks more interesting. He'd been a soldier and that showed in his erect bearing and weathered complexion, but his gray-green eyes were weary with experience.

Yet he was also a stranger. A powerful man with an air of quiet authority. Rather an intimidating man, actually. And why had the damned fellow scrambled her thoughts by gently calling her "my lady"?

She sipped her tea, wishing she'd brought the whole blasted pot. Control once more established, she said calmly, "Forgive my outburst of temper. It was a shock to meet you here after so many years, and in such an unexpected place."

She thought a moment, then asked, "Do you remember that night in Bombay?"

"Not as well as I should," he said tersely. "You may recall that I was appallingly drunk."

"I could hardly miss it," she said tartly. "You smelled as if you'd just been dragged out of a vat of whiskey. What do you remember?"

"We met at the George, a tavern on the Bombay waterfront that catered mostly to European sailors," he said slowly, as if dredging up long-buried pieces of the past. "It was a ... very low time in my life, and the idea of drinking myself to death was appealing. I was going from tavern to tavern. When I entered the George, a repellent degenerate who claimed to be your uncle was trying to sell you to the highest bidder, cash only."

Kate shivered at his words. "Yes, Rupert was my uncle, and calling him a repellent degenerate is more credit than he deserved."

"How did you come to be there?" he asked. "If you told me that night, I don't remember."

"I didn't speak of it. The feelings were ... too raw." She looked down at the mug she held in both hands. It was still hard to speak of it, but they needed to discuss everything that had happened. "My father was an official with the East India Company. He was quite good at what he did, so he'd been promoted to a better position in Bombay.

"We'd only moved there a few weeks before and there hadn't been time to make friends, so when my parents both died of cholera, there weren't many people to rally round or look after me. Uncle Rupert showed up and said he'd take care of everything. Because he was a close family member, there was no reason to disbelieve him."

"When I saw him, he didn't look very reliable," Daniel said.

"He was a drunk and a gambler constantly in need of money," she said in a hard voice. "He swooped in like a vulture and helped himself to anything he wanted."

"Surely you were your parents' heir?" Daniel asked with surprise.

"Yes, but there was no one to advocate for me." Her mouth twisted. "Uncle Rupert was furious when he found very little money or other goods to fill his pockets. He decided I was the most valuable thing in the house, so he was entitled to sell me."

Daniel sucked in his breath. "When I entered the George, I had trouble believing what I was seeing. A gently bred English girl being auctioned off? It was insane!"

"Perhaps Uncle Rupert was insane. When he took me to the tavern, I was so confused. All those *eyes*, staring at me! I couldn't believe what was happening." She bit her lip. "Then one of the men in the tavern came up and started pawing at me, saying he wanted to see what he was bidding on. Uncle Rupert pushed him away, saying that he wasn't allowed to handle the merchandise, but wasn't I a pretty little thing? Not a lot of redheads in India, which made me more valuable."

Daniel swore under his breath. "I wish I'd arrived earlier to spare you that!"

"I was frightened of you as well. You seemed so large and ferocious when you started bidding." She swallowed hard, remembering her paralyzing fear.

"As I said, I was at a low point in my life and looked like a thoroughgoing rogue." He hesitated. "That night I hit rock bottom. When I saw you, so young and innocent and in such distress . . . Seeing you was the first step in pulling myself out of the depths. I stopped wallowing in my own problems and started thinking of someone else. I couldn't let your uncle destroy you. So I started bidding." He looked thoughtful. "The price would have been higher if your uncle hadn't insisted that whoever bought you would have to marry you on the spot. He claimed he must make sure his little niece would be taken care of."

Kate snorted. "Rupert was a raging hypocrite. If he ever set foot in a church, I think the Almighty would have struck him dead. I can't imagine why he insisted on marriage. Most of those dissolute old sots would have gone through a ceremony without blinking an eye."

"Hypocrites can be very pious," Daniel said cynically. "Insisting on a marriage ceremony gave him a clear conscience over what he did to you. He was just arranging a marriage for his orphaned niece."

"He died several years later, and he's surely rotting in hell now even if he was trying for a clear conscience." She shivered again as she remembered that night. "Though you terrified me at first, I was soon very grateful that you were the one who bought me. You were much more gentlemanly than your appearance suggested."

He smiled a little. "I'm not sure it would be possible to be less gentlemanly than my appearance that night."

Kate had almost dissolved with relief and gratitude when Daniel said she was safe. "You proved yourself when you asked if I had family back in England who would take me in, then immediately arranged for an upstanding local merchant named Mr. Yorke to send me home." She smiled back at him. "You were more than a gentleman. You were my guardian angel."

He shrugged uncomfortably at the compliment. "As soon as I realized what was going on, I knew I had to get you out of there and to safety. I doubt if any of the other leering customers felt the same. I hadn't met Adam Yorke then, but he had a reputation for honesty, integrity, and compassion. He seemed like a good choice to take care of you."

She remembered all those eyes in the tavern: greedy, lustful, violent, and worse. "I'm sure you're right. I've wondered since what would have happened if you hadn't won the auction. I had the impression that it took most of your money to meet the price."

"You were right, it took just about all of my money." He hesitated again. "I had decided that if the price became too high, I'd rescue you by main force. Sweep you off the dais and take you away from the George. Which would surely have frightened you even more badly."

Startled, she said, "Would you have tried to abduct me from a room full of drunken ruffians?"

"I was a drunken ruffian myself, but also a soldier. I had a pistol and I think I could have managed. Moving quickly is the key. But I didn't want to do that if I didn't have to. The chances were too great that people would get hurt or killed, and you might have been one of them."

"So could you," she said, feeling chilled. "It would have been very dangerous and you would have been the target."

He shrugged. "As I said, I was at a low point in my life. I didn't particularly care if I was killed."

So Daniel had been young, drunk, and suicidal. Yet despite all that, he'd rescued her. "I am deeply grateful for what you did," she said quietly. "Sometimes I wake up from a nightmare about what would have happened if you hadn't come along."

"It doesn't bear thinking of," he said firmly. "The bidding didn't go out of my range, and after that drunken sot who claimed to be a vicar performed a travesty of a marriage ceremony, we were free to go."

He didn't know, Kate realized. Her mouth twisted. "Bad news, Daniel. That drunken sot was an ordained priest of the Church of England. You and I are legally man and wife."

# Chapter 3

"What?" Daniel jerked upright in his chair, horrified. "He didn't look like any vicar I've ever seen!"

"But ordained and legitimate George Fenwick was," Kate said flatly. "My marriage lines were signed by him and two witnesses."

Daniel rose and began pacing around the parlor, his movements tense. "It never occurred to me that the marriage might be valid. Never!"

"Have you taken another wife, thinking you were free to marry?" she asked in a cool voice.

He stopped pacing and stared at her. "Of course not. But I assumed you made it home safely to your family in England and by this time had married some decent man, perhaps had a child or two."

She shook her head. "Once I returned, my family looked into the legality of the marriage. Since the marriage took place in India, it took some time to confirm that Fenwick really was a clergyman. It might be possible to argue that there were no banns read, but when my grandfather investigated, he found that the Church is very reluctant to dissolve marriages, even those that take place under unusual circumstances."

"Have you wanted to marry? Seven years is a long time." She had been a budding beauty on the verge of her most marriageable years. Those had been stolen from her.

"I'm on the verge of marriage," she said hesitantly as she thought of Edmund. "I'm not formally betrothed because I am not legally free to marry, but my would-be husband has been investigating the possibility of having you declared legally dead."

Swearing to himself, Daniel said flatly, "That obviously isn't possible. I thought I'd rescued you. Instead I've ruined your life."

"Nonsense!" she retorted. "You saved my life. If you hadn't been there and willing to pay every penny you had to buy my freedom, I would have ended up in the hands of some vile drunk and heaven only knows if I would have survived."

"True, but I should have tried to get you out of there before the marriage ceremony."

"Uncle Rupert would have objected most strenuously. I didn't think the marriage was legal either until much, much later." She frowned. "You didn't ruin my life, but you certainly made it more complicated. There must be some way we can undo this."

"An annulment?" he suggested.

"We looked into that, but it was difficult because you weren't to be found." She smiled a little. "Since it's been almost seven years, we were going to try to have you declared dead. Yet here you are, looking quite splendidly healthy, so that won't work either."

"My timing wasn't very good," he said ruefully. "But perhaps an annulment might be possible now that I'm in England."

"More lawyers," she said with a sigh. "But it might work now that you're clearly alive and can cooperate. When did you return home?"

"Just a month ago. I'd been living and working in the East. Mostly India."

Surprised, she asked, "What brought you back?"

Preferring to keep his explanation simple, he said, "An unexpected inheritance of a nice-size property and the responsibilities that go with it. I was the black sheep younger son of a younger son and there were enough potential heirs that I never considered I might inherit. But here I am. As I said, there are responsibilities I couldn't ignore. It seemed the right time to come home."

"How do you feel about your inheritance since it upended your life?" Kate asked.

"No one has asked me that," Daniel said, surprised. "Rather odd, to be honest. I've been looking after myself for a long time and have done fairly well with it in the last seven years."

"Since you rescued me?" she asked, brows arched. "Is there a connection?"

"There was. I recognized how far I'd fallen and realized that it was time to accept my failings and move on." That was true, but even more, meeting the young Kate Macleod that night had made him realize that life held people and possibilities worth living for. She'd been a brave and lovely girl. Now she was a beautiful woman with strength and depth.

And legally his wife.

"We all have our failings," she said. "Wallowing is useless, which means moving forward is the only real choice."

"To return to the subject of our unexpected marriage," Daniel said. "Obviously you can't have me declared dead unless you're in a homicidal mood."

"Shooting you might free me from marriage," she said with wry humor, "but it's not a good solution if I end up hanged for murder."

"That would be a bad choice all around," he agreed. "Besides annulment, perhaps there is some other way to dissolve the marriage based on lack of banns or another technicality."

"It does seem like the only solution," she agreed.

He studied her lovely features, the hazel eyes that could laugh or storm. The bright hair and elegant female figure that could warm a man at night. Most of all her intelligence and character, and the fact that he'd never been able to forget her. "There's another possible solution," he said carefully, amazed at his own temerity.

When Kate raised her brows encouragingly, he continued, "Since we're both here and likely to be snowed in for at least two days, we . . . could give this marriage a chance."

# Chapter 4

Kate gasped. "That's ridiculous! We're complete strangers!"

"Not quite," he said. "We did share a very dramatic adventure and ended up legally married. We might not suit at all, but we do have an opportunity to get to know each other better." He smiled a little. "It's not as if we have much else to do until the roads clear. Of course there would be no point if one of us can't bear the other."

She tried to conceal her shock, and the treacherous excitement that his words stirred in her. Telling herself that the fact he was handsome was not enough for a marriage, she said, "I don't find you unbearable. I find you . . . intriguing. You were an imperfect hero who swept in from the night and saved me from an unspeakable fate. After you secured my safety, you vanished as mysteriously as you'd appeared. You were my private hero."

Looking relieved, he said, "You intrigued me as well. You were clearly terrified, yet you kept your head up and never broke down despite the circumstances."

"I did break down after you left me with Mr. Yorke," she said, "but that was mostly relief."

"Then shall we learn more about each other and see if we agree that we can make something of this marriage?"

She kept her gaze steady. "There are complications. The man whom I might have married has been working diligently to help me end my marriage. He was the one who suggested it might be possible to have you declared legally dead. We're not betrothed, of course, because of my status as a married woman, but . . . he has been a good friend to me."

Daniel became very still. "Are you in love with him?"

How to answer that? "I would have married him by now if I'd been free."

"That doesn't actually answer my question," Daniel said thoughtfully.

"I have not allowed myself to think of love because it would be dishonorable and painful," she retorted, knowing that she was still avoiding his question. Edmund was a good man who respected her intelligence and didn't mind her red hair. He was pleasant looking and prosperous. They had many interests in common.

She had wanted to marry, to have a beloved companion and, God willing, children. But did she love Edmund? She certainly liked and respected him. She would have thought that was enough if she'd been free to marry. But *was* that enough?

"If you were in love with him, things would be different. But since you're unsure, doesn't it make sense to spend the time we're stranded here to become better acquainted?" Daniel gave her a teasing smile. "If we decide we like each other enough to make our marriage real, it will spare us from having to deal with more lawyers!"

"There is that," she agreed, unable to hold back a smile.

He crossed the room to stand in front of her. "There is something I very much wanted to do that night, but it would have been wrong then." Moving with slow deliberation, giving her time to stop him if she wanted to, he caught her hands and raised her to her feet. Cupping her face in his palms, he gave her a light, sweet kiss. "I so much wanted to do that," he whispered. "But it would have been horribly ungentlemanly to kiss you when you were alone and vulnerable."

"You did kiss me that night," she said unsteadily. "A quick kiss on the forehead before you said good-bye and wished me well in the future." She wouldn't have wanted a real kiss then, but to this day, she remembered the warm brush of his lips, and her wistful knowledge that she'd never see him again. Now he was warm and real and present, and even this light kiss took her breath away.

But seven years had passed. "I'm not that innocent young girl anymore."

"And I'm not that drunken, disgraced soldier. We met as strangers, and now we meet again as strangers who have grown and changed," he mused. "It's an interesting situation, isn't it? I'm very glad that our paths have crossed again."

"So am I," she admitted. "But you are a complication!"

He grinned. "Complications make life interesting. We both need to get settled into our rooms. Dinner isn't that far off and I assume that the inn will be able to provide at least a simple meal. I'll see you then." He held the door open for her as she left.

Rest and food. Both sounded wonderful. Feeling a wave of fatigue, Kate made her way to the kitchen to ask what time they'd dine.

"Five o'clock, miss. A gong will be struck ten minutes before," Alice said, looking up from grinding peppercorns in a mortar and pestle. "The guests will dine in the public room and the servants here in the kitchen. But I warn you that the meal won't be up to the White Rose's usual standards!"

"Anything warm will be wonderful," Kate assured her before she headed to her room. It was a very pleasant bedchamber, spacious and nicely furnished. Someone, probably Craig, whose job included looking after her in whatever ways were needed, had brought up her bags, laid a fire, and lit a lamp to dispel the rapidly growing dark.

She checked that he'd also brought up her carbine in its case, concealing the weapon and ammunition under the bed. She doubted she'd need it here, but when she traveled, she kept the carbine close to hand in the carriage.

After turning the lamp up a bit, she considered lighting the fire. With the storm rattling the windows, she would have been glad of the warmth, but with so few servants, it would be wiser not to use up fuel this early in the evening.

She had about an hour before the dinner gong, so she succumbed to the lure of the bed, kicked off her half boots, and slid under the covers. Bliss! Her weary body sank into the comfortable mattress. Her whirling brain was less willing to rest.

She now had a husband *and* a suitor! Edmund was solid and kind, and they shared goals and values. He'd be a very comfortable husband.

But Daniel? He'd been her dream hero. There was no denying his appeal or his dashing good looks, and they were legally married. But what kind of man was he? Brave, certainly, he'd proved that. He had a directness that she appreciated. But did he want the same things from marriage that she did? Would he be a good husband?

There was no answer to those questions short of spending the time available to become better acquainted. Would a day or two be enough? She hoped so. Giving in to her fatigue, she drifted into sleep, hoping that getting to know Daniel better would give her a clear answer. . . .

Quietly thrumming with excitement, Daniel found his room. The bedchamber was sizable and had two beds as well as chairs, a wardrobe and table, and a fireplace. Rob was there, having brought up their saddlebags and enough fuel for a fire now and through the night. He was lazing in a chair by the fire, holding a glass with amber-colored fluid inside.

Rob glanced up at Daniel's entrance. Compact and easygoing, he had the capable air of the sergeant he'd once been. "The

White Rose stocks some very nice brandy. Plus there's some ale in the pitcher if you're interested." He took a sip and set the glass aside. "Care to tell me how you acquired a wife I didn't know about?"

Daniel poured himself a tumbler of ale, then sat opposite his friend and pulled off his boots. "I'm sure you remember that time when I hit bottom and dived into a whiskey bottle after being cashiered."

Rob grimaced. "Oh, I remember. When you vanished, I thought you were a goner. By the time you reappeared, you had pulled yourself together and were returning to sanity. Did you meet and marry the lady during that lost time?"

"Yes, though it wasn't what you would think." Daniel explained how he'd entered the tavern and bought Kate's freedom, then arranged for her to return home. "It never occurred to me that the marriage was legal, so I didn't ever think of her as my wife, but that night was a turning point. I realized it was time I started acting like an adult, not a heedless boy. It was quite a shock to meet Kate here and find that the marriage was performed by a real clergyman. I'd unknowingly trapped her in a husbandless marriage. In the years since, she and her family have explored getting an annulment or having me declared legally dead. Which I'm obviously not."

Rob gave a low whistle. "Your good deed went awry, Daniel my lad. What will you do? Mind you, if I'd accidentally misplaced a wife who looked like your lady, I'd want to keep her. Though the red hair might be a warning sign."

Daniel studied the gently rising bubbles in his glass of ale. "I suggested to Kate that we spend the time we're snowbound here to learn whether we might make a go of the marriage. She's rather cautiously agreed, but there is a worthy gentleman in her life whom she might prefer."

"Hmm . . ." Rob considered. "If you want to keep her, you'll have your work cut out for you."

260 • *Mary Jo Putney*

"Indeed." Daniel frowned. "Will you be mortally offended if I ask you to dine with the servants tonight? I think that Kate and I have much to discuss, which will make us both poor company."

Rob smiled peaceably. "No offense taken. You know me—I'm comfortable on either side of the social divide." He sipped at his brandy. "Since I'll be dining with Miss Macleod's driver and guard, I might learn a bit more about her situation as well as what they think of her."

"I wouldn't mind knowing that," Daniel admitted. "This isn't a real investigation, but it's worth knowing the opinions of people who work for her."

"It sounds as if you really want this marriage to be real," Rob said shrewdly.

"I think you're right. From the moment I first saw her, she moved me," Daniel said hesitantly. "It's hard to explain. I never thought to see her again, but when I did, I had that same feeling. Even more so. I hope she's what I feel she is."

"Then you'd better be your most charming self," Rob said. "You might use the time before dinner to wash up a bit since you smell like horse."

"Agreed." Daniel got to his feet. "So do you, by the way."

"Yes, but I'm not trying to impress a fair lady," his friend pointed out.

Knowing Rob was right, Daniel dug into his baggage for his shaving kit. The first time he'd met Kate Macleod, he'd been drunk for a fortnight and looked it. Now he looked like a man who had ridden through a blizzard. He could and would do better than that for tonight's dinner!

# Chapter 5

*Booooong!!!* The deep boom of the dinner gong jerked Kate from her sleep, and it took a long moment to orient herself. Blizzard. The White Rose.

Her long-lost husband.

That last thought sent her scrambling from the bed and thinking about her appearance. If only Bridget hadn't caught that cold and had been able to come on this journey!

Well, it was better that Daniel see her as she was rather than looking unnaturally polished. Time was short so they should be honest with each other. Her golden brown gown was a little wrinkled, but not badly since it was wool.

Her hair—best not to think too much about her hair. Its neat traveling style had come unraveled and was all over the place, an explosion of red mischief. She must have looked a fright when she and Daniel had talked in the private parlor! That was honesty with a vengeance.

She brushed out the tangles, then braided the thick tresses into a long red rope that fell down her back. The effect was unexciting but neat.

A glance in the mirror led to pinching her cheeks to bring out some color, but she still looked plain as a wren. Inspiration struck. With the storm still raging outside, the inn and its corridors were cold, which was a perfect excuse to pull her Indian paisley shawl from her luggage.

Richly patterned in crimson, gold, and darkest blue, it was a powerful reminder of the lush color and beauty of India, where they'd met. It also complemented her coloring and her gown. She glanced at the mirror and decided that she looked reasonably presentable for a snowbound traveler.

But she had the awkward realization that she'd need help with unlacing her gown and her stays after dinner. Now she *really* wished she had Bridget! Perhaps there was another female guest who could help her then.

She had a brief, scalding image of Daniel unfastening her gown, letting it fall open over her shoulders. Then unlacing her stays, his fingertips brushing the bare skin of her nape. . . .

As she left her room, she ruefully recognized that her face no longer lacked for color. To her surprise, she found Daniel waiting for her at the top of the stairs. He'd also taken the time since they parted to clean up, shave, and change his appearance from weatherworn traveler to elegant country gentleman. His navy blue coat was well cut and his tan breeches and brown boots were perfectly suited to an informal dinner.

She took a closer look at the boots. They were the same ones he'd worn earlier but now they were polished. He'd looked good before. Now he looked even better. The advantage of having his servant with him.

He gave her a warm smile. "You're looking very fine. Is that the same paisley shawl you wore the night we met?"

She swallowed hard, touched that he remembered. "Yes, it was a gift from my mother. I cherish it for that reason."

"It's beautiful and suits you well. She surely knew that when she gave it to you," he said quietly as he offered his arm. "I thought we could go down together."

She was pleased to take his arm, but asked, "How shall we present ourselves? Saying we may or may not be married is too complicated."

"We can say that we met years ago in India, and it's pleasant chance that our paths have crossed again," he suggested.

"That has the advantages of being simple and true." She smiled. "I'm a terrible liar so I try to stick to the truth when possible."

"I find that a good philosophy also." Arm in arm, they proceeded down the stairs.

"The man you were with earlier," she said. "He's your valet?"

"No, Rob Matthews is first of all my friend. In recent years he's been . . ." Daniel frowned. "My right-hand man is as good a description as any. I told him that you and I would be doing a lot of talking at dinner so he decided to join the servants for supper. He's comfortable anywhere."

"Did he know about our maybe marriage?"

"No, that happened when I was wallowing and I never got around to telling him later."

"That's admirably candid," she observed. "I'm glad you didn't stay in the wallow. After disaster, a certain amount of wallowing is allowed, but too much makes a person all soggy."

He laughed. "I was definitely in danger of sogginess until I met you."

The look in his eyes was warming and a little alarming. There was an air of unreality in being with him after all these years and seriously exploring whether they had a real marriage. Their first meeting had been a pivot point that changed her life, and this second meeting might be doing the same.

They'd come to the public room, and when Daniel opened the door Kate saw that another party had arrived and seated themselves at one end of the long table. There was a rather grand lady of mature years and a dark blond young woman with a shy smile.

Kate smiled cheerfully. "Good evening! Under the circumstances, it's hard to maintain the formalities. I'm Katherine Macleod, usually of London but on my way to friends for a holiday visit." She glanced at her companion. "This is Daniel Faringdon. We met years ago in India, and by pure chance our paths have crossed again."

The rather grand lady smiled with welcome. "This is rather a time out of normal time, isn't it? I'm Lady Whitmarsh and this is my companion, Flora Younger."

"It's a pleasure to meet you," Kate said, and Daniel added his agreement.

The door opened and an attractive man with poetically long blond hair entered. As he joined Lady Whitmarsh and Miss Younger, he said, "Good evening. I'm Konrad Juncker. I'm glad you also made it through the storm to this fine refuge."

"I'm very grateful we found the White Rose," Daniel agreed and more introductions were made.

"Our supper is informal," Miss Younger said. "Soup and bread and drinks are on the sideboard." She gestured to illustrate her words. "Alice in the kitchen said there will be stew later."

"The soup smells delicious." Daniel said. "Miss Macleod, would you like some wine?"

"Please. I'll get bread and soup for us." Kate ladled out two bowls of soup, chicken with vegetables by the looks of it, then buttered bread for them both.

After the initial pleasantries, the three people at the other end of the table began talking among themselves, leaving Kate and Daniel to private conversation. Daniel swallowed several warming spoonfuls of soup before asking, "Obviously you made it safely home, but what were the details of your journey?"

"It was quite easy, actually." Kate sipped her wine, which was excellent. "Your Mr. Yorke lived up to his reputation for integrity and efficiency. He handed me over to his housekeeper, who fed me and had a bath drawn, then put me to bed in a quiet, comfortable room. I had the first good night's sleep I'd known since my parents had died." She'd dreamed of Daniel that night and given thanks for him. "By the next morning, she'd produced clothing for me as well."

"I'm glad of that," Daniel said in a low voice. "I prayed I was doing the right thing. How long was it before you were able to leave for England?"

"Only five days," she replied. "Mr. Yorke found an English widow returning home and I traveled as her companion. Mrs. Lowe was very kind and good company. We still write each other."

"You told me that you had family in England?"

"Oh, yes. My mother's parents welcomed me with open arms. I'd been very young when we left for India, but I'd corresponded with my grandparents once I was old enough to reply to their letters." Her eyes narrowed as she looked at Daniel. "I gave you their address before we parted, but you never wrote me. I thought you'd send at least one letter. Why didn't you?"

He sighed. "I lost the address. You gave it to me, I looked at what you'd written, then put the slip of paper in my pocket. I never saw it again. I remembered the address was London and the name wasn't Macleod, so I thought it must be your mother's family. But I couldn't remember anything specific. I'm sorry." His mouth twisted wryly. "If you recall, I wasn't very reliable at that time."

Considering his drunken state that night, Kate supposed that it would be more surprising if he hadn't lost her address. "What brought you to that low point in your life?"

A spasm of pain showed in his face. "I'd rather tell you in a more private place."

"As you wish." Though the guests at the other end of the table were involved in their own conversation, this setting wasn't really private. "You said after that eventful night, you began to sort yourself out. How did you do that?"

Daniel smiled. "You weren't the only one Adam Yorke saved that night. After his housekeeper took you off, he said he'd heard of me, and if I could stay sober for three months, he'd give me a job."

She glanced at his wineglass. "Apparently you managed to stay sober?"

"I did. I haven't drunk spirits since that night. I've since learned through cautious experimentation that I can drink wine or beer in moderation." He laughed. "If I start feeling too good, it's time to stop. I found that I could accomplish a great deal when I stayed sober, and my life is better this way."

"What sort of job did Mr. Yorke give you?" she asked with interest.

"It's rather hard to describe." He frowned, looking for words. "My official title was chief liaison."

"What did that mean?"

"Whatever Adam wanted it to mean. He had a variety of business interests," Daniel explained. "He was ambitious but scrupulously honest. My job was to see that his businesses ran smoothly and all transactions were to the benefit of both the company and the customers. Sometimes that meant traveling with shipments, other times it might mean visiting warehouses or business associates of Adam's."

She studied him thoughtfully. "Was your presence a form of quiet intimidation in some situations?"

"Yes. And sometimes not-so-quiet intimidation." He fingered a faint scar on his left cheekbone. "My friend Rob Matthews worked with me. We made a good team."

"I presume that you resigned when you learned of your inheritance," she said. "Did you mind having to return to Britain?"

He frowned. "I had very mixed feelings. I was restless and ready for a change. I'd even briefly considered returning home but didn't have the courage to do so. Then I had change thrust upon me, and here I am."

"It's interesting that you still consider England home."

He gave a slow nod of acknowledgment. "There was much I loved about India, but I never thought of it as home."

Following her intuition, she asked, "Most people would look

upon a substantial inheritance as a great blessing, but you seem somewhat uncomfortable with it?"

"You ask awkward questions," he said wryly.

"You don't have to answer," she said quietly.

"We promised each other honesty, so yes, I do have to answer," he said. "The trouble is that I'm not really sure of the reason."

His brow furrowed as he considered. She watched his fingers tighten around the stem of his wineglass. He had strong, capable hands, equally well suited for work and for wooing.

A little embarrassed by the thought, she concentrated on finishing her soup. Daniel said slowly, "It feels as if I have no right to the inheritance. My grandfather despised me, my father thought I was worthless, and both of them were glad that I would never inherit. The fact that I have just seems wrong."

Her brows arched. "Both of those men are gone. Is it that you yearned for their approval and now you'll never have that?"

He blinked. "That's a very interesting thought. You may be right. I need to think about it."

"What will it take for you to be comfortable with your new lot in life?"

"I'm not sure," he said slowly. "Acceptance by what family members are still around?"

"The appearance of confidence is usually helpful," she observed. "It must be a fairly substantial inheritance to make you this uncertain. If you act as if the property is yours by right, other family members may be more inclined to accept you." She gave him a wry smile. "But it's much easier to give you advice than to face down disapproving family members of my own! I'm fortunate that, except for my horrid uncle Rupert, my family is generally quite nice."

"But you do give good advice, if I can manage to follow it. Has your life flowed smoothly since you left India?"

"Yes, I was welcomed into my mother's family and thoroughly cosseted. As I said, I was fortunate."

"How have you spent the years since that return?" he asked, curious. "I presume a young lady is presented to society and goes to crowded social events, where you would be greatly courted because you're so pretty. All that plus embroidery and music?"

Blushing a little at the compliment, she said, "I like music, but I have a profound distaste for embroidery." She chuckled. "I'm not a lady by the standards of society, you know. My father's people were lawyers and civil servants, and my mother's family is in trade, not at all aristocratic. I had no grand presentation to society, nor did I want one."

"How have you used your time if not in embroidery?" he asked. "The church flower guild, attending improving lectures, running your grandparents' household?"

"A bit of all of those things, but much of my time has been spent working in my family's business." She watched him closely, wondering what his reaction would be to learning that she worked.

Interested rather than disapproving, he asked, "What kind of business is that, and what is your part in it?"

"We're merchants who do a good deal of importing and exporting of goods," she explained. "I have a knack for numbers so I often work on the accounts. Sometimes I meet with customers. Half of them are so stunned to be confronted with a female that they become very cooperative."

"And the other half?"

She laughed. "They ask to see my grandfather or one of my uncles. Which does the customer no good because the men in my family send them back to me. Scots are great believers in strong, independent women."

"I'm glad they're so supportive," Daniel said warmly. "Your skills sound very useful. When I met with the family attorney, I was inundated with accounts and ledgers and other financial matters. If you'd rather not be my wife, might I hire you to be my business manager?"

"That actually sounds quite interesting." She chuckled. "I fear I have just proved myself a boring person."

"Never!" he said firmly.

Kate was about to reply when the door to the public room opened. She looked up with interest. New guests?

# Chapter 6

Daniel was pleased when Alice and another woman entered the room, Alice carrying a steaming cauldron that smelled like a nice meaty stew. The bread and soup had been good, but it had been a long day and he would appreciate more food.

Lady Whitmarsh nodded to the newcomers. "I'm glad you could join us, Mrs. Waverly."

So this was the landlady. She was younger than Daniel had expected, certainly under thirty, with blond hair and an air of brisk competence. As Alice encouraged people to help themselves, the landlady served herself and settled down to eat.

There was a period of quiet as everyone enjoyed the savory mutton stew. Then Mrs. Waverly laid down her fork and called for attention. Her voice unapologetic, she explained that the inn was officially closed for Christmas so the food and service were considerably below the White Rose's usual standards. To a large extent, guests must do for themselves.

Daniel said, "I think I speak for all of us in expressing gratitude that we have a roof over our heads and a warm fire in the hearth." Others around the table nodded agreement and volunteered their services.

The landlady's expression eased. "If I may impose on the gentlemen one more way," she said. "If you desire anything other than the barest of boards, you may want to hunt once the worst of the storm is over. It would be helpful."

Mr. Juncker said, "Of course."

"You have met Peter, who is in charge of the stables," the landlady went on. "He has firearms, and also wraps and warm garments. With the ice on the ground, it will have to be on foot. I will leave it to you to arrange how you will do this."

"Two together seems wise to me."

"We will set out in the morning."

Daniel said, "I'll be happy to help fill the larder, and my companion, Mr. Matthews, will also want to participate."

To his surprise, Kate said, "I'll join the hunters. I'm a pretty fair shot and I have my carbine with me." She gave Daniel a challenging glance.

He smiled at her, wondering how she could have said that she was a boring woman. "Miss Macleod, will you be my companion when we set out far too early in the morning?" Daniel asked in a low voice as the others went on talking.

"With pleasure," Kate said, then rejoined the general conversation. "Perhaps I could also help with the cooking. I'm no expert, but I can chop vegetables and follow directions, and perhaps do a bit of baking."

"I'll help also," Miss Younger volunteered. "I've always wanted to try my hand at making pies."

"You don't know how to cook," Lady Whitmarsh said.

"I can follow instructions. I can chop onions and such. It can't be hard. Or bake bread or pies. I should like to try a pie very much, in fact."

"I think bread is more necessary," Lady Whitmarsh said. "I will try my hand at that. It can't be too difficult."

The landlady looked skeptical but accepted the offers of kitchen help. She rose and draped her shawl around her shoulders. "I hope the hunters have good luck in the morning or we may be reduced to bread, soup, and cheese. Now I must see to my duties. Luckily there are ample supplies of wine, ale, and spirits, including port if any of you gentlemen are so inclined." With a nod, she left the room.

"Both hunting and baking?" Daniel asked Kate with interest as they left the table to go upstairs.

"We stranded travelers will have a more comfortable time of it if we all help where we can," she said mildly. "To be honest, I'm rather enjoying this experience, particularly since the other guests seem to be a cooperative lot."

Alice entered the room, opening the door so Rob could bring in a tea tray with a large pot and several mugs. "Tea for those who wish it," Alice announced as she and Rob moved everything from the tray to the sideboard.

The two of them began to stack plates and eating utensils on the now empty tray. Daniel said, "Rob, I've volunteered you for tomorrow morning's hunting party."

"I'll be glad for some fresh air," his friend replied. "For now, Miss Alice is keeping me busy!"

"Which gives me more time for cooking!" she retorted. Daniel suspected that the girl was doing a good job of persuading the visiting servants to help her, to the benefit of everyone at the inn.

Miss Younger rose and poured tea for the other guests. After thanking her, Daniel said to Kate, "Shall we go into the private parlor to continue our discussions? There is still much to learn about each other."

She agreed and they headed into the smaller room. Daniel built up the fire while Kate took the same chair by the fire she'd occupied earlier in the day. She was lovely in the flickering firelight, both vital and serene. It occurred to him how pleasant it would be to spend a lifetime sitting by the fire with her, talking and not talking. Sharing a bed and a breakfast table.

His musings were interrupted when a gray tabby cat materialized and began stropping Kate's ankles. "Well, aren't you the fine fellow?" she cooed.

Hearing invitation in her voice, the cat jumped on her lap, circled twice, and settled down with his head well positioned for petting. Kate obliged with a laugh. "I think this puss is the kitchen cat, since he looks well fed and content."

"I heard Alice call him Ivan, and he certainly seems to be living a good life," Daniel said as he took the opposite chair and tried not to think of how it would feel if she stroked him the way she petted the cat. Reminding himself not to rush his fences, he asked, "What was your destination when you became snowbound here?"

Her brow furrowed. "Edmund, my not quite suitor, invited me to spend Christmas with his family near Leicester. He had to travel several days before me to take care of some business."

Daniel did not like the sound of that. "Traveling so far in chancy winter weather is not something one does lightly. It's very nearly a declaration of intent to marry."

"We have been moving in that direction," she said. "If it had been possible to declare you legally dead, Edmund would have posted the banns by now."

"Were you ready for that?"

She hesitated. "Our families are in similar businesses and have been friendly for years, so a marriage between us would be very sensible. Everyone has been in favor of it. But I realize now that I've been drifting along with the idea of marrying Edmund because it seemed natural and easy. I haven't really thought about it deeply. It's going to be . . . awkward visiting his family now that you've proven to be alive!"

"I could travel there with you," he said. "That would be even more awkward."

She regarded him thoughtfully. "I'm not sure if you're joking or not."

"I'm at least half serious, Kate." He took a sip of his tea. "My existence can't be wished away."

"When my family discussed the possibility of annulment, I was told that might be possible if you were in England and cooperative. Now that you're here, we can file for that annulment."

He studied her expressive face and knew that she wouldn't like what he had to say. Nonetheless, he would say it. "I will not cooperate so you can marry a man for whom your feelings are so mild."

For a moment she just stared. Then she slammed her tea mug down on the side table, startling Ivan off her lap. "You intend to force me to stay married to you?"

"No, but I won't jump through all the legal hoops only so you can marry a man because everyone expects you to," he said firmly. "You deserve better than that."

Her brows arched. "And you are that better choice?"

"Almost certainly not, but you can do better than me or Edmund," he said with rueful humor. "Will Edmund support your talent and independence as much as your family does?"

She hesitated. "He seems to like those qualities in me now."

"Have you discussed that with him? Do you want to continue working in your family business, or perhaps in Edmund's? If so, what does he think of the idea?"

Kate drew a deep breath. "No, we haven't talked about that. It's something that needs to be done."

The gray tabby arrived at Daniel's leg and patted his knee in quiet request. Understanding the question, Daniel scooped Ivan onto his lap and commenced petting. Ivan had a very substantial purr. "You've never been free to actively search for a better husband," he said as he formed his thoughts into words. "Now is the time to think hard on the subject rather than drifting into a marriage that will change your life dramatically."

Kate shook her head. "I can't decide whether you're noble or a twit."

"A twit," he said promptly. "But a twit who would like to see you happy. Perhaps I'm a romantic, but I think one should be enthusiastic about one's marriage, not drifting toward it like a drowning leaf in autumn."

Her expression turned thoughtful. "Apparently I need lessons in how to marry properly. But if I decide I'm enthusiastic about marrying Edmund, will you promise to cooperate in getting an annulment?"

He nodded a little reluctantly. He owed her that even though he was becoming quite sure that he wanted her to keep her for himself. What mattered was that she was starting to think more seriously about what kind of marriage she wanted.

"Your turn for interrogation now," Kate said with an obvious desire to change the subject. "Where were *you* bound on your interrupted journey?"

He grimaced. "I'm heading to Faringdale, the family estate which I haven't seen since I was packed off to India at the age of seventeen. In theory I'm the owner, but I feel like an interloper. I'm supposed to spend the holiday with a number of female relations, including my terrifying grandmother. I don't expect to be welcomed as the new head of the family because, as I mentioned before, that's a result of so many male relatives dying childless or not spawning suitable heirs. I feel like a captured eel that will be cut into pieces and used as fish bait."

Looking as if she was trying not to laugh, Kate said, "I can see why that will be uncomfortable, but it's not your fault that you were chosen as the heir."

"True," he said glumly, "but whatever anger they have over the situation will be aimed at me."

"Some, perhaps," she agreed. "Are many of these females financially dependent on you because you're head of the family?"

He considered a moment. "About half."

"Is the estate prosperous enough to meet all the Faringdon family needs?"

He thought of his meeting with the family lawyers and managers. "I'm told it is."

"So you won't be tossing widows and orphans and spinsters into the street?"

"Of course not!" he said. "As head of the family, my first responsibility is to ensure the welfare of all my relatives."

"I suggest that you make that clear from the start," she said thoughtfully. "You might want to say that you wish to meet with each of your kinswomen privately to determine what their needs are and whether there should be adjustments. Some people will try to get as much out of you as they can, but depending on the generosity of your predecessor, some may be barely scraping by and genuinely need help."

"That's a splendid idea! I don't remember that my grandfather was particularly generous, so surely some of those dependents need more than they've been getting." He grinned. "Thank you, Kate. Now I have worthy ways to use some of my inheritance."

"As I said, I come from a merchant family," she said in dulcet tones. "I am always happy to help people spend money."

"For years I've concentrated on saving," he mused. "Strange to think I need to learn how to spend."

"I've found that spending money to help others is rather easy," she said seriously.

Ivan jumped from Daniel's lap and moved to the door, batting it in a clear sign that he wanted to be let out. Daniel rose and opened the door enough for the cat to exit. He could hear soft talk and laughter from the public room as he closed it again. "Ivan has a good point. It's time for bed now since we'll be getting up early to go hunting."

Kate stood and covered a yawn. "I'd rather sleep late but even more I want to eat well."

He caught her gaze and said softly, "Earlier I kissed you, which I'd wanted to do seven years ago. Do you have any interest in kissing me?"

Her eyes widened and he wished he hadn't made such a foolish suggestion. After a long, awkward moment, she said, "That's quite an interesting idea."

She stepped forward, her skirts rustling sensuously around her ankles, and cautiously flattened her palms against his chest.

As she spread her fingers wide, he enjoyed the warmth of her nearness, the subtle fragrance of lavender twined with the essence of Kate.

"Take your time," he said softly. "Husbands and wives are encouraged to explore each other's bodies."

She glanced up with a redhead's blush. "We are still working on whether we really are husband and wife."

"But touching, hugging, kissing, enjoying each other's bodies is a large part of marriage," he said. "At least it should be."

She paused to consider. "That makes sense."

He wondered how much touching there had been between her and Edmund. His guess was that it hadn't been much.

Her hands moved upward to his shoulders, then slowly and carefully down his arms. He liked the confident strength of her touch and held still under her interested caresses.

Then she raised her hands to cup his cheeks and looked up into his eyes. Her hazel eyes were golden with interest and the beginnings of desire. His breathing quickened, and now he had to force himself to stay still. To allow her all the initiative.

She stood on her tiptoes and drew his head down into a kiss. Her mouth was warm and delicious and he would have liked to put his arms around her and draw them together.

No. She must set the pace. She licked across his lips in gentle exploration. Then, to his delight, her tongue shyly encouraged his mouth to open. He guessed that she was inexperienced but interested.

Not only interested but she had a budding talent for kissing. He felt a rush of intoxicating desire. Barely managing to keep it in check, he allowed himself to put his arms around her waist to draw them closer together. The whole soft yielding front of her body pressed into him, alive and alluring.

He wanted more, but he told himself he could wait. For now,

it was enough to savor the kissing and closeness of a woman who stirred him as no other woman ever had.

After a lovely long interval of increasingly intimate kisses, she drew her head back and said breathlessly, "Well, this is certainly interesting!"

He laughed and drew her yielding body closer. "It is indeed, and other things that husband and wife are permitted to do together are even more interesting. But not so soon, I think."

She stepped back out of his embrace. "I am beginning to understand why chaperones are considered essential for marriageable young females!"

"It's a good rule, Kate," he said seriously. "Passion can dissolve good sense and you make me feel . . . very passionate. My mind keeps saying 'Not yet!,' while my blood is singing, 'This one!' "

She laughed a little. "Should I be flattered?"

"I hope that's how you feel, because I find you almost irresistible." It was his turn to draw a deep breath and step back. "But part of being a gentleman is knowing when to resist."

"I appreciate that." She touched her fingertips to her lips with a kind of wonder. "You have given me much to think about. But now it's time to withdraw to my room. I'll see you when the hunters gather far too early in the morning." She opened the door and slipped out.

He spent a few minutes settling his unruly blood. On the one hand, he knew better than to rush her, but he didn't know how long they would have this time together. Surely no more than two or three days. Would that be long enough? Her responses had been promising. But he was competing with a man she'd known for some time and who was already part of her life, approved by both families. The thought sobered him up quickly.

After banking the fire, he headed up to his room. Rob was already there, relaxing by the small fire. He glanced up with a smile. "How is the courtship of your wife going?"

"Reasonably well, but it turns out that she was heading north to visit the family of a man who wants to marry her." Daniel peeled off his coat and cravat. "How was your evening?"

"Very pleasant. The other servants are a decent lot and Miss Alice is a charming persuader, very good at encouraging everyone to help her. Not that we need much encouraging."

More interested in Kate than Alice, Daniel asked, "What do Miss Macleod's men think of her?"

"They thoroughly approve of her and her family. Very fair employers. Miss Macleod is a particular favorite. She's always courteous and even tempered." Rob grinned. "It sounds like she has the makings of a good wife."

Daniel nodded, unsurprised. There hadn't been a trace of spoiled beauty in Kate. "I took a look outside before I came up, and it appears that the storm has blown out, though it's still very cold. Do you know where the hunting ground is?"

"Peter, the head ostler, said that the land behind the inn runs into the back of a sizable manor. Apparently Mrs. Waverly and the owner of the other property have agreed that exact boundaries don't much matter," Rob replied. "We're only likely to see small game like rabbits and waterfowl, but if we can bag a few, we'll have a better dinner."

"I hope we have good luck, or we might end up eating stone soup," Daniel said. As he washed up and prepared for bed, he wondered how good a shot Kate was. He suspected that anything she did, she did well. She'd certainly shown a talent for kissing! It was a warm thought to take to his bed.

# Chapter 7

Kate felt a little unsteady when she left Daniel and headed for her room. She'd never thought much about the physical side of marriage. So many people married that she assumed it was something that would work out naturally when the time came.

Strange that she'd never thought about passion and the role it might play in marriage. Daniel's comment about husband and wife being free to explore each other's bodies was a new thought. An exciting one.

Edmund had kissed her very nicely, but she'd never had so intense a reaction to him. The prospect of sharing a bed with Daniel was far more intriguing. Exciting, in fact. But was passion a solid foundation for a marriage, or was it a passing madness that could lead people to disaster?

Thoughts in turmoil, she slipped outside before going upstairs. The storm had blown past and the air was still and numbingly cold.

A few deep breaths cleared her mind. Surely the foundation of a good marriage must include trust and understanding. She had that with Edmund. Passion, she suspected, was like icing on a cake—delicious as an extra but not in itself a firm foundation for building a family and a future.

Daniel was still in many ways a stranger, but he had proved himself trustworthy in the past. He was behaving very well now and their long conversations were rapidly increasing mutual understanding. She hoped they had at least two more days of being snowbound together since this was a rare opportunity for a man and a woman to deepen their acquaintance. Surely in two more days she would be better able to decide on her future?

Feeling calmer, she stepped back inside and headed up the stairs. She saw Lady Whitmarsh and Miss Younger about to enter their room, and called out, "Miss Younger! I hate to ask this, but I need help with . . . undressing."

"Oh, of course!" Miss Younger said. "We're all in the same situation here, aren't we?" She turned to Lady Whitmarsh, but before she could even speak, the viscountess said, "Go on, then. It's fine. I can wait."

"It won't take long," Miss Younger assured her employer, then followed Kate to her room.

"Are you enjoying being snowbound, Miss Younger?" Kate asked.

"I am! It's a holiday from normal life and a chance to meet new people." She gave Kate an interested glance. "Are you enjoying catching up with your old acquaintance from India?"

Kate opened the door to her room and hoped she wasn't blushing. "Yes, it's interesting to discuss our time there. I came back to England years ago but he's only just returned." She turned her back so Miss Younger could unfasten her gown, then unlace her stays. It was a relief to have them undone. "Thank you. I hadn't realized how much I would miss my maid."

"I'm happy to help out," Miss Younger assured her. "Will you need help dressing in the morning?"

"No, I plan to wear garments I can manage on my own."

"I need more clothes like that!" Miss Younger said. "I'll see you tomorrow."

Kate changed to her nightgown and robe, then laid out her clothing for the morning. As she climbed into her bed, she wondered how large a place passion should hold in marriage.

Kate woke when the soft chime of the mantel clock told her that it was time to get up. This was one of the longest nights of the year so it was still dark out. She spent a moment rewinding the clock since there were no servants to perform the task.

Then she washed up and dressed for the hunting party. She liked taking long walks in winter weather and she'd brought her winter walking clothes, though she certainly hadn't expected to go hunting.

As she donned heavy trousers, knee high boots, a shirt and warm knit tunic that fell to the middle of her thighs, she wondered how many men she'd shock. She chuckled at the thought.

A heavy overcoat and fleecy scarf and hat completed the outfit. Then she pulled her carbine out from under the bed and slung her ammunition bag so it hung across her body and required no attention. She made her way downstairs quietly so as not to disturb anyone still sleeping.

The rest of the hunting party had gathered in the kitchen, all of them holding large cups of steaming tea.

The room fell dead silent when she entered.

Peter, the inn's head ostler, looked mildly scandalized. Mr. Juncker and Mr. Matthews appeared surprised but not deeply shocked, and Daniel looked downright amused. He poured a cup of tea and added milk and sugar the way she liked it, then handed her the beverage. "Something to warm us up before we head out."

She took the cup and swallowed the tea gratefully while Peter described the area behind the inn where they were to hunt and the best places to find game. He ended with, "If you angle off to the north and come to a small road, don't go any farther because that will take you off our property. And come back with enough meat for a proper dinner!"

"We'll do our best," Mr. Matthews promised.

Daniel asked, "Are you ready to head out with me, Miss Macleod?"

"It will be my pleasure," she said formally, but she couldn't hold back a smile. This would be an interesting change from sitting in front of a fire and talking. The more she learned about his personality and character, the easier it would be to make a decision. Though he was very appealing, validating her marriage to him would be a leap into unknown territory, while Edmund would be a known and comfortable choice.

The hunters left the inn, their breaths puffing into white clouds as they walked. She and Daniel angled a little to the north to give them some distance from the other group of hunters. The sky was beginning to lighten enough to see game if there was any to be found. Kate knew that the early hour had been chosen because wildlife tends to be most active at dawn and dusk, but in this weather, many animals might prefer to stay in their burrows.

The snow was only six or so inches deep, but Kate's and Daniel's boots crunched through layers of treacherous ice in many places. A bitter wind sent little spirals of icy crystals whirling upward. "You came prepared for the weather," Daniel remarked.

"Yes, I like walking in winter and trousers are much more practical than skirts," she replied, glad he wasn't critical of her costume. Edmund liked her intelligence and understanding of business, but he was rather conservative in his views of proper behavior for females.

"I missed seeing snow in India," Daniel mused as he gazed over the silvery white landscape. "So beautiful and still."

"Are you minding the cold?" she asked. "When I returned to England, I spent my first winter wrapped a dozen layers deep in woolens."

He smiled as wisps of dark hair danced below his hat. "I do feel the cold today, but it's also refreshing. I'll adapt."

A couple of shots sounded from the direction of the other group. "I hope that means meat for tonight's dinner," Kate commented. "It will take a good amount of small game to feed everyone properly. We may dine on stew again because it will extend whatever meat we have."

Daniel laughed. "There's always the cheese so at least we won't starve." He glanced at Kate. "That a fine-looking carbine. Do you do much hunting?"

"I've never actually hunted," she admitted. "I carry the gun mostly for protection when traveling and I do target shooting to keep in practice."

"How did you get started?" he asked curiously. "Do you come from a family of hunters?"

After a long silence, she said, "You're probably thinking that hunters are almost always landowners, and I come from a merchant family."

"That thought had occurred to me," he admitted. "But I know that if you wanted to learn to shoot, you'd find a way."

"I did," she said in a steady voice. "Because after that night in Bombay, I swore I'd never be helpless again."

After a long silence, he said quietly, "So that is how you've become so strong. Not just as a markswoman, but in strength of character."

"Is that how you see me?" she asked, glancing up at him.

"Yes," he said simply. "And that is much of the reason you are so interesting. I've never been interested in drooping damsels."

She had to laugh. "I have my flaws, but I definitely do not droop!"

"I have a theory that drooping damsels never have red hair," he said firmly.

"You're probably right." As she spoke, she skidded on a patch of ice. He caught her arm to prevent her from falling.

"Thank you!" she said as she regained her footing. "There are advantages to being larger and heavier when walking in these conditions."

"True. Do you want to take my arm? That way we can stay up or go down together," he said cheerfully.

Three more shots sounded to their right, the booms echoing over the frozen landscape.

"We should stop talking and get serious about hunting!" Kate said. "The area ahead looks like one that Peter suggested might be good for rabbits."

Daniel agreed, and in the next half hour they shot five rabbits between them. Kate got two with her single-shot carbine while Daniel brought down three with the fowling piece borrowed from the inn, which shot a spray of buckshot.

As they headed back to the inn, Kate said, "I think this is my first and last hunt. I'd have to be much hungrier to shoot animals again."

"I don't love hunting myself," Daniel admitted. "But since I enjoy eating meat, it would be hypocritical to refuse to kill it myself."

"That's a good argument," Kate said. "But I'd rather eat potato soup than go hunting again!"

"You've proved you can hunt if need be, so now you can save your fire for highwaymen," Daniel agreed. "They're larger targets and probably deserve shooting."

He was right. She was pleased that she could handle a gun well if necessary, and glad she probably wouldn't have to ever do it again. The fresh air and time spent with Daniel were certainly enjoyable, though.

They came across the road Peter mentioned. It was more of a lane, but there were marks of carriage wheels and several horses. "I suppose they were also heading for shelter yesterday," Daniel said after studying the tracks. "No traffic moving today."

"I'll be glad to get back to our warm inn and have that breakfast we were promised," Kate observed. "It's a good day to be inside."

"*MRROOOOW!!!*" They were turning away from the lane when she heard a shrill, frantic cry. Startled, Kate went in search of the sound. Though it sounded rather like a baby, it must be some sort of animal.

With Daniel following, she tracked the sound to a snowdrift by the lane. "*MRROOOOW!!!*" Another piercing cry rose from a small hole in the snow.

She handed her carbine to Daniel, then knelt and peered into the hole. A bedraggled striped face looked up at her. Shocked, she said, "It's a little cat!"

She scooped the cat from the hole with both gloved hands and found herself holding a small ball of wet gray fluff that was shivering uncontrollably. "The poor little thing!" she exclaimed.

It clawed its way out of her cupped hands and scrabbled up the left sleeve of her coat, making small, piteous cries. Kate opened her coat and tucked the little cat inside against her breasts, cradling it with one hand. "How do you think she got here?"

Daniel shook his head. "It must have jumped or been thrown by someone traveling that lane. You think it's a girl cat?"

"I'm sure." She peered into her coat, where the cat was snuggling in, breathing hard but no longer crying. "Male creatures are much more stoic and likely to freeze to death rather than admit they're in trouble."

Daniel laughed. "You have a point there, though maybe male cats are more sensible than male humans."

"What kind of brute would throw away such a sweet little creature? I may rethink what are suitable targets for shooting!" Kate said angrily. "She must have been here for hours. I wonder how she survived?"

"I think she was insulated by the snow." Daniel looked cautiously inside Kate's coat. "From the strength of her cries, she's in reasonably good shape."

"I hope so." As she started walking toward the inn again, Kate crooned, "Don't worry, darling. You're safe now. Soon you'll be warm and well fed."

She was answered by a softer meow. She thought the little cat understood.

As Daniel carried the firearms and game bag with one hand, he used the other to hold Kate's arm and steady her on the slippery footing. He couldn't get the image of her cradling the half-grown cat from his mind, because it was heart-stoppingly easy to imagine her cradling an infant with equal tenderness. A child that belonged to both of them.

He'd never thought much about having children beyond assuming that he'd probably have some if he ever married. Now for the first time he really contemplated what it would be like to have children. Kate would be a wonderful mother, and probably fill the house with stray cats and dogs and possibly children in need. He rather liked the idea.

Even if Kate weren't legally his wife, he would still feel this intense pull to her. He had the strange but undeniable feeling that he'd been waiting for this time and this woman his whole life.

When they reached the inn, he was allowed to hold the cat while Kate took off her overcoat, hat, and scarf. The cat was definitely female, a skinny little thing under her saturated long hair, and with mesmerizing green eyes. She would be a lovely example of her breed when she was dried out and combed. "Do you have a name for her?"

Kate thought a moment as she fashioned a sling from her scarf to hold her new friend against her. "Princess Flufferbella because clearly she is of noble birth."

"She does look rather special," he agreed. "But why Flufferbella?"

"It means 'beautiful fluff' in Italian," Kate explained.

"Really?" Daniel asked skeptically.

Kate grinned. "If it doesn't, it should."

Daniel laughed, enjoying Kate's streak of whimsy. Another thing he hadn't considered was how necessary it was to marry a woman with a sense of humor.

He hung his own coat, scarf, and hat on a peg, then carried the game bag into the kitchen. The other hunting party had also just returned and the men were taking seats at one of the tables.

They all enjoyed a substantial breakfast of scrambled eggs, porridge, toast, and mugs of tea. Alice was satisfied by the results of the hunt, which had produced enough rabbits to provide a nice addition to their night's dinner. Kate begged small amounts of the scrambled eggs and milk to feed Flufferbella, who dived into the rations as if she was starving, which she probably was.

Kate also used her scarf to dry her new friend. By the time breakfast was finished, Flufferbella was looking more like a proper cat and less like a scraggly dust mop.

"I think she needs a good rest now," Kate said as she rose from the table, cradling Flufferbella against her. "I'll take her up to my room. Alice, can I help you this afternoon with chopping vegetables or something else simple?"

Alice looked up from cleaning a skillet. "That would be very welcome, Miss Macleod. We'll be having braised root vegetables and they need a good bit of cutting up."

"I'll see you later, then," Kate said. "And thank you for a fine breakfast!"

Daniel followed Kate out of the kitchen. "I noticed that in the public room there are old newspapers used for starting fires. I'll rip some of them up and find a box that your little princess can use for her sanitary needs."

"That's a very good idea!" Kate said. "She certainly shouldn't go out in this weather."

As Daniel headed off to find a box and claim some of the old newspapers, he told himself ruefully that he really should not be jealous of a cat. But he would love to be cradled by Kate the way Flufferbella was!

# Chapter 8

When Kate released Princess Flufferbella into her bedroom, the cat turned out to be an intrepid explorer, investigating everything, running under the bed, and jumping much higher than one would expect. She was very amusing to watch as Kate changed from her hunting outfit into a simple morning gown.

She had just finished dressing when a tap on the door heralded Daniel with the promised box filled with pieces of torn newspaper. She invited him in. "Thank you. I wonder how she'll take to the box. Cats are normally tidy little creatures."

"I must admit I've had little experience of keeping cats indoors. Ivan, the White Rose cat, seems to come and go as he pleases."

"I'm not sure he'd welcome another cat into his territory so little Fluff should stay in here." Kate set the low-sided box out of the way against a wall, then scooped Flufferbella up and set her amidst the ripped papers.

The cat nosed curiously through the papers, then squatted and used the box for the intended purpose. "She's a clever little thing," Daniel said admiringly.

Finished with her task, she jumped from the box and trotted over to Daniel, her bushy tail waving like a fluffy banner. "She's fearless," he said as he lifted the silky fur ball in both hands. She gazed up at him with interest. "She seems to be mostly air."

"I'm sure that will change with regular meals."

Daniel handed the cat to her, his fingertips brushing Kate's palms and leaving a pleasant tingle in their wake. "I shouldn't linger in your bedroom. I'm off to the stables to see to my horse. I'll see you later."

"In the kitchen, perhaps?"

"In the kitchen," he agreed with a smile.

After he left, Kate set Flufferbella on the bed. The little cat had the most adorable tufts of fur between her toes. Kate had always liked cats, but Fluff was without question the most endearing one Kate had ever met.

Having woken early, Kate decided to take advantage of the quiet day to nap before kitchen duty. She pulled the bed's coverlet back and slipped under it. Flufferbella promptly burrowed under the coverlet and curled up by the pillow, purring gently.

Kate dozed off with a smile. She wasn't sure of her future with Daniel, but she'd be leaving the inn with at least one new friend.

Kate woke refreshed from her nap. After neatening her appearance, she headed downstairs, leaving Flufferbella snoozing on the bed.

When she entered the warm and enticingly scented kitchen, Alice looked up with relief from the bowl she was stirring. "I hope you're good at cutting up vegetables, Miss Macleod! There will be enough roast rabbit for everyone to have a few bites, but there's none to spare. We'll need a goodly amount of braised root vegetables to fill empty bellies."

"Since we're working side by side here, call me Kate. Cutting up vegetables I can do," Kate said. "Do you have an apron to spare?"

"Over there on that peg." Alice pointed with her wooden

spoon. "Your helpful driver, Howell, washed the vegetables. They're in baskets on that table, along with a cutting board and a proper knife."

"Perfect." Kate started with the basket of turnips. Carrots and potatoes would come later, then onions last. Cut up and braised with a bit of butter and seasoning, the vegetables would make a tasty and filling dish. "How are you preparing the rabbit?"

"Cut into pieces and roasted on a spit. I'm making the mustard sauce now to serve with them. Then Miss Younger's apple pies for a sweet."

"It sounds like a fine and filling supper," Kate said. "We all appreciate what you and Mrs. Waverly and Peter are doing for us unexpected guests."

"It's not the quiet holiday we expected," Alice agreed. "But we can't leave people starving in the snow. Speaking of starving, if you get hungry there's a nice pot of potato soup warming on the hob and bread and cheese on that side table."

"I'll take you up on that later," Kate said as she started in on her first turnip. "By the way, do you have any nuts in the pantry? If so, perhaps tomorrow I can make some tea cakes from my grandmother's recipe. It's quite simple, just flour and butter and sugar and nuts, but they're crumbly and delicious and rather festive."

"We have a good supply of hazelnuts, and tea cakes would be lovely, especially since tomorrow night is Christmas Eve," Alice said. "I believe that Mrs. Waverly is going to cook a ham for the meal."

"That's good of her since we're all likely to be here still unless the weather warms rapidly," Kate said, privately admitting that she wasn't ready to leave the inn yet, not when she needed to spend as much time as possible with Daniel.

Kate knew enough about cooking to realize that the vegetable pieces should be of a similar size so they would cook evenly. She'd always liked kitchens, and it was good to be doing something useful.

Since she'd be able to make tea cakes the next day, perhaps she'd ask Daniel to grind some sugar to powder fineness to roll the cakes in after baking. If he refused to help, it would tell her something more about him.

Daniel was leaving his room with the intention of heading down to the kitchen when he heard a piercing wail. He recognized that cry. Moving to Kate's door, he knocked but got no response. Cautiously he tried the knob, thinking there was a good chance it was unlocked; this snowbound inn felt very safe. The knob turned and when he swung the door open, he was immediately charged by a frantic fur ball.

"*Maioww!*" Flufferbella wailed as she climbed his trouser leg, her tiny claws pricking through the fabric. She ended on his shoulder, nosing his cheek.

"Poor kit." He petted her until she stopped crying. "You're hungry or lonesome or both, aren't you?"

She looked at him with great green eyes, apparently agreeing. "I'd better take you with me or you'll scream the house down, won't you? But I need a way to entertain you."

She didn't comment, apparently content to cling to the shoulder of his coat. He returned to his room and found a worn cravat that would do. Then he took his companion down to the kitchen. He opened the door and found Kate efficiently cutting up carrots. Flufferbella saw Kate and gave a happy little *miaoww* of greeting.

"When I passed your bedroom, I heard howls of misery," he explained apologetically. "Since your door was unlocked, I checked to see if she was all right. She climbed right up me and doesn't want to let go. She was lonely, I think. And obviously a talkative little thing. "

"The poor puss!" Kate paused her chopping. "Lonely and perhaps hungry again. Alice, can Mr. Faringdon give her a bit of cheese?"

"Yes, but keep her away from the food," Alice said. "Don't

want her to end up in the soup. Speaking of which, Mr. Faringdon, help yourself to some of that soup if you're hungry."

"Thank you, I'll do that soon," Daniel promised as he cut several small pieces of cheese from the wheel and set them on the floor to lure Flufferbella from his shoulder. "I'll do my best to keep Miss Kitty out of trouble."

He took a seat at the table next to Kate's so he was out of her way but could watch her. He liked watching Kate chop vegetables, as comfortable in the kitchen as she was everywhere else.

After Flufferbella finished the cheese and started exploring, he trailed the old cravat in front of her, causing her to go into a frenzy of playfulness as she chased the strip of fabric. Kate looked at the two of them and laughed. "You've found the perfect toy."

"I'm hoping to wear her out so she'll fall asleep," he explained.

Alice glanced at the clock. "Do you mind keeping an eye on things here? Mrs. Waverly had some tasks she wanted me to perform about now."

"Of course not," Kate said. "We'll make sure nothing burns."

Daniel was glad they now had the kitchen to themselves for a while. "Given the mountains of cut vegetables in front of you, you may be ready to sit down for a few minutes. I was about to have some soup. Would you like some?"

"I would indeed." Since Kate was closer to the soup pot gently steaming on the hob, she used the ladle to fill two bowls and moved them to Daniel's table while he cut up bread and cheese to go with the thick, creamy soup.

"Warm food on a cold day. Delicious," Daniel said. "The White Rose may not be able to offer its usual levels of food and service, but I'm thoroughly enjoying being here."

"So am I." Kate's hazel eyes regarded him warmly over her soup.

Thinking it was time to increase his knowledge of Kate's life, he said, "Will you tell me about the man who wants to marry you? The fact that you're considering his suit suggests that he's a good and honorable fellow."

"He is," she agreed. "Edmund is kind and hardworking and devoted to his family. He's a good businessman as well."

"A paragon," Daniel said rather dryly.

"Well, I wouldn't want to marry a bounder," Kate said reasonably.

"True, but if he were a bounder, it would be easier for me to change your mind," he said seriously.

Her gaze became challenging. "When you put it like that, I have to wonder how much you really want me, and how much you simply like the idea of defeating another man."

Daniel winced. "I can see why you might think that based on what I said. But I don't see you as the prize in some foolish manly contest, Kate. I would prefer that there was no Edmund in your life because that would give us more time to get to know each other before you make a final decision. As it is, I'm praying for the ice to last so we'll have several days at least."

Flufferbella jumped on Kate's lap, turned twice, then settled down to purr. Kate smiled and stroked the cat's furry throat. "Time I started asking questions again. What kind of life would we lead? You've inherited a reasonable-size estate. Will you become a country gentleman with a pack of hounds and no interests beyond your crops?"

"My inheritance includes a London house. I haven't seen it because it's currently leased, but it's in a pleasant neighborhood," he said. "I'd have to visit the country estate occasionally to ensure that it's well managed, but London could be our primary residence if that's what you prefer."

She glanced up, startled. "You would do that for me?"

"I'd do a great deal for you, Kate," he said quietly. "You're very special. I'm grateful that fate has brought us together so we can have a chance to explore what is between us. You don't seem to dislike my attentions."

"I don't," she said hesitantly. "But I keep feeling disloyal to Edmund. Not to mention being disloyal to both our families, who see Edmund and me as a perfect match."

"Loyalty is a great virtue," he said, sure that it was a bone-deep part of Kate. "But marriage is too important to undertake primarily because of loyalty to others. What about loyalty to yourself? What kind of life do you want to live? Will Edmund frown upon your work?" Daniel looked at her lap. "Does he like cats?"

Kate smiled at that. "He'd better like cats!"

Her expression turned thoughtful. "It's occurring to me that perhaps I don't know Edmund as well as I should. I had assumed that if he and I married, I'd continue to work indefinitely. But I've never asked him directly how he felt about that. I just assumed he wouldn't mind if I carried on as I do now."

"This sounds like a conversation you should have with him before you try to get our marriage annulled," Daniel said seriously. "If I may weigh in, it appears to me that being a working woman agrees with you, so I certainly wouldn't object to your continuing to work in your family business." He chuckled. "I hope they pay you what you're worth!"

She smiled. "I'm paid as much as the men who do similar work. There are few businesses where that can be said."

"Impressive!" he said with real interest. "And this suggests a new topic for discussion, which is the difference between landed gentry and merchants."

Kate looked thoughtful. "Napoleon claimed that Britain is a nation of shopkeepers, though I don't think he meant it as a compliment. This could indeed be an interesting topic of discussion."

Before Daniel could continue, Alice returned to the kitchen, smiling and looking rosy. Kate handed the sleeping cat to Daniel and rose to her feet. "It's time I got back to my vegetables! Daniel, if you're willing, there's a kitchen task I'd like you to undertake." Her eyes glinted. "Or would that be an insult to a man of your rank?"

He laughed. "A task that keeps me in a warm kitchen with two lovely females"—he looked at the cat and corrected himself—"three lovely females . . . is something I'll be happy to try. Just a

296 • *Mary Jo Putney*

moment while I put the Fluffy One on my cravat. With luck, she'll continue to sleep for a while."

"That should work for at least five minutes," Kate said. "Alice, where may I find a mortar and pestle and a cone of sugar?"

Alice obligingly produced everything needed and Daniel received his first lesson in grinding sugar. "Make it as fine as possible," Kate instructed. "When I take my tea cakes out of the oven, I must roll them in the ground sugar while they're still hot. That creates a nice sweet coating on the cakes."

"Delicious," he murmured while gazing down into her lovely, piquant face.

She rolled her lovely hazel eyes, but returned to chopping her vegetables with a smile.

# Chapter 9

Kate thoroughly enjoyed her afternoon in the kitchen. After cutting all the vegetables into bite-size pieces, she followed Alice's directions on how to sear the pieces in butter in a large skillet. Then the vegetables were piled into a very large cast-iron pot with beer added for flavor and to prevent burning as the food was simmered over a low flame. Kate found it very educational.

Others in the inn, both guests and servants, were coming and going to have soup and conversation. The atmosphere was easy and convivial, very different from any stay at other inns Kate had visited. Being snowbound together seemed to have loosened some of the usual social barriers, in a good way.

Daniel proved to be adept with the mortar and pestle and he produced more than enough powdery sugar for all the tea cakes she planned to make the next day. By the time he finished with the sugar, Princess Flufferbella was awake and in the mood to play.

Distracting the cat with the trailing cravat was a full-time occupation, but Kate and Daniel continued to chat on all kinds of topics, from merchants and landowners to current politics. She loved how well he listened, and that he treated her opinions as if they were as valid as any man's. Was the same true of Edmund? She realized that she'd never had such wide-ranging conversations with him. They usually talked about business or family or mutual friends.

By the time Kate had finished all the tasks Alice had set her, the sky was darkening as the short day ended. Kate glanced at the window, then removed her apron and hung it on the original peg. "Time I left to dress for dinner. Thank you for letting me help, Alice. I thoroughly enjoyed doing so."

Alice chuckled. "I'd be happy to give you a reference to be a kitchen scullion. With enough training, you could make a proper cook."

"I'm honored," Kate said with a laugh. "Now where is my cat?"

Daniel tossed her one end of the long cravat he'd been using to play with Flufferbella. "Pull this across the floor and see what happens."

Kate obeyed, and a gray ball of fluff rushed out from under the table and seized the end that was being dragged across the floor. Kate found herself pulling a strip of fabric with a feline attached to the other end like a fish on a line.

Laughing, she reeled her cat in and detached her claws. Wild-eyed, Flufferbella scampered up her arm onto her shoulder, where she teetered as she surveyed her domain.

"She certainly has a lot of energy!" Kate observed. "But your cravat is no longer fit for polite society."

"It was old and worn. The Fluffy One will get the best use out of it," Daniel said with a smile. "I'm heading upstairs also so I'll escort you both."

Kate took his arm and together they left the kitchen and headed up the stairs, Flufferbella on her shoulder between them. It was so easy to be with Daniel, and she loved that he doted on Flufferbella as much as she did.

He escorted her to her door and left her there with a bow. "I'll see you at dinner. It might be best if the Fluff doesn't attend."

"You're probably right. The young seldom have manners." She inclined her head and entered her room. Inside, she set the cat on the bed, then rolled up the cravat.

Her smile faded as she sank down on the edge of the mattress and thought about the relative merits of Daniel and Edmund. Daniel was playful and romantic and listened well and kissed even better. And, incidentally, was legally her husband.

Her thoughts of Edmund were all bound up with the Camerons, her mother's family. She'd met him four years earlier when he'd come to the office to discuss a business matter. His family had started their business in Leicester and had decided to open a branch in London. Edmund had come to set up the new office, and because the families were friends, he'd been taken in as if he was a Cameron cousin.

He often came to dinner and spent holidays with the Camerons and attended the theater with them. Eventually his attentions to Kate had become more particular. When he learned her marital situation, he'd actively worked with her grandfather and uncles to free her of her absent husband. All of the Camerons liked and respected him.

Thinking of Edmund made it hard to breathe. Rejecting him would be like removing herself from the family that had embraced her when she'd arrived in London as an orphan. She didn't think she'd be ostracized, but she would disappoint everyone by choosing a stranger over a man who was already part of the family.

Was it worth doing that just because he liked her cat and kissed well?

But Daniel was more than that, and as he said, she owed loyalty to herself as well as to her family.

Now her heart was starting to hurt. She curled up on her bed and tucked Flufferbella close. Maybe she didn't need a man. Just a cat.

When the dinner gong sounded, Daniel walked to Kate's door and knocked lightly. As she opened it, Flufferbella made a dash for the door. "Stop that!" Kate exclaimed as she bent to grab her errant pet. "I told you that you have to stay in my bedroom for the evening!"

"*Mroeww?*"

"Yes, you," Kate said firmly as Flufferbella gave her an injured look.

"This might help," Daniel said. "I have cheese and milk so she won't starve in the next few hours. If we're really lucky, she won't even yowl."

"Thank you!" She stepped back to let him in while keeping a firm hold on her furry friend. After he put the food down, Flufferbella was interested enough in her supper that they were able to leave without her darting out the door.

As they headed to the stairs, Daniel said, "You look a little tired. Too many vegetables, or too much cat care?"

Kate smiled and looked more relaxed. "That plus getting up too early this morning! I look forward to sleeping later tomorrow while you hunters brave the wilds in search of dinner."

"Peter is going to tell us where we might find ducks," Daniel said as they headed down the stairs and turned along the passage. "Alice says there will be a ham, so we should have a fine Christmas Eve feast."

They entered the public room and greeted the other guests. He noted that the table was set with plates that held a serving of the roasted rabbit. Presumably that was to prevent any guest from taking more than his share.

Conversation was light and pleasant, with speculation about the weather and a general belief that they would all be here for at least another day.

The rabbit and vegetables made for a filling meal, and Daniel was eyeing the apple pies on the sideboard when Kate said to the group, "Since tomorrow is Christmas Eve and none of us will be where we expected, perhaps we might create our own entertainment after we dine? Sing carols or perhaps play some games?"

"I like that idea," Daniel said, "though the only entertainment I might be able to provide would be cravat tricks with Princess Flufferbella."

That provoked general laughter. "I agree that we should make the evening special," Mr. Juncker said with a glance at Miss Younger. "Definitely music, and I have another idea or two."

Lady Whitmarsh nodded approvingly. "Quite right that we should make Christmas Eve special, Miss Macleod. I would like to read the Christmas story since the tale of travelers seeking shelter is akin to our own situation."

"Indeed, though our accommodations here are much better than a stable!" Daniel said to a chorus of agreement.

"After dinner, I'll let Mrs. Waverly know what we have planned," Kate said. "I hope she will join us so we can thank her, and perhaps her mysterious patient will be well enough to join us as well."

The meal ended with apple pie and laughter, and once Lady Whitmarsh and Miss Younger departed, discussion of a special surprise Mr. Juncker planned. As the other guests were leaving, Daniel suggested to Kate, "Shall we remain a bit longer for more conversation?"

Kate nodded. "I have a topic in mind. I'll inform Mrs. Waverly of our plans for tomorrow evening if you'll pour tea for us."

Daniel agreed, and had added wood to the fire as well when Kate returned. She collected her cup of tea and took a seat closer to the fireplace. "It's strange to think that after several days of living in each other's pockets, we travelers will go our separate ways and are unlikely ever to meet again."

"In Bombay we didn't think we'd ever meet again either, yet here we are," Daniel pointed out. "I quite like the idea of you and I living in each other's pockets."

Kate dropped her gaze, and he had the feeling that she was withdrawing. After a long silence, she said, "I asked once before what brought you to the breaking point in India. You did not want to discuss that then. Now is the time, I think."

Daniel drew a deep breath. They'd agreed that they must be honest with each other, which meant she needed to know him in all his weaknesses. He took a long swallow of tea, then stood and began to pace.

# Chapter 10

"It's a rather simple story," Daniel said as he paced around the public room, "though ugly. The great battles for India had been fought in earlier years and the British won, but when I arrived there was still skirmishing with rebels and outlaws. As a captain in the Indian army, I spent a good deal of time patrolling and digging out nests of bandits.

"I was good at it, a hard-fighting, hard-drinking officer. I was much respected and commended. Until the night I drank so much that I was senseless the next morning when I was supposed to be leading out a patrol. When I couldn't be roused, my new young lieutenant led the patrol.

"He was inexperienced, there was an ambush, and several of my men died, with most of the rest wounded. Rob Matthews was one of the ones who survived, though it was a near thing. Because of my past work and reputation, I was allowed to quietly resign instead of facing a court-martial.

"I traveled to Bombay and set out to drink myself to death. I was beginning to think that a bullet would be quicker and less painful when I wandered into the George tavern and found a brave young lady in dire straits. The rest you know."

He halted, staring blindly at a landscape painting on the wall, remembering the horror and the guilt. "I betrayed my men, my rank as an officer, and my honor. I imagine you can see why I avoid speaking of this."

"It's a terrible burden to carry," Kate said quietly. "The lives lost are forever gone. But you saved me, and I suspect that since then you've gone out of your way to help others as well. Am I wrong?"

He turned to face her with a deep sigh. "You're not wrong. When I began earning decent money after I started working for Adam Yorke, I set up annuities for the families of the men who died in that ambush. But the wives and parents and children would rather have had their men alive."

"I don't know if you can ever forgive yourself," she said bluntly. "But you seem to have moved forward as a better man than you were."

He smiled wryly at that. "There was much room for improvement. I was a good soldier but not a very good man."

"Thank you for revealing your past," she said, her face solemn. "It makes me appreciate how far you've come since then. As a near-suicidal drunk, you could have walked into the George tavern, seen me on the auction block, and just shrugged and walked away. It would have been the easy course. But you didn't walk away. I see why you consider that the turning point in your life."

Her gaze held his, steady and accepting, and he felt a great burden lifting from him. Guilt and grief remained but were now leavened by the acceptance in her eyes. "Thank you for listening and not spitting in my face," he said. "Rob is the only other person in my life who knows the story."

She beckoned for him to come and sit again. "How did you first meet?"

"We grew up together at Faringdale. When I was packed off

to India, he thought it sounded interesting so he went with me. I became an officer and he eventually became the kind of sergeant that is the blood and sinew of a good army. We're making our homecoming together."

Daniel joined her by the fire, moving his chair next to hers so he could hold her hand because he very much wanted that connection. Her warm hand turned under his, her fingers clasping his.

"Does Mr. Matthews want to settle down in Faringdale again?" she asked.

"He isn't sure what he wants, but like me, he feels that he needs to see his family again. After that, who knows?"

"At least you have the responsibilities of your inheritance to keep you busy," she said thoughtfully. "That's simpler than having many choices, as he does."

"The one thing he's sure of is that he doesn't want to take orders from anyone in the future." Daniel smiled a little. "I told him in that case, he'd better not marry."

Kate laughed. "I like the idea of a marriage where neither partner gives orders. Instead, husband and wife discuss issues and decide together. My grandparents are like that."

"That sounds like an excellent approach to marriage," Daniel agreed. "Would you consider staying married to an imperfect man who has made many mistakes, but is willing to listen and discuss rather than giving orders?"

"As my grandfather says, natural virtue is all very well, but it's our mistakes that build our character." She slanted her gaze at Daniel. "You seem to have a great deal of character."

"I am a work in progress," he said wryly.

"Isn't everyone?" After long a pause, Kate said hesitantly, "I've led a fairly blameless life. But while Uncle Rupert was bruising me with his grip to prevent me from escaping while he called for bids, I thought very seriously about how I would kill any man who bought me to be his whore. Most households have a good variety of knives in the kitchen."

Her voice hardened. "Then, if possible, I planned to hunt Uncle Rupert down and kill him." She raised her gaze to Rupert. "Luckily I didn't have to murder anyone, but the intent was quite clear and surely was a mortal sin."

"I'm glad you didn't have to do that," he said, not flinching. "But you have enough steel in your soul to commit such deeds if necessary. I respect your strength." He raised their joined hands and kissed her fingers. "I've never known a woman like you, Kate. My wife."

After a long silence, she withdrew her hand. "I don't feel like a wife, but I do feel like a cat mother. It's time I went to my room and made sure my little princess is fed and happy."

He stood, reluctantly releasing her hand. This was not a night for kissing, he felt, not when they'd both revealed their darkest secrets and were feeling vulnerable. "I'll see you in the morning when I come back from the hunting trip."

"If you find another lost cat, bring it home," she said with a faint smile. "Until tomorrow."

He didn't try to accompany her, feeling that this evening was best ended in silence. He was quite sure that he wanted Kate for his true and forever wife.

It was equally sure that she was far less certain about him.

Once more Kate's sleep was troubled by the tension of the most stressful decision she'd ever faced, a decision that would utterly change her life. Her grandmother once said that a woman didn't just marry an individual but a family. Kate would become part of her husband's family and, to a lesser extent, he would become part of hers.

Hence, it was sensible to consider a man's closest relations. Was there a mother-in-law who would make her life difficult? A bullying father-in-law who would terrorize everyone in the family? Jealous brothers- and sisters-in-law?

She'd met most of Edmund's family and found them to be pleasant, decent people. It was easy to imagine becoming part of the Meadows family and finding warmth and support with them when she needed it.

In contrast, Daniel didn't seem to have much family, and he feared that what relatives he had despised him. How would they feel if he brought home an unexpected wife? He was an unknown quantity still, and his relatives would be complete strangers to Kate.

But there was a new and enthralling closeness growing between her and Daniel, not to mention the fact that he was attractive and interesting. And of course he was legally her husband.

Had she ever felt so close to Edmund? No, but perhaps they hadn't tried to become emotionally closer.

Perhaps she should decide she didn't want either man. That would be much simpler than having to choose between them!

# Chapter 11

After a long and restless night, Kate was woken by the sound of quiet footsteps in the corridor. It was still dark so she guessed that the hunters were heading out for the day's hunt.

Wishing she could sleep, she rolled onto her side. Flufferbella promptly walked up her side and settled down with her small paws on Kate's shoulder as she made a soprano purr.

Kate smiled and dozed off, to be woken later by the sounds of gunshots. The hunters were at work. Since further sleep was impossible, she dressed and headed downstairs, carrying her cat in a sling made from her outdoor scarf since Flufferbella seemed fond of it.

Alice was already at work. She glanced up from frying potatoes. "Good morning, Miss Kate! After you and the little moggy have had your breakfast, will you be helping with the cooking for dinner?"

"I want to bake my tea cakes this morning," Kate replied. "Later I can help with simple dishes if you tell me what's needed."

"We'll have several side dishes along with the ham and whatever the hunters bring back." Alice considered. "Boiled potatoes dressed with butter and herbs. That's simple and will go well with the ham."

"I should be able to manage washing and boiling potatoes." Kate prepared breakfast for the Fluffy one, then made a nest of her scarf under the farther table where the cat would be out of the way. Having eaten a substantial breakfast, Flufferbella curled up on the scarf and went back to sleep.

As Kate ate her own breakfast and began sifting flour for the tea cakes, the hunters returned bearing ducks. Daniel was carrying two, and he gave her a smile that made her blood hum.

After Alice had given orders about cleaning the ducks, Daniel served himself to a substantial breakfast and sat down by Kate. "Will you need help making your tea cakes?"

"How are you at chopping up hazelnuts?"

"I'm trainable," he assured her. She laughed, thinking that a man who could make her laugh was very appealing.

The kitchen filled with hunters and other guests in search of breakfast. Miss Younger was already there, rolling out dough to make mince pies since she'd learned much about pie making the day before.

When Kate started on her tea cakes, Daniel proved an able assistant. As he chopped the hazelnuts, she showed him how to cut butter, sugar, and flour together. After she added the nuts and mixed everything together, he helped her roll the dough into little spheres like tiny cannonballs.

When the cakes came out of the oven, Daniel volunteered to roll them in the powdery sugar he'd ground the day before. He muttered an oath under his breath as he burned his fingers rolling the first cake. It was so hot that the sugar immediately melted on the surface in a delicate white glaze.

Naturally he ate the first one. "Delicious! Very rich and crumbly. They taste like Christmas."

He reached for another cake and was on the verge of eating it when Kate rapped his knuckles with a wooden spoon. "We need to save them for dinner! If you roll the rest in the sugar, I'll let you have two more."

He grinned. "You're a hard taskmistress."

"The cook sets the rules," she said firmly as she ate one herself, then gave a purr of satisfaction. She lifted another and offered it to Daniel.

His eyes dancing with amusement and affection, he took it from her fingers with his lips, giving her fingertips a teasing lick in the process. She blushed as she considered all the possibilities if one flirted with food.

They managed to finish baking the rest of the cakes, only eating half a dozen between them. Alice suggested letting the cakes cool in the pantry, where they would be out of sight and safe from greedy fingers.

Kate noticed Mrs. Waverly's regal gray tabby, Ivan, drift into the kitchen and find his breakfast. After clearing the bowl, he raised his head, looking suspicious. Then he stalked down the room to the table that sheltered Flufferbella. She flattened her ears and whiskers and made a small, nervous "*Miaoow!*"

Looking interested, Ivan began licking her ears and head. Soon she was licking back. Kate gave a sigh of relief. "I was worried what might happen when those two met, but they're getting along well."

"What sophisticated cat of the world could resist a young female charmer who looks up at him with adoring green eyes?" Daniel remarked.

"Are youth and adoration all that a male wants in his mate?" Kate asked tartly.

He chuckled. "Discerning males want mates who are intelligent and good company. But they still want their ears licked."

"If that's a parable, I don't know what it means!" Kate said as she swooped down and removed Flufferbella. "Time to take you to my room, little Fluff. Alice, I'll be back later to help you with the vegetables."

Daniel followed Kate from the kitchen, dodging Miss Younger's energetic mince pie project. Outside he said, "Once you've stashed away your little ruffian, Kate, I have something interesting to show you down in the public room."

"What is it?"

"You'll see," Daniel replied with a smile.

As Kate started up the stairs, Flufferbella scampered up to her shoulder. "This is going to be more difficult when little Miss Puss becomes a large, full-grown Lady Puss," she observed.

"You must hope that she's as trainable as I am."

Kate laughed. He loved making her laugh.

When they reached Kate's room, she set the cat on the bed and used the wool scarf as a blanket to cover her. "Now we leave quickly before she decides to follow us!"

They exited, followed by a mildly accusing "*Meoooow.*"

"I think she's less afraid of being abandoned now," Kate said to Daniel as they returned to the ground floor and headed to the public room.

Once there, Daniel turned Kate so she could see that under the gallery was a tall pine tree. "It's Mr. Juncker's Christmas tree! Now that I see it, I understand the appeal. I've heard that some of the royal family members have trees like this because of their German heritage, but I've never seen one."

"Mr. Juncker said he wanted to provide something special for everyone," Daniel said. "But I suspect that he particularly wants to surprise and impress a certain young lady."

Having seen the looks exchanged between Miss Younger and Mr. Juncker, Kate had no trouble guessing the object of the gentleman's affections. "Mr. Juncker encouraged everyone to add decorations. I've been thinking about that. I don't have any suitable jewelry, but I have a good many ribbons of different colors."

She glanced at Daniel. "Holly and other greens were to be gathered this morning. We could tie holly leaves and berries together with a ribbon bow that has a loop so they can be hung from the branches."

Daniel blinked. "We? I always think of such projects as occupations women enjoy, but if you want me to help, I'm game. Bring down your ribbons. I'll collect some clumps of holly and berries and meet you in the private parlor."

"Brave man!" she said with a laugh. "You may surprise yourself and enjoy making pretty little ornaments."

Kate was right; Daniel was surprised how much he enjoyed making pretty little ornaments with Kate and Flufferbella, who had insisted on joining them. He loved laughing with Kate over the cat's hysterical delight in the ribbons. He loved the bright clusters of holly and ribbon which would enhance the Christmas tree and please everyone marooned in the White Rose Inn.

Most of all, he loved the results when he produced a sprig of mistletoe and held it over Kate's head. The first kiss was sweet. The second produced a flare of mutual heat. And the third kiss ended when Flufferbella chose to climb Daniel like a tree.

In revenge, he tied a jaunty red ribbon around the little cat's neck. She looked adorable. All three of them left the private parlor feeling pleased with themselves.

Kate dressed for the feast in the burgundy velvet gown she'd bought to wear for Christmas dinner with Edmund's family. Then she put her hair up in a simple twist, and added gold earrings, a garnet and gold necklace, and her always reliable Indian shawl, which looked well with every gown in her wardrobe.

When she was ready, she looked in the mirror and decided she looked as polished as she could be without the help of Bridget, who was particularly good at doing hair. Kate would be very glad when she was reunited with her maid!

There was a knock on the door. She responded swiftly and opened it to find Daniel in formal dinner wear, looking every inch a landed gentleman. She ran her gaze over him appreciatively. "I'm impressed by the amount of clothing you're producing from your saddlebags!"

"I'm an expert at packing." His warm gaze traveled from her face to her feet, making her feel desirable and desired. "And you, my lady, are dazzling." He leaned forward and brushed a light kiss on her lips. "Shall we join the feast?"

"I look forward to it." As she took his arm and closed the door behind them, she added, "I gave the little princess enough ham and cream to put her to sleep. I don't think she'd be reliable in a room containing tables covered with food."

Daniel laughed. "A wise decision."

They both fell silent as they went down to the public room together. She could hear talk and laughter coming from that direction.

She caught her breath in amazement when they entered the room. It was gaily decorated and pine-scented with greenery. Mr. Juncker's Christmas tree was stunning. Careful placement of Argand lamps made light shine through the branches and sparkle on the ornaments.

"A lot more decorating has been done since we hung our holly and ribbons!" Daniel said admiringly.

"I'm glad we were able to contribute," Kate said. After they seated themselves at a table with the other guests, she continued, "It's rather magical how a group of strangers have become a kind of family this evening."

His voice equally soft, Daniel said, "I've found that brief, unexpected meetings can turn out to be unexpected gifts." He looked down at her, his eyes serious. "And some gifts can last for a lifetime."

"I will treasure these days," she said before looking away, unable to tell him what he hoped to hear. Her gaze moved over the room. "Your friend Rob seems to have appointed himself the master of the drinks, and he looks very much at home as he dispenses them."

"He should," Daniel replied. "His parents ran the inn and tavern in Faringdale. When he left at age seventeen, he couldn't wait to get away, but the old skills seem to have survived."

For the next hours, Kate concentrated on enjoying the celebration. The food was less varied than at a grand feast, but it was delicious and a source of special pride since so many of them had contributed to it. She was especially pleased by the enthusiastic reception of her tea cakes, which disappeared quickly once dessert was served.

When the table was cleared and it was time to begin the entertainment, Lady Whitmarsh read the Christmas story from her own worn Bible, her voice surprisingly sonorous. Kate realized that she was tearing up as she remembered so many other Christmases, in India with her parents, more recently in London with her grandparents and other family members.

Daniel silently handed her a handkerchief. From his expression, she saw that he was also moved by the way a group of strangers were now celebrating this ancient tradition.

After that, the mood lightened as Mr. Juncker and Miss Younger sang a holiday song they'd composed together, with a simple chorus that all were invited to join.

That led to the singing of carols that were familiar to all. Kate didn't think she'd ever spent a more enjoyable evening. The celebration ended when one of the men entered the public room and announced, "The temperature is rising. The roads should be passable by morning!"

There was a moment of absolute silence before Daniel said in the carrying voice of an army officer, "This has been a grand, unexpected gathering." He stood and raised his glass. "My thanks to Mrs. Waverly and Alice and Peter, and to everyone here for making this such a special time."

All glasses were raised in the toast. Then the room dissolved into chattering as groups formed to make plans for leaving.

"We need to talk," Daniel said to Kate, his eyes so bleak that she guessed he knew what she was going to say.

She nodded and left her half-full glass of negus behind as she walked to the private parlor, which had been their special refuge.

The end had come too soon.

\* \* \*

Daniel lit the fire while Kate turned up a lamp, but neither of them sat down. He gazed at her in silence, scarcely able to breathe. She was lovely in all ways, with a graceful, feminine figure, elegant features that were infinitely expressive, her hair shining like dark flame in the firelight. A strong woman. Her own woman, not his.

She was very calm as she gazed at him, her hands linked in front of her waist. He felt with a terrible certainty that he had lost her without ever really having her.

Yet he had to try. "Katherine Macleod," he said quietly. "I think I've loved you from the moment I first saw you. In all the years since, you lived in my heart as an impossible ideal of what a woman should be. Surely it's one of God's own miracles that we met up again. Will you be my wife in truth and for always? Because I love you still, and I'm sure I always will."

Her linked hands clenched and her knuckles whitened. "Daniel, you are asking too much, too soon. You were my dream hero, and now that we've met again, I see you as a hero in truth as well as in my dreams.

"But as much as I like you and have delighted in getting to know you, you are still something of a stranger. The future you offer is uncertain to me. Just as Edmund is a known quantity to me, do you think you love me because I'm something familiar to hold onto while the rest of your life is in turmoil? Do you love me, or is it just the idea of me?"

He felt as if she'd slapped him. "It's you I love, Kate. In all your beauty and bravery and stubbornness," he said tightly. "Together we can make the future you want. Are you going to choose Edmund merely because *he* is familiar?"

"If I do choose him, that would be part of the reason. But even more, when I think of him, I also think of family, of how well he fits with mine, how well I will fit with his. It's a future that I know will suit me."

"So familiarity matters more than *this*?" He stepped forward and kissed her, hugging her close as he tried to show how much he needed her and how much he believed she needed him.

She dissolved into fire in his arms, returning his kiss with desperate intensity. "Kate, we can be so much better together than alone," he whispered as he drew her even more tightly against him. They fit together so well, in all ways. Surely she could see that as clearly as he could? "Isn't this enough, Kate?"

With a gasp she stepped away, covering her lips with one hand as if trying to cool them. "Passion is *not* enough!" she said in a ragged voice. "It's an intoxicating distraction that clouds my judgment when I'm with you. But I can't truly understand what you and I have without seeing Edmund again."

He stared at her, hope draining away, sure that when she saw her damned Edmund, she'd slide right back into the peace of comfort and certainty with him.

There was nothing more to say. "As you wish, my lady," he said, his voice unsteady. Then he turned and left their private trysting place for the last time.

Daniel spent the sleepless hours of the night preparing to say good-bye to Kate in a composed manner if they saw each other as they were leaving. He didn't want to hurt either of them more.

Hoping to avoid seeing her, he and Rob had a quick early breakfast. Unfortunately Kate must have had the same idea because as he and Rob led their horses out of the stables, he saw that her servants had her coach prepared and ready to leave.

He smiled a little sadly when he heard an indignant "*Meoowwwww!*" emerge from the vehicle. He'd miss that fluffy little imp.

The hand of fate that had brought Kate and him together twice before had not given up on them yet, because she was emerging from the inn. She looked beautiful, composed, and very pale.

Mrs. Waverly came outside to bid her guests farewell, which

was fortunate because her presence made it easier for him to control himself. After thanking the landlady again, Daniel inclined his head to Kate. "Miss Macleod, I wish you a safe journey."

"And the same to you, Mr. Faringdon," she said, her face calmer than her eyes. "I hope your journey ends better than you expect."

After that, there was nothing left to say. He watched her climb into her coach and waited until it pulled out of the yard and on its way. Then he and Rob mounted their horses and followed. He wondered if he'd ever see her again. Perhaps in a lawyer's office as an annulment was arranged. He wondered if he would be able to bear that.

# Chapter 12

Kate maintained her composure as she climbed into her carriage and they rumbled out of the inn's courtyard. The roads were in surprisingly good condition, firm from the recent freeze and not yet warm enough to turn muddy.

The carriage turned north. She knew from her driver, Howell, that in less than a mile they'd reach a split in the road. Her carriage would turn left to continue west to the Meadows family home. When Daniel and Rob reached the intersection, they would turn right toward Faringdale, where an uncertain reception awaited him. She suspected it would be easier for him to face an ambush by hill bandits than to confront a platoon of disapproving female relatives, but she was sure he'd manage.

She had left him with a "not now," not a "never," but she was sure that after opening his heart to her without success, he would turn away and not look back. How long would it take him to arrange an annulment? After that, they'd both be free. Wasn't that what everyone wanted for her?

She began to weep, and her tears were joined by cries from the traveling box Craig had made for Flufferbella. She sounded so desolate that Kate learned forward to unlatch the lid of the box. "I should have named you Meowser since you certainly know how to meow!"

The little cat swarmed up Kate, small claws scrabbling on her skirt until she came to rest on Kate's chest, no longer crying but breathing hard. She began nuzzling her small furry face on her mistress's chin.

Kate began to weep again as she petted the small, warm body. "I'm so glad I have you, my little poppet. We can be two single ladies together."

When Daniel and Rob reached the intersection where they would head east and Kate would have turned west, Rob said quietly, "I'm sorry things didn't work out with Miss Macleod," he said. "She's a fine lady."

Daniel sighed. "That she is. But our marriage came about by pure chance. It never should have happened. When I return to London, I'll find out how it can be annulled."

"Did you ever tell her that you're Lord Elland now?"

Daniel snorted. "No. Quite apart from the fact that I'm still uncomfortable with the title, I'm not sure I'd want her if she decided to stay married just for the sake of becoming a baroness."

"I don't think she's that sort of a woman," Rob said.

*No, she isn't,* Daniel thought, though all he said was, "If she is, I'd rather not know."

They rode in silence for another half mile. The snow was starting to melt in some places, but there was still enough to make this a white Christmas, his first in many years.

Strange to think this was Christmas Day. It didn't feel like a holiday.

After they passed a hay wagon that was lurching along the road, Rob said hesitantly, "I think I've decided what I want to do with my future."

"Oh?" Daniel asked, his voice encouraging. Rob and he had

discussed this regularly, but up until now, his friend hadn't come to any conclusions.

"Our stay at the White Rose decided me," Rob said with a slanting glance at Daniel. "I want to become an innkeeper of an establishment like Mrs. Waverly's. A comfortable haven that caters to travelers and is a welcoming gathering place for people in the area." He smiled wryly. "My parents are getting on in years. The Black Swan is mine for the asking if I want it."

Daniel had to laugh. "When you left, you swore that you'd never, ever return! You couldn't wait to leave. Are you sure you want to take the inn over?"

Rob smiled, unabashed. "We change with time. I needed to get away and see some of the world to appreciate what I left behind."

"You'll make a fine innkeeper if that's what you want, Rob," Daniel said sincerely. "Though you wouldn't have had to face death anywhere near as often if you'd stayed in Faringdale and married your sweetheart."

This time Rob's face colored. "Interesting you should mention Maggie. My mother wrote that she was married but has been widowed. She's head housemaid now at Faringdale."

Daniel's brows arched. "It sounds as if your love life is going to work out much better than mine!"

"We'll see," Rob said. "Maggie and I haven't seen each other in fifteen years. But there was always something special about her."

"Is it possible to wish you well in all sincerity while being profoundly envious?" Daniel asked.

His friend laughed. "Of course it's possible! I've done enough traveling. I want to stay in one place and run a business that makes people happy. The business is waiting for me, and as for Maggie . . . well, we'll see." His voice turned serious. "I think you'll find your peace at Faringdale, Daniel. It's always been your home, you know."

Yes, Daniel did know that, though he'd refused to recognize

that simple fact for many years. There was work to be done at Faringdale, and he'd do it because it was his home.

Petting Flufferbella, Kate regained her composure while trying not to think about Daniel and whether she'd made the greatest mistake of her life. She snapped to alertness when she heard shouting outside the carriage.

Surely not highwaymen! If so, Craig would be shooting at them.

The carriage rumbled to a halt and the door swung open to reveal a familiar face. "Edmund!" Kate exclaimed in shock. "What are you doing here?"

"Happy Christmas, Kate!" Smiling, he climbed into the carriage and sat beside her. "With the dreadful weather, I assumed you'd had to stop at some wayside inn. Since the roads are passable this morning, I decided to ride out and see if I might intercept you." His smile widened into a grin. "Besides, both Brutus and I needed some fresh air."

"Horses and men both need regular exercise," Kate agreed. "Happy Christmas! Is your family well?"

"Yes, and anxious to see you."

Craig appeared beside the door. "I've tethered your horse to the back of the carriage, Mr. Meadows, so we'll be on our way again." He closed the door and climbed up beside the driver, and the carriage started moving again.

"I've missed you, Kate." Edmund leaned across the seat to kiss her, then halted. "You seem to have a cat attached to your chest."

Flufferbella glared at him with narrowed green eyes. "*Mrowwwp!*"

Kate smiled. "This is Princess Flufferbella. I found her in a snowdrift when we were stranded at the White Rose Inn. Isn't she lovely?"

Edmund's brows furrowed. "I suppose every kitchen needs a cat."

"She's not a kitchen cat," Kate said firmly. "She's a bed-and-lap cat."

Edmund looked skeptical but jumped into a topic that interested him more. "Great news, Kate! My London lawyer has explained how we can have that pesky husband of yours declared dead." He took her hand. "Then we can finally marry!"

Unaccountably irritated, she pointed out, "You've never actually asked me."

Edmund looked startled. "Asking would have been improper when you were legally married, but I assumed that we'd marry when you were free. Everyone expects it. I've hoped to marry you for years."

He wasn't being unreasonable, based on what the situation had been. "Things have changed, Edmund. One of the other travelers stranded at the White Rose turned out to be none other than my long-lost husband, Daniel Faringdon, very much alive."

Edmund stared, his face turning pale. "That's not possible! He vanished after the night he married you and has been presumed dead for seven years."

"Daniel lived and traveled widely in the East after our marriage, which is why it was so difficult to find proof of his continued existence," Kate explained.

"Nonsense!" Edmund said angrily. "Surely this man is an imposter who knows you're an heiress and wants to claim your fortune for his own!"

"He is most certainly the man I married," Kate said firmly. "We recognized each other at once."

"He may be the man you married," Edmund said grudgingly, "but he could easily have learned that you're one of the heirs of Cameron and Kin, and now that he knows, he doesn't want to let you get away."

She shook her head. "He's not a fortune hunter, Edmund! He knew me as Kate Macleod. I had never mentioned my mother's maiden name or the name of our family business. He's only been back in England for a month. He was as shocked to learn the marriage was legal as I was."

Edmund considered her words. "If he's telling you the truth, I presume he'll be willing to cooperate in getting an annulment. It will be complicated, but the marriage was a farce from the beginning."

Kate remembered that Daniel had said he wouldn't cooperate if she intended to marry a man she didn't love. Did she love Edmund? How deeply did their relationship run? She needed to find out.

Watching his face carefully, she said, "Edmund, you've often complimented me on my understanding of business and for the work I do at Cameron and Kin. We've never discussed this, but I have every intention of continuing to work there after I marry."

Edmund looked shocked. "Naturally I assumed that you would leave your job after marriage. My wife will have no need to work."

"I have no need to work now," she pointed out, suppressing her irritation. "But I *want* to! All my lowbred Scottish relations seem to think it's a fine idea." So did Daniel.

Edmund's face hardened. "I'm beginning to wonder if you're the woman I thought you were."

"We should have talked seriously long before this, because we appear to have a number of misunderstandings between us." Kate drew a deep breath, then threw away one of her possible futures. "I can't and won't marry you, Edmund. You have been a dear friend and I hope you will continue to be. But I am not the woman for you, and you are not the man for me."

His expression froze. "Are you going to stay with that fortune hunter?"

"He's not a fortune hunter!" Kate said again. "I don't even know if we both want to stand by the marriage."

Her mind snapped back to that desperate night in Bombay. Her terror, the dangerous-looking rogue who took her hand and promised that she would be safe. Her uncle's greedy face as he counted Daniel's money while insisting they must wed *right then*. The drunken vicar who performed the ceremony. All was painfully vivid in her mind. Most of all she remembered the kindness in Daniel's eyes and the tumbling of her heart as she gazed into them.

She continued slowly, "Even though I didn't really mean those vows when I took them, I said the words before God and man. I promised to love and honor my husband." She frowned. "I wish I hadn't agreed to obey. I think I'll just ignore that one. But marry we did, and he and I are the ones who must sort our marriage out. Not you, not my family. Only Daniel and I."

She caught the gaze of her friend, her eyes compassionate. "It's time for us to go our separate ways, Edmund. Please give my apologies to your grandmother for me."

She banged on the roof panel. When Craig opened it, she called up, "Stop the carriage and bring Mr. Meadows his horse. He's leaving now, and we're turning around."

Edmund stared at her as the carriage rattled to a stop. Then his expression turned wry. "You're right, Kate, you're not the wife for me. If you decide you want to keep that fortune hunter, I hope he takes good care of you." He leaned forward and brushed a light kiss on her cheek. "Yes, let us be friends. Good-bye, Kate. At least I won't have to sleep with that ragged fur muff."

Kate laughed and held on to the cat as Edmund climbed from the carriage. "You've had a lucky escape."

"I suppose I have." He gave her one last regretful glance, then crossed to mount his horse.

Craig looked into the carriage with a deeply interested expression. "Now what, Miss Kate?"

"We're going to turn around, go back to that intersection, and turn east toward Faringdale. Do you think we can catch up with Mr. Faringdon and his companion?"

Craig grinned. "Count on it, lass!"

\* \* \*

Daniel and Rob had slowed to ascend a long hill when they were startled by the sound of a rifle shot behind them. As old soldiers, they both yanked their horses to the side of the road and looked back to see a carriage pounding along behind them, the guard waving a rifle in the air to catch their attention.

Daniel was reaching for his pistol when Rob said, "Isn't that Miss Macleod's carriage?"

Daniel's heart accelerated. "Yes, and it appears they want us to stop."

They waited by the side of road until the carriage rumbled to a halt beside them. Kate opened the door partway and looked up at Daniel anxiously. "Will you ride with me, Daniel? Once more we need to talk."

Praying that this meant what he hoped it did, Daniel dismounted and handed his reins to Rob. "Take charge of my horse, please."

Smiling, his friend said, "Of course. I'll continue on to Faringdale, and I expect the carriage will follow?"

"Please do," Kate said, her expression uncertain.

Daniel climbed into the carriage. As it set into motion again, he heard a piercing "*Meeoowwww!*" and Flufferbella leaped at him, landing on his chest.

He laughed and petted her. "Did the little princess say she wanted to be with me rather than you?"

"She wants to be with both of us," Kate said in a shaky voice. She had pushed herself against the other wall of the carriage and was regarding him uncertainly. "When we spoke last night, you offered me love, and I said I needed more time. Can you forgive me for that?"

"I can forgive you for anything, Kate," he said, his breath tight. "Anything other than leaving me permanently. But I thought you needed to see Edmund again before you could decide?"

"I did see him. He rode out to intercept my carriage. We

talked." She smiled a little mischievously. "By the time I sent him away, I'd convinced him that he'd had a lucky escape. He wasn't at all keen on sleeping with Flufferbella."

"Foolish man!" Laughing, Daniel set Flufferbella on the opposite seat, then leaned across the carriage and scooped Kate up in his arms and across his lap. "Yes, we'll talk, but first . . ."

He kissed her with all his passion and renewed hope, loving her warmth and softness and strength. She responded with no hesitation, sinking into him as if she could never get enough of his embrace.

When they paused to breathe, she said haltingly. "I wasn't sure what love was until I saw Edmund. I love him as a friend. If you didn't exist, it would be easy and comforting to marry him and become part of his family."

Her gaze intensified. "But I realized that I love you much more than I crave familiarity and comfort. I love you so much that I'll willingly take on any of the complications and difficult relatives that come with you. Together we can manage anything, Daniel. As you said, we are better together than apart."

He kissed her again. "I love that you're trainable, my Kate Cat."

She laughed. "I have decided to ignore the vow to obey that's in the wedding service. But I will happily vow to discuss and decide with you."

With every word she said, he loved her more. "I will happily make that vow also."

She leaned back in his arms. "Edmund is convinced you're a fortune hunter."

Mildly interested, Daniel asked, "You have a fortune?"

"As I said, I'm from a merchant family." She eyed him a little warily. "My full name is Katherine Cameron Macleod. My mother's parents founded Cameron and Kin."

Daniel blinked with surprise. "Aren't they the largest merchants in Britain and the colonies?"

"Possibly, but there are some other very large merchants," she said meticulously.

"That's interesting," he said, "but if they decide to disown you because you've married a useless landowner, I promise that you and Flufferbella won't starve."

"They might be disappointed that I won't be marrying Edmund, but they won't disown me," Kate said seriously. "And when they get to know you, they'll also love you."

He hoped so, but he had a confession of his own to make. "While we're on the subject of things not mentioned, it's time for me to confess that the property I inherited is the entailed estate of the Lords Elland. I'm the seventh Baron Elland."

Kate's brows rose. "That explains why the estate came to you, and female relations might resent you. So nice to meet you, Lord Elland. I hope I like you as much as I like that roguish kinsman of yours, Daniel Faringdon."

"Daniel and Lord Elland are one and the same, Kate." He kissed her again. "Finally!"

"I'm glad for you," she said softly. "I've never craved a title, but I want a husband who is happy with his station in life."

What had he ever done to deserve a wife like this one? He kissed her again, knowing there was a lifetime of kisses ahead of them.

The carriage jolted in a particularly large rut and she pulled back a little. "A carriage is no place to consummate a marriage," she said with regret.

"True," he said tenderly, "but we can explore the possibilities a bit more."

Kate smiled up at him. "I presume we have several miles to discover what you mean by a bit more?"

"Indeed we do!" He kissed her again, tempted to tell the driver to slow down.

"Let the explorations begin!"

As the carriage drove up the sweeping drive that led to the entrance of Faringdale Hall, Kate moved from Daniel's lap, knowing that she was blushing and happier than she'd ever been in her life. Telling herself she must order her senses, she said rather primly, "Your home is very beautiful, Lord Elland. Palladian, I think?"

He nodded and clasped her hand, but he didn't speak as he gazed out the window at his ancestral home.

She continued, "I'm imagining you and Rob and perhaps a dog or two racing across these lawns."

His expression eased. "You have an accurate imagination, my Lady Elland."

The carriage rocked to a halt in front of the entrance. "Courage, my love," Kate said quietly. "If they're mean to you, I'll insist we spend the night at the local inn."

"The Black Swan, which is run by Rob's parents, would welcome us gladly but I hope it won't come to that."

They climbed from the carriage, holding hands and with Flufferbella riding on Daniel's shoulder. Their arrival had been noted and the great doors swung open.

Daniel led Kate into the massive entryway and nodded his head to the elderly butler. "It's good to see you, Jackson. Will you inform my grandmother that Lord and Lady Elland have arrived?"

Jackson looked at Kate with unconcealed interest. "Your arrival has been expected, my lord. The family is taking Christmas tea in the main drawing room."

He solemnly escorted them to a door on the right and swept it open, announcing, "Lord and Lady Elland have arrived!"

Kate saw that there were ten or twelve females in the room, running the gamut from a small child to a grand lady in the middle of the group. Surely she was the dowager Lady Elland.

The old woman rose to her feet. "I imagine you were delayed by the weather, Daniel." Her gaze ran over him appraisingly, lingering on Flufferbella. "You always did like animals."

"That hasn't changed." He bowed and Flufferbella leaped to Kate's shoulder, where she clung with her tiny claws. "Happy Christmas, Grandmother. It's been a long time."

"Indeed it has." The old woman's face crumpled and Kate saw tears in her pale blue eyes. "Too long. You were not treated as well as you ought to have been."

"I agree but must admit that I didn't always behave as I ought to have," Daniel said mildly. "Let us put the past behind us, Grandmother. Allow me to present my wife, Katherine Cameron Macleod." He gave Kate a fond glance and his hand tightened on hers. "My Kate."

"I look forward to become better acquainted, my dear," the dowager said, her curiosity masked by courtesy. "Now let me present the rest of the family to you since you surely won't recognize most of them after so many years."

As the old lady began to introduce the various females, Kate's gaze moved over the room. She saw eagerness, shyness, and some uncertainty, but no resentment. Daniel's fears of this homecoming had been proved baseless.

Her gaze was caught by a small drama on the right side of the drawing room. Rob Matthews had slipped in behind them and he was making a beeline toward one of the maids who was serving the tea. She was a pretty, sweet-faced blond, and her eyes were huge as she stared at the man approaching her.

Rob caught her hands and they gazed at each other raptly. Feeling that was a moment too private for her to watch, Kate turned her attention back to Daniel and the introductions. Her roguish rescuer was calm, kind, and unutterably handsome as he accepted the role he was born to.

She leaned in and whispered, "Welcome home, my lord husband, and Happy Christmas!"

He looked down at her, his heart in his eyes. "The happiest Christmas ever, my love!"

"*Mroowp!*" Flufferbella meowed in complete agreement.

Looking for more from Sabrina Jeffries? Don't miss the
Duke Dynasty series, beginning with . . .


**Project Duchess**

From *New York Times* bestselling author Sabrina Jeffries comes
a sparkling new series about an oft-widowed mother's grown
children who blaze through society in their quest for the truth
about their fathers . . . and in the process find that love just
might conquer all . . .

A series of stepfathers and a difficult childhood have left
Fletcher "Grey" Pryde, Fifth Duke of Greycourt, with a guarded
heart, enviable wealth, and the undeserved reputation of a rogue.
Grey's focus on expanding his dukedom allows him little time to
find a wife. But when his mother is widowed yet again and he
meets the charmingly unconventional woman managing his stepfather's funeral, he's shocked to discover how much they have in
common. Still, Grey isn't interested in love, no matter how
pretty, or delightfully outspoken, the lady . . .

Beatrice Wolfe gave up on romance long ago, and the arrogant
Duke of Greycourt with his rakish reputation isn't exactly
changing her mind. Then Grey agrees to assist his grief-stricken
mother with her latest "project": schooling spirited, unfashion-
able Beatrice for her debut. Now that Beatrice is seeing through
Grey's charms to his wounded heart, she's having trouble keeping him at arm's length. But once Grey starts digging into her
family's secrets, she must decide whether her loyalties lie with
her family . . . or with the man whose lessons capture her heart . . .

*Available wherever books are sold from*
*Kensington Publishing Corp.*

# Chapter 1

*London, September 1808*

One fine autumn afternoon, Fletcher Pryde, 5th Duke of Greycourt, strode up the steps of his Mayfair town house, caught up in thinking through his business affairs. Which was probably why he missed the speaking look on his butler's face as he stalked through the doorway.

"Your Grace, I feel it is my duty to make you aware that—"

"Not now, Johnston. I've got a dinner at eight, and I hope to catch old Brierly at his club before then. He's unloading property near my Devon estate that I must have if I'm to continue my improvements. And I have reports I have to peruse before I can even talk to him."

"More land, Grey?" said a decidedly young, female voice. "Sometimes I think you shop for properties as eagerly as women shop for gowns. Judging from your reputation for shrewd dealing, you probably pay less for them, too."

Grey whirled toward the sound. "Vanessa!" He scowled over at Johnston. "Why didn't you tell me she was here?"

332 • *Sabrina Jeffries*

His butler lifted his eyes a fraction, as close as the man ever came to rolling them. "I did try, sir."

"Ah. Right. I suppose you did."

Grey smiled indulgently at Vanessa Pryde. At twenty- four, she was ten years his junior and more like a little sister than a first cousin.

He removed his hat, driving gloves, and greatcoat before handing them to the footman. Grey didn't recognize the servant, who was gawking at Vanessa like a pauper at a princess. The footman's fascination was understandable, given her heart-shaped face, perfect proportions, and wealth of jet-black curls, but it was also most inappropriate.

Grey cast the fellow one of the quelling glances at which he excelled.

When the footman colored and hurried off, Johnston stepped up to murmur, "Sorry, Your Grace. He's new. I will be sure to speak to him."

"See that you do." Then he turned his attention to Vanessa, who didn't even seem to have noticed the exchange. "I wasn't expecting you."

"You ought to have been, Cousin." With an elaborate curtsey, Vanessa flashed him a mischievous smile. "Or should I say, 'prospective fiancé'?"

"Don't even joke about that," he grumbled. Every time he tried to think of himself married to Vanessa, he remembered her as a babe in swaddling, being held by her father, his uncle Eustace Pryde, and he knew he couldn't do it. He'd seen her grow up—he couldn't imagine her as his wife.

Fortunately, she had no desire to marry him, either. Which was why whenever her ambitious mother sent her over here with instructions to get him into a compromising position so they could be forced into marriage, they spent most of the time drumming up a plausible reason for why Vanessa had "just missed him."

"Don't worry." Vanessa gave a little laugh. "My maid is with me. As usual, she will swear to whatever excuse we concoct for Mama. So come join us for tea and cakes in the drawing room."

Leave it to Vanessa to take charge of his household. As they strolled down the hall, he said, "You look well."

Preening a bit, she danced ahead and whirled to face him, forcing him to halt as she swished her skirts about her legs. "So you like my new gown? I won't tell Mama. She picked it out herself to tempt you. I told her yellow was your favorite color."

"I hate yellow."

Her blue eyes twinkled at him. "Precisely."

A helpless laugh escaped him. "You, my dear, are a hoyden. If you would put a tenth of the energy you expend in provoking your mother into hunting down a husband, you'd have twenty men begging to marry you."

Her spirits seemed to droop. "I already have that. But you know how Mama is. Until you are off the table, she won't allow me to accept a lesser man's suit." She wagged her finger at him. "So will you please get married? To *anyone* other than me? Or I shall surely die an old maid."

"That will never happen to you, and we both know it." He narrowed his gaze on her. "Wait a minute—is there someone in particular you have your eye on?"

Her blush alarmed him. Vanessa had terrible taste in men.

"Who is he?" he demanded.

She tipped up her chin. "I'm not going to tell you."

"Because you know I'd disapprove, which means he's entirely wrong for you."

"He is *not*. He's a poet."

Damn. Vanessa needed to marry a poet about like he needed to learn to cook. Then again . . . "A *famous* poet?" he asked hopefully. If the fellow had money, it could work. Anyone who married Vanessa would need pots of money, if only to keep up with her gown purchases.

She turned and marched on to the drawing room. "He will be. With my support and encouragement."

"God help us all." He almost felt sorry for this poet, whoever he was. "I suppose your mother disapproves."

"As if I would ever tell her," she scoffed as she entered the drawing room.

Vanessa's lady's maid sat erect on the settee, her expression bland. No doubt she was used to being the foil to her volatile employer.

"Then things have not progressed to a serious interest," Grey said, relieved not to have to deal with that, too. He was still hoping to get to Brierly's club before the man left.

"How could things progress at *all*?" Vanessa picked up a tea-cake and devoured it with her usual gusto. "Mama is so focused on my marrying you that I cannot get her to bring me to events my . . . friend might attend." She shot him a dire look. "And thanks to the latest on-dit about you, she's on a tear again. She actually believes all that rot about your running a secret cabal of licentious bachelors."

He snorted. "I'd never run anything so tiresome and predictable. I don't have the time or inclination for it, and that level of discretion requires too much effort to maintain, people being who they are. I hope you told her I'd rather focus my energy on my estates."

"I did. She didn't believe me. She never does."

"Yet she sent you over here to engage the leader of this secret cabal of debauchery. She makes no sense."

"The gossip only made her more eager to marry me off to you. Hmm."

"She's probably afraid I'll spend all my wealth on 'licentious' living before you can grab me and my dukedom for our progeny."

"Or she thinks that a man with such ungoverned desires would be easy to manipulate. She ought to know you better than that. I certainly do. There isn't a single ungoverned thing about you." Vanessa tapped her finger on her chin. "Then again, there's another possibility—that Mama started the rumor about the cabal herself."

"To what end?"

"By making you sound unappealing, she hopes to eliminate my competition."

"I hate to tell you, my dear, but rumors of a man's wickedness rarely seem to eliminate the competition. If that was your mother's plan, it's a foolish one. And it proves my opinion about gossip: Rumors are nothing more than entertainment for the bored. If people in society would put a tenth of the energy they expend in—"

"I know, I know—we're all frivolous, with not a whit of usefulness between us," she said archly. "You're the only one with any sense."

When her maid looked as if she might explode with holding in a laugh, he shot Vanessa a rueful glance. "Do you think me as pompous and arrogant as all that, pet?"

"Worse." Then she softened the accusation with a smile. "And on that note, I shall leave you." Her maid cleared her throat, and Vanessa said, "Oh, I almost forgot! I have this for you." She fished a sealed letter out of her reticule. "It came to us rather than you. Which is curious. Perhaps your mother heard you hadn't been here in weeks. Though why she thought *we* would see you any more often is anyone's guess."

He ignored the sudden tightness in his chest. "You know perfectly well why."

With a sigh, Vanessa stepped nearer to speak in a low voice meant only for his ears. "Must you still punish your mother?"

"Don't be nonsensical," he said lightly, to hide the guilt that swamped him. "I'm not punishing her. Besides, she has her other children to keep her company. She doesn't need me fawning over her."

Vanessa sniffed. "As if you would ever fawn over anyone. And yes, you are punishing her, whether you admit it or not."

The pity shining in Vanessa's eyes made him regret having said anything about his mother.

He reached for the letter, but Vanessa wouldn't release it. "She does love you, you know."

"I do." What else could he say? He loved her, too, in his own way.

Grey started to shove the letter into his coat pocket, then paused. The missive seemed awfully thin for one of Mother's. With a sense of dread, he opened it to find the briefest of messages:

> *My dearest Grey,*
> *I regret to inform you that your stepfather has passed away. The funeral is at Armitage Hall on Tuesday.*
> > *With much love,*
> > *Mother*
>
> *P.S. Please come. I can't do this without you.*

Grey stared numbly at the words. Maurice, the only father he'd ever really known, was dead.

*Please come. I can't do this without you.*

Holy hell, Mother must be devastated.

Apparently, his distress showed in his face, for Vanessa snatched the letter and read it, then lifted a horrified gaze to him. "Oh, Grey, how *awful*. I'm so very sorry."

"Thank you," he muttered, though he felt like a fraud. He'd barely seen Maurice since the family's return from Prussia a few months ago. He had let his bitterness keep him away, and now it was too late.

She was now rereading the letter with a furrowed brow. "Maurice . . . that would be Sheridan's father, right? I suppose he will now become duke."

The odd note in her voice arrested him. "*Sheridan?* Since when are you so chummy with my half brother? You only met him once."

"We've met thrice actually," she murmured. "We even danced together twice."

Uh-oh. Sheridan had best watch himself around Vanessa. When she fixed her affections on a man, she could really dig her teeth in. "Don't tell me he's the 'poet' you have your eye on."

His sharp tone made her glance up. "Don't be ridiculous. Sheridan doesn't have a poetic thought in his head."

She was right, but how had she known that? "You'll have to call him Armitage now that he's duke."

"All the more reason for me not to have an interest in him. I will *never* take a duke for my husband, no matter what Mama wants. You're all too . . . too . . ."

"Pompous and arrogant?"

As if realizing she shouldn't be insulting a man who'd just lost a close relation, she winced. "Something like that." When he said nothing, she added, "You certainly have a number of dukes in *your* family."

"That's what happens when one's mother marries well three times."

"She'll be leaving quite a dynasty behind her. Some would say that's excellent planning."

"She didn't plan on being widowed thrice, I assure you," he said sharply.

Vanessa looked stricken. "Of course not. I'm sorry, Grey, that was most thoughtless of me."

He pinched the bridge of his nose. "No, it's . . . I'm just unsettled by the news."

"I'm sure. If there's anything I can do . . ."

Grey didn't answer, his mind having already seized on the reminder that Sheridan had become Duke of Armitage. Maurice had only been duke a few months, and now Sheridan was being forced to take up the mantle. His head must be reeling. Grey needed to be at Armitage Hall, if only to help Sheridan and Mother with the arrangements for the funeral on Tuesday.

Wait, today was Sunday. But *which* Sunday? Damn it, had he already missed his stepfather's funeral?

"When did this letter arrive?" he asked.

It was the maid who answered. "I believe it was this past Friday, Your Grace."

"That's right," Vanessa said. "Friday."

Armitage Hall was near the town of Sanforth. If he caught the footmen before they unpacked his trunk, Grey could be changed into his mourning clothes and back on the road in an hour. He'd easily reach Lincolnshire by tomorrow. "I must go," he said, turning for the door.

"I'll go with you," Vanessa said.

"Don't be absurd," Grey snapped before her maid could protest. "You will go home as usual and tell your mother I wasn't here. You have the perfect excuse for missing me this time. Just say I'd already been notified of my stepfather's death and had left for Lincolnshire. Understood?"

"But . . . but how could you have been notified if I hadn't yet brought you the letter?"

"Say that the servants told you I'd already received one here." His common sense finally asserted itself. "Indeed, I probably have, since I haven't looked at my mail yet. Mother wouldn't have left anything to chance. She would have sent multiple notices." No matter how distracted by grief she might be.

Vanessa laid her hand upon his arm. "Grey, you need someone with you. You're clearly upset."

"I'll be fine." He would, damn it. "Now go on with you. I have preparations to make before I can leave."

"Of course." She nodded to her lady's maid, who joined her. "I shall tell Mama of your loss. Perhaps that will keep her machinations to a minimum for a while."

"Somehow I doubt it." He leaned close to whisper, "Take care with your poet, my dear. You deserve better."

She made a face. "I don't suppose I'll get a chance at him, anyway, now that you're in mourning. Mama will make me wait to see *anyone* until you're available again."

"Good. I shouldn't like to think of you marrying someone beneath you while I'm not around to prevent it."

Tossing back her head, she walked toward the door. "There's something to be said for marrying for love, you know. I swear, sometimes you remind me of Mama in your opinions about marriage."

With that parting sally, she waltzed out, with her maid trailing behind her.

How ridiculous. He was nothing like Aunt Cora, that grasping harpy. He was merely sensible. Love didn't enter his equations because it had no monetary value. When *he* married, it would be to some sensible woman who'd be content with having a wealthy dukedom at her disposal, who had no dreams of cloud castles and no hope for sentiment or love or any of that romantic nonsense from him.

He had learned the hard way to guard his heart.

Looking for more from Madeline Hunter?
Don't miss the Decadent Dukes Society series,
beginning with . . .

## The Most Dangerous Duke in London

From the *New York Times*-bestselling author, "an intelligent,
fast-paced romance, chock-full of sensuality and spiced with
mystery" (*Publishers Weekly*).

## NOTORIOUS NOBLEMAN SEEKS REVENGE
Name and title: Adam Penrose, Duke of Stratton. Affiliation:
London's elite Society of Decadent Dukes. Family history: Scandalous. Personality traits: Dark and brooding, with a thirst for
revenge. Ideal romantic partner: A woman of means, with beauty
and brains, willing to live with reckless abandon. Desire: Clara
Cheswick, gorgeous daughter of his family's sworn enemy.

## FAINT OF HEART NEED NOT APPLY
Clara may be the woman Adam wants, but there's one problem:
she's far more interested in publishing her women's journal than
getting married—especially to a man said to be dead-set on
vengeance. Though, with her nose for a story, Clara wonders if
his desire for justice is sincere—along with his incredibly
unnerving intention to be her husband. If her weak-kneed
response to his kiss is any indication, falling for Adam clearly
comes with a cost. But who knew courting danger could be such
exhilarating fun?

*Available wherever books are sold from*
*Kensington Publishing Corp.*

# Chapter 1

The Dowager Countess of Marwood could be a formidable enemy if she so chose. Her mere presence dared one to take her lightly so she might have an excuse to rain destruction, just for fun.

Adam Penrose, Duke of Stratton, knew at once what he had in her.

He had called at her grandson the earl's country estate at her request. *Let us attempt to bury the past*, she had written, *and allow bygones to be bygones between our families.*

He had come, curious to see how she hoped to accomplish that, considering that some of those bygones were not gone at all. One look at her and he knew that whatever plan she had concocted, it would not benefit *him*.

The lady kept him waiting a half hour before entering the chamber herself. She finally sailed into the drawing room, angled forward, head high, her ample bosom leading the way, like a figure on a ship's prow.

Mourning for her son, the late earl, forced her into black garments, but her crepe ensemble must have cost hundreds. Abundant gray curls decorated her head, suggesting that she also mourned the dead fashion for wigs. Shallow, large, pale blue eyes examined her caller with a critical gaze while an artificial smile deepened the wrinkles of her long face.

"So, you have returned." She announced the obvious when they sat on two sturdy chairs, after his short bow and her shorter curtsy.

"It was time."

"One might say it was time three years ago, or two, or even several years hence."

"One might, but I did not."

She chortled. Her whole face pursed, not only her lips. "You have been in France a long time. You even look French now."

"At least half so, I assume, considering my parentage."

"And how is your dear mother?"

"Happy in Paris. She has many friends there."

The dowager's eyebrows rose just enough to express sardonic amusement. "Yes, I expect she does. It is a wonder she did not marry you off to one of her own kind."

"I think a British match would suit me better. Don't you?"

"Indeed I do. It will help you enormously."

He did not want to discuss his mother or the reasons why a solid match would help. "You wrote of bygones. Perhaps you will enlighten me regarding that."

She opened her hands, palms up, in a gesture of confusion. "The animosity between our families is so old that one wonders how it even started. It is so unnecessary. So unfortunate. We are county neighbors, after all. Surely we can rise above it if we choose to."

Unable to sit and listen to her blithe references to that history, he stood and paced to the long windows. They overlooked a spectacular garden and on to the hills beyond, not far away. The house and its immediate grounds occupied a shallow valley.

"How do you suggest we do that?" He asked the question while he corralled the bitterness in his mind. The dowager knew damned well why the recent animosity had started and probably knew about the older history too. To acknowledge any of that would make her peace offering peculiar, however. *We stole your property and savaged your mother and helped drive your father to his death, but you should rise above that now.*

He turned to see her watching him. She appeared puzzled, as if he had done something unexpected and she could not determine if he had won a point without her knowing it.

He raised his eyebrows, to encourage her to speak.

"I propose that we resolve this the ancient way. In the manner of political dynasties down through time," she said. "I believe that our families should join through marriage."

He barely avoided revealing his astonishment. He had not expected this, of all possible overtures. She did not merely suggest a truce, but rather an alliance bound by the strongest ties. The kind of alliance that might keep him from pursuing the truth about this family's role in his father's death, or seeking revenge if he learned his suspicions about the last earl were correct.

"Since I do not have a sister for your grandson, I assume you have set your sights on me."

"My grandson has a sister who will suit you perfectly. Emilia is all any man could ask for and would make a perfect duchess for you."

"You speak with great confidence, yet you have no idea what *this* man would ask for."

"Do I not? As if I have lived this long and learned nothing? Beauty, grace, demure obedience, and a fine settlement. Those qualifications are high on your list, as on all men's."

The temptation to add other requirements, ones that would shock her, almost conquered his better judgment. He only won the battle because he had learned never to let the enemy know his thoughts.

"I can find that in many young women. Shall we be honest

with each other? What is it about this particular match that would be to my advantage?"

"A bold question, but a fair one. We will be allies instead of enemies. It will benefit you just as it will benefit us."

"Well, now, Countess, we both know that is not true. I have been invited to negotiate peace now when my father never was in the past. I would be a fool if I did not wonder why you think I would be agreeable. Considering the rumors regarding my activities in France, I can surmise how you may think this will protect your grandson, but not how it will help me."

Her eyes narrowed. Her skin's wrinkles froze like stone carvings. She displayed no fear. Adam admired her strong poise, but then she was not the one she assumed to be in danger.

She stood. "Come out on the terrace. I will show you my granddaughter. Once you see her, you will understand how you will benefit."

He followed her out into the crisp April air. The garden spread below them like a brown and red tapestry, punctuated by small new leaves and early flowers of yellow, pink, and purple. Bulbs, he assumed. They had not yet begun blooming when he left Paris.

A girl sat within the reviving growth, on a stone bench thirty feet away. She had a book open, held up so her face did not angle down. The dowager must have given her a reprieve from mourning because the girl wore a pale blue dress. She was pretty, and perhaps sixteen years of age. Her blond hair sparkled in the sun, and her fair skin and lovely face would appeal to any man. Add a fine settlement and she would do well enough.

The dowager stood beside him, her expression one of supreme confidence. He did not trust her, but he admired her skill at this game. He admitted to himself that her offer did have its advantages, and not because the girl was lovely. His father's name and his family's honor had been badly tainted in the best circles, and if he wanted to overcome that curse, this marriage would definitely help.

It would mean forgetting the reasons he had turned his back on England as well as his only good reason for finally returning. Which was why the dowager had invited him here in the first place, he assumed.

"Emilia is as sweet in disposition as any girl I have known. She is of good humor too and has a fair amount of wit, lest you worry that she might be dull," the countess said.

Sweet Emilia pretended not to see them, just as she pretended to read, posed so he could see her face and form. No wrap warmed her, and no bonnet protected that fair skin. He wondered how long she had been sitting like that, waiting for her future intended to inspect her.

He did not know why she held no appeal. Perhaps because while she might be lovely and witty, she was too young, and from the look of her compliance with her grandmother's instructions, probably lacked spirit.

The doors opened and the earl strode out. Tall and blond, he had not yet completely shed the gangly thinness of boyhood. He glowered at his grandmother while he passed her. She pursed her face in return. His arrival apparently had not been part of the dowager's plans.

He advanced on Adam like a man greeting a friend, but his rushed, loud welcome and the glisten of sweat on his brow told another story. Theobald, Earl of Marwood, was afraid of his guest. Many men had shown the same reaction since Adam arrived back in England two weeks ago. His reputation had preceded him, and society apparently expected him to issue challenges left and right at the slightest provocation.

Adam had done nothing to correct their assumptions. For one thing, he might very well issue a challenge or two, depending on what he discovered about events five years ago. For another, there were men, like Marwood here, who were more pliable when motivated by fear.

"I see Grandmother has already broached the idea of this

match," Marwood said heartily. He looked down at his sister Emilia, still posed in the garden. The two of them looked much alike—fair, pale, handsome, and young.

The earl could not be more than twenty-one. Adam wondered if Marwood knew about the rumor that had haunted Adam's father to his grave. Marwood's fear suggested he might, and that Adam's long-held suspicions about these old enemies might be true.

"Are you amenable to the idea?" Marwood asked.

His grandmother drifted closer. "Forgive my grandson. He is still young enough to think impetuous impatience is a manly virtue."

Marwood looked to heaven as if praying for that patience. "He knows by now if the notion appeals or if it does not."

"The notion appeals, in a general way," Adam said. He did not lie. He still weighed the implications of the dowager's plan. This offer to simply turn the page on the past tempted him more than he expected.

The young earl shot his grandmother a glance full of bright optimism. The dowager managed more circumspection.

Adam focused his gaze on the girl. The dowager retreated. The earl sidled closer. Eager to complete negotiations, the earl extolled his sister's charms, man to man. Out of the corner of his eye, Adam saw the dowager shaking her head at her grandson's lack of finesse.

A movement on the hill beyond the garden caught Adam's eye. A flash of black streaked along the crest, took flight over a large, fallen tree, then abruptly stopped. A woman all in black, on a black horse, looked down on the house.

"Who is that?" he asked.

Marwood squinted and feigned lack of recognition. He glanced sideways at Adam, and thought better of it. "That is my half sister, Clara. She is the daughter of my father's first wife."

The black spot named Clara managed to communicate a good deal of hauteur even from this distance. She paced her horse back and forth on the hill's crest, watching the show below as if the rest of them put on a pageant for her amusement.

He remembered Lady Clara Cheswick, although they had never been introduced. She had been out in society before he left England, though. Bright-eyed and vivacious. Those were his impressions absorbed in passing.

"She does not allow mourning to interfere with her pleasure in riding," Adam said.

"She would probably say she honors our father this way. They liked to ride together."

"Since she is the eldest, why am I not being offered her hand?"

Marwood glanced askance at the dowager, then smirked. "Because the goal is to keep you from killing me, isn't it?" he said in a low voice, with unexpected bluntness. "Not give you another reason to want to."

Adam chose not to reassure Marwood about the killing part. Let this pup of an earl worry. "You are intriguing me now, not discouraging me."

Marwood bent his head closer and spoke confidentially. "I am doing you a great favor now in speaking honestly. My father spoiled and indulged her and allowed her to build notions unfitting for women. He never demanded she marry, and now she thinks it beneath her. He left her a good bit of property in her own name, a handsome tract with rich farms." His voice turned bitter on the last sentence. "She is my sister, but I would be no friend to you if I sang her praises when in reality she is something of a shrew."

Clara was the old earl's favorite child, apparently. Adam wondered if the recently deceased father still had the ability to turn over in his grave. With a nudge or two, perhaps. "How old is she?"

"Far past marrying age. Twenty-four."

Old enough to remember. She might even know a great deal, if her father kept her close. "Call her down here. I would like to meet her."

"Truly, you do not want to—"

"Call her. And tell your other sister to put the book down. Her arms must feel like lead by now."

Marwood scurried to his grandmother to share the request. The dowager sailed over to Adam while trying to appear calm. "I fear you misunderstand. For this match to come to a satisfactory conclusion, the bride must be Emilia. Clara's character is above reproach, but she is not suitable for any man who desires domestic harmony."

"I only asked to meet Lady Clara. Nor have I agreed to any marriage yet."

"Before he died, my son specifically spoke with me about this alliance. I am only executing his own intentions. He said it should be Emilia—"

"He wants to meet her, Grandmother." Exasperated, Marwood raised his arm and gestured to his sister Clara to come in.

The horse ceased pacing. The woman had seen and understood the instruction. She sat on that hill, her horse in profile, her head turned to them, gazing down. Then she pulled the reins hard. Her horse rose on its back legs so high that Adam feared she would slide out of her sidesaddle. Instead she held her seat neatly while she pivoted her horse around. She turned her back on them and galloped away.

The lady had just slapped him in the face from a distance of six hundred yards.

The dowager's expression showed smug triumph beneath its veil of dismay. "How unfortunate she did not see my grandson's signal."

"She saw it well enough."

"She is a bit willful, I will admit. I did warn you," Marwood said.

"You did not mention that she is rude and disobedient and quick to insult others if she chooses."

"I am sure she did not intend to insult you." He gave his grandmother a desperate glare.

"Sure, are you? Then please tell the grooms to bring my horse to the garden portal over there immediately. I will go and introduce myself to Lady Clara so I do not brood over her unintended cut and allow it to interfere with our families' new friendship." Adam bowed to the dowager. "Please give my regards to Lady Emilia. I am sure she and I will meet soon."

Please read on for an excerpt from Mary Jo Putney's next Rogues Redeemed novel, *Once a Laird*!

# Chapter 1

*British Embassy*
*Constantinople*

The letter was dirty and folded, not surprising considering how far it had come. Ramsay was reluctant to break the seal because he had a strong suspicion of what it would say. He was right.

The letter was addressed to Kai Douglas Ramsay and said tersely:

> *Kai,*
>
> *Time to stop playing around and come home, laddie boy. Your grandfather is dying. He may be swilling ale in Valhalla by the time you get this. You know the price you promised to pay for your footloose wandering. Now the note has come due.*
>
> *Signy Matheson*
> *Skellig House*
> *Mainland, Thorsay*

Of course it would be Signy who had written him. Only islanders he'd known as a boy would call him Kai. Signy had become his grandfather's deputy as well as being the head schoolmistress in the islands. Ramsay smiled a little, remembering her as a knobby little girl with a tongue that could flay a whale when she was in a critical mood. She was the younger sister of Gisela, his first and only love.

His smile faded. Laying the letter on his desk, he moved to the window and gazed out at the domes and minarets of Constantinople, visible above the walls that surrounded the British Embassy compound. He'd been here five years, the longest time he'd spent in any one place during his wandering years.

His official position was Under Secretary for Special Projects, a vague enough title to cover his various nefarious activities. With all the layers of history in Constantinople, he could spend a lifetime here and barely scratch the wonders of this city and this land.

It was hard to imagine a place more different from the far northern islands of his homeland. But Ramsay had always known his time here was limited. He might have stayed in Thorsay if Gisela hadn't died suddenly of a fever when he was finishing his studies at the University of Edinburgh. The pain was so numbing that he'd been unable to bear the thought of returning to the islands.

His grandfather, the wily old devil, had known how Ramsay would feel. After giving him the news of Gisela's death, the laird had said that Ramsay could feed his wanderlust until his grandfather died or was near death. Then he must come home to assume his responsibilities as Laird of Thorsay.

Ramsay had seized on the proffered bargain, both because he couldn't imagine returning to Thorsay with Gisela gone, and because he'd yearned to visit distant lands and study ancient ruins. He'd had a dozen years of that freedom and had managed not to get himself killed, though it had been a near-run thing more than once.

That thought led him to recollections of a certain cellar in Portugal where he'd been held captive with four other men as they drank bad brandy and waited to be executed at dawn. But the five of them had worked together to escape and made a pact to meet up again after the war, if they survived. Now Napoleon was gone for good, exiled to a bleak rock in the South Atlantic to rule over the seabirds.

How many of his fellow captives had survived? They'd all been living risky lives. When Ramsay traveled through London on his way home, he could check for letters at Hatchard's bookshop, which had been their chosen locale for information exchange.

Ramsay forced his wandering mind back to practical matters. Though he'd wished this day would never come, he'd been mentally preparing. Over the years he'd shipped his finest archeological finds home. He hoped they'd safely made the long journey through the Mediterranean, west around the Iberian Peninsula, then north through the English Channel and North Sea to Thorsay.

The three island groups north of Scotland were closer to Norway than to London. Orkney was visible, barely, from the northern most coast of mainland Scotland. Thorsay lay beyond and far-flung Shetland lay west of Norway. All three archipelagos were inhabited by tough, stubborn islanders whose first language was Norn, a Scandinavian dialect. Over the centuries, Gaelic-speaking Celts had settled on the islands, and even a few English. No wonder the Thorseach, the people of his islands, were good with languages.

Ramsay turned to his painting of the Egyptian pyramids set against a blazing sunset sky. The picture was hinged on one side and he swung it away from the wall to reveal the mirror mounted on the back.

He concealed the mirror to avoid being accused of vanity. Its real purpose was so he could check his appearance when he was dressing up in local clothing in order to travel through the teeming city without being recognized as a foreigner.

He studied his appearance. Years spent in the sun had tanned and weathered his complexion so he looked more like a native of this part of the world than Scotland. He had also dyed his hair dark brown so he wouldn't stand out as a Northern European. He'd stop the dyeing so that by the time he reached the British Isles, his natural light hair would have grown out.

His gaze moved around his office and the many shelves holding his favorite archeological treasures. Constantinople had been a trading center for centuries, and goods of all nations could be found here. He'd shipped many objects back to London and had made a good deal of money in the process, but these items were the ones he loved. They'd have to be carefully packed for the journey home.

He lifted a richly decorated silver mirror from Renaissance Italy. Gisela would have loved it. If she'd lived, the shape of his life would be completely different, yet he could barely remember her face. She'd been sweet and funny and very, very pretty. He would have returned from Edinburgh and married her and they'd likely have children by now.

Ramsay would never have seen the sun set behind the pyramids, but he wouldn't have known the loneliness of his solitary years. Would his life have been better or worse if she hadn't died? Impossible to say. Certainly it would have been very different.

Face set, he left his office and headed down a floor to see the ambassador. There was no reason to delay handing in his resignation. Once he did that, his life here would be officially over.

He thought he'd have to make an appointment, but the secretary said, "Sir Robert is available so you can go right in."

No reprieve here. Ramsay knocked on the door, then entered. Sir Robert Liston glanced up from his desk. A Scot, he'd studied languages at the University of Edinburgh as Ramsay had done several decades later. Ramsay had used their common history to persuade the ambassador to create this unusual position as part of the British delegation.

Sir Robert started to rise, then settled back into his chair with a frown. "The evil day has arrived?"

Sir Robert was a perceptive fellow. Ramsay replied, "I've just received a message summoning me back to Thorsay."

The ambassador's frown deepened. "Have you considered refusing the summons? Surely there are others who would leap at the chance to become the next laird, but there is no one who can do the work you do here. Your skills are unique."

"My deviousness and affinity for disreputable rogues, you mean," Ramsay said dryly.

Sir Robert smiled. "Exactly. Most of the young gentlemen who join Britain's diplomatic corps are entirely too conventional. Good for many things, but not for what you do so well."

For a moment Ramsay allowed himself to consider the older man's suggestion. If he refused the call, another laird would be found and he'd be free to continue learning and exploring and quite possibly dying in some savage place.

*No.* He'd promised to return and take up his responsibilities not once but twice—first to his grandfather, and then again seven years ago in that damp cellar in Portugal. He and his fellow captives had spent a long night drinking and discussing what they would do with their lives if by some miracle they survived.

All had spoken of becoming better men and redeeming past sins. Ramsay had privately renewed his vow to answer the call to Thorsay when the time came. Though he'd make no wondrous discoveries during his travels, he'd gathered enough material to spend the rest of his life writing scholarly articles about what he'd observed in his wandering years.

The thought was not exciting, but at least his conscience would be clear. "This is one call I can't refuse, Sir Robert."

The ambassador nodded regretfully. "The trouble with honorable men is that they're honorable. When will you be leaving?"

"As soon as possible. The letter I received was written when my grandfather was still alive. Perhaps he still is." Ramsay would like to say good-bye if possible. He and the old laird had fought like two cats in a sack, but there had been real affection under the fireworks.

"You islanders are a tough lot. I hope he'll be there to swear at you one last time." Sir Robert unlocked a lower desk drawer and produced a bottle of good Scots whisky and two glass tumblers. "A toast to the old laird, and thanks to you for all the nefarious and useful things you've done for Britain."

He poured a couple of fingers of whisky in the glasses, handed one to Ramsay, and lifted his in a toast. "To auld lang syne."

"To auld lang syne," Ramsay repeated before downing the whisky in one long, burning swallow. "Next Hogmanay I'll be in Scotland."

"I envy you." The ambassador leaned forward and poured more whisky into Ramsay's glass. "Lift a glass for me, lad."

"I will," Ramsay promised. But by God, he'd miss this part of the world!

His voyage home benefited from fair winds and was swifter than expected. The light grew bluer and the winds more chill. By the time he reached London, Constantinople was only a distant sunburned memory.

He spent several days in town attending to business and staying at Thorsay House, which was owned by the Laird of Thorsay. The Browns, the couple who maintained the house, hadn't heard that the Old Laird was dead, so perhaps Ramsay's grandfather was still holding on.

Thorsay House, though owned by the Lairds of Thorsay, served as a way station for traveling Thorsayians. Ramsay found that he'd just missed a favorite cousin, Kendra Douglas, who'd taken refuge in the house after a disastrous scandal. She'd been a lively little thing. He'd taught her and Signy Matheson and several other younger children the basics of fencing.

He stopped at Hatchard's and found a trove of letters from the Rogues Redeemed of the Portuguese cellar. Impressively, they all had survived the wars and he managed to dine with one of the men while he was in London. Then he set sail again, first to Edinburgh and finally on a small coastal trading vessel that took him the last stretch to Thorsay.

Ramsay spent much of this last leg of his long journey in the bow of the boat, feeling a reluctant sense of homecoming. The silvery seas and austere scattered islands seemed to be bred into his bones.

When the vessel finally moored at the dock below Skellig House, Ramsay left the deckhands to unload his crates of antiquities. Impatiently he climbed the hill to the family home. Skellig House was a compact stone structure designed to stand against the fiercest winds off the North Sea. Behind it towered a massive stone monolith erected by the ancient inhabitants of these islands.

Nothing seemed to have changed in the dozen years since he'd left. His pace quickened as he wondered if his grandfather still lived.

As he approached the entrance to the house, the door swung open and someone stepped out, his gaze turned toward Ramsay. No, not a man but a tall woman, that was clear from the way the wind shaped her gray gown around an undeniably female figure. The same wind rippled her blazing red-gold hair like a banner of war.

When he was a dozen feet away, she brushed back her hair and said in a voice colder than an Arctic gale, "What took you so long, Kai?"

He stopped dead in his tracks and stared. In the years he'd been gone, bony little Signy Matheson had become a damned Nordic goddess!

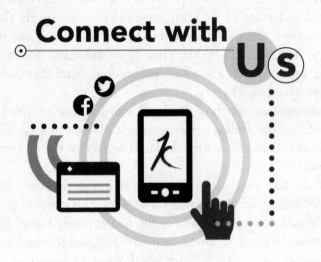